Paul Cobb was born in Yorkshire and has lived and worked in the landscapes he writes about, weaving his fictional characters around these landscapes as much as around the real figures from history.

THE BOOK AND THE KNIFE

Part One

Thegn *of* Berewic

PAUL COBB

Copyright © 2024 Paul Cobb

The moral right of the author has been asserted.

Apart from any fair dealing for the purposes of research or private study, or criticism or review, as permitted under the Copyright, Designs and Patents Act 1988, this publication may only be reproduced, stored or transmitted, in any form or by any means, with the prior permission in writing of the publishers, or in the case of reprographic reproduction in accordance with the terms of licences issued by the Copyright Licensing Agency. Enquiries concerning reproduction outside those terms should be sent to the publishers.

This is a work of fiction. Other than references to actual historical figures, places and events, all other names, characters, businesses, places, events and incidents are either the products of the author's imagination or used in a fictitious manner. Any resemblance to actual persons, living or dead, or actual events is purely coincidental.

Troubador Publishing Ltd
Unit E2 Airfield Business Park,
Harrison Road, Market Harborough,
Leicestershire LE16 7UL
Tel: 0116 279 2299
Email: books@troubador.co.uk
Web: www.troubador.co.uk

ISBN 978 1 83628 069 9

British Library Cataloguing in Publication Data.
A catalogue record for this book is available from the British Library.

Printed and bound in Great Britain by 4edge Limited
Typeset in 11pt Adobe Jenson Pro by Troubador Publishing Ltd, Leicester, UK

For Linda and Izaak

ðegn

A *thegn* holds land granted by the king, and ranks between an ordinary freeman and a hereditary noble

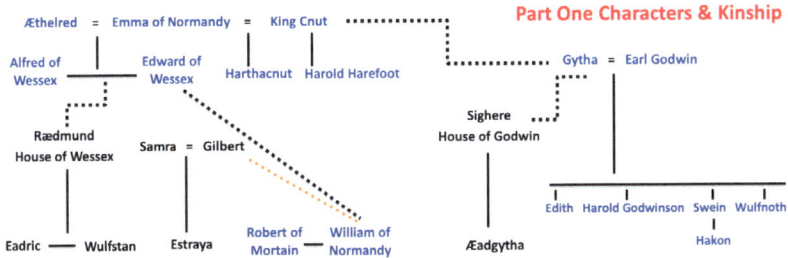

Other people:
Felip de Mazerolles – the Benedictine monk
Hugh de Bayeux – the Norman knight
Cuthred – the reeve at Berewic
Father Brenier – the priest at Berewic
Osbern – Edward's chaplain

Guðrun – Eadric's slave
Dudda and Mildrythe – the charcoal burners
Jaco Reuben – the ship's captain
Miriam Bonafoy – Samra's friend in Rouen
Beornwyn – the serving girl

Pronunciations

The Æ in Æadgytha and Ælfwyn was a letter of its own ('ash' – in Old English, æsc). It can be pronounced either like the 'a' in 'sack', or (my preference) like the 'e' in 'ten'.

The ð (Old English *eth*) in Guðrun is pronounced like the 'th' in 'then'.

Thegn is pronounced 'thane' and can be spelt that way.

Fyrd is pronounced 'feared'.

Estraya is pronounced 'es-TRAY-ah'.

Berewic is pronounced 'Berrick'. Although my Berewic will be somewhere in the area of present day Berwick in Sussex, it is a fictional place.

Place names

I use the present-day versions of all place names, except for the site of the Battle of Hastings, which was not at Hastings and not called Battle in 1066. The Normans called it *Senlac*, from the Old English *Sandlacu* or the 'sand-stream' near the English army's position. The English name *Sandlake* long survived as the name of a Tithing in Battle, and I have the English call it by this name.

Godwin and Wessex

The great Earl Godwin was father of Harold, and Harold and his brothers were Godwinsons, following the old Scandinavian naming tradition. But Earl Godwin also gave his name to his house, and so as part of his extended family Æadgytha and her father Sighere are Godwins, just as Eadric, Wulfstan and their father Rædmund are part of the extended family and the house of Wessex. Godwin was also the Earl of Wessex, though to avoid confusion with the house of Wessex I don't refer to him by that title.

Den or denn?

Landscape historians use the term 'den' for the woodland pastures where pigs were driven to in autumn, and which are the origin of the many place names ending in -den in the Andredswald, the vast wooded area that once covered the Weald of Kent, Surrey and Sussex. However, I use the Old English word *denn* here to avoid any modern misunderstanding in talking about a 'den in the woods'.

"I will bear it. For as long as it takes." - Eadric

Prologue

Nothing happens but for a purpose. Everything begins and ends at its given time. Everyone comes into and leaves your life to set you on or change you from a path.

The man who spoke those words took the book from me, and left me to be sold as a slave; but I forgave him. Another man traded my daughter's life for the book, and I forgave him too. Another was sent to kill me because of it, and I forgave him. I was told once that my power to understand, and to forgive, was humbling. But forgiveness is not a power. It is the gift of time, and time is something we Abravanels have in abundance, for we trace our line back to the house of King David, and we date our arrival in Spain from the destruction of the Temple in Jerusalem.

Many years after that and yet many years ago, when the book held nothing but charts of the stars, one night a young girl was playing on the steps of her father's house near Toledo. It was the year of 732, the year that her Moorish rulers in Spain were halted in their advance into Europe at the battle of Tours.

The steps went up to the flat roof on which her father, a metalsmith and instrument maker, was observing the stars.

It was a fine and clear night, and the stars seemed unusually brilliant and close. The girl was throwing a ball up the steps, seeing how near to the top she could pitch it so that it would bounce back to her as fast as possible. On one throw the ball went too far and she had to follow it onto the roof. Her father smiled at her; dark hair, dark eyes that briefly met his before she scampered after the ball. He turned away to his quadrant and his chart of the stars, measuring, making notes in a large leather-covered book.

The ball had come to rest in a puddle left on the uneven roof by recent rain. As she reached over the water, the girl saw the night sky reflected, the swirling patterns of galaxies and stars on a fabric of inky black. She looked at a shape made by one small cluster of stars and its milky background, and began to speak.

'I save a life. I take a life. I make a life.'

Her father looked round at her. She pointed at the puddle. He came over quickly, the vibration of his feet rippling the water until he stopped and looked too. The script in the water was minute but clear; three lines of text, spelling out in stars the words his daughter had just spoken. He looked up at the sky, shifting position, moving closer to the puddle, then further away, searching for the pattern he had seen reflected; but in vain. It could be seen only in the dark water on the roof. He fetched his book and wrote the lines down, and carefully sketched the shape of the background around them.

The girl grabbed the ball and ran off down the steps. Once the water had settled, the pattern of words was gone.

As her father sat in his workshop the next day, he found himself looking across his bench at a small, unfinished piece of steel. No more than a flat outline, he recognised the shape it made at once. He reached for his bag of tools, and opened the book at the page with the three lines.

My name is Samra Abravanel, and I was born keeper of the book, and of the knife. Because of this, the people in these pages came into my life, and the book and the knife came into theirs.

Everything begins and ends at its given time.

Sophia

Toledo, Spain, December 1031

A woman's voice.

A woman's voice, clear and light, ringing round the domed ceiling of the room beneath the observatory. A voice that should have been deadened by the rows of shelves around the room that held book after book, and the benches below them on which lay instruments and devices of all kinds. But it was not.

'Who calls on me?' said the unseen voice. 'Who intercedes between heaven and earth?'

Startled, Samra gripped the hands of the men on each side of her. Whatever eagerness she had shown for what they were about to undertake had deserted her, replaced by a dread, the origins of which she could not place. But one of the men was speaking in response.

'It is I, Sophia, spirit of wisdom, bringer of light to the world. I, Alhacen. I called on you before, when I was in Egypt and in fear of my life.'

The man who had spoken was seated with Samra and the other man at a small round table in the centre of the room. The three had all linked hands. Alhacen's long beard was grey;

a turban covered his hair. The light from the candles flickered in his eyes, and though age had creased the skin around them, it had not dimmed their brightness.

'You are a long way from home,' the spirit voice went on, 'Alhacen, bringer of knowledge to men, seeker of the truth. And this time you are not alone.'

Alhacen nodded to the young woman on his left. Like him, Samra had angular features, dark skin and dark eyes that shone in the candlelight. Slender and, even seated, taller than her companions, her black hair fell across the shoulders of a finely patterned red robe, trimmed with gold and silver thread. For a moment she sat breathing heavily, staring at the table in front of her, unable to speak. *Take your strength from Alhacen; he is not afraid.* Samra drew breath, and now her own voice was steady and firm.

'My name is Samra Abravanel and this is my home – and yet not, for I am one of the Sephardim, the Jews of Spain, and we left our true home centuries ago.'

Sophia's voice rang out again. 'Then you must be a seeker after truth and knowledge also, Samra Abravanel, for you are surrounded by many books and instruments.'

'We are all seekers after truth here.'

The young man with deep brown eyes and brown hair on Alhacen's right who had spoken these words wore the tunic, scapular and cowl of his Benedictine order.

'I am Felip de Mazerolles, and I am also far from my monastery in the south of France,' he went on eagerly. 'Yet I have made this place my home, for Moorish Spain is the centre of a knowledge unsurpassed in the world of men.'

The spirit voice spoke again. 'And knowledge is the realm

of men, while wisdom is the realm of heaven. What would you know from me?'

Alhacen got up from the table and went to a shelf behind him. He came back with a bundle wrapped in a velvet cloth decorated with a moon and stars, placed it on the table and sat down again. Slowly he unwrapped the cloth to reveal a large, leather-covered book.

'This book has become our life's work. Begun in the family of a Jew, taken up first by a Muslim and now by a Christian, within its pages are centuries of knowledge. Knowledge acquired through observation, through experiment and the repeated venture of the mind; from what is known and possible into what is unknown and seems impossible. Knowledge in many spheres – philosophy, logic, mathematics, astronomy, optics, medicine, metallurgy. From the humblest insect, to the stars that even now wheel above our heads.'

Samra looked at him. Alhacen seemed to be devouring the book with his eyes.

'All this is recorded here,' he continued, 'in a book that we have come to realise is greater than any of us can imagine, and is bound to the future of men. But the realm of men is troubled. Great forces wax and wane around us like the moon, and in my dreams I see the book destroyed. Yet I know its truth is universal to all men; a truth that glorifies the God that each of us worships and yet which could be lost. What should we do?'

There was no answer. Instead, a sound; the sound of a wind, a wind that grew from nothing, then increased in strength until it whirled around the room behind them. It whirled past the shelves and over the benches, as if it would fling their contents from them. One by one the candles were extinguished, and the room went dark. As the wind faded away, above the three figures at the table, pinpricks of light began to appear in the blackness that had swept the whitewashed dome when the candles died. As the lights grew in number, Samra looked up, and gasped as the thrill of recognition ran through her. The entire dome was a star-map, an inner likeness of the night sky beyond the roof above them.

Sophia's voice spoke again. 'Know, then, that the book you have before you is great indeed. For the wise, it is the way to treasure beyond price. For the foolish, it is the way to hell.'

'It is not treasure that we seek,' Felip cut in, 'but knowledge.'

'And that knowledge is the treasure beyond price, Felip. Without it, you are but creatures that labour on the face of Earth. With it, you have the key to the mysteries of Earth and you can change the lives of men.'

'When I turn my gaze from the stars to those around me,' said Samra, 'I see that the power to restore the body from injury or sickness can be learnt and passed on to others. For that alone I pledge myself to the book.'

'And when I lift my gaze,' added Alhacen, 'to be able to see and record the true motion of the planets that move above us even now, for all that follow me to understand, I pledge myself.'

'And what do you bring to, or take from the book, Felip de Mazerolles?' asked the voice.

'If my friends here are servants of the book,' replied the monk, 'then I am but their servant. We sit here in Toledo between two worlds. North of us is Christian, where Latin is the common tongue; for those who study, teach and write, it surpasses all languages. South of us lies the Muslim world, where Arabic was brought on the point of a sword, from the deserts of Arabia to the plains of Iberia. I am the portal between these worlds. My task is to render the book from the Arabic of its authors into Latin, so that the knowledge of the Muslim south can reach the Christian north. But I have only just begun.'

The dome above them faded to black again, and in place of stars, images began to form on the dark space. Now Samra found herself watching men and women at work with tools and instruments; people setting limbs, examining the inner structure of a flower, pouring molten metal, looking into lenses. And the images moved across the dome, forming and fading as quickly as clouds cross the sun.

'But all this is for nothing,' said Felip firmly, 'if not done in the service of God.'

'Then consider,' spoke the voice, 'that there is no better way to God than through searching for truth and knowledge. Do not be afraid to serve Him in what you do.'

'We are not afraid, Sophia,' said Alhacen, 'we fear only that what we have found will be destroyed before it can be passed on.'

Now the pictures on the dome changed again. A horde of men on horseback, armed with swords and spears, was sweeping across a valley to meet another mass, similarly armed. As the two groups merged in bloody battle, other images appeared of women and children fleeing burning houses, turning to look back in terror. These images too dissolved into scenes of armed men bursting into a library, ransacking and burning as they went. Samra wanted to close her eyes, but the voice was speaking again.

'This is the world of men. A thousand years since he that was called Christ died on the cross, princes wield their power, armies clash in the name of their Gods and chaos follows. We are as far from the kingdom of heaven as when He walked the earth.'

Sophia's voice was soft with sadness, but picked up strength as it went on.

'Yet it can be otherwise. Through you, a ruler will arise who will use the knowledge that you and those before you have poured into the book, for the good of all. A ruler who will govern wisely and justly. A ruler whose power is based on the knowledge within the book, who will need no God who demands that men suffer and no faith that demands their blind obedience for its own ends.'

At the table, the three looked at each other.

'When will this come about?' Alhacen asked. 'And where?'

'How do we keep the book safe?' said Felip.

Bewildered, Samra added, 'What part do we play in this?'

'I cannot answer these things; except the last. Open the book, Samra. Open it at the inscription.'

Samra nodded and, pulling the book towards her, turned through the pages until she came to the one that she knew had just three lines of text, with a shape roughly sketched around them. Above her head, the night sky had reappeared, only now with a single pattern of stars forming three lines. She looked up at them and spoke the words she had spoken many times before, which her mother had spoken to her, and her mother's mother before her. Words that so many Abravanel women had uttered, mother to daughter, reaching back through the generations.

'I save a life. I take a life. I make a life.'

'You carry the knife that your forefather crafted here nearly three hundred years ago, Samra Abravanel, when among the light of ten thousand stars his daughter saw those words reflected from the night sky.' At her ankle, Samra could feel the knife in its soft leather sheath. 'He wrote those lines on its blade; it is the foretelling that will bring about what I have described to you all. Its time is beginning.'

Alhacen was the first to break the silence that followed.

'What you describe, what you say will come about – to put on a throne, a ruler who finds his own way to God, with no imam, or priest, or rabbi; a ruler for whom the truth of science is word enough – such a belief is a heresy in any of our faiths.'

'So the book must be kept secret, and safe, until its time comes. It is dangerous, and in danger. But it is not finished; there is more to add to it. There will always be more. You and those that follow you will do this. And you will show men what you can do with the knowledge within it.'

'Why do you say that for the foolish, the book is the way to hell?' Felip asked.

'Fear and respect its power,' replied the spirit voice. 'What it holds can be used for good or for evil. Those who look into the book will covet its knowledge for themselves. None of you is immune. You must prove yourselves worthy of the book, and of its knowledge. How, I cannot tell you. I have already said enough. Now I must leave you.'

As she fought to understand, Samra asked, 'I would know one thing: why did the knife come into my family? We are Jews. We only serve the powerful; we do not create them.'

'Your humility is misplaced, Samra. You are of blood royal, and into your line blood royal shall come. And the ruler I speak of will come from your bloodline. But the journey will be long, and hard.'

The stars faded from the dome and new images appeared.

Samra, Alhacen and Felip looked up. A young man and a young woman were running from the door of a squat stone building, hand in hand. They were finely dressed, but their clothes were splashed with blood and their faces were masks of horror. Samra stood up. Pity and anguish overwhelmed her as she watched the scene unfold, and she dropped again onto her chair, reaching for the book. Before her, the three lines on the page glowed a fierce red. She felt she would fall into them and be consumed.

The images faded, and the dome went black.

'Wait – I must know more,' Samra managed at last. 'One of these you have shown me is my flesh and blood. You have to tell me how this will be.'

'I cannot,' Sophia's voice in the darkness replied, 'it is not given to me.'

At once the candles relit. Samra slumped forwards onto the book, her forehead meeting the three lines on the open page. Alarmed, Alhacen and Felip leapt to their feet, pulling Samra upright in her chair. Her head tipped back, eyes rolling, and her mouth moved as she tried to speak.

'What is it?' Felip said urgently. 'Tell us!'

And Samra spoke; a single word, that meant nothing to any of them.

'Berewic.'

On the table, the book slammed shut.

The Manor

Berewic, Sussex, December 1031

Leaving behind him a sleeping young woman a little younger than his eighteen years, Cuthred stepped out purposefully over the threshold and breathed in the crisp winter air. Although it was not early, the woman did not need to stir and he did not need to be about the village, for there would be no work done for twelve days, until Epiphany. And after the village meeting and the mass in the church last night, Cuthred had come home for the first time to a Christmas Eve in his own house, his father having died in the summer. Now as his own man and one of the *folcfry*, the freemen of Berewic, owning a yardland of thirty acres on which to keep his mother and the family he expected to have, he relished walking the village alone. Tightening his belt around the tunic over his plump body, Cuthred set off on his short legs.

The streets of Berewic were that in name only, for the collection of timber houses with thatched roofs Cuthred was moving through had come together haphazardly over the years, with only here and there thoroughfares of beaten earth that people could move along in a straight line. Around him the village was quiet, the fields and meadows, the woods and waste, springs and streams, farms, houses and church still slumbering under the pale rising sun. England had greater manors, in size, wealth and status, but Berewic had what it needed to prosper. It had a thegn of standing, freemen and villeins to work their own land and do his service, and slaves to do theirs. It had light, workable land on the slopes above the village to go with the fertile wet meadows in the valley bottom, woodland behind it to draw fuel and timber from, and the river that provided fish and brought vessels and trade from the sea to its little quay.

If this were later on another day at another time, the sounds and smells of the village would be reaching him. The rise and fall of the treadles on the weaver's loom; the carpenter sawing and the bone worker filing; the anvil ringing at the blacksmith's. The aroma of round flat loaves from the baker's; of thick, cloudy beer from the alehouse; of salted fish from everywhere. Above and behind all these, the everyday sounds of people and carts, livestock and birdsong; the smells of animals and dung, of earth and air.

Passing the church with its square-set tower, the only stone building in Berewic, Cuthred saw lines of great timbers being set into the ground, the foundations of the hall house the thegn was having built. He tried to imagine the four great bays he could see topped with beams and roofed over. His thegn had had the church built too, and the new hall house would be another mark of Sighere's hold over his manor. There were rumours of a mill to be built, powered by the river. Not that Sighere's hold was in any doubt; in the fifteen years since King Cnut had granted him Berewic, king and thegn had enjoyed trouble-free rule. Of course, small child as he was at the time, Cuthred would barely have been aware that the previous thegn had been removed to allow Sighere's installation, and that there were uneasy times after this, but it was long ago and Berewic had settled undisturbed into its yearly routine of ploughing, planting and harvest.

As he pondered how happily unremarkable the manor he lived in was, Cuthred found himself almost at the edge of the village and was surprised to see another man abroad. Walking haltingly away from the houses, this old man was a *gebur*, living from a yardland he held from Sighere in return for service on the demesne, the thegn's own landholding.

'An early hour, and to be working at this time of year,' Cuthred called after him, noticing the man was holding an ox goad.

'I have land to plough of my thegn's,' the old man replied as he turned round, 'and he won't thank me if I fail to get it done. My slave is waiting in the fields with an ox team. What did you want?'

Cuthred knew that his chubby face with its piggy eyes and fleshy lips led others to dismiss him, and he bridled at the man's tone. But he knew how to put on a smirk and mask his menace.

'What if the priest knew you weren't upholding this holy time?' he said in an oily voice. 'You'd be better off giving yourself to Sighere as a slave,' he added, 'than drudging away at your age.'

The other man took a step forwards and slapped the end of the goad, a hazel rod, onto the palm of his other hand.

'If you were more my age, Cuthred, you might remember when I had land of my own here under the old thegn. Then Cnut took the throne and the Wessex royal family fled from England, while his Godwin henchman Sighere ousted the royal family's Wessex kinsman Rædmund from Berewic. My fortunes have withered since.'

Cuthred raised his eyebrows; he knew where his allegiance lay. 'And Berewic's have flourished.'

The old man shook his head. 'God gave his judgement, when two years gone Sighere's wife died in childbirth, leaving a baby girl as his future hope. That hope will not last when the Wessex come back.'

Cuthred smirked. 'If they ever do, you will be long dead. Speaking of which, you'd better get to the fields – you don't want to pass away before you get your work done.'

Stooped and swaying slightly, the other man glared at him, slapping the hazel rod onto his palm a few times more. Then he turned and walked slowly away. Cuthred's eyes bored into his back, and he clenched his fists.

You'd be wise, old man, not to declare for the Wessex in this place, or to gainsay me. One day, I will be something in this manor, and your yardland will be mine.

Into the Unknown

Toledo, Spain, January 1032

The order in the room beneath the observatory was gone. As he stepped over the threshold, Alhacen saw books pulled from the shelves, some piled roughly into large chests on the benches, others on the floor. The instruments now made a muddled heap on one of the benches, save for a few laid out carefully on another bench. On the small table in the centre of the room lay the book, wrapped in its cloth. As he put out a hand to touch it, Alhacen realised Samra was behind him.

'Are you sure of this?' he said, turning towards her. 'You cannot know what awaits you.'

'I know what awaits me here, sooner or later. You are returning to Egypt, and I must think of the book and its future.'

'Felip has convinced you its future lies with the Christians. And you believe him?'

Samra's dark eyes flickered with a moment of uncertainty.

'He knows their world, and their growing power in my country. It is a chance I must take.'

'And what if you fail? Draw a line just north of where you live here, and beyond that the world of ignorance begins.'

Alhacen took her hands in his, and felt her tremble a little. 'Samra... you are going into the unknown. The Christians do not prize knowledge as we do. They may destroy what they see as infidel, or what they simply do not understand.'

'They will understand. And I will be the one to make them understand.' She pulled her hands away, went to the bench with the few instruments, and picked up a long, cylindrical object.

Alhacen looked up at the whitewashed dome above them, remembering the night sky and the array of the stars they had seen there with Felip.

'You mean to show them the transit of Venus? To take my work and put the Christians in awe of it – and of you?'

For a moment, Samra looked abashed. 'In awe perhaps, though not of me.' But the eagerness shining in the young woman's eyes did not diminish. 'What better way to show the power of the book? Come with me – we can work together, as we have done! Who would not listen to Alhacen, so renowned in Egypt as a scientist?'

'A renown that brought me to the caliph's attention, who thought I might use my science to dam the Nile and control its flooding. It was only the gift of Sophia of a kind of madness that saved my life, as you know, when I told him this would be impossible. A ruler who thinks that as a scientist you are a god is as dangerous as one who thinks you are a devil.'

'Yet it was during your house arrest that followed, that you wrote your great *Book of Optics*, and the works you produced after your release – on the physics, astronomy and mathematics you have shared with me – made you even more famous. I wonder that you ever thought to leave your fame behind and travel to distant Spain.'

'Because when the Jews in Spain wrote to the Jews in

Egypt, they spoke of another book and of a woman who studies the stars, here at the edge of the Islamic world. I came to see her, and I have not been disappointed.'

'Then let us study the stars together still; beyond the edge of the Islamic world. Come with me.'

'You know I cannot,' Alhacen sighed. 'I must return, while my health holds out. And what can be demonstrated in Castile must be demonstrated in Cairo also. I owe it to my masters there.'

Samra laid the cylindrical object down again. For a moment she seemed lost, her purpose gone. Then she turned back to Alhacen and nodded.

'I understand. And I must carry on with my preparations. There is much to be made ready, for me and for my family. But be sure to call on me before you leave.' She turned to a chest of books and began to arrange them.

'Of course.' At the door, Alhacen paused and turned back. 'Samra, let me take the book.' He took a few steps into the room, and towards the table.

She turned to him, her voice hard. 'Why?'

'In the Fatimid caliphate in Egypt, knowledge is also appreciated, and learning encouraged. I can take the book to the library in Cairo – the House of Knowledge. The book will be treasured there, and protected.'

By now, Alhacen had reached the table.

'If that was what I wanted,' Samra countered, 'I could take the book to one of the libraries in Toledo.'

'You know there is no Umayyad caliphate in Spain any more, Samra – only war between the faithful. It pains my heart to say it, but the Muslims here are no longer fit to hold on to the book that was created in their realm.'

Alhacen was gazing down at the cloth covering the book, with its moon and stars.

Samra shook her head. 'You do not understand. The book needs to be in the world, dangerous as it is. It cannot be put away on a shelf, out of reach and forgotten.'

'It will not be forgotten, I assure you.'

'There is more to add to it, Sophia said to us. You and those that follow you will do this, we were told.'

Alhacen looked up at her. 'Keep it secret and keep it safe, we were told.'

'The book belongs in my family. I will decide what is safe.'

For a moment, the two stood, looking at each other. Alhacen felt his whole body straining towards the book on the table. Then he relaxed.

'Sophia was right. I am coveting the book and its power. Forgive me.'

'Then perhaps I am, too. Yet if you were with me, I would know what to do.'

Alhacen looked at the woman with whom he had sat poring over books in this very room, and whose insight and hunger for knowledge had astounded and inspired him. Suddenly Samra looked very young and afraid. He went over and put his arms round her.

'I will leave here today, and you will not see me again in this life.' Samra pulled out of his embrace, looked up at him and made to speak, but he put a finger to her lips.

'No; this has to be, for both our sakes. If I saw you again, it would be to take the book from you. The book and the knife are your destiny; follow it, wherever it leads. Your journey will be long and hard, Sophia said. But it is yours to make, not mine.'

He took her in his arms again, then let go and turned and walked away.

At the doorway, he did not look back.

The Book

North of Toledo, Spain, February 1032

In the dangerous high country between Moorish Toledo and Christian Castile, a young monk from the Languedoc in southern France was waiting anxiously, looking across a piece of flat ground to the mouth of a narrow valley. In the previous year, the caliphate of Cordoba had fallen, and civil war had split the once rich and powerful land into rival *taifas*, Muslim states fighting among themselves. The Christian states and their mercenaries to the north were exploiting the rivalries, gaining territory and encouraging the Christian enclaves in the *taifas* to revolt. The Jews in the *taifas* were uncertain where their safety lay, fearful that their peaceful co-existence with Christians and Muslims, a world in which Felip the young monk had once moved with ease, was ending.

He was not alone. Beside him, a group of the most feared fighters in Europe formed a line on horseback, in their mail tunics and with their swords by their sides. Their fair skin and short hair shaved at the back of the head made them alike, except for one – a sandy-haired young man of about thirteen, who wore no armour and served the leader of these Norman knights.

Snow was on the ground; a few flakes were falling from a grey sky. Suddenly, Felip rose in his saddle. A horse-drawn cart was slowly coming out of the valley. A small group of people was with the cart, the older riding in it, the younger walking beside; two children were astride the horse. They were all dressed against the cold; their clothes, of a quality fitting to the family of the astronomer to the ruler of the *taifa*, marked them out as Jews of Toledo. Ahead of them was another small group, an escort of lightly armed Berber foot soldiers.

As they saw the line of knights at some distance in front of them, the Berbers escorting the group with the cart stopped. One held up his arm, and the cart stopped too. The leader of the Normans motioned his line to advance. Felip and the young man followed. The Norman knights bypassed the Berber foot soldiers and went to the cart, which was heavily laden and covered with sackcloth. One dismounted and lifted a corner of the sacking. Dismounting, Felip spoke to one of the Toledans on the cart. The knight opened the neck of a large cloth bag and saw the glint of metal before he pulled the bag free and tipped it out in the cart. In the cold air his breath steamed onto plates, cups and bowls; gold and silver, many decorated with emeralds, rubies and pearls.

More knights dismounted. The Berber soldiers behind them began to stir, some calling out in the same language Felip had used with the Toledan. The knights at the cart had pulled the sackcloth right back, looking into more bags. The Toledans jumped down and moved away, except for one, a tall young woman in a long, red robe, who stayed at the front of the cart. The first knight tipped out another bag, revealing silver metalwork, this time instruments and devices he did not recognise. As he ransacked, other knights began to gather up objects and stuff them roughly back into empty bags, clearly making some judgement on their value as they did. Felip saw one of them pick up a long cylindrical object made of silver and finely engraved. This man puzzled over it a while before dropping it to the ground and stamping it flat, then bending it in half so as to fit it more easily into a bag. The man did not notice the two spheres of a transparent material that popped out, one from each end, and shattered on the hard ground.

The Berber soldiers were becoming more agitated. The two knights still mounted moved towards them; Felip felt his stomach tightening. The first knight had moved on, to a set of chests at the back of the cart. He opened one and found in it books; large, leather-covered books. Another chest held more books, and another. Frustrated in his search, he began to throw the books onto the ground behind him. One bounced, and fell open in front of one of the Berbers at a richly decorated page. At this the man gave a great shout and rushed at the knight at the cart.

As the knight turned, the Berber drew a long, curved sword, and in one sweep sliced off his head. It bounced onto the hard ground beside him, eyes wide, throwing a spiral of red across the snow. The body toppled slowly, the arm still moving a hand towards the hilt of his sword.

Instantly the two mounted knights drew swords and rode at the Berber, hacking him to the ground. As the other Muslim soldiers rushed the knights at the cart, the young woman in the red robe reached in and pulled out something wrapped in a cloth, which she held to her before running back towards the mouth of the valley. Felip followed her. The young man watched them go, turning his horse back and forth around the bloody fight breaking out in front of him.

The valley into which the woman had fled tapered quickly until it was little more than the width of the cart that had come along it. High boulders lay on either side, and a few bushes. Felip stopped; he could hear the sound of rushing water, behind him screams and shouts. Then a stone, falling. He moved onto a narrow path to his left and followed it. At its end stood the woman, clasping the cloth bundle to her stomach. Her black hair fell across the shoulders of her finely patterned robe, trimmed with gold and silver thread. She was reaching down to her ankle, but as she saw Felip, she straightened.

Neither spoke. The rushing water was behind and below the woman, a long way below, and louder now. She held the bundle tighter and turned to the void. Felip froze. The woman looked down; to him the seconds that passed felt like hours. Then she turned back and he saw her dark eyes burning with anger.

He stretched out an arm. Slowly, he raised it to the sky.

'If this were night, ten thousand stars would be looking down at us.'

'Ten thousand witnesses to this betrayal!'

Felip lowered his arm, and shook his head.

'I cannot save you, Samra; but I can save the book.'

He saw her looking past him at the sandy-haired young Norman who was now standing just behind him. She turned away again and closed her eyes; pressing the cloth-covered bundle to her, rocking it in her arms like a baby, whispering softly. The abyss was a step away.

Felip tensed, ready for a dash to her that he knew would be hopeless.

Samra turned back. She came slowly towards them and held out the bundle. The monk took it, and as she walked past, her eyes met the young man's; light blue-grey and set deep in his face. For an instant they were connected; the woman whose predecessors had walked the streets of Babylon, the young man whose forebears had sailed from the shores of Scandinavia. Then she was past. The young man followed Samra out of the valley, to where his master and two other knights were waiting. These two led her away; he could see the blood on them. All was quiet now, and not a single Berber soldier was left alive.

The young man spoke to the leader of the Normans. 'You swore the Jews would have safe conduct.'

'I said I would deliver them to the Christian lands, Hugh de Bayeux. And I will.' He went after his men.

The young man turned and went back into the valley. Felip was still in the same spot, turning the bundle over in his hands, looking at the velvet cloth decorated with a moon and stars.

'Do you have the book?' the young man asked.

'I do.'

'Is it the one?'

'It is.'

'Then you must make it safe. My father will find you a place in a good monastery in Normandy.'

'Normandy? They say Normandy is wet, Hugh — wet and cold.'

'No colder than this,' the young man replied.

And the monk saw that his hands and face were blue.

The House of Godwin

Winchester, Wessex, May 1032

The Thegn of Berewic looked around him at the torches burning on the walls of the New Minster, lighting up the paintings of saints and angels in their bright colours. Sighere was nervous to be far from his Sussex seat and in the home of the royal treasury and capital of one of England's ancient kingdoms, which by gift of the great King Cnut had become the earldom of the kinsman he was meeting. It was not lost on him that this man, who had risen from lowly origins to become Cnut's chief adviser and enabler, was now ruling over the lands that gave their name to the house of Wessex that his own house of Godwin had helped the king to destroy or exile.

Alerted by the sound of the great door closing, he turned to find Earl Godwin striding down the nave towards him, banishing such of his company as had dared follow him with a wave of his hand back to the outside.

'Sighere! No time to waste, cousin; the queen will be here soon. What news do you bring us?'

His kinsman looked back to the door. 'Why here? Why does Emma want to meet us here and not at the royal palace?'

'Because this place is safe. Like me, she can shake off her followers with their spies and tale tellers to come in here and talk freely.'

Sighere shook his head, and his red hair shook with it. 'Well then, you should know…' he began, but too late, for there was again a noise from the doorway, and again a figure entered the minster with a retinue behind, which was commanded to wait outside. As the figure paused to make its devotion towards the rood screen, through the open door a little of the evening light came in, and with it a sparrow that began to flutter around the great space, going from a niche with the figure of a saint to the rood screen and back again. Godwin laughed; his blond hair shook with his laughter, and his great frame with it.

'Poor sparrow! If it only knew what company it keeps in here. And the queen hasn't even seen it.'

Berewic's thegn looked at England's foremost earl, then at the figure now moving quickly towards them. Wife to Cnut, the Dane who had been England's king since he had ousted Ethelred, its last king from the house of Wessex, Emma was also Ethelred's widow, and in marrying her Cnut had rubbed salt into the defeated country's wounds. Sighere had seen the queen before, but not this close, and he was surprised at how slight she was; she might have been a servant hurrying through a hall house on some errand. But her richly embroidered gown spoke of her status, and her upright bearing of her rule over others. Then, when Emma opened her mouth to speak for herself, her voice was steely and commanding.

'Godwin, is this the man you spoke of?' She looked at Sighere as if he were a cup bearer.

The earl bowed. 'Sighere, a cousin and kinsman to me, and Thegn of Berewic, my lady.'

'Berewic?' Beneath her wimple the queen's dark eyebrows raised slightly. 'The manor Cnut took from the Wessex and gave to the Godwins? Does this man wish to return it?'

Sighere's mouth fell open, and Godwin laughed.

'No, my lady, no such thing. Berewic prospers under him, and it will ever be the manor of a Godwin.'

He shot a glance at his cousin and Sighere knew what he was thinking. The thegn's wife had died leaving him with one child; a three-year-old girl was the slender thread now holding the succession of Berewic in her tiny hands. He thought of Æadgytha back in Berewic, playing with a little doll that stood for her mother talking to her. *You are a Godwin, my child, and one day you will be the Thegn of Berewic.* Words the little girl had never heard her mother speak, yet knew in her heart.

'Well?' Queen Emma demanded.

Sighere pulled himself back to the present. 'I- I-' he stammered, 'I have news from Normandy, my lady. It concerns your cousin, the duke – and your sons. Your sons by Ethelred,' he added quickly, seeing the flash in her eyes and remembering that Emma had only one son whose fate concerned her now; Harthacnut, her son by Cnut.

'Yes?' she snapped.

'If it is true, then Duke Robert is allying with your sons… pardon me,' Sighere faltered again, 'with Edward and Alfred, to invade England and restore the Wessex to the throne.'

Letting this sink in, Sighere watched the queen's face. If she was moved, she did not show it, but the steel in her voice was edged with irritation when she spoke.

'How do you know this? How does a Godwin have news from the Wessex exiles in Normandy?'

'When the king – blessed be his name – took Berewic from him, the old thegn, Rædmund—'

'I know his name. He used to hunt with Ethelred. Get on with it.'

'Rædmund went to Normandy with Edward and Alfred, but a woman who stayed in Berewic kept contact with her sister, who went with them. It is a letter from this woman that has alerted us.'

Emma shook her head. 'Duke Robert already made clear his support of the Wessex in this matter, when he sent envoys to Cnut to demand their restoration.'

'And we sent them packing,' added Earl Godwin, glaring at his cousin. 'Is there more?'

'The sister's husband is a shipwright,' Sighere went on. 'She says he has lately been at several places along the Normandy coast, at Robert's bidding, overseeing the building of ships. Not many in one place, but if brought together, many, many ships.'

He looked at Godwin, who looked at the queen. Emma was gazing past them and towards the rood screen, as if lost in thought.

'Did you know, Berewic's thegn, that a few years ago, I came here with the king to present a cross to the altar through there – a great cross of gold? All who saw it marvelled at the splendour of it, and how it spoke of the dedication to our Lord of we who gave it to this minster.' Now she looked straight back into Sighere's eyes. 'They say it is a wonder that my husband has become so saintly and peaceable, given that his wresting of England was bloody and violent. That he gives such gifts – and so many – to our religious houses, that he went as a pilgrim to Rome, that he venerates the bones of an archbishop his Danes slew for their amusement. Some say they see my hand in this,' the queen went on, 'urging my husband to a show of piety to win favour with a pious people. But his devotion is heartfelt. Only one who knows the horror of war knows the value of peace. Cnut has brought that peace.'

'A peace we are all thankful to our king for,' Earl Godwin added.

'Do not forget, Earl Godwin,' Emma rejoined, 'that I have seen both. I was still a young woman, married four years to Ethelred, when the Danes invaded England again. Here at Winchester, I watched with everyone else as their army passed the city gates on their way to the coast, laden with booty from miles around. They were so sure of themselves they hardly glanced in our direction, let alone take care lest they be attacked from within our walls. And we who looked on knew what death and devastation they had left behind; we women were especially thankful that they passed us by.'

In the silence that followed, the two men shuffled their feet, until Emma spoke again.

'This sister who stayed in Berewic – who is she? Do you trust her to keep this to herself?'

'She became my wife, my lady.'

Earl Godwin cleared his throat. 'We should make such preparations as we see fit. I will alert the fleet.'

'Do it quietly; tell the commanders only that we are practising against an attack, as we do from time to time.'

The earl bowed. 'As you wish, my lady. Will you tell the king?'

Emma shook her head. 'My husband is not a well man. Leave him to his prayers, Godwin.' Addressing Sighere, she went on, 'I will have my own letter delivered to you to send to Rædmund, through your wife and her sister in Normandy. Let your wife send nothing back until then.'

Emma turned on her heel and was gone; her royal figure sweeping down the nave, the door opening as she reached it. In the light that flooded in, she stood and made her devotion towards the rood screen once more before calling back to the earl, her raised voice echoing round the minster.

'Never hide anything from me, Godwin. Like the sparrow in here, the truth will find the light.'

Quickly Emma was surrounded by her retinue and ushered outside. At the exact moment everyone had passed through and before the door shut, the sparrow made a dash from the head of the saint and bolted into the light.

Earl Godwin turned to Sighere. 'We are lucky that your dead wife still has news from her sister.'

'It sits ill with me to get my priest to write back in her name,' Sighere growled, 'as much as it does that he has to read her sister's letters to me. But it makes us of greater value to the queen…'

'And through her, to the king,' Godwin returned. 'Do not forget, cousin, that when other families among the English had been devastated by the wars with the Danes, when other men felt Cnut's vengeance by the sword, wherever they fled or hid, I stepped forwards and took the king's part. I have ever been at his side, in England, in Denmark, in peace and – if it comes to it – in war. Our family's fate is bound to his now, for good or for ill.'

'What of Leofric, Earl of Mercia? His rise does not worry you?'

Godwin grinned. 'I have an asset he does not: Gytha. My wife is Cnut's sister-in-law.'

The thegn pursed his lips. 'Still, for Emma to turn against her own sons in Normandy; will she see Edward and Alfred slain as they step ashore? Emma who comes from the Norman ruling house – for all the English name they gave her when she came here – and is cousin to Duke Robert?'

'Like the Godwins, Emma made her choice and cannot go back on it.' The earl looked around him as if he might be overheard, then leant in closer to Sighere. 'Do not fail the queen, cousin, for Emma is a she-wolf; the cub she has now in her lair with Cnut is the one she will defend tooth and nail. The cubs she had with Ethelred, and that plot against her in Normandy, when Edward is not hunting and Alfred in his books, she will tear to pieces if they come near Harthacnut.'

'And if she orders us against them?'

'Then we will tear them to pieces.' Godwin straightened. 'I must go – there is work to do. Go back to your manor, Sighere, for you have preparations to make too.'

The earl spun on his heel and strode away. The door closed behind him, leaving the Thegn of Berewic alone in the torchlight with the saints and angels. Sighere turned to the rood screen and made a devotion to the unseen altar beyond. *God help me if Edward and Alfred return. For if they do, they will bring with them the man I turned out of his manor. And Rædmund and his sons will want retribution on me, and on my daughter.*

A Devil

Bay of Biscay, France, July 1032

Shielding his eyes from the sun, Jaco Reuben looked across the stretch of water that separated him in the stern of the *Tita* from the thin smudge of land disappearing into the sea to the east. Brittany; they were nearly clear of the Bay of Biscay, that bringer of storms and wrecker of ships. His other hand rested on the ship's side, though it was not for support, for his tanned, wiry body clung to the deck like a crab, but with the pride of possession. Under the clear skies, the squat little ship he captained would soon be past the mouth of the narrow sea that lay between Brittany and England, and passing beyond Wales to Ireland; Jaco's destination. Looking up at the square sail filling in the fresh breeze, he nodded to the man at the steering oar, and turned to another of his men.

'Bring the woman up to me – the tall one, in the red robe.'

The man grunted and headed to where a group of people was huddled in the prow, his rolling gait easily taking in the movement below his feet. Jaco crossed to the other side of the *Tita*, where a rough shelter of planking and old sails gave him some private quarters. Pushing through a gap in the sails, he waited inside. There was little around him: a sword hanging from the ship's side, some things on a shelf, one stool, and a rough bed of more old sails and some furs.

From outside, the sound of someone being dragged grew louder before a young, dark-haired woman was pushed through the gap and towards him. Once alone with her, Jaco studied the woman as she stood, almost a head height taller than he, breathing heavily and staring at him with fierce, dark eyes, rubbing her wrists where a rope had tied them. He saw her dark skin, and a long red robe that was finely patterned, but so dirty now it was almost black. Jaco reached out a hand and ran it along the tears on a seam where the trim had been pulled off.

'How you are come down in the world, my proud beauty.'

If she was startled to hear him speak in what he knew was her own language, the woman did not show it, though he could tell she was looking at his sun-bleached hair and sea-green eyes, and thinking, *He is one of us?* Nor did she flinch when, as he spoke, he pulled his hand away from her robe and brushed her cheek with it.

'What was it?' Jaco went on. 'The trim on your robe.'

'Gold and silver thread,' she answered. 'And here and there, lapis lazuli, for the stars in the night sky, which are my love and my calling.'

The captain nodded. 'Who took it? The Normans who captured you?'

The woman shook her head. 'The Christians in the north of Spain that they sold me to.' Seeing the stool, she went to sit on it, where she hunched in thought for a while before looking up at him. 'When the Christians heard I was in the service of my Moorish ruler in Toledo, they thought he might pay ransom for me. So they sent a message and pulled a piece of trim off my robe to go with it. But he answered that he had no money to pay a ransom. They pulled another length of trim off, and sent another message that they were sure he could find the money.'

'And did he?'

'He said yes, he could find it, but they would have to wait.'

'He was stalling; I would do the same.'

'The Christians sent word back to him, with another length of trim. The trim on my robe was running out, they said, and their patience with it. My ruler replied that he was trying to borrow the money, but it was difficult to obtain credit.'

'A good tactic.'

'The rest of the trim followed, with another message – that months had already gone by, there was no more gold and silver thread, and there would be no more waiting. Next time, it would be one of my fingers; then a hand.'

Jaco glanced quickly down at her hands. All of her long, elegant fingers were there.

'What happened?'

'My ruler sent back that if the Christians could cut off the hand of an astronomer, they were clearly barbarians, and he did not trade with barbarians.'

'So the Christians sold you to me. Did you really think the Moor would buy back a Jew?'

The woman got up and stood before him, the light burning in her eyes.

'I was held in honour. I was privileged.'

'Honour? Privileged?' Jaco laughed. 'Everywhere in the world, we are others' servants, nothing more. The higher we rise, the more servile we become. Oh yes, the Moors in

Spain tolerate us, and there have been many like you, rich and rewarded in the times of plenty. But wait; the hard times will come, and when there is a defeat or a plague or an earthquake, we will be blamed. Then there will be sword and fire in place of honour and privilege.'

'So this is your answer?' The woman motioned towards the prow of the *Tita*. 'To trade in your own people? To make slaves of us, because we are servants?'

Jaco's eyes hardened. 'I trade in any people, if they let themselves be caught like animals.' Going over to where his sword hung, he ran a hand along its scabbard before turning back to the woman. 'When I was young, I vowed I would be no man's servant. The sea and a ship gave me the freedom I sought. I had to take orders but I bit my tongue and bided my time; I made alliances. A day came when the captain refused to go after a prize the rest of us thought worth the risk. While the others muttered, I killed the captain myself and took over. Now, at twenty-one, I own my own ship. I speak four languages and I don't say please or thank you in any of them.'

'And the prize?'

Jaco spread his arms to indicate the ship. 'You are on it. But I am bored with this talk. Take off your robe and lie down.'

Her eyes followed to where he had pointed, to the bed. When they looked back at him, there was a flicker of alarm in them, yet she said nothing. As she turned away and stooped to lift the hem of her robe, Jaco saw only compliance; he began to pull his shirt up over his head. The instant the captain's head came clear, he saw the woman facing him, and a blade moving fast towards him. Still trapped in their sleeves, his arms met the blow from the knife; there was a sting of pain and blood welled along a forearm. The woman struck at him again and he had to dodge her, awkwardly, arms still trapped.

'Help! In God's name, help me!' he called out.

Another blow, and another dodge before he shouted for help again, louder. Two of Jaco's men appeared through the gap in the sails. One paused and laughed at the sight of his captain, half out of his bloody shirt. The other made a grab at the woman but she turned swiftly and he got a cut to his cheek as she lunged at him. But it gave Jaco time to pull his arms free, and he grabbed her from behind, while the cut man seized the wrist of the hand with the knife and the man who had laughed grabbed her legs. Between them, the three wrestled her to the deck, face down, and the cut man sat on her, twisting her arm behind her back until she screamed and dropped the knife.

'Fetch rope to tie her with,' Jaco said to the other man, wrapping his shirt around his bleeding arm.

When the man had gone, Jaco dropped to his knees and looked at the half-turned face of the woman, listening to her heavy breathing. He pointed to the gap in the sails through which the man who had laughed had gone to fetch rope.

'When we approach Dublin,' he said to the cut man, 'he takes an oar with the slaves. Now, pass me the knife.'

The cut man handed the knife to his captain, who took it and wiped the blood from it, before turning it over in his hand. He saw an inscription on the blade, with three lines of text.

Now the other man was back with rope, and they put the woman in a sitting position on the deck and tied her arms to the stool behind her.

'Where did you have this hidden?' Jaco asked the woman, holding out the knife, but she said nothing.

A Devil

Jaco remembered her lifting the hem of her robe and pointed at it, nodding to the cut man, who stooped and moved a hand to her feet. She tried to pull her legs away, but he had seen a small sheath tied to an ankle. He grabbed the ankle with one hand while the other the man undid the thongs fastening the sheath to it and passed it to his captain. Jaco studied the sheath a while, wondering how the knife that had attacked him, still in his other hand, would fit in it. Yet it did, perfectly, as if it had become smaller.

'Do not take the knife from me,' the woman called out.

'You think I should leave you with this? So you can slash me again?' He went to put the knife on the shelf.

'When I lost all that is dear to me,' the woman went on, 'only the knife remained. Without it, I am nothing.'

Jaco looked at her. 'You became nothing the day you were captured. The next man that has to handle you will be the one who buys you in the Dublin slave market.' And he threw the knife onto the shelf.

On the floor, arms tied behind her to the stool, dirty robe now splashed with blood, the woman did not speak. She threw back her head and let out a wail; a long, devastating scream, which seemed to leave her body as if it had never belonged to her, but was returning to heaven – or hell. The cut man beside her covered his ears; the man who had laughed crossed himself.

For some moments the three men in the shelter stood staring at her. There was no sound except the wind in the sail, no movement bar the steady lift and drop of the ship beneath their feet. But the noise of the sail was growing louder and the *Tita* was beginning to pitch more heavily. In an instant, the sun outside was gone and in the shelter it was nearly dark.

Pushing outside, Jaco looked up; the sky was rapidly covering in a suffocating blackness. The strengthening wind was beginning to push the ship along; he glanced at the man at the steering oar, who pointed out to sea.

'Storm! Storm coming!'

But the man could not say more, for already he was having to wrestle with the oar in his hands. Now Jaco had been joined by the other two men, looking around them and up at the sky, panic on their faces. Shouting over the wind, the cut man spoke in his captain's ear.

'We should take in the sail.'

Jaco shook his head. 'Too late.'

Even as he spoke, the wind was rising ever more fiercely from the west; all his men together would not furl the sail now. And at least the sail gave them direction; without it they would be helpless, tossed this way and that.

'All we can hope is to outrun it. Take two men and go to the steering oar; I want two on it at all times, taking turns.'

As the man left him, Jaco knew his order was a token; there would be no steering in this sea. He turned to the other man.

'Fasten down everything that can be. Make sure every rope is tied.'

'And the slaves?'

Jaco looked along the *Tita* to the prow, pitching violently against the sea.

'They are fastened together, and to the ship. Keep them or lose them, there is nothing to be done.'

The man turned away, and Jaco looked back at the shelter. *God help us.* Inside, the woman had fallen over and was beginning to be rolled along the deck with the stool. Finally, she fetched up against the bed, the stool wedging her from behind. And there she lay, the ship groaning beneath her like a wounded creature.

In the storm, the *Tita* ran and ran. No man dared move in the open; anyone crossing the deck would have been plucked from it by wind or water. The storm howled over it, the waves crashed onto it and the rain lashed it like a whip. Jaco held on to the mast, feeling the huge strain in the timber, and hearing the wind screaming in the sail over his head. He knew that at any minute, the sail could tear free or the mast could snap. He had no idea where they were or where they were headed; but if they had not sundered on a coast, they must have passed between Brittany and the tip of England, and were heading still further east beyond that. Through the rain driving across the ship, the prow was a misty outline as again and again it plunged into the sea and lifted, with the water pouring onto the deck and rushing towards him. The grey, sodden mass behind the prow that was taking this deluge might have been a pile of rags, not people.

When the storm dropped, it was as suddenly as it came. The blackness swept away to the east, the sun came out, the wind slackened and the rain stopped. Men turned their backs to the sun, letting the warmth through their soaking clothes and into their chilled bodies. Only one man was now needed on the steering oar. The sail flapped a little idly, as if it had never had to face a strong wind. Below it, Jaco let go of the mast and shook the stiffness from his body. The cut man appeared beside him and pointed to the prow questioningly.

'Untie them all. Throw the dead overboard and let the others dry out a while.'

The man went to do his bidding, and Jaco watched as

he loosened ropes, and the huddled mass became individual figures once more. Among them, there was movement everywhere.

'Alive!' the man shouted up the ship. 'All of them, alive!'

Jaco pushed through the gap in the sails and into the shelter. Everything from the shelf was on the floor, among the debris that had washed in from the rest of the ship. The woman was face down on the bed, the stool at her back. For a moment he wondered if she was alive, until she turned a little. He picked up the knife, pulled it out of its sheath and cut her ropes. Freed from the stool, she lifted it upright and sat on it, rubbing her arms and legs, before looking up at him. The ferocity in her eyes was gone; their darkness was fathomless. It brought back to Jaco memories of the sea in a night of dead calm, under cloudless skies; when the light of the stars falling on the water did not penetrate, as if the deep refused to give up its secrets. He looked at the writing on the knife blade.

'What does it say?' he asked.

The woman shook her head. 'I have a destiny you cannot understand.'

He looked at the shirt still wrapped around his forearm, and its dark bloodstain, and at the marks of his blood on her robe.

'I should have you thrown overboard,' he said. 'But a woman who can conjure storms must be a devil – who knows what you can do? Besides, I paid money for you. Your destiny is to be sold as a slave. We are at the mouth of the River Seine; Normandy. Tomorrow we will be moored at Rouen and soon I'll be rid of you.' He pushed the knife back into its sheath. 'And of this.'

After the Storm

Forest of Lyons, Normandy, July 1032

The messenger who left Rouen and struck east towards the Forest of Lyons was taking the route of his Viking ancestors. They had followed the River Seine into the rich heartland of what was to become Normandy, the land of the Northman. But when the king of the West Franks gave the Viking raiders land and their leader Rollo accepted baptism into the Christian faith, the pirate leaders became settlers. The messenger was a servant of their descendants, the dukes of Normandy, and they were founders of and donors to many abbeys. It was the abbey of St Ouen at Rouen that had appealed to Duke Robert to mend the damage to its roof from a sudden storm, and the duke had sent to his hunting forest of Lyons for timber. There was nowhere better than among the great oaks and beeches of the forest to find it, and none better than the forest warden to the dukes of Normandy to choose it.

Gilbert was at work when the messenger arrived, clearing up the damage around his forest home. The wind was still stirring in the trees, a restlessness that his big shire horse felt, as it shook itself in its harness while waiting for Gilbert to lash on another great branch to drag away. The advancing messenger saw a tall, powerfully built man with very short hair and light blue eyes, square-faced, with a strong jaw. The hot weather had returned after the storm and below his cap, Gilbert's forehead was pricked with sweat. Under his tunic, close-fitting like a brown woollen jersey reaching to his knees and open at the neck, a damp patch showed on the white shirt at his chest. Hearing the order for timber, Gilbert spoke as he moved; slowly and deliberately.

'Tomorrow, you say? It will take a while to find and to cut. There may be some fallen timber I can use, but my men are away clearing roads and paths…' He shrugged. 'There aren't so many trees that will be good enough. Tell the duke I will do my best.'

The messenger was gazing around him, his nose puckered. Gilbert looked at him in his fine livery, with the leg bindings he would have been loath to get muddy from the road. He would have hated just as much to get the coat on his fine black horse dirty. Gilbert knew what was coming next.

'I was told I was coming to a wood. Where are all the trees?'

Gilbert sighed. All twenty-six years of his life had been spent among trees – and there were trees in the forest. It had taught him to be patient.

'A hunting forest is not a wood, my friend. To hold good game and provide good chase for the hunt, it has to be a mix of open ground and scattered trees – in small stands or singly – and thickets of scrub. This is what you see around you. It's my job to keep it so, never to let the trees take over, and to manage these to provide timber for many purposes. And all the while I have to uphold the forest law for my duke;

I protect the animals of the hunt, the deer and wild boar, against poachers and wild beasts, and allow those with rights in the forest to go about their business, like grazing livestock or collecting wood.'

'So are you axeman or herdsman?'

'A little of both. My father was forest warden before me and I never expected, or wanted, to be anything else. You learn a bit, living in a place like this.'

Gilbert was being modest. He knew every hill and vale of his forest, every stream and river, and every track and path, even where there looked to be no path at all. His animals moved across this landscape and he moved with them, counting, observing, ready to intervene if needed, but otherwise happy to let the round of seasons and of birth and death follow their course, so long as there was enough to hunt without risking the survival of the whole. His trees sprang from seed in this landscape and he watched them grow, saw how they formed, straight as arrows or with their limbs aslant, saw them ready to cleave into the timbers of a hundred houses; or perhaps of one great cathedral.

So as the messenger rode away, Gilbert set about finding the timbers he would need, cutting down and to size great trunks and limbs and using his horse to pull them out into the open on roller logs, then up onto a long cart. Once satisfied with the amount and quality of timber he had loaded, he backed the horse into the cart shafts and left it food and water while he took a little of both for himself for the journey to Rouen.

The house was quiet as Gilbert left, after he had said a prayer before the cross on the wall. As he passed the rowan tree that stood at the centre of the clearing where his horse and cart waited, he saw its delicate leaves still moving in the wind and put out a hand to feel their touch.

Something is changing.

Turning to go, Gilbert made a silent wish to Víðarr, the god of the forest, and as an afterthought he could not explain, to Nótt, the goddess of the night.

A Traveller's Tale

St Ouen, Normandy, July 1032

The man Gilbert had asked for when he arrived at the gatehouse of the abbey of St Ouen, just outside Rouen, wore the black habit of his Benedictine order. This was a new man in charge of repairs to the buildings and Gilbert was curious to meet him. He saw a young man with an oval face and a strong nose, and on a tonsure he wore too long, dark brown hair that fell over one eye and had to be flicked back with a quick movement of the hand. Not tall, and stoutly built, since he had exchanged the life of a travelling scholar for the cloister, Felip de Mazerolles tended to get fat from living too well. Quickly the monk's glance took in Gilbert, and his horse and laden cart waiting beyond, before dropping to his muddy boots and the trousers with leather leg bindings crossing them to knee height that Gilbert always wore, which were just as mud-spattered.

'Such a storm we have had, and at this time of year,' Felip said.

'My apologies,' said Gilbert. 'I am late – the roads are bad. You will not want such a dishevelled guest.'

'Nonsense. You are arrived safely and your timbers with

you, to mend our damage. That is all I asked for, and you are welcome.'

Felip's handshake was strong and his words were warm as he introduced himself; Gilbert felt a liking for him at once.

As usual Gilbert oversaw as the heavy timbers were unloaded, many monks now working in place of his one horse that had loaded them in the forest. While the horse was seen to, Gilbert was brought into the shelter of the monastery and his guestroom in the outer parlour of the western range. Here was the welcome of a fire to dry out, and he was seated at a table with food to restore him. Around him the life of the abbey was going on: prayers, work, food, rest – a daily round whose quiet energy Gilbert could appreciate, even if he could never exchange the self-reliance of his forest for such a close community. Beside and above him was a more familiar world, for the abbey buildings were made from wood, and some of that had come from the Forest of Lyons. As he ate, Gilbert could admire in the strongly upright timbers of the walls and the delicate curves of the roof supports both the choice of wood, and its setting in place.

Gilbert was finishing his meal with some walnuts when Felip came into the parlour and joined him at the table. The monk pushed a cup of wine towards the man from the forest, then poured one for himself.

'Fine timber, as they say we always have from the Forest of Lyons. Be sure to thank the duke warmly when you see him.' As he drank, Felip's deep brown eyes moved restlessly and searchingly, and Gilbert sensed there would soon be a question. 'But listen… tell me what you know about timber.'

'What do you need to know?'

'Duke Robert is reconciled with the church and with the

Bishop of Bayeux. He wants to found a new abbey beyond Bayeux, at Cerisy, on the site of the old monastery founded by St Vigor that the Vikings destroyed. I am to go there and begin the clearing and building work.'

Gilbert cracked another walnut in his hand. 'Timber?'

'The timber you bring, you have chosen and cut to size for its use for building. I need to know what to look for in a virgin tree, or my monks will chop everything to bits.'

'Ah…' Gilbert thought a while, then went on, 'wood moves and settles as it dries, and is stronger the more bent it grows. Look for trees with a natural shape, for roof trusses especially, and set them aside. Use them green, or if you let them dry, then not too quickly.'

Felip flicked back his hair. 'They said you would know everything. But I badly need someone like you, with your skill. I can plead with the duke for you to come with me. Cerisy is not so far from the Forest of Valognes, a hunting ground he would love for his sport.'

'Not me. I am too settled at Lyons. And why has he asked you to go to Cerisy?'

Felip refilled both their cups with wine.

'The Cotentin is rough country, with its ignorance of God barely left behind. It seems my travels in Spain make me an obvious choice to forge the way.'

'Spain? A long way from Rouen.'

'It is a long story. My birthplace was across the Pyrenees, in the Languedoc, but like many others I was gripped by the tales of the Moors of Spain, their fabulous cities and their learning, and how they lived in harmony with their Jewish and Christian subjects.'

'And you found them, these fabulous places?'

'And more. Imagine cities with streets with running water and gardens full of scented flowers. With libraries where men — and women — of all faiths and none, work together and argue together, pushing the limits of what we know of the world beyond anything you or I can imagine.' Felip leant closer across the table towards Gilbert, his eyes bright in the firelight. 'The Great Library at Cordoba once had over four hundred thousand books, Gilbert, with nearly fifty volumes to catalogue them all. Imagine! A whole building, with row on row of shelves, as high as the ceiling. Between the rows of shelves, scholars sat reading at tables, or gathered outside to debate what they had read. The head librarian to Caliph Al-Hakam, who founded it, used to send his deputy, a woman called Labna, to the bookstalls and merchants of Cairo, Damascus and Baghdad in search of new acquisitions. Toledo, where I lived and worked, has several libraries, linked to its centres of faith and learning.'

Gilbert was shaking his head.

'Four hundred thousand? Where would you get enough calf-, goat- or sheepskin to make the parchment for that many books?'

Felip smiled. 'Not parchment; paper. Only paper can produce that many books quickly and cheaply, and the Arabs have been using paper for two hundred years. You can make paper from many things: rags, plant fibres, even wood. Imagine if the trees you nurture were to end up in books, not buildings.'

Gilbert nodded slowly, taking this in. 'Why did you leave Spain?'

'The old order has collapsed; the land is in turmoil. If this learning was to reach us here in the north, it needed to be saved. So I sent books back, unsure if they would even reach the Languedoc. But then I worked on a great book written by two scholars, one an Arab and one a Jew. My part was small – to translate some of it into Latin, so it could be read and understood. But as I worked, I knew I had to save it myself, to bring it out from Spain. When I came by it early this year, I was offered a place to study it at St Ouen by the father of a young man who was serving a group of Norman knights in Spain.'

'This book – it's made of paper too?'

'Alas, no,' Felip laughed, 'it is many centuries old, and paper had not reached the Arab world from China when it was made. It is parchment, a material but few can afford, and it might have taken three hundred skins to make it. Yet what is in it will be brought to the world by books made of paper; only paper can bring knowledge to the many.'

'You are working on this book now?' Gilbert asked.

'Yes, though I make little progress. It is the most extraordinary thing I have ever come across. Even though I translated some of it with those who wrote it, still it astonishes me. The knowledge in the book, of astronomy, optics, mathematics, medicine, is so far beyond what we have, and often beyond what I can understand, if I am to translate further.'

'The Moors – they have this knowledge, then?'

'Yes, and we call them unbelievers, ignorant. Even now, Christian armies are ransacking their libraries, looking for loot, burning the books they find. To get as many to safety – and this book above all – before it is too late, became my life's work.'

'If God gave them all this knowledge, then we are the ignorant ones?'

Felip shook his head sadly. 'I cannot tell you what it is like, to see people discover the world together, and each offer that discovery to the glory of his or her God and the beauty of the human spirit, without question. And then to see the mob, driven by ignorance and hate, refusing anything outside its own set of laws, and destroying what it cannot understand. But do not misunderstand me; many of the books in Toledo came from the library at Cordoba after it was purged by the fanatic Al-Mansur. Intolerance is not confined to the Christians.'

Gilbert was thoughtful a while. 'Optics?'

'The working of the eye; how we are able to see.' Felip put a hand over the other man's eyes, and the room went black. 'The moment I take this away, you make the world.' And he took his hand away, and Gilbert made the world, as he had said.

Suddenly a man burst into the parlour, followed closely by the abbey porter, an old man who could scarcely keep pace with his charge. He had not been able to stop him, said the porter; the man had insisted on seeing Felip. The man was captain of a ship from the north of Spain, the porter went on, where Christians fighting the Moors had sold him some captives. He had put them on board to take to Ireland, but the storm had driven him into the narrow sea beyond Brittany and to Normandy.

A slaver, thought Gilbert.

The man's skin was dark from the sun and the sea; his face, with its sea-green eyes, deeply lined and weather-beaten. His clothes were salt-laden and one arm was roughly bandaged. He was clearly troubled but calmed a little when given wine. Felip asked what he wanted.

In answer, the man pulled something from inside his clothing and hastily threw it onto the table as if it burnt in his hand. Gilbert saw a small knife in a sheath. For what felt to Gilbert like an age, Felip stared at it.

'Where did you get this?' Felip said at length. Gilbert heard the shake in his voice.

'From the woman who slashed me and one of my men,' the captain replied. His accent was strong, but he spoke French well enough. 'And who was nearly the end of my ship.'

'What do you want from me?' Felip asked him.

'The knife – it has some writing on it; three lines, like a curse. I was told that you will be able to read it, and I don't want the thing near me. Or the woman; she is a devil. I have brought her into Rouen, looking to sell her. But now I am here, I'm afraid what might happen if she is in a crowd of people.'

'You can take her to the market place tomorrow,' Felip said calmly. 'I will be there to protect the crowd. And do not fear the knife; it is now in my possession.'

Quickly he picked the knife up and put it up the sleeve of his habit.

The Knife

Rouen, Normandy, July 1032

Leading his horse, Gilbert made his way from the monastery into Rouen. The now-empty cart behind swayed as it travelled along ruts deepened by the recent heavy rains. Along the streets, with their broad thoroughfares and narrow alleys, people were making repairs to the closely packed houses; someone atop a ladder mending thatch, another man hauling a timber up on a rope and pulley to where the corner of a building had come away. Gilbert found a man who would guard horse and cart for a fee, and went with the money he had made from selling his timber at St Ouen to buy food, cloth and new tools.

He had just come back with the last of the sacks he had bought and was preparing to leave when he heard the noise: a roar from the direction of the market place. They must have brought in the devil woman. He took up one of the loaves of bread he had bought, gave the man he had left minding the horse and cart promise of further payment if he waited a while, and made his way there. Many others scurried past as he went; by the time he reached the market place it was full of a jeering, jostling crowd. Felip was at the back, hands folded in front of him, hood pulled up, observing. Gilbert pushed his way through to the monk's side, parting the crowd easily with his size. Faces turned to look at him; the tall, squarely built man of the forest, out of place among the squat townspeople.

In the centre of the square, on a rough raised platform with a couple of steps up to it, were a man and a young woman. The man was the ship's captain who had burst into the monastery the night before. He stood facing the crowd, occasionally saying something Gilbert could not hear over the noise. The woman had a wooden pole across her shoulders behind her neck, to which her outstretched arms were tied by the wrists. Her thick black hair, matted with dirt, fell across bare shoulders, which showed a dark, olive brown skin. Part defiant, part terrified, she glared out at the crowd, from time to time lifting her head and calling out in a howl of pain and anger that carried far into the tense and sweaty air of the market place. Every time she cried out, many in the crowd crossed themselves, and no one bore her gaze, instead looking away or hiding their faces.

Gilbert pulled a piece of bread from his loaf and chewed it thoughtfully.

'She is a Moor?' The sun was climbing in the sky now, hot on the back of his neck below his cap.

'You might think so, from this.'

Felip held out his left hand. Sitting in the palm of his hand was the knife the man on the platform had thrown onto the table the night before. Looking at it more closely now, Gilbert saw a small sheath of soft, pale leather from which showed the handle, wound round with a thin, polished cord of darker leather. The sheath had short, slender thongs attached at the bottom and top.

Gilbert took the knife and pulled it from the sheath. In his fat, wide palm the sheath had looked even smaller; he would have said the knife must have a short blade, almost square. Yet as he withdrew it, the blade was longer and more pointed than he expected. He turned the knife and the steel flashed in the sunlight. He ran a thumb across the blade and felt the wicked sharpness of the edge. Gilbert was used to blades, for skinning, cutting, felling and chopping; he knew this was the most superb piece of craft he would ever see.

Felip's voice called him back. 'See the writing on the blade?'

Gilbert looked. Three tiny lines, and if it was in words at all, there were none he recognised. Not his Norman French, not English runes, not the monks' Latin.

'Arabic; not her tongue, though she both speaks and writes it,' Felip went on.

'What does it say?'

'It says "I save a life, I take a life, I make a life".'

Gilbert looked again at the writing and then over at the woman, who was quiet now, her head sagging. He recalled Felip's words of the night before, about the mob destroying what it could not understand, and felt anger. Gilbert replaced the knife in the sheath and tied it by the thongs to the inside of his left wrist. Then he pushed his way to the front of the crowd. Felip made no move to stop him. On the platform the ship's captain barred Gilbert's way at the top of the steps.

'Go home, woodsman,' Jaco growled. 'This is no place for you.'

By way of reply Gilbert took a fistful of coins from his pouch and threw them onto the planks. The other man gathered them up, and examined them; hardly enough. But

Jaco was nervous. Unlike in Ireland, or England, selling a man – or woman – for a slave was unusual in Normandy, and he was risking the authorities' wrath by even being there. He grabbed the coins, jumped down from the platform and made off through the throng of people as fast as he could.

As Gilbert took the two strides that brought him in front of the woman, the crowd fell silent. No one moved except for Felip, who had now begun to make his way to the front. As soon as Gilbert had come to the steps the woman had lifted her head. She did not take her eyes from him now, and he was looking right back into hers. Their blackness, their depth, and the light in them, spoke to him of lands he would never know. Lands with bright, burning blue skies, with fabulous cities, and a dark-skinned people like her, for whom it was not their home, despite their years there. Now he was close, he could see her robe was made of a fine cloth, for all it was filthy and darkened with bloodstains. It was torn in places, where trim perhaps of a yet more costly material had been ripped off.

Gilbert brought his left arm across and pulled out the knife with his right hand. When she saw it, the woman stiffened and let out a cry; if an oath or a prayer he could not tell. He went to cut the bonds on her wrists and felt the rope melting away before the blade; left wrist, then right. The crowd stirred again, some cried out, and those at the front began to move back. The pole fell from her shoulders and the woman lurched, then steadied herself and began to move her arms to shake off the stiffness. Gilbert replaced the knife, pulled out his water bottle and splashed a little onto her wrists and the back of her neck, where the pole had rubbed her skin raw. Seeing the water, she grabbed the bottle and began to drink, gulping it down, all the while keeping her eyes fixed on Gilbert. He picked up the pole and she handed back the empty bottle. He gave her the rest of his bread.

As Gilbert led her down from the platform, the crowd began to stir again. Felip met them, hood now pulled back. When the woman saw him, she started back and spat at his feet. Felip said nothing. Holding aloft his crucifix, he turned and began to make a way through the crowd, whose mood had changed. They had expected something more from the show than a quick sale, and now the devil woman had spat at a monk. Those nearest the woman began shouting and spitting at her; Gilbert pulled her round between him and the monk's back for protection. He pushed her along in front of him, holding the pole like a club. Stones began to fly in their direction. A man to his left was reaching under his tunic. Gilbert took no chances and felled him with a blow to the temple. Those nearby roared in anger and surged forwards, halting any progress.

Gilbert tugged at Felip's sleeve. 'What do we do?' he asked, trying to shield the woman between them.

The monk looked around. 'If we have any sense, we will leave her and make our escape. It is her blood they want, not ours.'

'You forget something. I've paid money for her.'

And Gilbert stood up to his full height and let out a roar of defiance, like a wounded stag. Wielding the pole in both hands he made a circle of space around them and began to push all three of them forwards again. As the crowd resisted, Gilbert sensed a stronger force had entered the square, and felt a surge of bodies coming towards them, pushing back against them. With people now pressed against him on all sides, shouting and screaming coming at him from all directions, he felt his feet almost lift from the ground. The heat of the sun was forcing the humid air from the rain-sodden ground of the square. From between the jostling bodies rose a stench of sweat, mud and offal.

Surely we three must go down, beaten and trampled into this square.

Suddenly Gilbert could see men above the height of the crowd – men on horses, men with helmets and spears. A small group of men-at-arms was pushing back the throng, clearing a way for them.

'Make way! Make way in the name of the duke!'

Jeering followed them out of the square, but no blows or stones. Outside, a horseman in the same livery as the messenger who had come to the forest, and holding the banner of Duke Robert, was waiting among a group of anxious-looking monks. Felip spoke with him, then returned to Gilbert.

'It seems that, despite his apparent reconciliation with the duke, the bishop is not trustworthy. I am to have an escort to the country of Bayeux.'

The woman was standing in front of Gilbert, looking around her uncertainly, and eating hurriedly what was left of the loaf of bread. From behind the group of men-at-arms, a sandy-haired young man, not yet himself a knight, was watching. Gilbert saw her body tense as she caught sight of him. Then Felip came across and spoke to her in a strange and throaty language Gilbert had not heard before. She replied only twice, but Gilbert could hear the anger in her voice. When the monk had finished, she looked across at Gilbert; the same steady gaze as she had had on the platform.

Felip knows her.

He looked at Felip in puzzlement.

'I speak little of her language,' Felip said, 'but we both speak the Arabic tongue of the Moors. Her name is Samra Abravanel. She would have a story to tell, if there were time. But she understands she must go with you for her safety, and quickly.'

*

The man Gilbert had left with his horse and cart was surprised to see him return with a man-at-arms, a monk and a weird woman in a soiled robe. Gilbert lifted Samra up into the cart and signalled her to lie down among the sacks before covering her with a blanket.

Then he turned to Felip. 'God speed.'

'And to you. Will you not change your mind and come with me?'

Gilbert shook his head. 'I love my own forest too well to change it for another.'

More of the day had gone than Gilbert would have liked and he led his horse at a good pace away from Rouen, the sun at his back. The packed streets gave way to a few houses, then to open countryside, with here and there someone turning a field of hay, or herding a few rough-coated sheep. Stopping to refill his water bottle at a well he trusted, he lifted a corner of the blanket and saw the woman, Samra, was asleep. She slept right through the journey, right through their stopping when they had reached the edge of the forest and Gilbert felt safe, right through his lighting a fire and making food. He had eaten and night had fallen when she sprang lightly down from the cart and sat on a log across from the fire. The dancing light of the flames highlighted her dark hair and skin, her angular features. He took a pot of food over and gave a little nod as he handed it to her. She gave a scowl. Samra examined the food and said something, in a different, softer language to that Felip had used with her at Rouen; a question, he could tell. He shrugged. She sniffed hard at the pot and finally began to eat.

Later, he lifted her back into the cart and climbed in beside her. He pulled the blanket over them. They lay side by side on their backs, in silence, looking up at the sky. It was a clear and mild night, bright with stars. After a while she took his hand, and extended his forefinger towards the pattern of stars he knew as the Great Bear. Arm raised, Samra directed his finger with her hand and began to move it around the sky, saying words in the same tongue he had heard Felip use with her.

'Kochab… Dubhe… Alioth… Alkaid…'

She is naming the stars.

Samra moved his finger to another part of the night sky and continued. Gilbert began to repeat the words, haltingly, or getting only part way through before faltering.

'Alhena,' she said.

'Elena,' he responded.

'Betelgeuse.'

'Yard–el…'

'Elnath.'

'A gnat.'

'Aldebaran.'

'Adab-dab…'

Samra began to giggle, then to laugh. She said other names, he mangled them again, she laughed and he laughed too. She tried to say more names, but now could not speak for laughing – and crying. Laughing and crying together.

As he lay listening to her, looking at the stars, Gilbert felt his body move, without moving. He, Samra, and the cart had swung round; earth and sky had changed places, so that he was looking down, not up, at the endless star-pattern. At any minute he could fall, fall the immeasurable distance into the galaxies below him, and be lost forever in the glimmering light of the universe. Panicking, he grabbed the side of the cart on one side, and Samra's arm on the other, so tightly that she gave a little whimper.

Suddenly, with the fast, lithe movement he would come to admire in her, Samra was sitting astride him, pinning his arms back against the sacks. Feeling the knife on his wrist, she must have sensed him tense, for she spoke again, urgently yet gently. He unfastened the knife and gave it to her; at once, she strapped it to her ankle. Now she was looking steadily into his eyes, saying something he could not understand but smiling. He reached up and took her in his arms.

The Star

Forest of Lyons, Normandy, April 1033

In the dark, Samra lay listening to the wind sighing gently in the trees outside; beside her, Gilbert was snoring gently. She had been sleeping only fitfully, the mound of her belly keeping her restless, as it had done since it began to show in earnest. Gilbert's delight in it, his holding her from behind to put his great hands on it or kneeling in front of her to watch intently for any sign of their unborn child moving, were a recompense she had clung to through her discomfort.

It would be much later that Samra was able to tell Gilbert what she had said to him on the cart, as she looked down into his eyes; that she knew the panic that had gripped him, the star-falling and the self-losing. It had first happened to her as a young girl as she had lain on the roof of her father's house in Toledo, between the puddles left by the rain, while he studied the stars above her. That her springing up and sitting astride Gilbert had been only to stop him from falling. The rest had followed, astounding to her but natural; as if the object of her life had been to bring her to that point, at that time, where she belonged. *Nothing happens but for a purpose. Everything begins and ends at its given time. Everyone comes into and leaves your life to set you on or change you from a path*. For now, the two of them were trapped in the space between their speech, she no more able to make him follow her own language of Ladino or the Arabic she had learnt than Gilbert could have Samra understand his rough Norman French. Yet other things filled the space – a touch, a look, a gesture, or the contented silence of twinned souls. She thought of Gilbert pointing at some object and saying its name over and over while she tried to copy, and of him on the cart, mangling the Arabic names of the stars. Smiling inwardly, she began to doze.

Samra awoke in the early morning. Gilbert was gone about his work already, and slowly she got up to go to the door and look out. The wind and the mild air that came with it were bringing the smells of moist earth and catkins; a renewed promise of spring. In the trees, a chiffchaff was singing its steady two-note song.

Suddenly seized by a pain in her abdomen and lower back unlike any she had ever known, Samra lurched and grabbed at the doorpost. Even before she called for help, she knew. *It is beginning*. One of Gilbert's men came quickly towards her with a concern on his face that needed no words to express. She gave a gasp and dropped to her knees. As quickly as he came, the man was gone, soon replaced by two women who calmly helped Samra to her feet and back to her bed. Through the long day that followed, these two watched over her, and by making hand gestures or with their own bodies, showed her what to do and how to sit, kneel or lie. In between bouts of racking pain, she saw them chatting to each other, smiling, heedless of the woman below them in the throes of labour. Samra found it oddly reassuring that these women who several times had gone through what she was now going through could be so casual. Childbirth? We know about childbirth – it will take its time. Be easy, and all will be well. She could not have said what time of day it was when the waiting stopped, and after examining Samra, one of the women took charge between her legs while the other held her hand and mopped her brow with a cold cloth, whispering the same words over and over; a prayer or a folk saying. But she remembered the smell of steaming water, and the pungency that arose when something was thrown into it. *Lavender; I know this from the book. It soothes, and heals.* And she laughed; a laugh of joy at what was to come, and that her part in the story now was to give life from her life. The two women looked at each other, and went on with their work.

It was dark when Samra was at last handed a tiny, dark-haired bundle to hold to her breast. Drained as she was, she could see the sign the woman at her legs made, looking a little concerned now, by bringing her splayed forefingers and thumbs together. A girl; you must have wanted a boy. But Samra laughed again and held the child to her, closely but gently. She felt the knife in its sheath at her ankle. *It will stay with me until the time comes to pass it on to you, my love, when you will be the fourteenth generation of daughters to carry it.*

Samra was nursing her daughter when the two women finally left and allowed Gilbert to come in. She smiled to see him look so exhausted, when it was she who had given birth. He sat beside her, kissed her, and tenderly stroked the baby's head, his great paw dwarfing its little skull. With her free arm Samra motioned to Gilbert to open the shutter on the window. He got to his feet and as he opened the shutter, she saw a sparkle of light, low and bright in the distant sky: Venus, the evening star. She pointed at it.

'Estraya.'

Gilbert looked back at her. 'Es-traya? This star is called Estraya?'

Samra shook her head and pointed at the suckling baby. 'Estraya.'

'Ah, I understand. Our daughter will be called Estraya, the star.' He took her hand in his and looked into her dark eyes. 'I love you, Samra Abravanel.'

Samra smiled at him and looked again through the window at the star. *You are of blood royal, and into your line blood royal shall come.* She looked down at her daughter. *And the ruler I speak of will come from your bloodline. You are my bloodline, Estraya Abravanel.*

*

Sixty miles to the west, two of England's blood royal were standing on the cliffs at Étretat, looking over to the moonlit great arch of the Falaise d'Aval. Behind them lay the encampment and tents of their forces, banners with the Wessex wyvern quivering in the breeze, lit by the many fires burning among them. Along the coast at Fécamp were gathering the greater forces and the ships of Duke Robert of Normandy. Edward and Alfred of Wessex turned at a noise behind them to see a man approaching along the cliff top, fair-haired, short and stocky.

'Well, Rædmund?' Edward asked the man as he neared. 'Are we ready?'

'Yes, my lord,' came the reply. 'We are ready. As soon as the duke sends word he is ready too, we can join them at Fécamp, and set sail.'

Edward nodded, his long white hair shaking in the moonlight. He looked over the sea below them and into the distance. 'For England.' He clapped his younger brother beside him on the back. 'Yes, Alfred? Seventeen years of waiting, a day's sailing, and England's throne will be ours again.'

Alfred's soulful dark eyes looked troubled. 'We must hope so, brother.'

Edward laughed, a silvery peal of laughter, and turned to Rædmund. 'Oh, more than hope, eh, my Wessex cousin? For we have fire in our bellies, do we not?'

The man looked out across the shimmering moonlit waves. 'And vengeance in our hearts, my lord. Vengeance on those who took from us what is ours.'

Rædmund's knuckles shone white on his sword hilt.

A Letter

Berewic, Sussex, December 1033

In the mild air of a gentle westerly breeze, the Thegn of Berewic was standing beneath a great beech tree with sagging lower branches that overlooked the river. Closing his eyes, he breathed in through his nose; wood smoke and earth reached his senses. *The year has gone well, and it will close with no hunger looming, thanks be to God. Tonight is Christmas Eve, and I will stamp my mark on my manor for another year.* Hearing a cough behind him, Sighere turned to see a man of about twenty, short, with a plump face atop his plump body, and a smirk on his fleshy lips. The man bowed.

'There is something I would raise with you, my lord, before tonight.'

Sighere gazed up into the tree above him. 'This will be the first year we don't meet under here, now that the new hall house is finished,' he murmured, almost to himself. 'This night our meeting will be a hallmoot; as it should be for a thegn of my standing.'

'I remember all the village meetings here, my lord, back to when I was young. Rain or shine, we villagers have gathered under this tree to listen to you.'

'Mostly rain, as I recall, especially at Christmas; even snow.' He turned his gaze back on the other man. 'I was your age, Cuthred, when I became thegn here. In my first village meeting I came face to face with the folk of a manor where many loyalties lay with Rædmund, the old thegn.'

'That I don't remember; I was too young. It can't have been easy.'

'It was my wife, who had links to Rædmund's people, who stood up to quieten the throng that day.'

Cuthred lowered his small piggy eyes, but the smirk did not leave his face. 'She was a great loss to you, and to Berewic,' he said in an oily voice.

'We men think we are the ones to rule the world, my friend, but we are wrong. It is women like her who hold everything together. And now my daughter will have to rule Berewic after me. Æadgytha will need to be strong like her mother, and to know where her friends – and her enemies – are to be found.' Sighere looked over the river, moving slowly through the village, and sighed. 'But tell me what you want. I have much to do today.'

Another bow before Cuthred began, 'There is a man in the village, a *gebur* who holds a yardland from you, and who is old and of broken body. He has no family—'

'He has a slave,' the other man cut in.

'My sister, who as you know is a midwife and healer in your manor, says the slave is sick and will not live long, my lord. And in any year, this tenant struggles and needs help from the other villagers on his own land, let alone in taking his turn on your demesne land and in his other duties to his thegn.'

Sighere shrugged. 'We help each other; that is the way in the village, and ever will be. You know this.'

'But, my lord, it takes resources from Berewic, if such a man needs constant help. I'm sure with your keen concern for the best working of your manor, you will have thought on this.'

The oil in Cuthred's voice was being heavily applied now, and his thegn looked at him curiously.

'What would you have me do?'

'At the meeting tonight, take his land and give it to me.'

The thegn's eyebrows were raised. 'You own a yardland now – what would you do as tenant on another thirty acres?'

'I have a wife with a baby boy, and God willing more sons will follow. I support my sister, and her work has costs that I have to meet. With more land and more crops I can do this, and I can buy more slaves. My standing in Berewic grows. I might hope to become something in your manor, and in a position to serve the interests of my fellow villagers. And yours,' Cuthred added quickly, his smirk widening.

'As my manor reeve? That position is taken.'

'Another old man, if I may say, my lord, and another upholder of the old thegn who still mutters Rædmund's name when you are not in earshot.'

Sighere shook his head. When his younger self of seventeen years ago had needed allies in his new manor, he had made a pact with the man Cuthred was speaking of; manor reeve in return for his support. Now as the man who oversaw the daily business of his manor, and mediated between his thegn and his fellow villagers, the reeve was an important figure, and Cuthred was openly angling for his position, as well as for more land. As the other man smirked and looked at him with his piggy eyes, Sighere felt uneasy, yet he could see Cuthred had ambition that would take him higher in Berewic, and might serve him as thegn. He put a hand on the other man's shoulder.

'Not yet, my friend. But I will give you standing at the gathering this night; as a juror in the drawing of lots for those holding land from me to be allocated their parcels of my demesne land to plough and seed. You've seen how this is done?'

Cuthred nodded vigorously. 'From a cloth bag with pegs in, each with the mark of its own field. The jurors take turns to pull out a peg, and the field on it goes to the man who has been called forwards.' He bowed again. 'Yes, my lord. It will be an honour.'

Berewic's thegn pulled his hand away, and stood hands on hips, waiting for the other man to leave. But Cuthred was looking at him.

'I… do you mean to include Bottom Flatt, this year, in the lots?' he asked hesitantly.

Sighere blew out through his lips. 'I– it's rich ground but heavy, and a hard field to work if the weather turns. I don't know. I should keep it in grass.'

'We have had a run of years when it could easily have been worked, and it would have yielded far more than your light land. To fill your grain store.'

Sighere grinned. 'Are you saying you would take it on?'

'Only that we should include it in drawing lots. It will fall to whoever its peg is pulled for; that is fair.'

This is a shrewd man, Sighere thought. 'Very well. Include it – you'll find the bag with the pegs in my chamber in the hall house. The peg for Bottom Flatt will be nearby; you can put it in with the others,'

A bow, slight this time, from Cuthred. 'Might I keep hold of the bag, until tonight?'

But Sighere had looked away, seeing a man hurrying through the village; a man with a leather bag slung round his shoulder, heading straight for the church. The thegn turned to Cuthred.

'You have had enough of my time – now go.'

If Cuthred was annoyed at being cut short, his chubby face did not show it. Giving another bow, he turned and walked away on his short legs, leaving his thegn alone under the moot tree.

*

Walking quickly towards it, Sighere took in the church in its honeyed stone and with its squat tower, and felt a swell of pride. *My church, ten years in the building; the first great thing I undertook when I became thegn here, and it paid my debt to God for this place.* He was in time to see the porch door close behind the man with the bag. Pushing it open, he went quietly through the main door and into the church. Under the light of a candle, the man was now in front of the priest, an old man with white hair and a stoop, and handing him something he had taken from his bag. Seeing his thegn moving towards him, the priest looked up, startled. He gave a slight bow.

'My lord. More news, from the sister in Normandy, I believe.'

Ignoring him, Sighere addressed the man with the bag, who was bowing in turn. 'Take refreshment at my hall house before you leave. But speak to no one about what you are here for.'

The man nodded, and left. As the church door closed behind him, Sighere turned to the priest.

'What does she have to say?'

As the light flickered and danced on the figure of a saint on the wall behind him, the parchment made a slight cracking noise when the priest unfurled it. Sighere saw the other man's eyes moving across the page as they scanned the letter; narrowing a little, then widening. The priest's lips moved soundlessly and his mouth fell open.

'Well?' the thegn snapped. 'What does it say?'

'My lord, I… I… there must be some mistake…'

'Read it!'

The other man cleared his throat. 'As you wish, my lord. "To the man who calls himself Thegn of Berewic. I know you will read this, as you have all the letters I have sent to you, through the sister who is sister to the wife you did not deserve. It was not enough that death took her from you; you sullied her name by writing back in it."' The priest faltered.

'Go on,' Sighere said grimly.

'Yes, Lord. "It has amused you to think that you have misled me; you see now that you have not. It pleased you to think you had word of the Wessex plan to return to England to pass on to your Godwin kin and masters; word that I was ordered to vouchsafe, on promise of the restoration of my manor to me should my homecoming with Edward and Alfred succeed. Know now that that return was thwarted; driven by contrary winds away from England's shore. Its failure has determined me to never again take the devil's bargain, and feed you news of the Wessex that the one who bribed me to send it could use against us. Yet know this also: we will return and we will fall on those who have usurped our standing and our lands, and put them to the sword. Death, not exile, will be yours."'

The priest folded the parchment with trembling hands. 'The mark of Rædmund follows what is written, my lord—,' he began, but the thegn held up a hand to silence him.

'I know who it is from. Burn this.' Sighere pointed at the letter. 'And never speak of it to anyone – do you hear?'

The priest's white hair shook as he nodded hastily.

Sighere rapidly covered the short distance between the church, finished the year Æadgytha was born, and the hall house, his second great undertaking in Berewic. As the stone of the church spoke of its permanence and of his devotion to God, the freshly painted carvings over the hall doors with their scenes of past battles spoke of his power and his wealth, albeit he was helped in the building of the hall by his Godwin cousins with money from their trading in slaves, as much as in the building of the livestock pens and other buildings – such as storehouses, workshop, stables and servants' houses – around it and the kitchen beside it. Stepping inside, he found its four great bays, with their benches along one of the long walls opposite a table on a raised dais with chairs behind it along the other, warming from a large fire in the centre hearth that was to make it welcoming for the gathering later; the hallmoot. Laughing and chattering, his servants were busy decorating the great rafters, and the fragrances of holly, ivy and mistletoe were blending with the smell of fresh timber. But he saw none of this; only the messenger from Normandy with a leather bag in front of him on a trestle table put up so he could eat. The man looked up from his bench as he approached without pausing from his noisy munching on his bread and cheese. When he did stop, it was to lift a mug of ale to his lips.

Berewic's thegn approached and putting his hands on the

edge of the table opposite the man, leant across so his face was as close as he could bring it.

'I was unsure,' Sighere murmured, 'whether to send you back with a message for Rædmund.' The messenger paused in his eating and looked at him blankly. 'But there are no words for my hatred of him that you could convey; no blow you could land on him that would have the force of the one I would deliver.'

Sighere straightened and from a sheath on his belt he drew a short single-bladed sword like a fighting knife, his *seax*, as in front of him the other man's eyes widened.

'So let this be my message for Rædmund,' the thegn went on, 'that nothing will return to him from Berewic.'

The messenger from Normandy was trying to get to his feet as Sighere swept out his arm, and brought the sharp point of the *seax* back in a swift movement across his throat. The man dropped back onto the bench behind him, grasping with both hands at the rent in his neck that was spattering his blood onto the remains of the food in front of him and into the ale mug, as if he might put it back together. One by one, the servants hushed and turned to look, faces filled with terror. A man on a ladder swooned and was grabbed before he fell. Wiping his *seax* on a cloth, Sighere turned to them.

'Clear up this mess before the hallmoot.'

*

In Sighere's chamber at the end of the hall house, Cuthred was looking at a peg in his hand. Identical in its shape and length to the others that were in the bag in front of him, it was marked in runes with the name of a field of the manor's demesne. He could not read the name, but he knew the peg must be Bottom Flatt because it had been outside the bag. He also drew his *seax*, and although Cuthred's was shorter than his thegn's, more of a tool than a weapon and without the fine inlaid metalwork, it marked him as a free man. With the blade he made a small, neat notch at one end of the peg, before putting it in the bag with the others. This night he would be a juror at the hallmoot, and when the old *gebur* shuffled forwards to be allocated his field to plough, Cuthred would make sure he was the one to draw out a peg for him. He smirked.

The House of Wessex

Bonneville-Aptot, Normandy, December 1034

Alfred of Wessex peered up anxiously as his little kinsman clambered up the heaped sacks of grain. The only light in the great barn was coming from one of the large doors, half open.

'Have a care, Wulfstan – you will be hurt if you fall from the top.'

Next to him, the boy's father Rædmund looked on more fondly. Outside a little snow was falling, and inside the barn Rædmund's breath too turned to steam as he spoke.

'Herluin will be angry if you spill his winter stocks of grain on the floor.'

From beneath his mop of blond hair his six-year-old son looked down at him, and there was puzzlement in his bright blue eyes.

'But you said Herluin had given up fighting for fasting, and become a pious monk who didn't care for anything but his prayers?'

'Hold your tongue!' Rædmund glanced at the other man in the barn, a young novice of about fourteen called Brenier, who been sent to meet them when they arrived. Brenier had ushered them to the barn, past the mud and timbers that marked the beginning of the religious community Herluin was establishing on his own estate, having despaired of finding true faith in any of Normandy's present ones. 'Not surprising,' Rædmund had muttered in the ear of his son, sitting in front of him on his horse as they arrived, 'for a man who could swap his calling as a knight for a life on his knees, give up his horse for an ass, and dress in shabby clothes leaving his beard and hair to grow long.' But Brenier was looking to the open barn door with his arms wrapped around his body, shivering, hoping Herluin would not be much longer.

'Herluin is an example to us all,' Alfred came in. 'Life should not all be about fighting. There should be devotion, and contemplation – and books.'

Alfred also had his arms wrapped around his body, but it was to hold something draped in a piece of coarse cloth; a book that he had brought with him to present to Herluin's new foundation. Slight of build and with light brown hair and soulful, dark eyes, he looked younger than his twenty-two years. Rædmund eyed Alfred quizzically as he clasped his bundle.

'Books don't win battles.' He turned to Brenier, looking him up and down. 'What say you, young novice? You're not roughly spoken and your hands tell of a life in some rich family before you came here. What draws you to a man like Herluin?'

'I... he is to me,' Brenier began hesitantly, 'what our Lord was, who saw in riches and power and baubles and trinkets the false glory of the world. Who said, "Give these things up and follow me". And so I did.'

Rædmund shook his head and ran a hand through his

fair hair. 'You would feel differently if you had had these things taken from you; these baubles, as you call them. If a war had been lost and your king and kinsman were dead. If men came to your lands and house, at their head one of the new ruler's henchmen, to turn you out, not just from your manor, but from your own country, and take the woman who should have been yours. And this man is sitting now in your hall house, at your table, while your sons grow up in exile, knowing the man may send someone to murder them. How do you feel now?'

Brenier gulped and nodded, looking down. 'What is this place?'

'It is called Berewic, and it lies not far from the southern coast of England. The ship I left Fécamp on last year should have taken me north and there in a day, not west to Jersey to kick my heels till Duke Robert made his mind up what to do.'

Rædmund closed his eyes. The smell from the sacks beside him was taking him back to another barn, in another place, where he was talking with his priest about the stores of grain that would see him and his villagers through the winter. Villagers going about their work in the fields and meadows, among the hedges and the withy beds of the manor by its little river, the woods and hills beyond it. He opened his eyes, glad that the gloom in the barn would not let the other men see the tears in them. He turned back to Alfred.

'What is done is done. But if you spent less time with books and more time at the hunt and on the practice field like your brother, we Wessex would have more chance of regaining England – and our possessions there.'

'No amount of sword-wielding on a muddy field would

have saved us from the storm that blew us off course last year,' Alfred retorted. 'That was God's will.'

'God's will, was it?' Rædmund shrugged. 'Well, Robert abandoned our cause for his own, and took his ships, men and weapons to Brittany instead of England. Perhaps that was God's will, too. Speaking of God,' he said to the young novice, 'where is Herluin? This cold barn is doing my bones no good. Go see what keeps him.'

Brenier nodded and quickly left, glad to be moving his frozen limbs and to escape the barn. Rædmund looked up at Wulfstan, now dozing between two sacks at the top of the heap, then turned back to Alfred, speaking in a low voice.

'It is as well, though, that brothers are often as opposite as can be, as are you and Edward. When the world looks at Wulfstan and Eadric, it sees two brothers not the least alike. Wulfstan loves a ceremony and came for the adventure; Eadric disdains both, though as the eldest he should be here. He disdains Wulfstan too – and Wulfstan him likewise. When they are older, they will need to be kept apart.' He looked again at Alfred's bundle. 'Show me this book.'

Hesitantly, Alfred unwrapped the book from its cloth, placed it on a nearby sack and opened it. Rædmund stooped to look at it, smelling the leather and parchment over the grain in the sack. The neat script ran across the pages like runes on a sword hilt, and the decorated capitals were like jewels in a necklace. He straightened.

'I can't read it, of course. What is it?'

'The life of St Ouen. The abbot of the monastery at Rouen that is named for the saint gave it me, to gift to Herluin and to this place.'

Rædmund saw Alfred's lips moving and his eyes shining

as they scanned the script. Curious to touch them, he reached a hand towards the words on the pages below.

'No, please! It is delicate work,' Alfred cried.

'Don't worry,' the other man growled. 'I just want some of God's will.'

Before his hand reached the parchment, Brenier rushed in through the open door, breathing heavily, his tunic coated from the snow that was falling more heavily outside.

'You must give that to me and leave with Herluin. There is no time for any ceremony today.' He was looking down at the book that Alfred was already closing.

Rædmund stepped over to Brenier and stood hands on hips, glaring at him. 'What's happened? Where is Herluin?'

'The great churchmen and nobility of Normandy are being summoned, he says; one to give Duke Robert their blessing for the pilgrimage he is to make, the other to swear an oath to uphold his son William as his successor.'

'Pilgrimage… hear that, Alfred?' Grinning, Rædmund turned to Alfred, who was wrapping the book in its cloth. 'The duke will not be outdone by a king – just as Cnut prostrated himself before St Peter, Robert too will plod his way across the Alps to Rome.'

But Alfred was already handing the book to Brenier, who took it and went to the door, clasping it to him as the other man had done. At the door, the young man looked back.

'Not Rome; Jerusalem.' And he was gone into the falling snow.

Rædmund broke the silence that followed. 'We're not leaving in a snowstorm – we can spend the night in here if Herluin can't be bothered with us. I'll send Wulfstan to get us food; they won't resist his blue eyes at the kitchen.'

He went to the barn door and, stepping outside, pulled it towards him. As it creaked shut on its hinges, the gloom inside the barn deepened.

'Jerusalem!' Alfred murmured in the near darkness. 'The blessed city where our Lord lived and died! Happy the man that will see it!'

The other man brushed the dusting of snow from his body. 'There is no cause for joy here, cousin. Duke Robert blows hot and cold with the church, now endowing it, now stripping it of its riches. This is another whim, but we will all have to bide our time until he returns; and if he does not, Normandy will be thrown into chaos.'

'Why would Robert not come home?'

'The perils of a journey to Rome are enough; but to cross land – or sea – to reach the Holy Land and then put yourself in the hands of the Muslim infidel, in a place where the hot sun breeds all kinds of pestilence and vermin… I tell you, it is madness.'

'One of the monks at St Ouen, where I used to go to read, spoke highly of the Muslims in Spain. He said they surpass us in all things; great cities with running water, fields and gardens brimming with food – and knowledge that we cannot imagine.'

'How would a monk in Rouen know that?'

'He had travelled in Spain and studied there with Muslims and Jews alike.'

'Hah! The Jews, who put our Christ to death, have no more hold in their own country than we Christians who worship Him. And what does a Muslim know of the world, other than through assault and conquest?'

'I have seen a book that Felip – the monk I speak of –

brought with him from Spain, into which a scholar from the lands the Fatimid Muslims rule in the east, the Holy Land among them, has poured his understanding. From the heavens above us, to the inside of our bodies, what I saw astounded me.'

Rædmund felt his hand gripping the hilt of his sword. 'Well, Alfred, I tell you this; had I enough men and weapons I would go to Jerusalem myself, rid it of its infidel occupiers, and give its holy places to Christians to hold safe again. For if Robert meets what I fear there – the blade of a dagger or death from disease – our cause is lost. The seven-year-old boy that stands to inherit his duchy from him if he dies will have another concern, other than pressing the house of Wessex's claim to the throne of England: his own survival. I will not see my manor at Berewic again, you will not see England, Edward will not be king there; and the secret we three guard between us will die with us, as it dies with Duke Robert.'

'Then… then it should be revealed now; while we are all gathered to meet Robert. Let the truth be known!'

Rædmund saw Alfred's eyes shining again. 'No. This is not the time, cousin.' He stepped closer to the other man and took him by the shoulders to speak to him in a low, urgent voice. 'The day I regain Berewic, and Edward regains England; then he can tell the world.'

From the top of the heap of sacks, a small voice called out. 'I'm hungry. Can we go now?'

The Hunt

Forest of Lyons, Normandy, August 1035

On a sweltering summer day, Gilbert was on his knees outside his house in the forest, bare head bowed, holding his cap in both hands at his waist, as a group of armed men approached him. Inside, Samra was nursing their daughter, now a little over two years old and dark as her mother. The dozing child opened her eyes briefly at the heavy tread of the horses, but quickly closed them again with a little sigh.

Gilbert did not change from his position of submission, only raising his head when the group had stopped and its leader was off his horse and standing before him. When he looked up, his eyes were level with those of an eight-year-old boy. Recalling this first meeting with his new duke, Gilbert always claimed to see the man in the boy's robust figure and well-fleshed face; and in the grey-green eyes that returned his gaze steadily, in silence, he felt as though he was being searched.

Fumbling with his cap, he began to speak awkwardly. 'I'm sorry for the death of your father, my duke. And in everything I am at your service, as I was at Duke Robert's.' Gilbert bowed his head again.

The boy extended his hand and Gilbert kissed the ring on his finger.

'My father should not have gone to Jerusalem. I will never leave Normandy.' William's voice was surprisingly deep for one so young. 'And neither should you. You may get up. Who do you know among us?'

Once on his feet, his cap back on his head, Gilbert could see the rest of the group. Among the French were Duke Alain of Brittany, who was one of the guardians appointed to protect Duke William during his father's absence, and two more of his followers that William introduced as Ranulph de Bayeux, and his younger brother Hugh. From their previous visits to the forest Gilbert recognised Edward of the English royal house of Wessex, and his brother Alfred. With them was a distant relative of Edward from one of the families that had taken refuge in Normandy, along with Edward's, when the Danes took the English throne and Cnut became king. This time this man Rædmund had come with his two sons; boys about William's age, born in Normandy and who knew no other land. Gilbert knew that William's father had supported the exiles, and made an unsuccessful attempt to regain the English throne for Edward. Now young William was glad of Edward's support in his own struggle to keep power.

As Gilbert looked around at them, William went on.

'When my messenger brought news of our arrival, he will have told you of our purpose. My father loved this hunting ground, and I mean to use it as he did. We will take refreshment, then go out into the forest and see what we can put up.'

'Everything is ready for you, my duke.'

Indeed it was. On the preceding day Gilbert's men had

been out with their dogs, checking the main tracks were clear of obstacles and at the same time seeing where a buck or wild boar might be found lying up. Now, as his servants brought food and wine to the company and fed their dogs and horses, Gilbert slung a horn around his neck, fitted out his men and sent them off. Everything must be done to ensure that once a beast was flushed out, it went in the right direction to provide good sport for the duke and his guests. For a while, the usual quiet of the forest around Gilbert's home was broken by frantic activity, while servants dashed to and fro, men talked loudly over their food and drink, horses neighed and dogs growled and yapped as they tussled over scraps of meat. Overseeing it all, and everywhere at once, Gilbert was sweating heavily by the time the group was mounted and ready, each armed with one or more weapons – spears, swords and bows.

As they prepared to leave, Gilbert spotted a loose rein on Edward's horse. As he tightened it, he was struck as always by Edward's long hands, their white skin almost translucent. Head of the house of Wessex, son of the late English King Ethelred and Emma of Normandy who was sister of William's grandfather, nearly twenty of Edward's thirty-one years had been spent as an exile in his mother's native land. Not that she shared his exile; in the wake of the English defeat and Ethelred's death, Emma had married Cnut.

Edward leant down to Gilbert so that his long white hair was almost touching the forest warden's face. Glancing up, Gilbert saw the fine features and chiselled nose beneath cornflower-blue eyes; Edward's face would have looked well on a woman. Yet Gilbert knew the hands that gripped the reins and the legs pressing against the horse's flanks were strong from his years of hunting, and that Edward was a man whose passions extended beyond those of the chase.

'Have care for the young duke,' Edward said softly.

'As I did for his father, when he came here to hunt, my lord.'

'I do not speak of the perils of the chase.'

Gilbert knew the story of William's origins. Herleva, the undertaker's fair daughter, had come to the well below the castle in Falaise and captured Duke Robert's heart. The son born to them, declared Robert's heir by Robert before he left on pilgrimage to the Holy Land, was now prey to powerful forces that would exploit his illegitimate birth and his youth.

'To be close to the duke is to be close to power over Normandy,' continued Edward, 'and to attract the jealousy of rivals while giving every opportunity to strike at William himself. Any one of these Norman nobles could be his assassin.'

If the young duke's life was under threat, he had not shown it. Striding confidently from horse to horse before he himself climbed into the saddle of a nearly full-size mount, he had given instructions and encouragement to the riders in equal measure, and was clearly enjoying the prospect of the hunt. Riding at his side, Gilbert blew on his horn; William waved the group forwards and they moved off into the forest, dogs running round them, following the men on foot who were already well ahead, combing through the undergrowth and blowing their horns.

*

Quiet fell over the house once more, where Estraya was asleep in Samra's arms, tucked into the folds of the loose tan-coloured gown that had replaced the fine red robe her mother once wore. The simple scarf partly covering Samra's long, dark hair gave no hint of the proud and prosperous young woman of Toledo. She began to sing to her daughter, in a high, rhythmic melody that was not Jewish, not Arabic, not Spanish; but all of these.

Lullaby, baby, the child sleeps.
May great God guard them, keep the children from evil.

As she closed her eyes, Samra was in a garden, with a view over a great city of white buildings, seated beneath spreading citrus trees whose interwoven branches shaded her from a an azure sky and a relentless sun, and whose sultry perfume filled the air. Fountains flowed behind her, and a channel of water at her feet led down the hillside from terrace to terrace, each more elaborately laid out than the next with grottoes and arbours, rich with the colours of countless varieties of trees and flowers.

*

Under the Norman sun, the hunting party moved slowly along tracks that dipped and curved with the undulating landscape, past little thickets and larger stands of trees, around rocky outcrops and along the valleys of small streams. Gilbert could have told William this was not a good time to be out, and that they should have waited until dawn the next day. But he knew not to oppose his duke in his keenness; in matters of hunting as in every other skill the young ruler would need, those around him would in time bring their wise counsel. Any large game was sitting out the heat, and all morning they put up only a small covey of partridge and a single hare that loped away in no hurry. In mid-afternoon they stopped by a small stream for shade and water.

When the party began to move on, Hugh de Bayeux, who had been riding all the while not far from Alfred, came up beside him.

'I hear you have been to St Ouen.'

At twenty-three Alfred was some eight years younger than his brother, and did not share Edward's love of hunting; learned and well-read, he needed no excuse to go to the abbey.

'It has a good library, and one of the monks lets me read there.'

The young Norman beside him wheeled his horse round in front of Alfred, and stopped. Alfred stopped; Hugh's light blue-grey eyes were looking at him intently.

'Felip de Mazerolles.'

Alfred could feel the sun burning on his neck. 'You know him?'

'Does he still have the book?'

Alfred hesitated. 'He has many books.'

Hugh came closer now and leant across Alfred. As the younger son of a noble family with no choice but to make his way in the world by his skill at arms, at sixteen Hugh was already strong from his three years' serving another knight, thick-necked and broad-shouldered under his shirt. His legs showed below his knee-length breeches, bare so he could better grip his horse, and muscular. His whole presence was threatening.

'Do not take me for a fool. You know the book I speak of.'

'Felip gives one book special favour in his studies, it is true. But I can only read in it what he has put into Latin.'

Hugh's eyes flashed. 'Then you have seen it. When I was

coming back to Normandy with Felip, he had it locked in a chest. But I picked the lock, and I saw what is in the book. Although I could not read it, I could tell that who possesses it will have great power. Next time you go to St Ouen, bring it to me.'

'You want me to steal it?'

Hugh moderated his tone a little. 'I would only borrow the book, to study it for myself. But do not fail me in this.'

The others were by now a way off, and Alfred suddenly felt the silence of the landscape pressing in on him with the burning heat. He wiped sweat off his brow.

'Very well. Next time I am at St Ouen, I will look for it.'
'And Felip will not know?'
'Felip will not know I have been there.'
Hugh nodded and turned his horse away.
'We need to catch up.'
'My horse has a stone,' said Alfred. 'I will go back.'

*

Hugh needed to ride quickly, for the others had spotted game and were off. The beaters had flushed a young buck, and at the head of the group Edward was in full cry, his dogs running in front of him. The deer ran swiftly, doubling back then dodging the hunters before the dogs could reach it, and tiring little until a spear from Edward caught its shoulder. He pulled away to pick up the weapon and let William take over the lead. The young duke was skilful and fearless, steering his horse after the buck from cover to cover, then through a sudden outcrop of boulders that had others in the party pull up short. When they caught up, he was stopped in front of a low ridge. Raising his arm to signal a halt, he pointed with the other at the buck, lying in the long grass under the ridge, flanks heaving, blood spattered along its coat from shoulder to tail.

Edward came up beside him. 'I think the honour is yours, my lord.'

'Not so. As I was blooded in the hunt, so it should fall to one of your young kin to be blooded, my noble cousin.'

All eyes fell on the two boys, the sons of Edward's kinsman Rædmund, who had kept up with the chase and now waited a little behind Edward and William. Eadric, fair-haired, lightly built and with a thin nose and a thin, serious face that made the two years separating him and his brother Wulfstan look greater, knew that as the eldest he was expected to come forwards. Dismounting, he moved towards the deer. Although still breathless, it had laid its head to one side and was otherwise quite still. Eadric looked round at the others, anxiety in his grey eyes; some nodded encouragement and others waved him on. One came up and gave him his sword, and Eadric took another step closer to the animal. It looked up at him as he approached; its eyes were dark and full of fear. Swallowing hard, hand shaking, Eadric went to pull back his arm with the sword. He wanted to get near enough to despatch the animal through the heart from behind the shoulder, but he knew its fearsome set of antlers could still be turned on him. He could not move.

Suddenly his brother was at his side and pulling something from his belt. The jagged blade of a hunting knife flashed in the sun. As the younger boy reached it, the buck made a struggle to get up, which was instantly ended with a deep stab between the antlers and neck, severing the spinal cord. The deer's legs thrashed the last of its life into the grass. Wulfstan dipped a hand into its warm, ebbing blood and smeared his face with it, leaving his blue eyes sparkling in a mask of red below a mop of blond hair. Turning to the others, the boy stood sturdily holding his knife aloft, grinning in triumph, while his taller yet slighter brother stood still frozen beside him.

Laughing, Edward applauded. 'Wulfstan! Well done!'

*

Alfred had reached the house. Stepping inside, he found Samra with her daughter. As his eyes adjusted to the light, he saw she was sitting, writing on very thin strips of wood. Strips she had finished were hanging around her, drying out. He recognised some of the symbols and devices among the unfamiliar script. Samra smiled as she saw him; she liked the quiet young man with his soulful, dark eyes and gentle ways. Alfred looked down at the sleeping Estraya, then sat opposite them both, in silence awhile before speaking.

'I... you did not have much French, last time I came. And now?'

'A little more. I understand more. I do not speak well.' Another silence before she spoke again. 'Where is Felip?'

'Gone to Cerisy; this time for good.'

'And the book?'

'Gone with him.'

Samra nodded, and returned to her work.

*

There was to be another kill before the hunting party returned in the evening. Hugh de Bayeux finished an injured wild boar with a thrust of his boar sword down its throat, to the admiration of the rest of the party. As everyone milled around outside, William caught Gilbert coming out of his house where he had just gone in to see Samra. As the boy looked up gravely at his forest warden, Gilbert knew something was coming.

'My thanks for an excellent day, Gilbert. You are everything my father led me to expect.' Gilbert bowed. 'You know my sport means as much to me as it did to him. And my faith. I mean to carry on his work with both, in the Cotentin. His foundation at Cerisy makes progress, and I will make sure it is finished, as a light to the faithful in that region, where the darkness of superstition still sways some. And Cerisy is a great step towards the Forest of Valognes, a hunting ground the dukes of Normandy have long held but not used well enough.' *He is moving me*, thought Gilbert, *and I will have to tell Samra.* 'You will put that right for me. I see what you have laid out here and I want that for Valognes; it and Cerisy will be my monuments.'

*

As night fell and the party feasted outside in the warm air, Samra finally came out of the house. Alfred saw her, looking up at the starlit sky. As he came across, beyond him she saw Hugh de Bayeux, talking energetically to Edward of Wessex. Samra pulled Alfred towards her, keeping out of sight behind his body.

He could feel she was trembling, as she whispered to him. 'Who is he?'

Alfred looked behind him. 'Hugh de Bayeux is one of the Normans my brother keeps company with. I do not like him, though I fear Edward has made promise to him.'

'What promise?'

'Hugh lacks land of his own. If he helps Edward regain the throne of England, he will be rewarded there.'

'Then let your brother return to England quickly,' said Samra, 'and take this man with him. For I do not trust him.'

'As quickly as he may.'

Samra and Alfred turned at the voice, to find Wulfstan standing behind them. The blood streaked on the boy's face had darkened, and as he gnawed the last of the meat off a bone, in the flickering light of the fire the small, stocky figure looked more prey than hunter. He threw the bone to a dog that had been waiting nearby, watching him with its ears pricked.

'Wulfstan and Eadric also have cause to return to England,' explained Alfred. 'Their father Rædmund is a thegn – that is, an English lord – dispossessed of his manor; his house and lands.'

Samra looked at Wulfstan, as he chewed his mouthful of meat. Gilbert had told her how he had upstaged his brother in the hunt, leaving Eadric cowed and shame-faced. But she did not sense any malice in him; only the bravado of youth – and a strange sense of connection that she could not place. His blue eyes meeting her black, Wulfstan looked back with frank curiosity at the dark woman from the south in front of him, out of place in a northern forest clearing.

'Where is this… "man-or"?' Samra asked.

Wulfstan laughed at her pronunciation of the word.

'At Berewic.'

And Samra felt a thrill run through her body, like panic; but like hope also.

The Book and the Knife

Forest of Valognes, Normandy, October 1035

In the three years since Robert Duke of Normandy had sent him to Cerisy, Felip and his monks had begun work clearing the site and providing the timber that would build the new abbey. But it was Robert's son, Duke William, who would encourage the building one day of a great abbey in the Benedictine style at Cerisy, and not in wood but stone. And now the young duke had sent his forest warden to his hunting ground in the Forest of Valognes, much closer to Cerisy than the Forest of Lyons.

So on an early autumn day, with the sun still driving the mist from the trees around, a man in the tunic, scapular and cowl of his Benedictine order came to the new home of Gilbert, Samra and their daughter Estraya. Felip was not surprised to see the large clearing Gilbert had created around him, in which already stood houses for him, his men and servants, and the beginnings of what would be several other buildings for the likes of timber, horses, carts and tools. As he approached, the monk saw what looked like slates hanging in trees and fastened to fences and to the house. Looking closer, he saw thin leaves of beech wood, with writing and symbols on them. Gilbert got up from where he had been sitting on a tree stump sharpening an axe. Estraya was playing nearby. As Felip got off his horse, Samra came out of the house. Gilbert approached Felip and hugged him with pleasure at seeing him again.

'Got all the wood you need down there? Don't need any of mine?'

'More than I can handle. But I could do with your strength – I am worn out from all this woodman's work.'

As Felip pulled out of Gilbert's embrace, Samra rushed at him. She pushed him violently by the shoulders so that he staggered back and nearly fell. As he tried to regain balance, she pushed him again and again. All the while she said some words over and over, in the throaty language Gilbert had last heard when Felip spoke with her at Rouen.

Gilbert grabbed Samra round the waist and arms and pulled her away. When she stopped struggling, he asked, 'What is she saying?'

Felip straightened his clothes. 'She is asking where the book is.'

'Book? Your book? From St Ouen? Why?'

Samra spoke to Felip again, urgently but more calmly. He listened, nodding, and then said to Gilbert, 'Samra needs to speak to you, but she cannot in her language, or yours. So she will speak the language we share – Arabic – and I will put it into French.'

Gilbert sat down again and Samra sat opposite, looking at him as she began to speak. Felip stood to one side midway between them, and began to pass on her words.

'You know that I am not here, or yours, by choice. You know that in this place, to me cold and wet, my body suffers and it takes all my skill in healing to keep myself from giving way. You know that other than to nurture our child I do not cook or clean or mend or make. You know that while I have learnt some of your language, I cannot yet speak as I was used to, fluently and with passion. So you see me frustrated and angry, and wonder at my writings on the beech tablets, or my looking at the stars, or the stones and flowers of the forest. You are a good man, and my anger is not for you. I would have you know my story.'

Gilbert had smiled to himself when Samra talked about cooking and cleaning, but quickly set to listening again as she went on.

'In Toledo where I grew up, among the Sephardim of Spain, I was highest of the high. I trace my mother's line, the Abravanels, from the house of King David himself. But we had already been many generations of Jews in Spain when an Arab scholar called Alhacen, who had arrived from Egypt, came into our world. In my life I was astronomer to my Moorish ruler in Toledo, and Alhacen came to me and told me of his work; and he asked to know mine. And as he spoke, all that I knew fell into an abyss of unknowing compared with the light of his mind. He knew the stars in the sky and the motions of the planets in as much detail as he knew the workings of the eye that beholds them. Alhacen saw the science of numbers and the properties of the material world as a child might see its toy bricks; to be picked up and arranged again and again in so many patterns, yet never losing the joy of it. In the understanding and healing of the body he followed the work of his forbears, both the great Al-Zahrawi, whose knowledge of anatomy and surgery is unsurpassed, and of the practice of Jabir in medicine and the properties of plants of all kinds. And he knew the writings of Jabir on many other sciences, especially knowledge of the substances of the earth, and how their transformation might produce on one day the perfect steel blade, and the next, gold from lead. As I listened, and as we observed the stars together, I wrote every word in the book, a book that had come down to me through generations of my family and which was to me more precious than any gold.'

Samra paused, keeping her eyes fixed in front of her. Her child, who had been playing in the sand of the forest floor, picked something up and held it out to give to her, then went to sit on the ground between her father's legs. Samra saw a small red stone, and smiled at her.

She continued, 'The book is not the only object to be passed down.' She put a hand down to the sheath at her ankle. 'I am the thirteenth generation of my family to bear this knife; handed always from mother to daughter, each knowing the three lines on its blade came from the stars, to the book, to the knife. And every girl who received it from her mother asked, "What does it mean?" The question could not be answered; the foretelling of the knife – if that was what it was – had yet to happen. We knew only that the book and the knife are intertwined – if the book is destroyed, the foretelling of the knife will never come about. Without the knife, the book too is powerless.'

In the silence that followed, a little wind stirred in the trees around them. The first leaves of autumn began to fall. Looking at Samra, Gilbert saw in her dark radiance not just the woman before him in the square in Rouen, about to be sold for a slave. *She is the Jewish scholar in Felip's story.*

'Another man came into my life, and Alhacen's – a young monk from France and a scholar himself, eager to absorb the learning he found in the book. These were uncertain times, and when the last caliph of Cordoba and ruler of the Moors fell, this monk advised us it could not be long before the Christian princes to the north swept all away. "Take the book to the ignorant Christians," this monk said, "for your only hope is put your trust in their desire to acquire your learning along with your wealth." One day Alhacen left us to return home, and our family took our many books, our instruments and our possessions and went to meet this monk in the empty country between Toledo and Castile, where no man had sway, or rather any man who had arms could prey on the weak and unguarded. For this reason, we had an escort, for we were held as high by the new ruler in Toledo as we had been by the old, and he hoped our journey might buy him favour in Castile. But this monk had deceived us.'

Felip stumbled over these words, then continued with eyes fixed on the ground. 'There has been no disaster. I have spoken with the Jews in Rouen. Toledo is as it was. And when we found the monk, the Normans who were with him captured us and sold us into slavery, except the very young and the very old. These they killed.' Her voice caught, but she went on. 'He took the book for himself, and later I was separated from the knife also. In my days of captivity, I despaired. Then, three hundred years to the day that the knife was crafted in the workshop where I played as a child, and where I later made the instruments for my work, you, Gilbert, gave the knife back to me in the square at Rouen. And you were the man who bought me, and brought me to the Forest of Lyons and then to here. Felip has no power over me now, and he cannot promise me anything I will believe. But all the while the book is kept from me, it tears my soul.'

From between her father's legs, Estraya had been watching her mother, and now turned her face to look up at Gilbert, who was looking at Felip. Felip went across to where his horse was tethered, and pulled from a bag something wrapped in a velvet cloth, decorated with a moon and stars. He crossed back to Samra and handed it to her. She held it to her, just as she had done that day in Spain, as if it were a child, her body swaying, eyes filling with tears. Slowly she unwrapped the cloth to reveal a large, leather-covered book. Turning the pages, she came to where the outline of the stars and the inscription now on the knife had been traced. Samra began to speak again, and Felip relayed her words once more.

'When my mother gave me the knife, young girl that I was, I was proud; thrilled. Might I be the one to fulfil its destiny? In the world in which I moved – between workshop, library, observatory, gardens, synagogue – it seemed impossible I should kill anyone, or save them. And I never imagined the book or the knife leaving that world. Yet now they are both here, and I am here with them. I do not understand the reason we are here, but the time of the knife is beginning, I know. And Felip knows, too. Now I look at my own daughter and wonder; will she be the one?'

Estraya had come over to her mother and was looking at the book. Samra turned the pages with her, showing her the diagrams of instruments, the maps of planets and stars, the pictures of plants. The child went to the edge of the forest and picked up something, bringing it back to her mother grasped in her little fist. When she opened her hand, a tiny flower sprang out, perfect and uncrushed.

Felip had gone back to his horse and was making to leave. Gilbert joined him.

'Is it true,' he asked urgently, 'that you betrayed her?'

'That day will come, if not this year, or for ten years, or a hundred,' Felip replied, 'when Spain is at the mercy of competing armies, and all the knowledge of the Jews and Moors is no more valued than a grain of sand. Then we will look for the books in vain. What happened that day was not of my planning. And yet I admit, when I saw I could take the book, I wanted it for myself. But from the first day I sat in my reading room at St Ouen, I knew I was wrong. It is nothing without its author, and if I am to understand it, I must work with Samra.'

'If the time of the knife is beginning,' Gilbert went on, 'where will it take us all? Whose are these lives that will be saved, taken, made? When?'

Felip shook his head. 'If I knew that…'

'How could you know, then, that Samra and the knife would come to Rouen, to where you had brought the book? How could you know that I'd go to the square that day and buy her?'

Felip had got on his horse. 'I could not know. But nothing happens but for a purpose. Everything begins and ends at its given time. Everyone comes into and leaves your life to set you on or change you from a path, Gilbert. And now you are part of what is happening here.'

Gilbert reflected on this for a while. 'I would talk with you more. Won't you stay, refresh yourself at least?'

'I cannot. My party are waiting for me, just beyond. They will want to make good progress before night.' He leant down to Gilbert. 'Two weeks ago, armed men came to the abbey at Cerisy and asked after the book. One of my monks died rather than reveal it.' Gilbert looked over at Samra and

Estraya poring over the book, their heads together in one mass of dark hair. 'Take care, Gilbert. Someone wants the book more than I do, perhaps even more than Samra, and will stop at nothing to get it.'

He turned his horse and rode away.

A Crossroads

Berewic, Sussex, August 1036

Under the high summer sky that lay over the south of England, two children were walking on the bank of the river in Berewic. By the measure of the age, one was no longer a child; at nearly fifteen, Harold Godwinson was a young man. Tall, strong, fair of hair and fine of face in a way that revealed his Danish heritage, as the son of the leading earl of England, he had borne arms from a young age. So it was with an easy strength that he lifted his cousin down from the bank onto a sand flat by the quietly moving water. Graceful and tall for her age – only half his – Ædgytha was already showing the beauty of face, with its high cheekbones and under soft light brown hair, that would mark her out in a few years' time. Harold stooped to pick up some flat stones and skimmed them one by one over the water. Ædgytha followed him, but picked up stones too round and heavy that only plopped into the river. Patiently he showed her how to find better, and to throw them with a low movement of the arm that brought one or two bounces off the rippling surface, which he applauded earnestly. And the river made its languid way south towards the coast and the narrow sea that separated England from France.

That day a ship of some note was tied up at the quay on the river, one that carried the banner of Earl Godwin, Harold's father; England's leading nobleman and the most powerful man in the realm after its king. The earl had come from his own seat of power along the coast at Bosham, and his slaves were waiting at their oars. Along with Harold's older brother Swein, he was in earnest discussion with his kinsman, Æadgytha's father Sighere, the Thegn of Berewic, among the cups of wine and the refreshments at the high table in his hall house. It was not going well with the thegn.

'How long since King Cnut died?' Sighere growled at the earl. 'And still no successor?'

'Ten months,' Godwin replied. 'There was a compromise for the succession between two of his sons, but it is breaking down.'

'Harthacnut, and Harold Harefoot? The half-brothers – each of them as unworthy of being king as Cnut was worthy. Good luck with that, I say.'

'We will guide the next king of England, as we did the last,' said the earl. 'We Godwins have prospered under the Danish kings, but now with each of the two men's mothers actively promoting her own son, all this uncertainty makes what we have guarded against for twenty years thinkable – a return of the house of Wessex to the English throne.'

'And which half-brother does the earl uphold now?' asked Æadgytha's father.

'I was always for Harthacnut,' answered Godwin, 'but he will not bring himself back from Denmark. Now that Emma has begun to make contact with her exiled sons in Normandy, I am minded to swing behind Harold Harefoot for king.'

'Their mother makes contact with Edward and Alfred of Wessex? Now I have heard everything.'

'Emma is no stranger to changing sides,' Swein cut in. 'Remember that after the death of her boys' father King Ethelred, she married again, to Cnut – Harthacnut is her son too, and half-brother to Edward and Alfred.'

'I know this well,' Sighere retorted quickly. 'So is it one of Ethelred's sons, or Harthacnut, who she backs for the throne? What game is the witch of Winchester playing?'

'We cannot tell,' Earl Godwin said grimly, 'and the more pity that we have not had insight through your dead wife's sister in Normandy these three years gone into the house of Wessex and its handlings. What we chose to make Emma privy to then, partial as it was, was to our benefit, and without it I fear this matter will come back to haunt us.'

Sighere thought of Rædmund's letter that the priest had read to him in his church, and the threat it contained, and grimaced.

'Do you believe Edward and Alfred will try to take England back?'

'Yes,' the earl replied.

'Then Rædmund will try to take Berewic.'

'That too. Be warned, my Godwin cousin.'

*

On the river bank, Æadgytha had been listening to Harold's account of the threat from the Wessex and thinking. She turned her serious hazel eyes on her cousin.

'Why should Edward and Alfred not come back? Are they not of the line of Alfred the Great, and their family once kings of England?'

Harold Godwinson sighed. 'Once. Now they are Normans, or as good as. When the history of this time is written, they should be a note in the margin, so my tutor says. And do we want Norman Kings, or English?'

'But Cnut was Danish and so his sons are.'

Harold frowned. 'The Danes have become English. In the north and east, where I have been, there is little difference between the incomers and the English after all this time. My own mother is Danish.'

'My father says we are all related, the Wessex, the Godwins, the Norman dukes.'

'Yes, that is true.'

And Harold drew a tree in the sand, where the roots went back three or four generations and the branches intertwined, with the houses of Wessex and Normandy linked through Emma, who through her marriage to Cnut was linked to the Danes, and they in turn linked to the Godwins by marriage.

Tiring of skimming pebbles, Æadgytha climbed out onto the riverbank. On a low bluff overlooking the river stood a solitary beech tree. Noble and massive, some said it was as old as the village itself. Its shade drew a circle of pure space around it, bearing no other plant or tree near. Radiance surrounded it in spring, green light falling through its soft leaves. Its huge lower branches sagged in summer, long arms spreading, touching the warm earth. In autumn it clung to its golden-brown leaves, letting fall instead a shower of crunching beech mast, food for pigs and people alike. It was a winter sentinel of the village, standing grey and unshaken through storm and snow. Until three years ago the village would meet under its shade or shelter, for then there was no indoor space large enough; no great hall house. The moot tree, they called it. As a small child Æadgytha's father would sit her on a fork of one of its lower branches, and it gently bore her weight as she listened intently to the officers of the village and the talk between them and their thegn.

Now she sat on the same fork, pushing herself up and down on the springy limb of the great old tree with her feet. Harold joined her, leaning against another branch, looking across the river to the hills and woodland vanishing in the haze beyond. A little way off, men were working, building a corn mill that the river would power. Their voices and the sound of adze on wood carried in the warm air to the two cousins.

'None of it really matters,' said Harold. 'In England the great council meets to decide who will be King. The *witangemot* chooses the one best able to serve his country. Claim to the throne, through blood or by battle, is not all that guides their hand. May it always be so.'

Æadgytha bounced up and down some more. 'How are we cousins, you and I?'

She saw his tawny eyes turn thoughtful for a moment. 'I think, my grandfather and your grandmother… or is it the other way round? At any rate, we are cousins of some sort,' he said.

The girl stopped bouncing. 'And both Godwins?'

'Yes. Never forget it.'

Æadgytha turned away, looking towards the church, completed the year she was born, but whose honeyed stone still looked fresh in the sun.

'What was my mother like?'

'I was only your age when she died,' Harold replied. 'I met her once, when she was carrying you. But I can recall her strength and nobility. And her pride, that when she gave birth to you, she would be assured of someone to follow your father in Berewic.'

'She would have hoped for a son.'

'She would have rejoiced in your coming, for the brief moment you were together on the day of your birth. And on another day, this manor will be yours, and you will not lack her qualities, I know.'

Æadgytha nodded slowly. Hearing footsteps, she turned to see Harold's father behind her; the bulk of the man, with his blond beard and hair shining in the sun, looming over her. Æadgytha screwed up her face when she saw Harold's brother Swein following him, dark like a shadow. He had all of his brother's strength in body and mind, but she had once seen him mistreat a servant so savagely that it now made her uneasy in his presence.

Earl Godwin lifted Æadgytha from the branch and held her in the crook of an arm, looking into her solemn eyes.

'I will borrow your father, my lady, if I may. I need Sighere's help to defend the coast of Sussex. The Wessex have been in communication with Emma, and we believe they are about to invade. England is at a crossroads. It must not take the wrong path.'

A Secret

Forest of Valognes, Normandy, September 1036

A year is a long time in a young child's life. At three, Estraya was no longer the waddling baby of Alfred's last visit, but a black-haired, elfin creature scampering around her father's forest home. Gilbert would watch as she melted into the trees beyond the now sizeable group of buildings he had created at Valognes, to reappear somewhere else; laughing, dark eyes shining. As Alfred climbed down from his horse, Estraya had taken his hand, and gently led him to the house where her mother was reading. Samra looked up as he came in and embraced the young man warmly. She looked older, tired.

'Alfred! Has it been a year since I saw you last? Are you come to hunt again?'

He saw her glance nervously towards the door, as if another, unwelcome presence might be about to enter.

'Not this time. Only Rædmund is with me, and some of his men. But how do you fare? It must be four years now since you were exiled from your home.'

'My people are everywhere exiles from our home. Normandy or Spain, it makes little difference. But yes, exiled from the place where I grew up, it is hard. When we were in the Forest of Lyons at least I could go now and then into Rouen, and be with others of the faith. Even if I had little of their language at that time, we could listen to the scriptures together, and that comforted me. Valognes is far away, and soon another winter will be on us, and the damp will seep into my bones once more.'

Now Alfred noticed her elegant hands, with their long fingers, were thinner than he remembered, and twisted.

'But I do not complain,' Samra went on, 'here there is peace, and the joy of seeing my daughter grow. She is a child of nature and at home in the forest in a way I will never be.'

'And I see you have many books.'

'I do; Felip brings them when he comes from Cerisy. His visits are a blessing.'

Among the books Samra had in front of her, one stood out; large, leather-covered and open at a page rich with symbols and diagrams. Alfred felt a thrill of excitement as he looked closer.

'This is the book – I recognise it from St Ouen. This page should be something about the working of the eye, is it not?'

'Of the eye, and of lenses; the bringing closer of distant objects.'

'And now there is a Latin text for the Arabic.'

'Felip's work, again. But if you stay, Alfred, you might add to it.'

Samra saw his eyes darken suddenly.

'I cannot stay long. And I wish I could have added something to the book of my own.'

From outside there was a noise, then Gilbert was at the door, calling for servants to bring the visitors refreshments.

He looked over at Alfred, sitting on the floor in front of the books.

'Is it true? The Wessex are returning to England?'

'Yes. Edward is already embarked. My ship will leave soon.'

Gilbert bounded across and, pulling Alfred upright, hugged him closely, his big hand ruffling the other man's light brown hair.

'Then God speed, and all success to you – the new kings of England!'

Locked in the woodsman's bear-like arms, Alfred glanced at Samra, and his eyes were troubled. She put her hand on Gilbert's shoulder.

'Show Alfred what you have made for the book,' she said softly.

'Of course.' Gilbert went to a corner and picked up a wooden box slightly larger than the book, with a hinged lid. 'It goes quickly from dry to damp here in the forest, and the parchment is vulnerable to the changes in moisture. But in the box, with the lid shut tightly, the book is protected, and the pages are kept flat and cannot warp.'

Samra smiled. 'Unlike my fingers.'

Gilbert handed Alfred the box. 'Made from beech wood,' he said. 'Strong, but light. I wanted to carve on it, but Samra said no; it should be plain, and pure.'

'It's beautiful.' Alfred turned the box over in his hands before passing it back to Gilbert. 'And it is fitting; beech boards were used to write on in ancient times. Beech is the tree of recorded knowledge; the book of the past.'

'When I did not have the book, it was beech strips I wrote on,' Samra added, turning to Gilbert. 'See to those outside, my love; they will be thirsty from their ride.'

When Gilbert had gone, they could hear him outside, giving orders, laughing. But Samra was looking at Alfred.

'What troubles you?'

He looked down at the floor, and when he looked up, she could see tears in his dark eyes.

'I fear no good can come of this venture. Our mother assures us we have support in England, but no other voice has spoken for us. What if Emma is wrong? What if she is...' he shook his head, 'deceiving us, to promote the cause of her son by Cnut?'

'If Edward has gone ahead, he can send word, if there is any doubt.'

'Perhaps.' A servant had come with wine, and Alfred took the cup and drank a little. When they were alone again, he continued, 'We are in God's hands. What will be, will be. But there is something that, if Edward and I should die, must be kept hidden from our enemies, but not from the world. And I feel driven to trust it to you.'

'A secret?'

'Yes. It concerns Wulfstan.' He looked at Samra, hesitating.

Samra felt herself tense a little. *Driven to tell me something about Wulfstan.*

'Go on.'

And Alfred told her. As he spoke, she felt herself lifted from the rough timbered house in the forest clearing and carried up to the sky towards the stars beyond, to look down on the world of men and their daily lives. Below her lay a land she had never known; a land of rolling hills, streams and rivers, green fields and deep, dark woods. And in a village, in a river, two men were fighting; everything depended on the outcome. *A ruler. My bloodline.* She struggled to speak.

'Wulfstan does not know?'

'No – he is too young, still.'

'He must never know.' Samra shook her head, and her eyes filled with tears. 'The moment Wulfstan learns it, he will die.'

Alfred stared at her in shock. 'How do you know this?'

'I know. That is all I can say.'

'And may none tell Wulfstan? Not even his father?'

'Especially not his father.' Samra took his hand. 'But you will add to the book, Alfred. You must confide this secret to it.'

Alfred nodded, and his voice was a whisper. 'Yes.'

'Then take it, and write.'

'But if it is in the book, what I write, others may learn also.'

'No. I am the keeper of the book and if it contains a secret, others will not uncover it,' Samra said firmly.

Alfred opened the book where she showed him, and began to write.

Just as Alfred had closed the book, Estraya came in, arms wrapped round something pressed to her stomach. She was crying. Samra gently moved one of her daughter's arms to reveal a trembling ball of brown fur.

'What is it, my love? Let me see.'

Carefully she took the ball of fur from Estraya and held up a baby rabbit. Across its face was a bloody gash mark.

'Did the men outside do this?' Estraya nodded. 'Poor thing; it cannot see. It will not live without help.'

Estraya stopped crying, and looked up at her mother with bright eyes.

'Can I keep it?'

Betrayed

Near Guildford, Surrey, October 1036

It was on a windy autumn day, with dark clouds shuddering across the sky, that Earl Godwin and his followers were to be found accompanying Alfred of Wessex on the high road west of Guildford. Alfred was not alone; with him was a hand-picked bodyguard of Norman mercenaries and some of his close followers, his kinsman Rædmund, who was father to Wulfstan and Eadric, included. Still ringing in Alfred's ears was the earl's loyalty sworn to him when he had met them in the town, where his men had been well rested and fed in the lodgings Godwin had chosen for them overnight. That morning both parties had set out together, for London, the earl said, where surely a great welcome awaited the returning king. But the high road west of Guildford does not lead to London. It would have taken Alfred to Winchester, and to his and Edward's mother.

Riding alongside Alfred, Godwin stopped his horse; so close that the young man had no choice but to stop his. Their legs were touching.

'Spectacular, is it not, the view from this ridge?' said the earl. 'So far over the Weald to the south, and almost as far as London to the north.'

Godwin leant in, pointing out features, putting an arm around the young man's shoulders and pulling him closer.

'What do you think of this vision of your new kingdom, Alfred?'

Abruptly Alfred heard voices behind him; urgent cries from his men. Trying to turn round, he was suddenly thrown from his horse by the earl, landing heavily on his back. At once men were upon him, pinning him down and blindfolding him, before pulling him upright. He felt the ground go from under his feet before being lifted and dropped on his stomach across what he knew was the back of a horse. He felt it startle under his weight, could smell its hide as his hands and feet were roped together under the animal's belly. The ropes tightened, forcing his face onto a warm flank. He heard a voice he recognised from the alehouse the night before as one of Godwin's kin; Sighere, who called himself Thegn of Berewic.

'What orders, Earl Godwin?'

'Decimate them. Let those who are left take the news back to Normandy, that the Wessex will have no sway here.'

Alfred struggled fiercely against his ropes, as the sound of sword after sword being drawn reached his ears on the wind. He was desperate to block them from what was to come next; the thud of metal into flesh. The Normans around him were being slaughtered; one in ten.

He struggled to raise his head and shouted, 'Godwin! Earl Godwin!'

The great earl spoke in his ear. 'Alfred? You have something to say?'

'Who ordered this treachery?'

'Harold Harefoot. My king.'

'When Edward learns of your betrayal—'

'Treachery? Betrayal?' Godwin cut in. 'For those holding on to or seeking power in our times, these are hazards to be expected, Alfred. Edward should have known that.'

'And murder?' Alfred sobbed. 'Butchery, with no mercy?'

'Weapons to be used. Oh, did I forget to tell you?' added the earl. 'Edward was turned away from Southampton. The good townspeople did not want a son of the wretched Ethelred for their king.'

All around Alfred the slaughter went on. The air was full of the cries of the dying and the smell of blood. He wept.

'Then kill me too! Do not let me live to see your carnage.'

'We do not need a Wessex martyr today. Take him away.'

The horse jolted and Alfred felt his body sway as it was led slowly away. The cries and voices receded, and now he was like a sack, being carried on the horse's back, bruised and weeping tears of fear and anguish. After a while they went past some woodsmen felling a tree; Alfred could hear the ring of their axes. He remembered the Forest of Valognes and the clearing where Gilbert's house stood, and Samra; and the book. And he knew he would never see them again.

*

Earl Godwin turned to the Thegn of Berewic. 'Are we done?'

'There are still many – too many to send back in one ship.'

'Then kill as many as you can stomach. The rest I will sell for slaves.'

Sighere turned, walked into the group of remaining Normans and found himself face to face with a man he had last seen twenty years before. On that day, on the road to

Berewic, he had passed a man hurrying in the other direction, into exile in Normandy. He looked at this man, whose hands were tied behind his back, whose face was bloody, and whose breathing was heavy.

'Did you think to take back your manor, Rædmund? Did you think to sit in my hall house? To eat and drink at my table?'

The man sneered. 'I would have done all that for my sons. And so that Godwin filth would soil Berewic no more.'

'Berewic is the heritance of my daughter. Not of a Wessex.'

'I had heard you have a daughter. Her mother was the fairest woman in Sussex, and meant for me.' The man of Wessex shook his head. 'And you used her as the Godwins like to use their women. Wed, bred and dead. How did she die?'

'In the gift of the child to me.' Sighere paused. 'When did you know she was dead? That the letters were coming from me?'

'She sent more than village gossip to the sister she wrote to, Sighere, and the sister shared it with me. When that changed, I knew. Your wife had kept her loyalty; and you the fool to think you were fooling me.'

Sighere drew his *seax*, and held the weapon out in front of him.

'Tell me one thing before you die, Rædmund. Who ordered to you to send me news of the Wessex return, and promised you Berewic for it?'

The other man laughed. 'Who else would bribe a Wessex with a promise she never meant to keep in order to ensure her own Wessex sons would be betrayed as soon as they stepped ashore in England? You are more a fool not to see Emma was behind this as soon as I sent my last word to you.'

As Rædmund was speaking, dark fury set in on the Godwin thegn's face. He stabbed the other man once, in the stomach, pulling the *seax* across and up as he did so. As the earl's men hacked and stabbed the others of Alfred's remaining followers around him, the man the world had known as the father of Wulfstan and Eadric of Wessex fell to his knees. With a huge effort Rædmund raised his head and looked into Sighere's face, eyes dimming, mouth slackening as it tried to form words between gasps of breath.

'There is no... Godwin victory here. Berewic... and England... belong to the Wessex. One day... we will reclaim them both.'

The light faded from his eyes, and Rædmund crashed forwards onto the ground.

Sanctuary

Forest of Valognes, Normandy, January 1037

Samra woke to the barking of dogs outside. Gilbert was gone; leaving Estraya asleep, she went quickly to the door. Over the sound of the rain that had been falling steadily since early afternoon, she listened in the dark. Voices sounded back and forth; those of Gilbert and some of his men, and others more distant and muffled. Samra tensed, recalling what Gilbert had relayed to her of the visit to the abbey at Cerisy, and the attempt to take the book.

Suddenly the door was opened and Gilbert rushed in with two servants. One tall and two smaller figures, all three of them cloaked and hooded against the rain, followed them inside. One servant was ordered to fetch food, and the other fed the fire in the hearth before being sent after the first. The cloaked figures crowded round the hearth as the flames flared up among the wood, and the smell of damp clothing began to spread into the warming room.

Samra looked questioningly at Gilbert. 'Are we in danger?'

The tall man threw back his hood, and Edward of Wessex stood before her. He gave a little bow.

'Forgive us; we have ridden long and hard, and we are come late among you. Eadric, Wulfstan – show yourselves.'

Hastily the two boys threw back their hoods likewise, and bowed. Starting to leave their boyhoods behind, they had grown; Wulfstan was more rounded, Eadric taller. Eadric shuffled his feet and looked around the room, while Wulfstan gave Samra the frank gaze that he had the last time they met. She did not notice; she was looking at Edward. The carefree huntsman from the Forest of Lyons with the broad smile was gone; the man who had left to be King of England looked gaunt, hollow-eyed, and dog-tired.

Over the crackling logs and the hiss of water dripping from cloaks onto the hot hearth stones, Gilbert spoke at last.

'Are you come to hunt? Is Duke William behind somewhere?'

Before Edward could answer, the servants returned. For a while the visitors busied themselves with taking food. Eadric and Wulfstan threw off their cloaks and settled in a corner to eat, while Edward remained before the fire, chewing slowly on a strip of meat, staring into the flames.

'And Alfred?' Samra's voice was a whisper.

Edward looked up and Samra could see he was close to tears. He shook his head.

'I may have fled here from nothing,' he said, 'from a rumour, or someone I imagined seeing on the road; an assassin sent to finish what Harold Harefoot and his Godwin helpers began. But they will have no more Wessex blood. So I took the two boys and came here. If I have troubled you without cause, I am sorry. We will leave at dawn.'

'It is no trouble, my lord,' said Gilbert, 'and you will stay here as long as you wish. The roads will be awash tomorrow, if this rain keeps up.' He looked to the door. 'But… might you have been followed?'

'I do not believe so. We left at night and have been travelling at night. Not even William knows where we are.'

'Gilbert,' Samra said softly, placing a hand on his arm. 'Will you take the boys to Hubert's house? There is room there and his wife is kind; she misses her own sons. Take food with you as you go.'

Gilbert nodded, and went to speak to Eadric and Wulfstan. They came back to the fire to get their cloaks. Eadric looked questioningly at Edward, who smiled and motioned to the door. When Gilbert had left, followed by the boys and the servants with food, Samra turned to Edward, arms held out. He fell into her embrace, sobbing, his head on her shoulder. When he had subsided, Edward pulled away and held her by the arms, looking into her face. The distress in his was clear.

'How do you tell two boys that their father is dead? That you led him into a trap, set by your own mother, their kinswoman? A trap that claimed your own brother?'

Samra felt a stab of anguish. 'Alfred… is dead?'

Edward turned away, and went to the table with the remaining food. He picked up a loaf and began to pull pieces from it. His voice was a distant murmur as Samra fought back her grief.

'They put red-hot pokers in his eyes to make him unfit to be a king. They did not need to do that to me. They already knew I was unfit. I turned tail at Southampton and ran.' He put a small piece of bread in his mouth and chewed it, staring at the fire. 'Poor, gentle, unworldly Alfred. From when we were boys, all he wanted was books and a cloister to sit in.

Now he will never see one again.' Samra came and took his hand, shaking her head, unable to speak. He turned back to her. 'I will hate the Godwins for as long as I live, Samra. But I will always know it was my foolishness and cowardice that let them do their work that day.'

Biting her lip, tears running down her cheeks, Samra struggled to master her grief.

'No, you must not blame yourself. You would have always known it was a risk. Alfred did. And you are alive; the Wessex may hope to be kings of England yet.'

'Not if Harefoot has any say. I am close to Duke William; I may be safe, but the boys… without a father to protect them…'

Samra nodded slowly and went to the table. From a flagon she poured two cups of wine, and brought one to Edward. He drank slowly, eyes closed.

Taking a drink, Samra said, 'We both know that is not true for Wulfstan.' Edward opened his eyes and found she was looking in to his. 'Alfred wanted me to know. In case none of you returned.'

He looked back at her and in her dark eyes suddenly he understood what Alfred had told him at moments when they were together – and Edward was not occupied with pleasures of the hunt or the table, or a girl – about the woman of the forest and her book. *She is wise, Edward; wise beyond anything you or I can grasp. And in her, I see our family's future.*

'It was you that told Alfred that Wulfstan must never learn the truth,' he said.

'Yes. I wish it could be otherwise.' Samra put down her cup. 'But it is not a father Wulfstan and Eadric need just now. It is a mother. Leave them here with me. Let the Forest of Valognes be their sanctuary.'

They both turned at a noise. Behind them, Estraya stood rubbing her eyes, face screwed up in part drowsiness, part crossness. She brightened when she saw Edward.

'Is Alfred here?'

A Manor in the Forest

Forest of Valognes, Normandy, April 1037

In the forest clearing, Wulfstan was annoying his elder brother. It did not take much from Wulfstan to annoy Eadric; he had a gift for it, and used it often. This time, he had found a devil's coach-horse, a large and fierce-looking beetle. He was holding its threatening rear end up to Eadric's face. Eadric was trying to evade the beetle and grab his brother's hand at the same time.

It was Gilbert who came up behind Wulfstan, grabbed him by the collar, and pulled him away.

'Enough! You boys have spent too much time in idleness and games. Spring is upon us, the days are lengthening, and it's time you took your places here.' Gently, he prised the coach-horse from Wulfstan's hand and put it on the ground, where it scuttled away.

Eadric looked at him seriously. 'What do you mean?'

'I mean, time you were put to work. Come on.' He had started to walk away, but turned back, realising neither boy was following.

Wulfstan was half laughing. 'We are English nobles. A manor in Sussex is our heritance.'

Gilbert walked the few steps back to Wulfstan and stood, hands on hips, looking down at him. 'Is that so?'

'My brother is right,' Eadric came in. 'We do not work.'

'Hmmm,' Gilbert mused, trying to restrain laughter, or anger; he was not sure which. He looked around him and saw a tree stump a few yards away at the edge of the clearing. 'Come over here.'

Wulfstan and Eadric followed him to the stump. It was broad and any roughness from its felling had long been worn down to leave a flat, if not perfectly level, surface.

'Just get on it, both of you.'

The boys looked at him, hesitating, then stepped up onto the stump. It was broad enough to hold both, albeit they had to stand close together, back to back. Wulfstan elbowed his brother in the ribs; Eadric elbowed back, scowling.

Beside them, Gilbert held up a hand. 'Listen!' Now he had raised his voice and both boys froze and looked at him. 'This stump is yours. It is your manor. I give you it, for all the time you are here with us. On it, you are lords. You may do as you wish. No one will disturb you, or ask you for your time or your service. Is that clear enough?'

Eadric frowned and Wulfstan nodded.

'But out here,' Gilbert waved an arm at the forest around him, 'I am lord. And you will do as I bid you. Here, none is so high that they can be waited on. We all work.' He bent down, until his face was close to theirs; they did not dare turn to look at him. 'So; stay on your manor as long as you like, my English nobles. But the moment you get off, you are mine. And by God, you will work.' He straightened, folded his arms, and waited.

A few minutes passed. It was Eadric who stepped off

first, giving Gilbert a hard but not impudent look. Wulfstan followed, grinning sheepishly.

'Good.' Gilbert put an arm round each of their shoulders. 'Now, let's see what we can learn, shall we? I hear your warriors fight with axes, so you should both know how to handle one.'

'Yes!' Wulfstan cried.

Eadric cringed.

Summoned

Bruges, Flanders, December 1038

If there were ghosts in the great hall of the ducal palace in Flanders, Emma of Normandy did not see them. Ghosts of the two husbands and kings of England she had seen buried. Ghosts of the many who Cnut, the second husband, had had pursued and killed – some said with Emma's knowledge – to assure his claim over the first, Ethelred, whom he had defeated. Not even the ghost of one of her sons by the first husband, beckoned back to England on her word and betrayed. Now she had summoned his brother from Normandy to meet her. But Edward did not advance to greet his mother, or even go to warm himself by the blazing logs in the hearth. Instead, he went to a window and peered through a crack in the shutters, down at the snow-covered street.

'Well?' In its fifty-third year, Emma's voice had lost none of its steel.

He turned, as if he had just noticed her. 'I was thinking… there are worse places you could be exiled, with Christmas coming. I imagine they do it rather well here.'

'Better than in Normandy; or England?'

Now Edward strode across the room to where Emma

sat in a high-backed chair. Her gown was a rich red and embroidered at the neck, while the girdle at her waist and the circlet round the wimple covering her head were of blue silk interwoven with gold thread. Even in exile, she was a queen.

Edward's long white hair brushed her face as he bent to her cheek, but there was no warmth in the kiss; and none in her hard blue eyes as she looked up at him.

'You did not bring me here to make me King of England,' he said, straightening. 'Not that you can; Harold Harefoot has seen to that.'

'Hah!' Emma almost spat. 'You will never be King of England, Edward of Wessex. You are too like your father; weak, dithering and bent on your own pleasure.'

Edward stiffened and turned away. As a boy, he had watched as Ethelred's chaotic reign failed to stem the tide of Danish invaders sweeping the country, and with Alfred was driven into permanent exile, with the death of his father following his final defeat. *Son of Ethelred*. It was a badge of shame he had borne through his long banishment in Normandy. He turned back, and his voice was as hard as the look he gave her.

'I need no lesson in kingship from the woman who married my father's enemy, and bore him a child to usurp my right. I need no lesson in loyalty from the woman whose last summons to me and my brother was no more than a trap. Thank God that one of us returned, to remind you of our eternal hatred.'

Emma returned his stare. 'You fool. To be so easily taken in by a forgery. If you seek the trap, you should look to the house of Godwin, our enemies, who threw themselves behind Harold Harefoot.'

'As they had thrown themselves behind Cnut, when he took the throne before that. You did not complain then, as you went to his bed.'

Emma looked away. 'I have lost a son, as you have lost a brother.'

'And now Cnut's other son has driven you into exile and menaces you from overseas.' He pointed at her. 'You thought to have a piece on every square on the board, when you had a son by Cnut to match yours by my father. But Cnut outwitted you when he put his son by his first marriage into power. Not to expect the unexpected is the downfall of all those who make plans, my mother.'

'Yet you came. And not only to give me the kiss of peace.'

Edward shook his head and went to the fire to warm himself. 'It is no matter. I came to tell you I have no interest in the throne of England. And now you know that, I will leave you.' He turned to go.

'Still you are a fool, Edward. I brought you here to support Harthacnut in his claim, not yours. You have resources he needs to contest the throne.'

Edward turned back, his mouth open. For a moment he could not speak. Then he laughed.

'You think I spent twenty years in Normandy, wondering if at any moment your husband's assassins might strike, now to help you put your son by Cnut into power? You are the fool – you and your endless scheming and conniving.'

Emma's eyes narrowed. 'It was only my place in Cnut's bed, as you put it, that stayed his hand against you and Alfred. With Harold Harefoot in power, no Wessex is safe. Put Harthacnut on the throne and I will see that he pledges your surety.'

Edward shook his head, but he was still smiling. 'You see? Scheme after scheme.'

'Better to scheme than to waste your life away in idleness! You have passed twenty years in what, Edward? Hunting – hunting and whoring.'

Her son came across to her. His cornflower-blue eyes were so full of fury that she stood up, ready to flee. Edward's voice shook as he tried to contain himself.

'She was no whore.'

'A serving girl who throws herself at a man of royal blood is a whore.'

He grabbed her by the shoulders, and pulled her towards him. 'She loved me!' Edward shook her as he shouted in her face. 'And she was the only woman I will ever love!' He threw her back into the chair and turned away, so she would not see his tears.

A moment passed as son and mother composed themselves, each lost in different concerns; of a lost love for one, and of matters of state for the other. Then Emma spoke.

'That brings us to the Wulfstan question.' Edward turned back. Emma went on, 'Who knows the truth now? With Alfred dead, and your Wessex kinsman who went to England with him?'

She had spoken so calmly of the deaths that Edward found himself obliged to think steadily again, despite his turmoil. He thought of Samra, keeping watch over Eadric and Wulfstan in the forest, guarding the secret Alfred had told her.

'Only we two. And I should not have told you.'

'Not Duke William?'

'No. The old Duke Robert, his father, knew of course, but not the son.'

'Then let it remain so. The truth will die with me. Ten years ago, when you wrote to tell me, I urged that it die with you. The old duke was right in one thing; if you ever hope to return to England – and you cannot tell me you do not hope for this – you must make an alliance with a daughter of a powerful family. Her son will be your heir – not that of a serving girl. You did right to let Wulfstan be brought up in your kinsman's family as one of their own. Yet I fear your recklessness, that you will tell him.'

'I long to, of course, as I watch him grow. Yet…' Edward hesitated. 'There is something that will bind me now.' Emma watched him, waiting, and he went on, 'When he landed in England, Alfred sent word to me. I thought it news of his success, or even that he had met with you, as he said he might. But it was something else. "One or other of us may perish here," he wrote. "If it is I, you must never tell Wulfstan what you know. For the moment that he learns the truth, he will die."'

Edward's voice had faded to a whisper, and he stood staring into the fire. Emma watched him as he stretched out his long, thin hands to the warmth of the flames.

Then he turned back to her, and said calmly, 'So you need not fear. I will never tell Wulfstan that I am his father.'

Hemlock and Hyssop

Forest of Valognes, Normandy, June 1039

'What are you doing here?'

Wulfstan had been watching Samra for some while as she moved around the herb garden, rubbing leaves between her fingers and smelling them, picking bunches from some of the plants to put in a basket she carried. She turned to see him on the path behind her, curiosity in his blue eyes. In the two years since he had come to the Forest of Valognes, he had already changed; he was on the cusp of being a young man.

'Collecting for the herbarium. All these plants have their uses. To cook, to preserve, or to heal.'

'No, I meant what are you doing in the Forest of Valognes? You're different from any around you. Someone told me you are from Spain and of noble birth. How did you come to be here?'

'It is not what I was born to, that is true. But I was brought here for my protection, like you. And now this is my life.' She gestured at the forest around.

'Protection from what – or who?'

Samra put down her basket. 'Sit down with me.'

She lowered herself onto a low timber wall that fronted one of the herb beds and motioned Wulfstan to sit beside her.

'You have seen me with a book that I study, and write in?'

Wulfstan nodded. 'Often, yes.' With his foot, he began to trace on the path one of the things he had seen in the book; a crescent moon.

'The book contains many things; it has great knowledge.' Samra hesitated. 'It confers great power on those who possess it.'

'Power to do what?'

'To use its knowledge. For good or for bad.'

Wulfstan stopped tracing and looked up at her. 'Who would use knowledge for bad?'

Looking into his guileless eyes, Samra felt a sudden relief. She remembered the night under the dome in the observatory in Spain when Sophia had spoken about the book, and how it could be used for good or evil. She felt again the connection she had with Wulfstan, a bond she sensed was greater than the name of a place she had never been to. And she longed to tell Wulfstan who he really was, for the blood of kings ran in his body, just as it did in hers.

Surely, of all people, he can learn this from me? What can happen, here in the forest, with the two of us, alone together?

She stood up and turned to him. 'Wulfstan…'

Wulfstan had turned round to a plant in the bed behind him that was tickling his neck. 'What is this?'

Samra looked at the spray of white flowers atop a tall stem. 'It is yarrow. When Achilles was injured in battle, he used it to heal his wounds.'

'Then a mouthful will be in order.'

'Wulfstan, there is something you must know. It concerns your father.'

His back to her, she saw him reaching to the plant, as if to break off a flower head. His hand had almost grasped it when she saw what it was.

'No! Do not touch it!'

Startled, Wulfstan found Samra grabbing his arm to pull it away.

'I should have recognised it,' she said quickly. 'It is water hemlock, and deadly. It must have come in from the marshes. I will have someone remove it.' And she sat down again beside him, shaking. 'I am sorry; how could I be so foolish?'

Wulfstan grinned. 'What would you have told Edward, when he comes back for us? That you had one less mouth to feed?'

Samra smiled weakly. 'Tell me about Berewic.'

He shrugged. 'A manor in England, with a river and fields and woods. Crops that grew, and oxen that ploughed the fields they grew in. Men and women, and children. My father… my father used to tell me about it. How one day he would take me and my brother there…'

Hearing the catch in Wulfstan's voice, Samra put an arm round his shoulders. For a moment he struggled to speak, then went on.

'What were you going to tell me about my father?'

'That I am sure you will honour Rædmund's name.'

'I will see Berewic, one day. Do you hope to see Spain once more?'

'I know I will not, and I am resigned to that. As long as I have the book.'

Wulfstan looked at her, frowning. 'Books do not interest

me. This is what will serve me, when I return to Berewic.' He put his hand to the hilt of his sword. 'I will kill this Sighere, who calls himself thegn there, and Eadric will take his place.'

Samra stood up and went to a plant on the other side of the path in front of her. She pulled a sprig of leaves from it and handed it to Wulfstan. He gave her a suspicious look, but she nodded.

'You may trust this; it is hyssop. Known to my people for thousands of years for its power to restore. I carry it with me always. Perhaps you should carry it with you too.' She looked down at him. 'You will see Berewic, Wulfstan, that is true; you and your brother. But I foresee danger, and blood.'

'Then you'd better find me the real yarrow plant,' said Wulfstan. 'I will need it.'

The Lens Tube

Forest of Valognes, December 1039

December had brought snow to the Forest of Valognes, more than it had seen for a long time – and, in her seventh year, the first deep snow Estraya had witnessed. She had emerged awestruck from the snug warmth of the house and ventured well beyond the clearing to find the valleys and the rocky outcrops cloaked, the contours levelled, and the trees white sentinels guarding a new world. In this creation, God had been playing a game, loading every twig of every tree with as much snow as it could bear. Now piled hand high but less than finger width, this snow teetered and wobbled in the slightly moving air, but did not dislodge. Here and there sunlight glinted in the icy crystals. Estraya pulled herself into a tree and began to climb, white powder showering her head and body, not to destroy this work, but to arrive at the pinnacle, from where she could look out across it all, her dress a little yellow sun among the tree branch latticework of black and white.

Estraya laughed in delight at God's handiwork, at the snow on the twig, and the twig on the branch, and the branch on the tree, and the tree in the forest, and the forest on the great ball of earth turning in the cosmos, as her mother had told her it did. A ball thrown onto the roof of the heavens, with the planets and stars whirling endlessly round it.

Beyond the edge of the trees she could see Felip, making his journey from Cerisy through a silent landscape, pristine save where the track of wolf or deer had marked it. And she laughed again, giggled to see the plump black shape of the monk on the plump black shape of his horse, ploughing doggedly on through the snow, the man of God furrowing God's creation without heed. Felip paused at a set of small shoe prints that circled and circled, reached the bottom of her tree, and vanished. Quickly Estraya descended the tree and plopped into the snow beside him. His horse startled a little, but he smiled and reaching down, pulled her up onto its back in front of him. She was icy cold, but still laughing as they rode on.

By the time they reached Gilbert's house, the toing and froing of people around it to harness horses, to fetch and chop wood, to butcher animal carcasses for the spit or the pot, had already churned the snow into brown slush. Steam was rising from warm roofs that were beginning to shed their load of snow, where it lay in piles beside the buildings. At the edge of the clearing, helped reluctantly by Eadric, Wulfstan had made Estraya a menagerie of forest creatures from the snow and a pen to keep them in. She leapt from Felip's horse, ran into the pen and put her arms round the neck of a deer, carefully so as not to break the antlers Wulfstan had made for it, and stood with her dark hair against its white snow body, eyes closed.

Felip himself had scarcely dismounted before Gilbert was at his side, pulling him into a bear hug. The monk had almost forgotten how strong Gilbert was. The woodsman's light blue eyes twinkled as he released Felip from his grip.

'Felip! It's been too long. Go inside and get something to eat, then I will show you what we have been doing here. I have a stack of oak timbers I am very pleased with. And I want to hear all about Cerisy.'

Felip hesitated; the message from Samra to come to the forest had been urgent and he wanted to see her. But it would have to wait.

'Of course.' He looked across to the snow pen. 'Estraya has grown since I was last here.'

'Children do,' Gilbert laughed. 'That is their way. Children, and trees.'

*

Now it was dark, and Felip and Samra were sitting in the warmth of the indoors, beside a menorah alight with candles. Wulfstan and Eadric were by the hearth with Estraya, roasting chestnuts at the fire. Felip was recalling a time he had sat in Samra's house near Toledo, when the whole household was celebrating Chanukah, the festival remembering the rededication of the Temple, when the Talmud relates that the oil that should have burnt for a day in the menorah lasted for eight. Samra saw him looking at the menorah.

'I bought it in Rouen,' she said. 'It is one of the few things I was able to bring with me from the other house.'

Felip looked around him, at the cross on the wall, and the holly and ivy hanging from the rafters. 'Happy the house that can celebrate Chanukah and Christmas together.'

'And Gilbert makes little offerings in the forest to his gods. He thinks I don't know, but I do.'

'Are you offended by these pagan idols?'

'We Jews have suffered worse in our time, and been left with less than a menorah to comfort us. Gilbert is good; at Christmas he makes little toys for Estraya, and puts nuts and sweet things in her shoes.'

'Then we will forgive him. But what do you have to show me?'

Samra opened the wooden box that Gilbert had made to keep the book in. Lifting it out, she unwrapped it from its cloth and opened it at a page with diagrams and writing. Felip saw lines drawn across the page, passing through objects and breaking into more lines, each going off in a different direction.

'Alhacen knows about light,' said Samra, 'and that it travels in a straight line and is split in different ways when it passes through a glass that is ground and shaped to be flat, curved or hollow – a lens. This is what Alhacen was working on when he left.'

Samra turned a page and Felip saw a diagram in which the light rays now passed along a tube with objects at each end, which he realised were lenses. As the rays passed through the lens at one end, they were gathered and passed through the second lens, to an object drawn in such a way it could only have been a human eye.

'I had made a lens tube like this, but the lenses in it were crude and the mounting was fixed. It brought what I was looking at closer, but it was blurred. I believe there should be two tubes, each containing one of the lenses, that slide one inside the other until a clear image is reached.'

'You want me to translate this part of the book?'

'Yes. But I also need lenses, exactly as Alhacen describes them here. One lens has one side curved out and the other curved in, one has one side flat and one side curved in; but they must be exact.'

'At Cerisy we have reading stones; glass spheres simply cut in half. They magnify, though not well. If I can cut two to these measurements, I will bring them back. How will you make your tubes?'

Gilbert had come in and was standing beside the hearth, warming the cold of his body. He looked over from where his daughter and the two boys were stirring the chestnuts.

'From wood.'

Felip nodded. 'And you will be looking at the stars, with your lens tube?'

'At the sun,' Gilbert said.

'The sun?' Felip looked at Samra in amazement. 'You may not look at the sun with the eye, let alone through a lens.'

'You will see,' replied Samra. 'But be sure you return here by May of next year. Before May the twenty-second, to be exact.'

The Reeve of Berewic

Berewic, Sussex, May 1040

On the low bluff overlooking the river, eyes closed in the sunshine, Æadgytha was sitting on a fork of one of the lower branches of the moot tree. After winter's harsh rule, a glorious spring was queen of all she touched. Above Æadgytha, the soft light-green beech leaves slowly spread and grew. Around her, the land was lush, dense and rich with promise, as England is in every May. The blossom of that name strewn along the field sides was a froth of white and pink, heady-scented and insect-buzzing. The willows along the river waved and startled with their fresh bright foliage, admiring themselves in the glassy reflection below. The fields were verdant with growth, grass assuring its future hay-heading, and crops their more distant grain-filling. High in the sky, a lark was stitching together its long, trilling song, and somewhere in the distance a sheep and lamb were bleating comfort to each other.

Æadgytha was not pushing herself up and down on the springy limb of the beech tree; at eleven years of age she was too sensible – and now too tall – for that. But she was acting to herself; and in her little play she was Thegn of Berewic, commanding her village meeting. She waved an arm towards the river, at someone beneath her in both senses.

'How does the village this year, Cuthred? And how is my demesne land?'

'Well enough, and already a better year than last. Hunger at our shoulder is no fit companion for your manor, my young lady.'

Æadgytha jumped at the voice behind her and, opening her eyes, turned to find Cuthred, her father's manor reeve, leaning against the trunk of the old beech, as if against the flank of some great animal. Although she knew he was important to her father and to the village, Cuthred's oily voice and ready smirk always made Æadgytha somehow uncomfortable. And now he had surprised her imagining her future self, demanding his report on her future manor. She bowed her head, so that her light brown hair fell forwards to hide her face and her blushes. Cuthred came up beside her and stood gazing over the river, shading his eyes with one hand.

'I can remember when we had to have the village moot under this tree, my lady. Good in weather like this, but a pain in the arse when it was raining, if you'll forgive me saying.'

Turning his head, he gave her a look that made it clear he needed no forgiveness from anyone. As reeve, Cuthred was the man chosen by his thegn to organise the daily business of the manor, and to act as a go-between with his fellow villagers. To Cuthred fell the task of ensuring the good working of the farmland of the manor and the good condition of its livestock. To him fell the collection of the yearly taxes due to the thegn, and of tithes due to the thegn's church, in penny and in produce, and what produce a villager raised over and above his obligation to his lord he could keep, if he satisfied Cuthred he was due it. His position, and the eighty acres of land he held in the manor as reward, made Cuthred a powerful man.

Æadgytha looked away and over the river. On the other side, a man was making his way to the bridge, carrying a burden of poles on one shoulder so large that his head could not be seen.

'I notice that man a lot. He works very hard,' she said.

'He's one of your father's *geburs*,' Cuthred replied. 'He holds land from him in return for service. He's fetching poles he's cut from the woodland to mend the fence round the hall house. Hard work indeed, on top of the ploughing and sowing and reaping he must do on his lord's fields – the demesne land.'

'But otherwise he is a free man.'

Cuthred smirked. 'A man who has freedom in name only is little better than a slave.'

'A slave might hope for his freedom, one day, if he earns enough to buy it, or his master on his deathbed releases him.'

'We all get our chance, my lady. A man who can take on more land from his lord and does well might buy himself out of being a *gebur*. Then he's fully free, not tied to his lord's estate – he can go where he pleases.'

Now Cuthred was in full flow. He turned to stand in front of the girl on her branch, waving his short arms.

'If his landholding rises to five hides, with church and kitchen, bell-house and burh-gate, he can even rank as a thegn, if he performs royal duties. And if he keeps his rank for three generations, it will pass to his heirs, even if his landholding later falls below five hides. Think on that!'

The glint in the reeve's eyes told Æadgytha that he was indeed thinking on it. She looked again across the river.

'You think the man over there has got that chance? Working every hour on his own land, when not on my father's? What does he have, at the end of each day?'

Cuthred subsided. 'He has his lord Sighere's protection. Like all of us.'

Æadgytha shook her head. 'The *gebur* who was mauled last winter when one of my father's hunting dogs attacked him was little protected.'

'One of his duties, also, to feed it. He hadn't been taking enough, and the dog was starving.'

'No less than the man.'

'My dear,' the reeve said, and laid a hand on Æadgytha's arm; she prickled at the oily voice as much as at the touch. 'You're young, and you have feelings towards people you might have had once towards one of your dolls, or a puppy dog. But a thegn rules over an order put in place by God and his king; a lord, then his truly free men, then men like the *geburs*, then his slaves. From the least obligation to him, to the most. That is how it will always be, and when you're married to the next Thegn of Berewic, he will rule over that order likewise, with your support.'

Æadgytha turned and stared at him. Never had it occurred to her that anyone but her might be the next Thegn of Berewic. Æadgytha thought of the day four years before, when she had been sitting on the very branch of the moot tree she was on now, with Harold Godwinson beside her, talking about how her mother had died giving birth to her.

And on another day, this manor will be yours, and you will not lack her qualities.

But she said nothing.

Transit of Venus

Forest of Valognes, Normandy, May 1040

Hugh de Bayeux got down from his horse and looked around him. The little group of buildings, home and workplace of Duke William's forest warden for five years, looked comfortable and purposeful in its clearing. Where this merged into the trees and bushes, spring flowers were blooming, craning towards the warmth of the sun when it appeared from between the clouds. The men on either side of Hugh dismounted too. Tall and strong as he was, Hugh was even so dwarfed by the first of these when he stood next to him. This man, aged about twenty and with dark curly hair and dark skin, was a head and shoulders above him, and twice as broad. Yet he stood and also looked around him, wide-eyed, nervously rubbing his huge hands together. The third man was dressed in the habit of a Benedictine monk, and he too looked worried. On their way through the forest, the three had met two boys – or rather young men – that Felip had recognised as Eadric and Wulfstan, the brothers Gilbert and Samra were sheltering. Wulfstan had stepped in front of Eadric, and the monk had seen that he was holding in one hand some snares, and an animal or bird of some kind. A lot to hold in one hand; but in the other he had held a sword.

'Are you come to kill us?' Wulfstan had said, looking at the small group of armed men behind the other three.

But Hugh de Bayeux had only smiled. 'Make sure you return to the clearing by midday,' he had said. 'We do not want to have come and find you.'

*

As he hurried to the door of Gilbert's house, Felip met Samra coming out. She looked straight past him at Hugh de Bayeux.

'Felip, you are just in time – but why did you bring him?'

Felip took her hands. 'I had no choice. He came to Cerisy and saw the lenses. He recognised the diagrams were from the book, and he wants to see the experiment.'

Samra saw in Hugh not the boy she remembered from the Forest of Lyons, but a grown man, powerfully built and moving with a long stride as he walked over to them. His deep-set, light blue-grey eyes looked into hers without expression, then he bowed.

'Felip has brought you the lenses, and I have been glad to be with him and assure their safe delivery.'

Samra did not reply, but looked questioningly at Felip. He pulled two cloth-covered objects from a bag on his belt and gave them to her.

As she unwrapped them, Felip said, 'Has Gilbert made the tubes?'

Samra called across the clearing. 'Estraya!' After a few moments her daughter appeared from between some trees, holding a bunch of flowers. Now seven, Estraya was slight and elfin-featured, and her dark bright eyes quickly took in the visitors as she came across. 'Find your father.'

As the girl scampered off, the other man who had arrived with Hugh and Felip walked over. He looked at Samra intently for a while, before saying to Hugh, 'Is she the one with the book?'

Samra, who had been examining the lenses Felip had given her, looked up, startled. *He spoke to him in Arabic.*

Hugh answered, in Arabic, 'She is indeed.'

The man shrugged and asked Samra if there was anything to eat.

'Inside. Ask one of the servants.'

'He speaks little French. I will go with him,' Hugh said, taking the man into the house.

Felip explained to Samra. 'The man was born in Egypt, but he has been travelling through France, making for England, where his mother came from. He was caught stealing in the Bayeux lands, but Hugh took him on in lieu of punishment.'

'He has taught Hugh Arabic?'

'Hugh had a little from his time in Spain. But yes, he has learned more.'

'Felip!' Gilbert called to the monk as he came across the clearing with Estraya. Felip barely had time to turn round before the tall woodsman had him in a bear hug. 'By God, it's good to see you! But you had better have these lenses, or Samra will send you packing.'

'I have them, though we have little time to spare. I hope you have done your work?'

'The tubes? I will show you. But first, why has Samra not offered you to eat and drink? Estraya, take our friend inside.'

'I have no great hunger, and I would see the tubes now if I may.'

Samra caught Gilbert's arm. 'Hugh de Bayeux is inside, with another man. See to them first; I will take Felip.'

Samra walked ahead of Felip across the clearing to an open area with a small wooden shelter. From one side of this stuck out a tubular length of wood, angled towards the sky. Samra took one of the lenses from its cloth and held it up to the open end of the tube above her head.

'A little too large. But we will be able to shape the inside of the tube to fit. Better that than too small.'

Putting down the first lens, she lifted a heavy cloth hung over a small opening in the side of the shelter, hooked it open on a nail, and ducked inside. Felip followed, and as his eyes adjusted to the near-dark he saw a second tube, fitted into the end of the first where it came through the wall and pointed at the far wall of the shelter, which unlike the others was smooth, and coated with a whitewashed clay. Samra held the second lens to the opening at this end of the tube, and took a deep breath.

Felip could feel her elation. 'It is with this that you will look at the sun?'

Samra sat down with her back to one of the walls and motioned Felip to sit opposite. She put down the second lens and began to speak.

'During the time that Alhacen and I made our contributions to the book, he was greatly preoccupied with the sun, the stars and the planets, and with light and the properties of light. He made experiments with lenses, mirrors and what he called a dark chamber, projecting light from a scene outside though a hole in one wall onto a wall on the other side. The motions of the planets fascinated him, and he was able to use mathematics to describe the true configuration of the seven planets in a way that resolved the contradictions in the theories of the great Ptolemy. The sections you see in the book, on the planets' motion, astronomical calculation and astronomical instruments, are sketches of a work that he had begun before he left Spain. To Alhacen, the movement of the planets through the sky was a matter of the laws of physics, not a mere theory. When he saw that the book held generations of my family's observations of the stars and the planets, he knew at once that his physics could be proved, and used to predict future conjunctions, eclipses and so on.'

*

Inside the house, Gilbert had brought food from the kitchen, then left to collect the lenses from Samra and begin their fitting. Estraya was in a corner, laying out her flowers. Hugh de Bayeux's companion was at table, already eating. Sat opposite, Hugh realised the book lay next to him, and it was open. He pulled it towards him, and started leafing through the pages.

*

In the shelter, Samra was speaking again. 'Now, Alhacen's physics and the observations in the book told him that from time to time, the relative motions of Earth, the sun and Venus bring Venus directly between the sun and Earth. During this transit, Venus must be able to be seen from Earth as a small disk moving across the great orb of the sun. By his calculation, such a transit of Venus would occur on May the twenty-fourth, 1032, and would be visible from Spain against the setting sun. When you persuaded me to go to the court of the Christians in northern Spain, I knew that within a few months I would be able to prove to them that I had a science far in advance of any then known. But in the attack in which the rest of my family was killed or taken as slaves, the lens tube was destroyed, looted for its value in silver alone. I would never know if Alhacen was right. It weighs heavily on me that in my eagerness and my pride, I brought about my family's destruction.'

Outside, they could hear Gilbert scraping at the end of the tube to make it fit the first lens; the sun had come out. Felip saw a small circle of light on the whitewashed wall, enough to illuminate the little shelter and Samra's face.

*

In the house, Hugh was looking at a page rich with text and diagrams. In one of them, a man was bent over a large crucible, adding something to its contents while two other men were stirring.

*

In the shelter, Felip saw the tears in Samra's eyes. The light died, and once again they were in near darkness. Samra went on. 'In my mind, I had seen myself – not in a rough shelter like this, but in the hall of a great palace, its walls hung with rich tapestries. At one end a king and queen are seated on gilded thrones. All their attention is on me as I explain what is about to happen; that an unimaginable distance away among the planets, Venus is about to cross in front of the sun.

I call for the shutters to be closed and the hall is in darkness, save for a circle of light cast onto a silk screen. As we watch, a small black disk enters the edge of the circle and begins to move slowly across. In the applause, I close my eyes with joy, the blood-red circle of the sun still filling my vision.'

*

In the book, Hugh was reading how, by reordering the qualities of one metal, it might be transformed into a different metal, if only one has the *al-iksir*, the mysterious catalyst that would make this possible.

*

In the shelter, Samra was still speaking. 'Now when I close my eyes, I see that January day in Spain. I see my grandfather, lying between my little nieces, a hand over both of their eyes, so they could not see what was coming, and the blood-red snow around them all. I hear my sister screaming, as she is dragged away.'

Her voice faltered; she stopped. Felip could not see her face, but he knew she was weeping.

*

Hugh's eyes had fallen on the words 'lead' and 'gold'.

*

Samra opened her eyes. 'It was several years before I could read those passages in the book again. But when I did, I saw a note at the foot of a page; the transit of Venus would come again in eight years, and then not again for over a hundred. Soon, from the image of the sun cast on that wall, I will know if Alhacen was right. And somewhere in the world, he will know too.'

Felip's voice sounded across the dark. 'The man with Hugh told me Alhacen died two months ago in Cairo.'

*

Hugh de Bayeux held a hand out to the man, who was cutting meat with his knife. The man paused, and passed him the knife. Hugh took a handful of pages from the book in one hand and put the knife to the top corner of them.

*

In the shelter, Samra got up suddenly. 'The book!'

*

'That is not yours.' Hugh had not seen Estraya come over, and now she was standing at his shoulder. 'It is my mother's. Put it down.'

He grabbed her and held the knife to her throat. 'Never speak to me like that again.' He pushed her away and turned back to the book.

'Estraya is right.' Gilbert had come back into the hall. He came across to the table until he was standing behind Hugh's companion. 'No part of that book belongs to you, and you will not leave here with any of it.'

Hugh said something in Arabic to the other man, who

made to get up. But he froze, as he saw Samra behind Hugh, her knife in her hand. In an instant, she had the knife at Hugh's throat.

'You will leave here now – both of you.'

And the man saw that the blade, which had looked so slight when the knife was first in her hand, was broad and jagged.

*

An hour later, Samra and Felip were again in the shelter, again seated on the ground opposite each other. Estraya was squatting next to her mother, and Felip was making small adjustments to the position of the lens tube, as he had been all the while, to keep track of the sun, and sliding one part in or out of the other as needed to keep a clear image. Just as earlier, the sun was elusive; the hour had passed with only fleeting images of it on the whitewashed wall. Suddenly the sun was fully out, and it stayed out. Samra got up. At the left of the orb of the sun, a small black disk had appeared. As they watched, it moved slowly from just inside the edge, crossing the face of the sun on a descending diagonal from left to right.

Felip gasped. Samra fell to her knees. Estraya went to the wall and caught the dark shadow of Venus in the palm of her hand.

'You are worthy of the book, Samra,' Felip said. 'And for what you have just shown us, you deserved a grander audience.'

'No,' Samra replied, 'for this is my lesson. What we know and confide to the book, we owe to God. For this we should be humble, not proud.'

Suddenly, the cloth over the opening was pulled back. Against the light that poured in, they could see Gilbert's large frame.

'Quickly,' he urged, 'they're taking Eadric and Wulfstan!'

As the others scrambled out to join him, Gilbert pointed across the clearing. Hugh de Bayeux had returned, and with him was a small group of armed men. Eadric was just mounting a horse, while Wulfstan stood beside another. Wulfstan turned as he saw Samra approach, but Hugh moved his horse between them.

Gilbert had come across to Hugh, and now stood in front of him. 'On whose authority do you do this?'

'I need no authority; but Edward will be glad to see his late kinsman's sons again.'

Samra had joined Gilbert and she looked defiantly up at the Norman knight. 'It was Edward that brought them here, for their own safety. They are at risk.'

Hugh de Bayeux looked down at her. 'That risk has passed. Word has come from England – Harold Harefoot is dead. Edward's half-brother rules in his place, and Harthacnut is well disposed to the Wessex. Eadric and Wulfstan are becoming men, and their place is among men; not hidden away in a forest with a woodsman and a wise woman.'

Now Samra went across to Wulfstan, where he stood holding the horse's reins. 'Would you leave us, without so much as a goodbye?'

Abashed, Wulfstan did not look at her, fiddling instead with the reins, as if he needed to make some adjustment.

'Hugh said you were too busy with your experiments, and that we must make some distance before nightfall.' Now he turned his gaze on her and his blue eyes met her dark ones.

'But I do not think he was honest in that. I believe he thought you would keep us here by some witchcraft.'

Wulfstan was grinning. Suddenly he flung his arms about Samra and held her in an embrace that surprised her with its strength. When he pulled away, she saw that Eadric had moved his horse closer. Leaning down, Eadric spoke calmly, but with a steely undertone in his voice that surprised her also.

'Hugh is right; we need to go. We are grateful – of course – to you both for our time here. Gilbert has been a diligent taskmaster, and we have learnt much from him. But this is about more than seeing Edward again. We hear that Harthacnut is not a well man, and without an heir. If Edward comes into view for the throne of England, we may also hope to regain the manor our father lost many years ago.'

While Eadric was speaking, Estraya had come up beside her father, and taken his hand. Now she looked over to Wulfstan, frowning.

'I know! Be... Be... Don't tell me!'

Wulfstan came over to her and bobbed down until he was looking into her face. Her took her hands in his and mouthed a word to her. Estraya's features brightened at once.

'Berewic!' she cried.

*

As Samra watched Eadric and Wulfstan ride away, she became aware of Felip standing next her.

'You must have known,' she said, 'that if Hugh came in force, it was to take Eadric and Wulfstan. Yet you said nothing.'

Felip nodded slowly. 'He offered the safe delivery of the lenses in return for my silence, and promised me the sword if I broke that silence. Hugh de Bayeux is not a man to argue with; we are lucky he has not left with the book, or at least part of it.' He turned to walk away then turned back, flicking away the hair that had fallen over one eye.

'You knew that the name you spoke in the room below the observatory at Toledo is a place in England. If Eadric and Wulfstan are heirs to Berewic, they are part of this. Yet you said nothing.'

Samra shook her head. 'I have wrestled with that knowledge, even disbelieved it. How can two boys, brothers who both give me cause to dislike them, share in this story and my destiny?'

'Dislike them?'

'Wulfstan is brave, but headstrong and arrogant. One day, he will pay a price for that. Eadric is timid, but watchful and cunning. One day, we will all pay a price for that.'

*

Quiet had settled over the clearing once more. Gilbert had returned to his work; Estraya was somewhere in the trees, singing to herself. Felip was in the house, watching the flames of the fire. He turned to Samra, who was at the table, leafing through the book, checking it was undamaged.

'It is just we two, Samra, now Alhacen has gone. We are the guardians of the book, and its purpose. We must be able to trust each other.'

Samra nodded, and as she turned the pages, she came to the one on which Alfred had confided the secret of Wulfstan's birth. *I should tell Felip who Wulfstan's father is.* And she drew breath, with a hand poised to open the book at Alfred's page.

'Felip...'

'Yes?'

She thought again about Wulfstan in the herb garden. *It is enough that I know. I cannot put him in more danger.*

'I will work with you, for whatever end the book and its foretelling bring,' she said. 'But after that day at the mountain pass in Spain, I cannot trust you again.'

The Way to Hell

Forest of Valognes, Normandy, September 1041

From high up in a tree, Estraya watched as two men on horseback approached her father's home in the forest clearing. Even from a distance she recognised them from their past hunting trips to the Forest of Valognes; one a count, one a knight. Now she saw them pull up in the clearing below her and dismount. They walked over to the shelter her father had built and one of them, Ranulph de Bayeux, pulled the sacking cover off the lens tube. He stood on tiptoe, trying to look into the skywards-pointing end. The words of the other man, Hugh de Bayeux, carried up to Estraya as he laughed at his brother.

'You need to be inside, where the other end comes through. There you will see the wonders of the universe. But not today.'

As Estraya watched, Ranulph walked across to a small pen and stood looking into it at a large rabbit that was loping stiffly around. When it reached the bars of the pen it bumped into them, then set off in another direction, until it once more collided with the bars. He watched as the animal did this over and over, then reached in and picked it up. Estraya tensed as

Ranulph held it up, looking into its sightless eyes. He turned to his brother.

'Hurry up. I need to get home.'

The girl saw Hugh leave him and go towards the house. He opened the door quietly and slipped inside. After a while he came out again with a wooden box and a velvet cloth that he put down by Ranulph, who was stroking the rabbit. Hugh went from building to building around the clearing, looking inside each. Unseen, Estraya began to climb down from the tree.

Finally Hugh came back to the wooden shelter that housed the lens tube. Lifting the cloth over the opening, he fastened it to the nail and looked inside. The shaft of light through the entrance fell across Samra, sitting against a wall, holding the book to her like a baby. As she passed the entrance to the shelter, Estraya paused. Hugh was squatting, facing her mother. He spoke, his voice cold.

'We met Gilbert and his men at the fair at Lessay, buying horses. Then they were going to Cerisy to help Felip. They will not be back this night.'

Estraya saw Samra look at Hugh a while before speaking.

'You are right,' her mother said. 'The wonders of the universe are to be found in this small space. But that is not enough for you.'

'You know why I am here.'

'And you know I cannot let you take it.'

Behind Estraya the rabbit began to squeal. She turned to see Ranulph gripping its throat.

Estraya ran across to the pen, pleading tearfully with Ranulph.

'Please!'

He gripped tighter, holding the rabbit above his head, where it began to kick. Estraya tried to reach for it and the squealing and kicking grew stronger, then stopped. Ranulph threw the animal down abruptly, and grabbed her. Holding Estraya by the arm, he dragged her over to the shelter and thrust her into the entrance in front of Hugh de Bayeux. Hugh pinned her to the ground by the back of the neck, took out a knife and put it to the girl's throat.

'I am not the crude knight you once saw. I am worthy of the book now. Read from it.'

Head pressed to the ground, from out of one eye Estraya saw her mother, paralysed with fear. Samra could only look at Hugh. He pressed the knife into Estraya's neck; she felt the sharp pain and her skin at breaking point, and screamed.

'Read!' Hugh shouted.

Hands shaking, Samra opened the book and began to read in Arabic, stumbling over the words.

As she spoke, Hugh repeated her words in French, then said to her, 'There is nothing I cannot do, Samra. I will be master of your book, and of the sun, the moon and the stars.'

On the ground, feeling a moment of slackening of the point of the knife, Estraya tried to pull her body away from the man's grip with her feet. But the hand on the back of her neck tightened, and with it the other hand with the knife pressed into her flesh again. She bit hard on her lip, whimpering.

Samra was shaking her head. 'You are blinded by greed, Hugh de Bayeux. When you open the book, you will read that Alhacen has written, "The book lives only in those who read it and know it. For the wise, it is the way to treasure beyond price. For the foolish, it is the way to hell." You will not make a slave of its learning, or bend it to your ends.'

'And you will not barter your daughter's life for it.'

Estraya saw her mother look from her to the book and back; she could not move. Struggling to breathe, she felt a tiny trickle of blood run down her neck from where the knife point pressed.

Samra hugged the book to her stomach and rocked to and fro, saying something in her own language of Ladino that Estraya recognised as a lullaby. Tears ran down her mother's face, as she slowly held out the book to Hugh.

As Hugh let go of her to take the book, Estraya made a grab at it. For an instant they held it between them, and she was looking into his hard eyes. Then he pulled it easily from her grip, pushed her aside and scrambled out of the shelter. As Estraya came out after him he was already wrapping the book in its cloth, and his brother was mounting his horse. Estraya saw where the rabbit lay in the grass and ran to it. As Samra emerged from the shelter, Estraya was holding the limp, warm body to hers, unable to take in the act of brutality that she had seen done to a blind, harmless creature. Samra went to her daughter, and hugged the child to her. Sobbing, burrowing into the greater warmth of her mother's body, Estraya looked up, to see Samra's face was a mask of grief.

Now Hugh had the book in its box and was mounted.

As he rode away, Samra called after him, 'I would have let you study the book if you had asked. I would have sat with you to read it.'

Hugh stopped his horse. He turned and looked back at her.

'Edward is leaving for England. He has called me to join him. The book goes with me.'

And he heeled his horse and sped away.

The Power Behind the Throne

Berewic, Sussex, September 1041

The Thegn of Berewic was a troubled man. Since the day in 1036 when the invasion of the Wessex was repulsed, fate had been unkind. It began as soon as Sighere returned in triumph from the Surrey high road, where Alfred had been taken prisoner and Rædmund lay dead. The land had slipped from high summer into an autumn of wretched harvest and a cruel winter. Hunger had followed as food stocks ran low. Cold and famished villagers listened to the rumours that Alfred had been cruelly blinded and left to die at Ely. They pointed to the man who, it was said, had been Earl Godwin's accomplice in the act, and who himself had Wessex blood on his hands. The good work the thegn had done and the past prosperity of his manor began to fade from memory. In the same winter Sighere became ill, suffering from a wasting disease that left him breathless at any exertion, and at times in an agony of pain.

And now the same Earl Godwin was here to tell him it had all been for nothing. Edward of Wessex was returning to England, invited by Harthacnut, who had named him as his heir. At his table in the great hall house he had built, with Æadgytha at his side, Sighere stared into his cup.

'Then Edward will be king?' he asked.

His daughter squeezed his hand. Now twelve, she was conscious that not only was she his heir, but the mantle of thegn might fall on her sooner than she wished. Æadgytha studied the faces of the earl and his son Harold, now a good-looking man of nineteen, and saw their own discomfort.

'When Harthacnut dies, yes,' said the earl.

'And the Godwins would support him? After everything that has passed?' It was Æadgytha who had spoken.

'We Godwins, yes,' Harold replied, 'and we would seek your support also.'

'Would you also have us abandon Berewic to a Wessex?' The girl's face was open and without guile, but her question was searching.

Harold shot a glance at his father, who cleared his throat.

'Æadgytha; I hear you have a falcon. Take Harold and show him – he has birds of his own, and can teach you much about the art.'

Æadgytha looked at her father, who nodded assent.

'Very well.' She went swiftly to the door, after giving the earl a hard stare. Harold followed.

Earl Godwin turned to Sighere. 'Edward will land at Hurst Head, and we are on our way to meet him, along with all the thegns of England. He will be received as future king, in return for an oath that he will continue the laws of Cnut. I believe he will have the sense to take that oath.'

'I will not be there to hear it. Give him my poor health for an excuse.'

'I would have you there in spirit. England needs stability. The peace we have created all these years is too great a prize to throw away.'

'Even if it means swapping sides?'

Godwin banged his fist on the table. 'Edward has claim. You know this.'

'It is not his claim on the crown of England that concerns me. He will return with Normans, and other English exiles. Among them will be the sons of the man I slew in Surrey, while keeping your precious peace. Will Edward swear an oath not to give Berewic to them?'

'Edward may not be king for some time. Once he is, he will be his own man, of course. I cannot say what he will do. But by the time that happens, things may be very different.'

'You mean I will be dead, and you will have married Edward to your daughter.' The thegn drank from his cup. 'I hope heaven has a place reserved for you, my kinsman, because you are too slippery to be kept long in hell.'

The drink started a coughing fit that left Sighere slumped over the table, exhausted. Earl Godwin looked down at him and poured himself another cup of wine.

*

Outside the hall house, Æadgytha's merlin was on a perch under its shelter. Æadgytha and Harold stood looking at it a while, with its striking brown and white chest with dark barring, below the ferocious beak. Making quick movements of the head, it fixed them with an eye of deep black. Æadgytha put on a leather glove from beside the perch.

'If the Wessex come here, will they want vengeance on us?'

'Edward remembers the Danish wars, when none were safe from retribution, and feuding ran through generations of families. He will not want bloodshed in Berewic.'

'My father says that your father is England's kingmaker. Since the days of Cnut, he says no king has held power but who had the Godwins' consent.'

Harold gave her a thin smile. 'Lucky then, that England has such a family behind the throne.'

'Yes. Unless you want to sit on it, of course.'

Æadgytha went to untie the falcon, then hesitated.

'Like this,' Harold said, swiftly untying the leash that ran from the merlin's perch to the jesses on its legs, and bringing Æadgytha's gloved hand across. The bird hopped from its perch to her hand, flapping its wings before settling down, using its tail to balance. Harold secured the leash to Æadgytha's glove. 'She is noble and alert. You have chosen her well.'

'I'm a little afraid. Her talons… and beak.'

'There is no need. Reward her, but show her that you are her ruler. The way to master a country, a falcon – or a woman.' He looked into the girl's hazel eyes and she lowered her head, blushing a little. Harold put a hand under her chin and lifted her face to him. 'When I come back from meeting Edward, I will pick up one of my birds from Bosham. I will come by Berewic and we can go hawking together. Would you like that?'

Æadgytha's face lit up.

'Oh, yes!'

A King Returns

Hurst Head, Hampshire, September 1041

Off a narrow spit of land on the south coast of England, a ship from Normandy had anchored. In a boat being rowed ashore were two young men. One, thirteen, blond and blue-eyed, was trailing a hand through the water and laughing, eager to be aground. The other, aged fifteen, fair-haired and with grey eyes, was looking intently at the approaching land, scanning the crowd of people he could see waiting. Then the boat scrunched into the shingle and the young men got out. Wulfstan and Eadric of the house of Wessex had set foot in England for the first time in their lives.

Beside them, a second boat with Edward of Wessex and his party was beaching; a third followed onto the shore on their other side. Soon a throng of men, some armed, was coming ashore. Eadric saw Hugh de Bayeux looking towards a line of men at the foot of a small cliff, shielding his eyes from the sun. Hugh turned and waved.

'Wulfstan! Eadric! Here!'

The two pushed through the men around them, hearing Norman and English voices as they made their way to Hugh.

'Come with me. I must speak with Earl Godwin.' Hugh

began to move up the shingle towards the cliff, then turned back to the men by the boats. 'No one leaves the shore until I order it. Is that understood?'

Hearing assent, he continued up the beach. Wulfstan and Eadric followed, slipping as the shingle moved under their feet. Soon they fell behind; when they reached Hugh, he was almost at the cliff, standing a few yards from the line of men at its foot.

Like Wulfstan, many of these English were blond-haired. Being brought up in an English family, speaking English as much as Norman French, the two young men had thought themselves English. But now that they could see the waiting line of men clearly – their long hair and broad features, the axes some had at their belts, the round shields with heavy centre bosses that one or two carried – they looked a different race. And everywhere the glint of gold; from fine metalwork on shield and sword, on belt and helm, to fine needlework on cuff and hem. Truly this was a race of gods, not men.

'Earl Godwin!' Hugh called out to the line of men. Some sniggered at his accent, but no one moved. He turned to Eadric at his side. 'Tell them Edward brings the kiss of peace. But he will not move until he has Godwin's sworn loyalty.'

'The loyalty the earl swore to our father?' muttered Wulfstan from his other side.

'Quiet,' said Hugh, as Eadric repeated Hugh's words in English.

From behind the left wing of the line, a man pushed through to stand in front of Hugh. A man whose purple tunic edged with fine embroidery at the neck and sleeves, and two-edged sword with a gold inlaid hilt, marked him out as a leader among those around him, as much as his size and bearing.

'I am Earl Godwin.'

Hugh looked him up and down. 'Where is your king?'

'Harthacnut is not a well man. I am come in his stead.'

Scanning the line of men behind the earl, Hugh asked, 'And these?'

'The great thegns of England, come to receive Edward. And to declare him our next ruler, so long as he vows to uphold the laws our late King Cnut established. Laws that have kept peace in this land since the great sundering that drove Edward into exile.'

Hugh listened to Eadric repeat this in French and clenched his jaw. 'It was Cnut's seizing the throne that drove England's legitimate heir to seek shelter with the dukes of Normandy. He will only take Harthacnut's word in person; even it means being received in his bedchamber.'

'We have followed the story of Edward's life in Normandy. It seems England's would-be king received many in his own bedchamber.' The smirk on Godwin's face faded quickly as he went on, 'Besides, that is not how we do things here. Among us are the *witan*, the king's council, and our advice to him to accept or reject Edward depends on what happens here today. Agree this, or leave.'

Wulfstan, who had been looking keenly up and down the ranks of the English, suddenly spoke to the earl.

'Which of these calls himself Thegn of Berewic?'

Godwin looked down at him. 'That man is not here. Who asks?'

Wulfstan pointed to Eadric. 'My brother and I are rightful owners of Berewic.'

'Are you, by God? And does the thegn know this?'

'Sighere – he who calls himself thegn – killed our father Rædmund. And I will kill him.'

The earl laughed. 'Then he should quake in his boots, young man.'

'What are they saying?' Hugh de Bayeux asked Eadric.

'Wulfstan says he would like to go to Berewic. The earl says not yet.' Eadric glared at Wulfstan.

Hugh turned back to Earl Godwin. 'I will report on your terms to Edward. If he agrees, I will signal you to advance, and he will come to meet you.'

*

A short while later, Eadric and Wulfstan were back at the shore, watching as England's future king and Earl Godwin advanced to meet each other. Beside the Earl, Edward looked simply dressed, with a brown tunic over a plain shirt; only the gold buckle pinning his blue cloak at the shoulder hinted at royalty. Behind Edward was Hugh de Bayeux; a short way behind the earl stood his son, Harold. Edward greeted Godwin with a stiff nod, to which the earl bowed slightly. Godwin spoke first.

'I bid you welcome, my lord. I trust that twenty-five years of Wessex exile will end today, when you take the oath.'

'If I take the oath, Earl Godwin, I will be no oath-breaker. But I wonder that you can stand here, knowing you have broken yours.'

'Whatever has passed between our families, Edward, England's future is at stake here. What we Godwins have done has been at the service and on the orders of the kings of England, past and present. As it will be in future, when you are king.'

'And the *witan* will agree what Harthacnut has proposed?'

'If I agree, the *witan* will – if you take the oath.'

'Then let the kiss of peace between us be my oath; and yours, for your future service to me.'

As the two men embraced, cheers rose from the ranks of English behind them, to be taken up by those waiting by the three boats from Normandy. Some unsheathed weapons and waved them. Sheltering from the onshore wind, with their backs to one of the boats, Eadric and Wulfstan saw the two groups of men advance towards each other, English merging with Normans and returning exiles in a swirl of exchanged greetings and laughter. Hand on the hilt of his sword, Hugh de Bayeux kept a watchful eye on what was happening, and on Edward, now the future King of England.

A man began moving away from the throng, towards the shore. Hugh watched as he picked up speed, walking faster, then starting to run. He was heading towards Eadric and Wulfstan; with their heads turned to talk to each other, the two young men seemed not to notice him. As he ran, the man drew something from his tunic; Hugh saw it was a *seax*.

'Eadric!'

Hugh's cry alerted Edward beside him, who turned to look as the man drew nearer to the two young men, *seax* in hand.

'Wulfstan!' he screamed.

Hearing Edward, Wulfstan and Eadric turned and froze. The man was bearing down on them; they could see his eyes glaring, hear his heaving breath and the scrunch of his feet in the shingle. Too late, Wulfstan reached for the hilt of his sword. The man was in front of him, and the outstretched arm with the *seax* was feet away from his chest.

From between two of the boats, a shape emerged. It was

a man, and if his dark curly hair and dark skin did not make him stand out, then his bulk did. He was a giant of a man; tall and broad, with arms like sides of beef, and legs like tree trunks. Yet he moved with surprising speed; the man with the *seax* saw him step out towards him as he went past. The giant did not try to grab the attacker; he simply stooped and took hold of one of his ankles, as one might catch a sheep, or a chicken. As he fell forwards, the man he had taken hold of found himself being lifted into the air; his view of Wulfstan and Eadric in front of him vanished as he was swung round. The shingle and the throng of men on it came briefly into his view, then the sky, before he was hurled against the side of a boat. His body slid slowly down the boat's side to the shingle, the back of his head leaving a smear of red down the planks. As his face crumpled, a sheet of blood appeared from under his hairline and began to run down his face. His eyes remained open and staring, still with a look of surprise.

Wulfstan and Eadric were still gaping at him when Edward, Hugh and the Godwins, father and son, reached them.

'That was well done,' Harold said to the giant, who had sat down in the shingle, leaning back against a boat. 'This young man owes you his life.' The big man nodded; but his dark brown eyes looked close to tears. Harold looked questioningly at him. 'Never set foot in England before, I am sure of it, yet he understood me a little. What is his story?' he asked Eadric.

'He has landed in his mother's country,' said Eadric. 'She was born here and taken as a slave to Egypt, to be kept in the palace of some great lord for his pleasure. She died somehow; Hugh knows, though he does not speak about it.'

Edward turned to Earl Godwin, and pointed at the slumped figure, with its bloody face. 'Do you know this man?'

'His head like an egg thrown at a wall – how would anyone know him?' the earl growled. 'But we have all spent enough time on this shore; we need to make for somewhere decent by nightfall. Somewhere more fitting for a king.' He smiled and gave a little bow before turning away.

Edward called after him, 'If this was any of the Godwins' doing, my lord, they will pay for it; you can be sure of that. See to it that you find this thing out.'

The earl stopped, and looked back. 'You are not my lord yet, Edward. So do not mistake me for your servant.' And he turned and went on.

Hugh turned to the boys; Wulfstan was eyeing the giant curiously, while Eadric was looking at the dead man.

'Come on; we have a way to go in this God-forsaken place,' Hugh said wearily. 'And no one here speaks French.'

'Would you mind closing his eyes?' said Eadric. 'He is staring at me.'

Wulfstan stepped over to the body. Pulling out his sword, he pushed the tip of the blade into one eye, and twisted it. Then he did the same in the other eye.

Retching, Eadric turned away. Wulfstan laughed.

Grief

Forest of Valognes, Normandy, January 1042

From the forest clearing, Felip took a path that led uphill through pine and beech trees to a rocky outcrop, before it dropped down to the edge of the trees and to marshland. In front of him, water fringed with dense stands of reed reached to a near horizon, on which clumps of willows were barely visible against a greyed-out sky and through lightly falling snow.

In the clearing, Gilbert had motioned with an arm towards the path, and shaken his head. *There is nothing I can do; she is lost in her grief.* For a moment, Felip had wondered if there was something more than the news that had reached him at Cerisy; but he had seen a movement behind Gilbert, and there was Estraya, waving and smiling.

Now he approached Samra, sitting at the water's edge, her knees drawn up and her arms wrapped around them. Snow had so covered her cloak that it was like an animal hide, dappled black and white. He squatted beside her, looking over the water, with the snow falling silently onto it and vanishing. It was some while before he spoke.

'Bad weather and much work have kept me at Cerisy. I

came as soon as I could, when I heard Hugh had taken the book.'

'They say he took Eadric and Wulfstan with him to England,' Samra murmured.

'Yes.'

She turned her head to Felip. 'Ten years. Ten years almost to the day, since you met me at the mountain pass in Spain. The snow was falling then. And now the book is lost to me again.'

Felip nodded. 'The day I brought the book back to you, Gilbert puzzled how you, he, the book and the knife came together in this place. I say to you what I said to him: that nothing happens but for a purpose.'

'Is that what you told yourself in Spain, as you took the book from my hands and my family were killed around us?' Samra replied.

'We must hold to the purpose, and believe,' said Felip. 'Sophia said, the journey will be long, and hard.'

'How can I believe in the journey and its end, when I mourn for the book? Its presence is so much a part of my life; I struggle to find my own purpose without it.'

'You have Estraya; the next keeper of the knife.'

Samra got to her feet, snow falling from her in a shower of powder. She turned to Felip, dark eyes burning as she looked down at him.

'And so that no more of mine should die, I had to let the book go. Estraya's life, for my family's heritance. What kind of God would have me make such a choice?'

Felip picked up a flat pebble beside him and rose to his feet. He sighed. 'I do not have the answer to that.' He turned to the water and skimmed the pebble across its surface. It bounced a few times before being lost in the falling snow; he heard a splash. Turning back, he took Samra's hands in his. 'We cannot know the future, Samra, and we often cannot make sense of the present. But we must trust that God has a purpose in what He does, for it has shown to be so in the past.'

'You do not need to tell a Jew that God must have a purpose, Felip. We have suffered much in clinging to this belief, through everything that befalls us. But you cannot stop me grieving for the book. That I will do, until the day I die or the day I hold it again.'

'You wrote before, without the book – on the beech tablets Gilbert made for you; I saw them.'

Samra pulled her hands free and went to the water's edge, looking across it, as if she would still see the stone that Felip had thrown. She shook her head.

'I will write no more. One day, if Estraya wishes to do so, in the hope that what she writes reaches the book, she may. I tell myself that if the book has gone to England, that is its destiny. That if Hugh abuses its power, that is its destiny too.' Samra turned back to Felip. 'Though after the bond I was sure existed between us, how Wulfstan's going will be part of what is written in the book and on the knife, or when it will all come about, I do not understand. No doubt you will have some sage words to explain it.'

Felip shrugged. 'I can only say again what I said here to Gilbert that day: that everything begins and ends at its given time; and everyone comes into and leaves your life to set you on or change you from a path.'

'What did I say? You always have an answer. Come. Our path must lead back to the clearing, and to Gilbert; the snow is getting heavier.'

Samra set off, towards where the path began to lead through the trees. As she reached it and started to climb the hill, she looked over her shoulder at Felip, a squat, dark shape in his habit, wheezing below her. In that moment, the clouds above the marshland parted and there was a flash of light on the water, and in the shallows at the edge she saw two figures; one broad and blond, the other slight and dark. As the pair embraced, Samra stopped and turned. She felt the same rush of pity and anguish that she had that night under the dome when she had seen the two running figures, although she knew these were different people. The clouds closed again, the light went, and Samra was left staring past Felip, struggling to regain herself.

Felip reached her, and turned round to where she was looking. He saw only the grey shoreline in the snow. 'What is it?'

Samra put an arm on his to steady herself. She shook her head.

'You know, Felip, of all that Alhacen has written in the book, it is not his descriptions of the working of the eye, nor his guidance on medicine and surgery, or even his calculations on the motions of the planets, that runs deep with me.'

'Then what?'

'Something about seeking after the truth. "If you study the writings of those that came before you, and blindly put your trust in them," Alhacen says, "you are wrong. You should question what you read; human beings are fraught with all kinds of imperfection and deficiency. It is hard to find the truth, and the road to it is difficult." We have no idea, Felip, how hard this road to truth, and the journey on it, will be.'

'You think we should question what is written in the book?'

'No. It is not the book that is imperfect; it is you and I. There will be suffering, and betrayal, before the foretelling comes about.'

Felip looked at her. 'You have already suffered – and I betrayed you, once. I will never do so again.'

A Choice

Berewic, Sussex, November 1043

When Edward of Wessex made the sweep round on his way to Winchester that took him through Berewic, it was not expecting such a train of nobles. For Harthacnut was near a year and a half dead, and Edward, now England's king, was in the company of its three greatest earls; Siward, Leofric and Godwin, whose kinsman Sighere, Thegn of Berewic, had lately died. Also with Edward were a Norman noble and two young men of his own house of Wessex who had returned with him from exile. Now fifteen and seventeen, Wulfstan and Eadric looked round them curiously as the group rode into the village at the heart of the manor that had once belonged to their father Rædmund.

The girl that greeted them was younger still. Slender but tall, even at fourteen, Æadgytha's bearing and her face, with its high cheekbones and hazel eyes, gave her a striking and noble beauty. The eyes were tired, and with the sadness of a recent grief. As the rest of Edward's party drew up alongside him, Æadgytha looked anxiously from one to the other.

'My lord, I...' Her light brown hair fell forwards as she bowed to her king.

A Choice

Edward held up a hand. 'Do not trouble yourself. We know you are still in mourning for your father and we will not put upon you. I will talk with you a while, if I may, with my kinsmen, Eadric and Wulfstan of Wessex. The rest of my party will ride on and wait for me.'

Edward said something in French to the two young men and to the Norman, who all dismounted. Earl Godwin had dismounted and was embracing Æadgytha. He let her go and held her at arm's length by the shoulders.

'Be strong.' He turned away and got back on his horse.

Æadgytha led the way into the hall; Edward, the Norman, Wulfstan and Eadric followed. Wood was put on the fire, a table was set up and refreshments were brought.

Edward touched nothing but began to speak. As he spoke, his thin white hands and long, almost transparent fingers moved, expressing the anguish his voice suppressed.

'The way that took us from London goes along the high road south of the city. It was there that my brother Alfred was taken when he returned from Normandy seven years ago, with a band of helpers, looking to win back England's throne. But he had been led into a trap. Most of his party were killed, and my brother was captured and then taken by boat to the monastery at Ely. As the boat reached land, and Alfred had sight of that place we both knew and loved from childhood, his eyes were put out. Although the monks looked after him, he died soon after.'

In the pause, Æadgytha looked uncertainly round her. Edward had been speaking in English, and it was clear the Norman had not understood. But the other two had. As the story unfolded, their faces hardened and they moved closer to Edward, and stood one each side of him as he continued.

'You can see the smoke of London itself from that high road. Can you imagine what that was like; to have promise of England held before you and then have it snatched away again? And it was Earl Godwin – that same earl, your kinsman, who has just ridden away – that had promised to help Alfred, but instead betrayed him.'

Æadgytha drew herself up and spoke firmly. 'If this was life and death to you, my lord, you would have had it out with the Earl. But when you came back to England, he upheld your cause, and without him you would not be king.'

'You may not speak to your king like this!'

Saying this, Wulfstan took a step towards Æadgytha and she saw him clearly now; a handsome face topped by a head of thick blond hair. His blue eyes flashed in fury.

Edward pulled him back and went on. 'Many died that day, in that place. One was a man of my house of Wessex, who had been with me in exile. His manor was taken from him by Cnut when he became king, and given to another of the Godwin house. And it was this Godwin who killed him.'

'My father Sighere.' Æadgytha's voice was a whisper now, her head lowered.

'And our father Rædmund, who he killed.' Eadric had spoken.

At once Æadgytha understood why they were there. She shook her head sadly.

'I cannot answer for what my father did. Now that I know what it is to lose a father, I feel for your loss. But I was a child. And the father that raised me – my mother dead in childbirth – was the man that made the Berewic that you see around you, and swore I would be thegn here one day. He built this hall, and rebuilt the church in stone, and built the mill. And when he sat me on a branch of the moot tree at a gathering of the village, and told me how before the hall they used to meet there rain or shine, I felt his pride. I beg you; do not take Berewic from me!'

And she fell on her knees in front of Edward. Wulfstan clapped mockingly. Edward put a hand out to stop him; but it was Eadric who spoke.

'We have seen how Berewic has been a place of order and prosperity, and for my part I do not doubt your father's hand helped shape it. But just so; Berewic is no denn, no pig pasture in the woods. It is a great community of many souls, and it looks to its thegn for its guidance, its strength; its peace. This wretched summer, and now a cattle plague, loom over that peace and threaten to bring famine in their wake. How can a mere girl take on such a burden?'

Æadgytha looked up at him, at his fair hair, his thin face with a thin nose. His grey eyes were hard, but his voice was calm; she felt in its moderate tones a searching of her that went far deeper than Wulfstan's anger. Unsteadily, she got to her feet. She looked around her, at the great timbers that had built the hall, at the logs burning in the hearth, at the rich hangings on the walls, and thought of the times when she had sat with her father at the table on the raised dais, with those at the tables around feasting and drinking. How her father had kept every man under his eyes, knowing them all.

'My father taught me well, and I learnt more at the hallmoot than just to hold my tongue. Sighere was a judge of men, and had the ablest to help him. His manor reeve has sworn to stand by me.'

In front of her the three were impassive. Æadgytha felt the tears welling up inside her; she struggled to hold herself in, clenching her fists by her side. But her voice was strong.

'I know my father was taken from me before I am ready. But I am his daughter, and Berewic's blood is my blood; my roots are in its soil. My father lies in the crypt of this place's church, and I hope one day to lie there beside him, knowing if I have done no better here than he, I have done no worse.'

Edward nodded hard, and his long, milky-white hair shook.

'You speak bravely, Æadgytha. And I am not here for vengeance. But what would you do, to keep Berewic?'

'What would you ask?' *He will marry me to one of them. The thin-faced one – is he the eldest?*

'Wait – we had your pledge!' It was Wulfstan again, rounding on his king.

Now Edward was angry.

'I pledged nothing. I said I would settle the matter – if you heard otherwise, it was your impatience, and you will learn to curb it.' Edward walked around the hall; then he turned back to face them. 'I give you all a choice. Æadgytha, you will keep Berewic. And you, Eadric, will have a share of it. While you, Wulfstan, will have the highest honour yet.'

'How can all that be?' asked Eadric.

Edward called to the Norman, who had been waiting on the other side of the hearth. Now he came forwards, and Æadgytha saw a man with sandy hair and light blue-grey eyes set very deep in his face, and a blunt nose, giving him a brutal look. And at the age of twenty-four, he had seen brutality enough, serving since boyhood for a Norman knight, and then as one.

'Hugh de Bayeux has served me well, in my exile and my return. To him I give the manor of Berewic. And Æadgytha I give to him as wife.'

Æadgytha's jaw dropped. She felt her head spinning. Even Wulfstan could not speak.

Eadric spoke. 'And we, your Wessex kinsmen?'

'Hugh and Æadgytha will give you, Eadric, a yardland of this manor, and settle you with the stock, crops and tools to husband it.'

'A yardland?' Wulfstan scoffed. 'Thirty acres, and with the lord's demesne to take his turn husbanding on, as the price for his holding?'

'His share of Berewic, yes. And you, Wulfstan, will return to Normandy, to serve as knight to the young Duke William, in honour of the pledge your father made to his father.'

Wulfstan looked at Eadric, then at Edward, and back again. 'No…'

Edward raised his hand. 'I give you free choice; but you must decide between you. What two of three choose will bind the other. And now I will take food and drink.'

He motioned to Hugh to sit with him, and the others withdrew, into what had been Æadgytha's father's private chamber.

*

As soon as they were inside, Wulfstan turned to Eadric, and spoke to him in French. 'Say you will not bear this, brother!'

Eadric spread his hands. 'I…'

'It is an insult to our family, and to the memory of our father. How long have we waited?'

'Long, and perhaps we must wait still longer,' Eadric replied. 'What is our choice?'

'To refuse; to fight!'

'Fight Edward – how? Who will be with us? We would be outlawed, and lose Berewic forever.'

'The shame! You a peasant, on your own land! And I, to hold William's armour for him! While another Norman lives at Berewic.'

Ædgytha watched the brothers' faces, trying to follow snatches of their argument; Wulfstan angry, Eadric detached. Then Eadric spoke, in English.

'Edward has settled the matter to his own satisfaction. Let us make our choices. Ædgytha?'

Ædgytha took a deep breath. She felt her whole life in the balance. Yet she was calm; her voice was firm.

'I take what Edward offers.'

Eadric turned to his brother. 'Wulfstan?'

'And I refuse. Brother, it is to you to decide our fates.'

Eadric chewed his lip. He closed his eyes and put his face in his hands. Then he pulled them away and looked straight at Ædgytha.

'I accept.'

Without saying a word, Wulfstan pushed through the door of the chamber into the hall, blinded by tears of rage. He left Ædgytha and Eadric looking at each other, still in shock at the choices they had just made.

'I hope we do not live to regret what we have done here today,' Ædgytha said.

'What choice did we have?' replied Eadric.

Ædgytha watched the muscles twitch in his thin, anxious face.

How young he looks.

A Choice

*

Seeming not to notice Edward and Hugh de Bayeux seated at the table, Wulfstan stumbled into the hall and headed for the door to the outside. Hugh made to get up, but Edward stayed him with a hand.

'They have chosen,' he said in French. 'And you are the Thegn of Berewic. How does that please you?'

Hugh shrugged. 'Is there more food?'

'Ask your future wife.'

Edward got up and went outside, in time to see Wulfstan going into the church. Following him, he found the young man standing at the rood screen, hands behind his back.

'He built well, this Sighere,' said the king, coming up beside him. 'You heard the church has a crypt, beneath the altar? A conceit on the part of a Godwin, to have himself entombed in it like a saint, or one of the royal house who has been saintly.'

'From what I've seen, the Godwins think they are the royal house,' Wulfstan said, without looking at him. 'Perhaps I should pray to Sighere, my lord. What should I pray for – to live long with William, or to die quickly?'

Edward put his hand on Wulfstan's shoulder. 'A pledge is a pledge.'

Wulfstan shook the hand off and turned to Edward, eyes burning.

'All that time, as I was growing up and Hugh was training me in arms, was for this – to be William's retainer? Why was I never told? I should have stayed in the forest with Gilbert and Samra.'

Edward rubbed his hands together, struggling with what

he was going to say to Wulfstan, and what he so desperately wanted to. He turned to face him, and drew breath.

'I... You are headstrong, Wulfstan.' *I see myself in you.* 'And you would have rebelled against your father's pledge to William's.' *The pledge I made him, as your father.* 'But you have learnt well; you are strong, skilled and capable.' *Everything I could have hoped for.* 'William is still young, and in constant danger.' *You are in danger – already someone has tried to have you killed.* 'I am sending you where you are needed, and you will be the duke's sword and shield.' *I am sending you where you will be safe, beside my friend who will protect you.* 'I know you will not fail me.' *I will be so proud of you.*

But Wulfstan only stared at him. Around them, Edward felt the peace of the little church, the fading afternoon light falling through the windows. Soon the priest would come to light candles.

What can it hurt, to tell him now, who he is? What harm can befall him, in this place?

Yet even as the words formed, ready to be propelled into his mouth, the walls of the church appeared to close in a little. The saints on the brightly coloured wall paintings seemed to incline anxiously towards him, and the other figures to stop their movement, and turn their heads. 'Do not speak this,' they all said, 'do not tell him.' Time stopped. Edward found himself looking down the years of his reign, suddenly able to see its triumphs and its tragedies, and the thread that would wind through it all, like a twist of dark wool through a pure white yarn: the Godwins. And he knew what he had to do.

'We must go,' Edward went on, regaining himself, 'and you must make ready to leave for Normandy. I will make my farewell to Hugh, and to Æadgytha. And to Eadric, of course. And you must make your peace with him before you leave. I can tell you have made different choices today. But you are still brothers.'

As his words echoed round the stone building, Edward's voice faltered. *Oh God, Wulfstan,* the voice inside him screamed, *let me embrace you, let me pull you into my arms, my son that I love, and I may never see again after today.*

'Hah!' Wulfstan spat. 'If Eadric can side with our enemies, he is no brother of mine. Say goodbye to whoever you want – I'll wait for you with Earl Godwin and the others.'

And he turned and strode from the church.

Checkmate

Winchester, Wessex, November 1043

'My mother has had a book written about her, Godwin. Did you know?'

Unusually for him, the great earl looked uncomfortable; he shuffled on his feet. Since he had become king on the death of Harthacnut, Edward had shown an energy and zest for command at odds with the image Godwin's spies in Normandy had conveyed to him, of the pleasure-bent royal exile. He had been everywhere in his new kingdom, issuing writs, marshalling its defences and wooing its people. Now here he was in his royal palace at Winchester, confronting his mother as she cowered in a corner of the cellar room where she had taken refuge, among the piled-up chests, pieces of broken furniture and old tapestries.

Godwin cleared his throat. 'I believe I had heard so, my lord.'

'And an astounding piece of self-serving falsehood it is,' Edward went on, 'meant to paint her and Cnut in the most favourable light, and to justify her every action. Is that not so, my mother?'

Emma of Normandy, the wife of two kings and mother

of two more, stepped forwards and drew herself up in front of her son. Her rich red gown was dusty; a cobweb hung from one side of her wimple. Still breathing heavily from her flight from Edward and his nobles – for he had come to Winchester in force – she looked up into his face.

'Everything I have done has been for this family, and for England. I worked to get Harthacnut to accept you as his successor. I have pleaded for your brother to be made a saint.'

'Let Alfred rest in peace; he does not need your intervention,' Edward retorted. 'And you salted Harthacnut's fortune away here for your own benefit, not for England's. Now you will give me the keys to my treasury.'

Emma stiffened. 'You think because you are England's master, you can buy its people's favour? A fool and his money are easily parted.'

'I will have my keys. And I do not believe you wish me to disrobe you in front of Earl Godwin to find them.'

The menace in Edward's voice was unmistakable. Godwin looked surprised.

'My lord—'

Edward raised a hand to silence him. For a moment he and his mother stared at each other. Then Emma reached under her gown, and her hand came out with a bunch of keys, on a large fob marked with the Wessex wyvern. Slowly she handed them to Edward. At once he passed them to the Earl.

'See that these fit the locks,' he said, eyes still on his mother. 'I do not trust her to have given me the right ones.'

Godwin bowed, turned, and left the room.

Watching him go, Emma smiled.

'You could never surround yourself with the right sort, Edward. The earl will do you service, while it suits him. Then he will turn against you. Now, if you have what you came for, I will return to my chambers.' She made to follow the earl from the room.

'And there you will gather such things as you need for your journey,' Edward said after her, 'and no more.'

At the door Emma stopped and turned back.

'You are sending me from the palace?'

'From here, and from any abode you thought to own. Your property and lands are mine now.'

Emma stepped over to Edward, and as she had before, looked up into his face; but now there was fury in her steely blue eyes, and her voice shook as she spoke.

'Take the treasure into your hands if you must; but you cannot banish me!'

'You think this was about treasure?' Edward responded. 'You think I do not know your newest plot: to put Magnus of Norway on the throne? To foist England with another foreign king? To deprive me of my heritance, now I finally have it, despite all your machinations?'

'Who told you this? The earl, no doubt, hissing my name in your ear, like the serpent he is. More fool you to believe him.'

Edward brought his hands together, rubbing his long, thin fingers against each other as he fought to control his anger.

'You play chess with England's kingship, and you think I will stand back and watch? At every turn, you have thought to win the game, with an alliance here, a letter there, and even a book, to serve your lying purpose.'

'Books are powerful, Edward; perhaps someone will write one about you one day, and we will see how the world views your kingship.'

'Oh, I mean the world to see me kindly, as I hope it will see you for what you are. I only wish I could tell it that you sent one of your people to kill my son on the very day we reached England's shore.'

'Wulfstan has no place here. He has no heritance, least of all the throne of England. But I still believe you are fool enough to try to put him there, after you are dead.'

'He should be England's next king. But I cannot tell him who he is; you know that. So I am sending him back to Normandy to serve Duke William. There he will also be safe from you. And I will marry as you have proposed; into a powerful family.'

'Then you have some sense. Where will you look? Normandy? Flanders? Denmark, perhaps?'

'Earl Godwin has a daughter; Edith.'

Emma looked dismayed. 'You will hand England's throne to our enemies? To the family that had Alfred killed?'

'Alfred came back with me, on your enticement!' Edward roared. 'How do I know you were not hand in glove with our enemies then, as you are now?' He turned away, twisting his fingers in an effort to control himself. 'It is my decision, and it will be my choice, if I settle on Edith.'

'A rash decision, Edward, and your choice will be either desperate or foolhardy; you will bind the fate of the house of Wessex to that of the Godwins, and keep them from taking power by all but giving it to them, in the next generation at least. And surely there will be a next generation; you will be much older than your bride, but Wulfstan is proof you can breed.'

At last Edward turned back. 'Delicately put, as always. But I tell you, whatever office the earl now has, he and his line will never rise higher. For I cannot trust the Godwins any more that I can trust you. Now leave me.'

'For the love of God, no, Edward; I beg you not to do this. Do not discard me.' Emma looked close to tears. 'Let me stay. I can make contact with other families that I know – there will be a royal daughter somewhere.'

Edward spread his hands, palms upward. He smiled.

'The game is over, my mother, and you have lost. You are overturned. Checkmate.'

A Wedding

Berewic, Sussex, December 1043

Hugh and Æadgytha were kneeling in the porch of the church at Berewic, heads bowed. The gold rings on their fingers felt heavy and strange to them both. Æadgytha was in the pale blue gown of fine linen she had had made for her wedding; the extravagance was part defiance in the face of the troubles besetting her manor, part the vow she was making to the future. Her father would have wished her to make every effort. Hugh was wearing a quilted jacket over a deep brown tunic and blue trousers with leg bindings and strong boots. He could not believe how much colder England was than Normandy.

Now a shaft of sunlight had fallen in the space between the couple and the priest, who had just laid his hand on each in turn. The light sharpened the contrast between Æadgytha, the young woman who was heir to all around her, and Hugh, the incomer ten years older, who did not even speak the language of his wife and his new subjects of Berewic. She was filled with hope and fear, he with boredom and indifference. Standing in the darkness behind them were Eadric, and Æadgytha's reeve Cuthred; the witnesses to the marriage.

Not far away at Bosham, the manor of the father of Harold Godwinson who was cousin to Æadgytha, Wulfstan was preparing to leave for Normandy and knight service with Duke William.

Suddenly the light had gone. The priest stopped and stood back, waiting as the new couple got to their feet. As a boy in Normandy, Father Brenier had been inspired to follow Herluin, the warrior knight who had famously given up riches and taken to prayer and fasting, and at fourteen Brenier had joined the religious community Herluin had founded on his own estate almost ten years back. Like Herluin, he wore his hair and beard long, and his habit was cheaply made, but he had parted company with him when his master moved the new community to Le Bec, and had come to England. Travelling in the south, Brenier had sought out the place he had heard of from its former thegn. Finding the old priest at Berewic had died, Brenier made his plea to Æadgytha's father for the position, and it had amused Sighere to allow one Norman in his manor.

As Hugh and Æadgytha stood a moment, heads bowed, behind them Cuthred turned to Eadric.

'Too late now. Berewic will never be yours.'

Eadric felt a cold dislike sweep over him for the podgy man before him, with the smirk on his fleshy lips and his oily voice. But he smiled blandly.

'And you are happy that it now belongs to a foreigner?'

'In name only... in name only. Hugh de Bayeux will rely on Æadgytha, and she relies on me to see Berewic runs properly.'

So that is how it is, Eadric thought. *You look to rule Berewic now.*

A Wedding

Æadgytha turned to speak to them. 'You will both join us now, for the wedding mass?'

Eadric bowed to her. 'If I may be excused.'

He thought of the little house with its mud floor and leaky thatch he had been given as lodging in Berewic, and recalled the castle of his childhood, with its solid stone walls and comfortable, well-furnished hall. He thought of the rain and the cold outside, and remembered the long, warm summer days in Normandy. He thought of the fine clothes he wore then, and the homespun woollen trousers and rough tunic he was wearing now, under a heavy cloak. He thought of the nudges and whispers his new neighbours gave each other when they saw him, and set this against the respect the tenants on the Normandy estate had shown him: 'He is of Edward's blood; Edward, great-great-great-grandson of Rollo, founder of our land, father of our people.'

At his side, Cuthred was smirking again.

'I will gladly join you, my lady.'

Led by the Father Brenier, Hugh and Æadgytha went into the church, followed by Cuthred. Eadric turned and went outside. As he walked across the space between church and hall house, in the wind-stirred trees by the river he saw a large bird; a bird usually black like a crow. But this raven was white. It called out harshly, once, and he remembered his words to his brother.

Perhaps we must wait still longer.

Life

Rouen, Normandy, December 1043

On the day that Hugh and Æadgytha were to grant Eadric a yardland of their manor at Berewic, Wulfstan was in Rouen, making his way up a long staircase, at the top of which armed men stood guard in front of a large studded door. They looked quizzically at the young man with his long, blond hair, then at a voice from beyond the door they made way. He passed into a large room with a high ceiling. The walls were covered with splays of weapons and rich tapestries showing scenes of battle and hunting. A young man, at seventeen a little older than Wulfstan, rose from a high-backed chair and came swiftly towards him. He was wearing a loose-fitting woollen tunic with a band at the waist, and a cloak fastened on the right shoulder with a brooch; only the glint of gold on this suggested he was anything but a common soldier. This man, who Wulfstan had last seen when they were both boys, embraced him, and in the strength of his grasp he became aware of just how much William of Normandy had changed.

'Wulfstan,' said William, holding him now at arm's length by the shoulders, 'you are angry. I can feel it.'

The grey-green eyes looked steadily at Wulfstan, who pulled out of the hold and turned away.

'Not I, Duke William. Weary from the journey is all.'

William crossed the room and pulled a spear from one of the weapon splays. Returning to Wulfstan, he held the spear out to him.

'You were pledged to serve me, and now you are here. Get it over with. Then take your place by my side. The honour I do you, and what you will do for me, outweigh your anger a thousand-fold.'

Wulfstan took the spear, and the knuckles on his hand went white as he grasped the shaft, turning the weapon this way and that, blue eyes burning. Then he stepped back from William and took the spear into a throwing position. Suddenly he turned and hurled it across the room, at a deer skull with antlers on the far wall. The skull split in half, the two pieces falling to the floor, leaving the spear embedded in the timbers.

William nodded slowly.

'Well, that answers one question. You have the skills I need. Now, sit and drink with me.' He waved Wulfstan to a chair near his own, sat down in his chair, and poured wine from a flagon on a table beside him into two cups. 'Tell me what became of you, after Alfred of Wessex and your father Rædmund were killed.'

Wulfstan stared into his cup, then looked up at William.

'Edward hid us with your warden in the Forest of Valognes until the king in England, who had ordered Alfred's death, had died. Then Hugh de Bayeux took us away and schooled me in arms, while Eadric learnt how it would be to order the manor in England that had been taken from our father.

When Edward returned to England, Hugh, my brother and I went with him.' Taking a draught of wine, Wulfstan went on, 'Two years later, in April this year, Edward became king, and not a month ago he took the three of us to the manor that was ours by right. I was glad. This was the day, I knew, when we would get Berewic back.'

'Berewic?'

'The name of the manor. But Edward gave it to Hugh. And sent me to serve you.'

'What became of Eadric?'

'He is to be given a peasant's holding on his own lands.'

The Duke of Normandy laughed a deep belly laugh, before taking a drink of wine. He laughed again.

'Edward has not lost his sense of humour, since becoming a king.'

Wulfstan slammed his cup down and stood up, glaring down at William.

'Should I laugh, too? Should Berewic being taken from us be a jest for others? When my father pledged me to you, he condemned me, Duke William, to losing my birthright forever. So send me on your errands, send me anywhere you like. I will do anything for you that brings my death a day nearer.'

Wulfstan turned, and stared at the spear in the wall. William drained his cup, set it down, and got to his feet.

'Sit down.' Wulfstan was still staring at the wall. 'Sit down!' William roared, and it echoed around the room.

Wulfstan looked at him, startled by the young man's ferocity. He sat down. William paced in front of Wulfstan a while, then turned to him. His face was grim.

'Birthright? You talk to me of birthright, for a few fields in England? Half my lifetime ago, Wulfstan, I came into my birthright; my father's dukedom, from the banks of the Seine to the borders of Brittany. Every year of my life since then, I have had to fight for it. Do you remember Duke Alain, my guardian? Killed, three years ago, fighting for me in a siege. My other guardian was assassinated soon after. A year later, my tutor was murdered, then my steward; his throat slit as he slept beside me. As a boy, I lost count of how many times I was smuggled out of my own castle by my uncle, and hidden in the house of a peasant on the estate, to be kept safe from the traitors who sought to usurp me.'

Wulfstan shook his head. 'Yet you survived.'

'I survived. But I learnt quickly who I could trust, and who I could not. Not the King of France, who the traitors helped to take my castle at Tillières. That was two years ago; Hugh de Bayeux had left for England, and I was in the hands of my advisers. But this year, when the king supplied soldiers to a man who had seized the castle at Falaise, where I was born, I needed no advisers. Only my own strength and the loyalty of those close to me. I laid siege at once. The man fled, and the King of France knows now to stay beyond my borders. My birthright is mine, and it will stay mine.'

William sat again, and filled his cup with wine.

'If you seek death, Wulfstan of Wessex, you will have every opportunity. But if you seek a life, taut as a bowstring, sharp as a sword, a life of sieges mounted and raised, of battles joined and won; if you want to wake the next day, your mail tunic bloody and your sword notched, and remember those who fought alongside you, how they lived and died, how you saved some of them and how others saved you, it is yours. Its rewards will be few, but by God, they are the most precious a man can have.'

Wulfstan got to his feet. He stood in front of William, and drew his sword. Dropping to one knee, he held the sword across in front of him, its hilt on one palm, its tip on the other.

'Then give me life, William of Normandy. And for as long as I live, I am yours.'

The Hallmoot

Berewic, Sussex, December 1043

After a wet and stormy summer, December in Berewic had turned savagely cold, and the ground was already hard frozen. Eadric was looking at the moot tree, the great beech overlooking the river, and that day the tree stood shrouded in the early morning hoar frost. He turned to see Æadgytha beside him.

'You have noticed, perhaps,' she said, 'that in my language, beech and book are practically the same word. This tree is the record of Berewic's history; it was here at our beginning, and perhaps it will be at our end.'

You said 'my' language, thought Eadric, *not 'ours', though I speak it as well as you. Even in this, you see me as an outsider.*

But Æadgytha was still speaking. 'Before my father had the hall house built, this was the place the *folcfry* of Berewic met with him to do the business of the village.'

'*Folcfry?*' Eadric's breath steamed into the cold air.

'The freemen, farmers and independent landed householders. It was here we settled the customs of the manor and the duties that bind the villagers and their thegn together; the service of the one given for protection by the other. Here we decided what should be allocated from the lord's own land to villagers and what given back, the use of the common fields, the appointment of officials, the rights of lord and tenants, and so on. Here we used to settle claims over property rights and other disputes.'

Eadric nodded slowly. 'I have heard of the English ways, the freedoms they cherish.'

'My villagers are not truly free, of course; just as the king grants their thegn lands in return for service, they hold theirs from me in the same bargain. But they have rights; the right to *wergild*, the compensation for injury or assault done to them; the right to bear arms and be part of the *fyrd*, the king's armed men; and the right to take part in the hallmoot.'

'The village meeting?'

'Yes. All the custom that was once done under this tree will be done this day in the hall house.' Æadgytha rubbed her arms. 'It will be warmer indoors.'

Eadric detected a tension in her action and saw worry in her hazel eyes.

'It will be your first hallmoot now Hugh is thegn, and the first since he married you.' He saw her purse her lips; saying Hugh was thegn had not pleased her, he could tell. 'It troubles you?'

'This year's crops have been poor in yield and quality, following on from a bad year before that. People are looking anxiously into what the next year might bring. A thegn cannot do everything. If you came here hoping to take Berewic as your own, this would not have been the year to do it.'

Eadric turned away, refusing the bait, silent.

'But it is Christmas Eve, and a chance to put that aside for a time.' Æadgytha's voice had brightened. 'From tomorrow, there will be no business done for twelve days, until Epiphany.' She turned to go. 'Don't be late – there will be much in the meeting that concerns you.'

Eadric watched her walk towards the church.

I won't be late. I need to be there, to get what is due to me, as one of your folcfry.

*

By noon, the villagers had packed the hall house. The hall was garlanded with holly, ivy and mistletoe, and a large fire burned in the centre hearth to keep out the bitter chill. Hugh sat at the table on the raised dais, watching as the villagers came in. Æadgytha, next to him, had on her other side Cuthred, who had been her father Sighere's reeve and was now hers. The next person to come in was Eadric. He looked round him, searching the faces of those who might have been his own tenants, but instead were his fellow villagers. They looked at him curiously, the young would-be thegn now a peasant.

Æadgytha stood. All eyes were on the young girl, calm and dignified. But her stomach was tight with fear as she looked back at the gathering.

'You know, all of you, that I stand here by my father's dying wish, and by the grace of King Edward himself. I am not thegn here,' she glanced at Hugh beside her, 'but I speak in his name.' Yet, as she began to speak, hesitantly at first, then growing surer, all who looked on had no doubt she was thegn, in deed if not in title. 'When Edward came here, he confirmed our old laws and rights that were set out when first the land was given to us, to make this manor from waste and wood.

Know, then, that we hold Berewic with those rights, from that time to this, and in time to come.'

Æadgytha held herself proudly and her words rang round the silent hall, as she named each right, knowing their power for a people bound together for the common good. The rights to have the very meeting they were in, to hold land, to raise money and to punish offenders, were the threads that held their lives together. They made men and women secure in their homes and their goods, knowing that the many would speak for those wrongly accused, or against a wrong-doer among them.

'Know that I will do my best to uphold you all, as my father did. That the practices and customs you have had will be yours, notwithstanding you belong to a Norman lord. Young as you see me, I am yours too and, God willing, I will serve you many years. Cuthred has pledged to serve me as reeve and I thank him for this, and I give way to him in the running of this moot.' She sat down.

A murmur went round the hall that Cuthred let run for a while before raising a chubby hand.

'We are all pledged to serve you, my lady. To serve you both. No other claim on your lands will be heard here. Now let the hallmoot begin.'

A jury chosen from among the leading tenants was sworn in. Once various appointments had been made, or confirmed, and some small parcels of land determined, Cuthred waved Eadric forwards to stand in front of the table. Æadgytha looked at him steadily, then began to speak.

'Eadric, we welcome you to Berewic and to our moot. As a *gebur* and a free man, yet bound to your lord, you will receive from us seven acres of your yardland ready sown, the implements to work it, and furniture for your house. For stock you will have from us two oxen, a cow, and six sheep.'

Eadric bowed and began to turn away, but now it was Cuthred who spoke.

'In return for this, you will work two days of every week in the year for your lord, and three days at harvest and between Candlemas and Easter. From the first breaking of the soil after harvest to Martinmas, you will plough an acre a week of the demesne, and fetch the seed to sow it from your lord's barn. You will further plough two acres a year for your pasture rights, and three as rent for your own land, and provide the seed for this from your own.' Eadric swallowed hard. He knew there would be obligations to work the demesne, the thegn's own land, yet these were hard. 'And if he so demands, you will plough a further three acres a year of the demesne.'

Cuthred looked towards Hugh, who was sitting stiffly, understanding hardly a word, and back at Eadric, with a thin smile. And Eadric knew that Cuthred would make sure the three acres were demanded, but he bowed his head. Yet Cuthred had not finished.

'In payments to your lord; ten pence a year at Michaelmas, twenty-three bushels of barley and two hens at Martinmas, and at Easter a young sheep. Or if you cannot lay hands on a sheep, two pence will do.' At this, some in the hall sniggered. 'For payments to the manor; as a freeman, a penny hearth tax to the priest, and six loaves to the swineherds when they take the herd to the denn in autumn. For duties to your lord; between Martinmas and Easter, you will take your turn in the watch over your lord's fold. And with another, you will share the feeding of one of his dogs. It is not beneath you to feed a dog, I hope?'

More sniggers in the hall. Eadric's fists were balled in fury, but he held himself in.

'Is that all?'

Cuthred nodded. 'Of course, you understand that if you die, all you have will be taken back by your lord. You'll leave the world as you came to Berewic – with nothing.'

Æadgytha looked uncomfortable. She wanted to rebuke her reeve, but needed his support above all. Instead, she smiled kindly at Eadric, who turned away to join the other villagers. Æadgytha now addressed them.

'And now we will allot the demesne land.'

The demesne, the land kept by the lord of the manor for his own use and on which those like Eadric, holding land from Hugh and Æadgytha, had to give free service, was part of the main farmland of Berewic. Allotment to the tenants was done by drawing lots from wooden pegs in a cloth bag, each bearing the mark of a particular field. The jury took turns to draw out a peg as each man's name came up. When Eadric's name was read out, Cuthred looked to the juror, who fumbled in the bag for an age. At last he pulled out a peg and looked at the runes on it; like the other jurors, he could not read them, but he knew from their pattern the name that he should give it. A sharp gasp went round the hall when he spoke. Cuthred gave Eadric a pitying look.

'Bottom Flatt. Difficult ground. Catch it right, and it'll work well for you. Catch it wrong, and… well, ten years ago a *gebur* died on it. Man's land, we call it. Let's hope you are a man, Eadric.'

He grinned from ear to ear, and his arms mimicked a man following behind a plough, struggling to keep control. The hall around him broke into laughter, then a hubbub of voices.

Eadric glared at Cuthred, face reddening. His mouth moved to speak, but no words came out.

Ædgytha got to her feet. 'Tomorrow…'

The racket went on.

Suddenly Hugh leapt up, and banged his fist on the table. 'Silence!' He spoke in French but it was clear enough, and the laughter ebbed away. All eyes turned back to Ædgytha, who spoke again.

'Tomorrow is Christmas Day, and the start of a new year. Let it be a new beginning and a blessed year for all of us. In the morning, we will celebrate mass together and the gift of God to the world on this night. Go in peace.'

*

Cuthred was sitting with the jurors in the alehouse some hours later, when Eadric came up and threw the peg for Bottom Flatt onto the bench beside him. Cuthred took a drink and looked at the peg, then at Eadric.

'Well?'

'It is marked. A small notch in the end of the peg would tell anyone feeling it to leave it – or to pull it out.'

Cuthred slowly picked up the peg and turned it in his hand, squinting.

'You read too much into a wooden peg, my friend.' He looked at the jurors, who nodded eagerly, and lifted the cup to his lips again.

'Have it your way,' Eadric went on, 'but I tell you this – you took every pain in that hallmoot to insult me, to mock me. And I with the blood of Edward himself in my veins. You offend my dignity.'

Cuthred slammed the cup down and ale bounced out onto the floor. Standing up, he grabbed Eadric by the tunic and pulled him close until their faces nearly met.

'If you have Wessex blood in you, it runs thinly. You and your brother are so many branches from the main stem, they say, it is a wonder you can even call yourselves by the name. As for your dignity, let me tell you, young man, the lady Æadgytha has more dignity in her little finger than you will ever have in the whole of your wretched body.' He looked around him at the approving jurors. 'This is her manor, and I am her man. And I had to watch while your seven acres was sown with wheat and rye the village could barely afford in this year of want. Had it been up to me, you wouldn't have had a bushel of it. When you take over your land at Candlemas for the spring planting, this is not the year to be a beginner at farming, I can tell you. But if you don't like it, you know the way out of Berewic. And if you make any trouble, I will kick your dignified Wessex arse all the way back to Normandy. Do I make myself clear?' He threw Eadric back onto the floor.

Eadric picked himself and brushed down his clothes. In silence, the jurors watched him leave. But it was not Cuthred's words that sounded in his ears as he went, but Wulfstan's. 'Say you will not bear this, brother!'

But I will bear it. For as long as it takes.

*

In the hall house, Æadgytha was asleep, exhausted by the labours of the day. Sitting by the hearth with a cup of wine, Hugh took the book out of its box, unwrapped it from its velvet cloth decorated with a moon and stars, and began to read a passage.

Now consider the elements. Each is composed from the four qualities, earth being cold and dry, air being hot and moist, fire being hot and dry, and water being cold and moist. The metals are but a combination of these four qualities, two inner and two outer, lead being cold and dry, and gold being hot and moist. Can we but order differently the qualities of a metal so we can create a different metal. The great Jabir says that to effect this transformation, the al-iksir is required.

Hugh took a drink.

I will find this al-iksir. And I will make gold.

An Accident

Berewic, Sussex, April 1044

Eadric was resting his plough team. Not that he wanted to, but oxen can only plough for a few hours at most, and he had been labouring in Bottom Flatt until well after noon. And so he was watering the two beasts from a wooden bucket as they stood yoked side by side in the breezy spring sunshine. The boy helping him was fetching them grass he had cut from the field edge. Eadric had not started as early as he wanted, after waiting – as he knew he would – for Cuthred to bring him the ploughshare and coulter to attach. Metal parts were too valuable to leave on a plough overnight, and so the reeve had taken charge of them after the previous day's work. The plough was not Eadric's and neither was the boy; he was hired to lead the oxen while Eadric came behind, steering the implement as it turned the heavy earth. And it was heavy; the clay soil of Bottom Flatt mocked man's efforts in winter and summer alike, going from slop to rock and back. Four oxen should have been the least to work it, but no one would lend another pair to Eadric. It was better suited to meadow, and had been in grass from time to time. Yet, when caught right, as Cuthred had put it, its crops yielded so well it was too tempting for the thegn in whose demesne it was to ignore. But neither Hugh nor Æadgytha had to cultivate it; that had fallen to Eadric, in the disputed drawing of lots at the hallmoot the Christmas past.

So at the end of a long winter, Eadric was anxious to finish the last acre. With his own lands to plough as well, he should have begun at Candlemas on the second of February, cultivating the fields that last year had grown rye and wheat to sow with oats, barley, peas and beans, and every third field ploughed for fallow. But not this winter. From before the hallmoot to well into March, Berewic, like the rest of this corner of Europe, had been in the pitiless grasp of the Great Ice. Land and water alike had turned to iron, snow covered and defying any implement to break it. Spring ploughing that should have been done by Lady Day on the twenty-fifth of March, and at latest by Easter, had dragged through April. Although he had turned the easier lands first and shunned Bottom Flatt for as long as he could, now Eadric had to break it. And black clouds were scudding along the hills on the far side of the valley, threatening rain. He motioned to the boy to urge the oxen on, and took his place behind the plough once more. As the coulter slit the ground, the ploughshare followed and the mouldboard turned over the dark earth. It was satisfying work when done well, and Eadric had had enough practice now to get it right; but he was too uneasy with what lay ahead to take any joy in his labour.

The final quarter of the field abutted a wood. While the weak sun had at last warmed up the land it could reach, here the tall trees cast a long winter shadow and the ground well out into the field was still white with frost. As the ox team plodded back and forth, the plough grew closer and closer to this dead earth, and Eadric braced himself. He knew at once when the share began to bite in to it, for the plough slowed noticeably. He shouted at the boy to goad the animals to keep up their pace, and held on grimly to the handles. It went better than he had expected, and the plough began to speed along under the beasts' new urgency. But as he turned at the end of the furrow, he saw why. The ground had stayed frozen below the surface, and the share was barely cutting into it, skimming the top and lifting not even enough earth for the mouldboard to turn. Cursing, he stopped the team and looked at the ragged ground. The sun went in and it was abruptly colder. The boy came to look, then made a lifting motion and went to the side of the field. In the long grass he uncovered a large rock brought up in an earlier ploughing, and began to lift one end. As Eadric went to take hold of the other end, rain began to fall. Struggling to stay upright on the slippery ground, the boy and the man, hardly any older, carried the rock to the plough and set it on to the frame. A second rock was fetched and put beside it, and a third. As the rain fell harder, the boy tried to get the oxen going, but this was not the weight of plough they were expecting and they stayed put. Only a flaying with a haw branch got them to move, lowing in distress, steam rising from their hot flanks. But the plough took hold, and with the rain lashing him, Eadric saw the furrow falling into place behind him as they went. Up and down they travelled, slowly, turning agonisingly on the headlands under the weight, then coming back into furrow, all the while the last of the unploughed land getting smaller and smaller.

*

An Accident

Æadgytha had taken advantage of the sunny morning to go out riding. Seeing the rain clouds gathering, she had turned her horse back towards Berewic and its hall. The track she would have taken had been made treacherous by frost heave, so instead she had skirted round the wood beside Bottom Flatt. Head down and riding apace, she rounded the corner of the wood into the field, and came sideways on to the plough team. Seeing the oxen too late, she pulled up and her horse reared, startling the animals. The oxen pulled out of the boy's hold and veered into the ploughed land, where they floundered in the soft, wet earth. Behind the plough, Eadric struggled for foothold and to keep in line; but in vain. The machine twisted out of his grip and tilted to one side. Eadric went alongside, desperately trying to keep it upright as the heavy stones made it lean more. He tried to pull these off to lessen the weight, but the oxen were still pulling sideways and the plough was turning on itself as well as tipping. The rain falling was now a steady downpour. Losing his footing, Eadric fell beside the plough in the same instant as it finally tipped over. On his back, in his futile scrabbling to get out of the way he could only watch as the plough with its heavy stones moved towards him, trapping his left leg against the cold, sodden ground. The land below the furrow depth was still frost hard, and as the plough settled on him the crushing weight grew.

It was Eadric's screams that reached Æadgytha and the boy, as the one sought to master her horse and the other to control the oxen. They turned to see him stretched full length below the plough, head lifted above the furrow he had just cut.

'Fetch help!' Æadgytha shouted to the boy above the rain beating down.

He turned to run, and gradually she brought the horse under control until she could dismount. Standing by the animal, stroking its nose and whispering to it, she became aware that she could no longer see Eadric. Going over to the plough, Æadgytha saw him, face pallid and distorted with pain. The water washing out from under the plough was brown tinged with red. He was weakening. The furrow was filling and as it did, his head began to sink slowly into the water until it was at his mouth. Æadgytha got onto her knees behind him, and took his head in her lap. Above him he could see her face upside down, looking down anxiously. Her lips were moving but he could not hear what she was saying; there was a buzzing in his ears and everything was fading from him. The pain was going from his body, and the cold. Warmth began to seep across him, and the rain beating on his face might have been no more than the gentle brush of a butterfly wing.

As the world retreated, Eadric was in a place of memory; but no memory his waking self had ever been able to call on.

Eadric was in his childhood home in Normandy. His head was cradled in his mother's lap, and she was looking down lovingly at him. She had been singing to him, a sweet lullaby, and now she was talking, telling him something. Somewhere a baby was crying. 'This is your new brother,' she said, 'and he will live with us and you will love him as I will.' And Eadric was confused and angry. He had had no forewarning of this new arrival, this cuckoo in the nest, this rival for his mother's love. And he reached up and gripped the side of his mother's face with his hands, digging in with his nails. She screamed.

Æadgytha was moving away and Eadric's hands were being lifted, then his legs, gently now that the plough had been pulled clear. Men had come from the village, Cuthred the reeve among them, and supporting his body and his crushed leg they bore him back to Berewic. Cuthred's sister set about mending him the best she could, cleaning and bandaging the leg and splinting it. Men rallied round and finished his ploughing, and did their best to sow the crops he needed. In the summer that followed, when the wretched planting in the manor was followed by a pitiful harvest, Eadric hobbled around the village on a stick until he could walk without it. But ever after he limped, and to the villagers he was the sign of the terrible famine that had settled on Berewic that year. To Eadric, his limp was the mark of the injustice done to him by Æadgytha, Cuthred and the rest of the manor. And sharp as the hunger in his belly was, it was nought beside the bitterness in his heart.

The Healer

Forest of Valognes, Normandy, December 1044

Wulfstan of Wessex opened his eyes. Overhead, the interlacing forest branches were rimmed with hoar frost. But all he could see was a blur of black, brown and white, and even this was lost as his sight faded again. Faintly, as if from another room in a house, voices reached him, but he could not answer. Wulfstan was aware something was wrong with his body, but he felt no pain. He drifted off, into a half-light of memory.

It is the Christmas before and Wulfstan has gone with Duke William to view the progress on his new abbey at Cerisy. They are met by a monk called Felip, an energetic man with brown hair that falls over one eye. From his accent, Wulfstan guesses he must be from the south. Felip proudly shows them around the emerging buildings, explaining how much land has had to be cleared and how much timber has gone into making the structures they see risen and rising around them. He seems to know a lot about timber. As he kneels in the new abbey church to pray with William, Wulfstan sees his master buried in his devotions, and understands how his piety, like everything else about him, is deep, heartfelt and unbending.

Wulfstan opened his eyes again. The voices were nearer now, and something was over his face – an oval shape blocking out the tracery of branches. A movement in the oval shape matched one of the voices; Wulfstan realised he was looking at a face, and the voice was calling his name. Closing his eyes, the voice receded.

Now he is in the forest, the Forest of Valognes, where he has come to hunt with William. Another voice is calling his name. But this is only days ago, and the voice belongs to the forest warden's daughter, Estraya. Eleven years old and dark of hair and eyes, Estraya has taken to following the young man with long blond hair as they prepare for the hunt. Her constant presence is as much a surprise to him as her mother's absence; for Samra is nowhere to be seen. As ever, William's party of Norman nobles has taken over the little settlement from where Gilbert runs the forest, and he dashes to and fro among the men, horses and dogs, keen that his domain should provide the best sport for his duke.

Suddenly pain flooded into Wulfstan, beginning in his right leg and sweeping through his whole body. He opened his eyes, hearing someone screaming in his voice. The voices around him became louder, and full of alarm. Arms reached down to Wulfstan and he was picked up. As he was lifted from the ground he saw a leg dangling at an odd angle, and it was some moments before he realised it was his. Something white came towards his face, wiped round it, and was taken away a vivid red. The other voices were gentle now; the arms were carrying him, turning him over. Wulfstan saw the back of a horse approaching, and as it reached him and he felt the warmth of its body, the pain seared through him one last time before darkness took him.

Now it is only hours ago. William and his younger half-brother Robert have taken most of the hunting party off into an area of outcrops and scrub, while Wulfstan and Ranulph de Bayeux are working through some small groups of trees with the rest of the beaters. Suddenly Ranulph's horse rears; a white shape hurtles out of some trees in front of it and is gone. A cry goes up from the beaters; this is a white hart, a deer rare and prized. Wulfstan digs into his horse's flanks and is off. As the hart weaves to and fro he follows, faster and faster, leaving any others on horse behind. After a while he sees nothing but the white shape in front of him, his horse bearing down but never quite catching up. Unaware the forest is getting denser, now he is hurtling through trees, branches whipping his face. Wulfstan will not give up. Leaning low over the horse's shoulder, he urges it on. Time and again he dodges branches, throws his mount over tree roots and fallen trunks. But the ground is becoming rougher. His horse stumbles and pitches to the left, then rights itself, but Wulfstan has lost his hold. For a few desperate strides of the animal he tries to regain his seat, until another lurch flings him aside and onto ground strewn with low boulders. He sees the sky, then quickly the ground comes up to meet him and there is a crunch; then blackness.

*

Estraya knew it was too early for the hunting party to be coming back into the forest clearing. She looked at her father's concerned face and at Wulfstan's limp form strapped across his horse, and froze. As they carried him into the house she followed; they laid him on a table and she looked down at his bloodied and twisted body. His breath was laboured, and he was still unconscious. Gilbert motioned the others with him to leave, and went over to a dark corner of the room.

'Wulfstan is hurt,' he said softly. 'He needs your help.'

Slowly a hidden figure got up and stepped out of the shadow. Samra looked gaunt, tired. She looked over at the prone body and shrugged.

'He is not the first man to be hurt while giving chase. Do what you must to make him comfortable.' And she sat down again.

Estraya looked up. 'Mother, please! We need your art in healing.'

A voice came from the dark corner. 'My art is in the book. Look for it there.'

'The book speaks through you.' Gilbert had taken Samra's hands in his. 'When you wrote your words on the beech strips, when you had me build the observatory and the lens tube, you and the book were one. It is not here, but you are.'

Her voice in reply was calm but distant. 'When I wrote on the beech strips, I was pouring out my grief for the loss of the book, and seeking to remember what it held. When I made what I needed to observe the transit of Venus, I had the book to guide me. Now the book is lost to me again and I am weary. Let me rest.'

Estraya looked up, and could see emerging from the shadow only Samra's hands, pressed between her father's. She went across until she could see into the corner and from the dark, the light reflecting in her mother's eyes.

'Then write again. Pour out your sorrow. But this time on the broken body of this man. Do it, please; help him!'

But there was only silence and the shadow. Estraya turned away and went over to Wulfstan. Taking one of his hands in hers, she held it up to her face and pressed it to her cheek, letting her tears warm the cold flesh. A noise behind her made her turn back. Samra had stood up and now she stepped again into the light. She looked more upright, taller.

Looking at Gilbert, Samra asked him, 'How is he injured?'

'His right leg is broken, for certain. Wounds to the head. What else, I cannot see.'

Samra turned to her daughter.

'Estraya, fetch hot water and as many clean cloths as you can find. Soon I will need from the herbarium, but first I will examine Wulfstan.'

Swiftly moving to his side, Samra ran her hands smoothly over his body, barely touching it or not at all, eyes closed. She gave a sigh.

'I will need the instruments I had made in Rouen. The break is bad; I will need to find the bone. The bruising is bad, but it will heal, and the head wounds are not serious, despite the amount of blood. Is the forge hot?'

'I will make sure, when I go to get the instruments,' said Gilbert. He turned to go, then asked, 'Should I revive him?'

'No. And I will give him a draught to make him drowsier still. Best he is not aware for what is to come.'

'Will he live?'

'If he does not die from my half-remembered surgery. But he will not walk again before Christmas. And he will not leave here or hunt again for some while.'

*

Three days later Wulfstan opened his eyes. He was lying in a bed and above him the beams of the house were hung with holly, mistletoe and ivy. By his feet, the dark girl who had followed him round before the hunt was busy with something. He looked at her as she concentrated, brow furrowed. Her elfin features amused him.

'What are you doing?'

Estraya jumped and blushed. 'Bathing your leg where it is sewn up, so it does not infect.'

He sniffed the air. 'With some witches' brew of your mother's, no doubt.'

Across the room Gilbert stopped sharpening a billhook, and smiled to himself.

Wulfstan will live.

*

It was another week before Samra approached Wulfstan, sat on a tree stump he had hobbled to across the clearing, his face turned to the winter sun, eyes closed. She sat down beside him on the broad stump.

'You are returned to your manor, Wulfstan – this one, at least.'

Smiling at the memory of the day Gilbert had made him and his brother stand on the stump, Wulfstan opened his eyes.

'Gilbert always treated us more kindly than we deserved. But if you expect me to pick up an axe or a sword when I get up from here now, you are mistaken.'

'The healing will take time; but it will come. Duke William will have to do without you a while.'

'It is no hardship to be here. I only realised how much I love this place, and the people in it, when I had left it.' He took Samra's hand. 'I owe you my life.'

'You owe Estraya and Gilbert more than me. It was they that brought me out of my darkness to tend to you.'

They sat a while in silence. Around them, the noises of work echoed in the trees, metal on wood, while the voices of men drifted across with the smell of wood smoke.

Hesitantly, Samra asked, 'Did you return to Berewic?'

Wulfstan released her hand and looked at her.

'Oh yes. Eadric and I returned.'

'Was it everything your father told you?'

'From what little I saw, yes, and more. I was there only long enough to see Edward grant Berewic to its new thegn.'

'Eadric.'

Wulfstan tried to stand up. His injured leg had stiffened and he struggled, almost falling. Samra made to help him, standing up and taking an arm. At length he stood upright, breathing heavily, sweat beading on his brow. He looked pale. Still holding his arm, Samra felt the anger in him as he spoke.

'Hugh de Bayeux is Thegn of Berewic. By now he will be married to the daughter of the Godwin who killed our father. Eadric serves Hugh as a peasant on his own lands.' He laughed coldly. 'This stump is the only manor he will ever have. And I am sent to serve William. He at least is true, and straight. I have the better part of this arrangement.'

Samra looked over to the shelter and the lens tubes. *The book is in Berewic.* She looked at Wulfstan, and smiled.

'Then we had better get you healed quickly. William is not a patient man.'

The Philosopher's Stone

Andredswald, Sussex, December 1045

By the Christmas of 1045, Hugh and Æadgytha had been married two years, and were without a child. The natural distance between them of ten years' difference in age was widened by lack of a common language, although the Norman knight – and English thegn – now spoke halting English. But it had been thrown further into relief by the savage hunger that gripped Berewic through another year. In this, Æadgytha busied herself with village matters, always in touch with her reeve about stocks of food, the state of land and crops. With its river and woods, it was luckier than some manors; even so Berewic's people became ghosts of their former selves, slow and apathetic, the gaunt faces and distended stomachs of many foreshadowing the corpses – the old, young and sick first of all – they would become. It was not lost on them that all this had come about with the arrival of the foreigner that now walked their streets, well fed and seemingly aloof to their plight.

In truth, Hugh de Bayeux had been preoccupied. The book he had brought with him, and which he had pored over while his wife was sleeping, was shaping in his mind a purpose that would surpass this world of suffering. Because it would make him rich, and people would beat a path to Berewic's door and bring food in exchange for his money. For now, what money he had had been spent on setting himself up to reach that purpose, with the materials needed to transform his raw material. Just as Samra had a shelter built to house her lens tube, Hugh had one built to house his alembic, the distillation device whose arrangement was taken from the pages of the book. In this, the book was following the design of the great Jabir, as recalled and set down by Alhacen. But the text in the book had remained obscure to Hugh, as much as he read it again and again. The principle, that by rearranging the qualities of one metal, another could result, was clear enough. But the process itself was hidden in number riddles, linked to the Arabic names of the elements such as sulphur and mercury, whose names he had read. It seemed he needed these, not to mention acids and other substances that might recover gold from alloys and ores of metal. And above all, he needed the *al-iksir*, the catalyst that could bring about the transformation of one metal to another. Berewic was a long way from the world of Moorish Spain, and the laboratory of Alhacen and Samra.

But there was one person who might help him. So he had ridden out of Berewic, taking the book with him, into the Andredswald, where he had been told he could find the man he was looking for. And the man who had greeted him by his hut in a woodland clearing, a giant of a man with dark curly hair and dark brown eyes, remembered the day more than five years before when he had first seen the book, in Gilbert's house in the Forest of Valognes, and the day a year later when he had landed on a shingle beach in England with Hugh and a returning king.

Apart from a rough wooden shelter, the only other structure in the clearing was a circular mound in a shallow, round pit. The mound was covered in turves, and a wooden stake stuck out from the top centre. Underneath the turves was a pile of wood covered in bracken and earth, except at the footings where the wood was still visible. A fire lit in the pile was slowly charring – not burning – the wood, and driving all the water out of it to leave a dry, clean fuel.

Hugh looked around him, at the frost on the leaves and trees, at the smouldering turf-covered pile and at the man with his soot-sodden clothes and grimy face.

'So this is your life now, among the charcoal burners, Fa—'

The other man held up a hand to stop him. Hugh had spoken to him in Arabic, but he replied in English.

'My name is Dudda. I have no Arabic name, and I will speak no Arabic. This was my mother's land. When she taught me some of its speech, and told me of its beauty, of its green hills and its deep woods, I little thought I might come here one day.'

'Until the day the walls of the palace in Cairo ran with blood; hers among it.'

Dudda dropped his head, and the big man wiped his eyes with the back of a hand, but not because of the smoke.

'Until that day. But I have come here, and now this is my land.'

'And here you found bed and board. First a charcoal trade to help run, then the owner's widow to marry when her two sons were made fatherless. You fell on your feet, as they say, in this land.'

'I work hard and I make my own luck. Charcoal is

valuable; it's light and easy to carry, and burns at a high temperature. The villages around the Weald pay well for it. But you did not come here to see my good fortune, Hugh de Bayeux.'

Hugh came over to Dudda, brought his face as near to the other man's above him as he could and lowered his voice to a threatening undertone.

'Were it not for me, Dudda, your bones would be hanging from a tree in Normandy. Some would say that makes you mine.'

Dudda breathed in and drew himself up to his full height. His great barrel of a chest forced Hugh to step back.

'I am no man's servant here, and I belong to no thegn. Tell me what you want.'

Hugh went to his horse and came back with the book. Unwrapping it from its cloth, he began to turn the pages to where Alhacen described Jabir's experiments.

'What does it mean?'

The other man looked at the script and the diagrams, then shook his head.

'So you came by the book after all. And now you mean to make gold. The woman was right not to let you have it.'

'It was you that started me on this path. When you told me you had been apprenticed in Cairo to an astrologer and alchemist, and what he had tried to do, I knew at once this was the work that is described in the book – and that I could succeed where he had failed.'

'He and countless others. I am a simple man, Hugh, and I don't know what can be done with one metal or another. But I know that for every alchemist who swore he was close to success, another said that the gold you seek is only to be found inside a man, once he knows himself. If you look for it in a flask or a crucible, you will find only your own destruction.'

'Then why would men like Jabir and Alhacen give so much detail about their experiments, if it is only to deceive?'

'Because the path is the goal. In following it, in the experiments, the wise man finds all he needs to know.'

A woman a few years older than Dudda had come to the edge of the clearing, carrying a basket. Like Dudda she was large and curly haired, but fair-haired and fair-skinned. Two young boys were with her, playing at sword fighting with sticks. When she saw Hugh with Dudda she stopped, and looked across at them.

'Dudda?' she called, concern in her voice.

'It's all right, Mildrythe. This man has lost his way.' Dudda turned back to Hugh. 'I cannot help you.'

Hugh grabbed his arm. 'But it is all here.' He pointed at the open pages. 'Lead, turned into gold by changing its properties. Only the *al-iksir* is needed.'

Dudda looked at him. 'The *al-iksir*? The philosopher's stone? The red stone, to create gold?'

Hugh's grip on his arm was tight. 'Is that its colour?'

'When ground to a powder, it shows its true colour. And yes, they say it will make gold.'

The other man's blue-grey eyes were blazing. 'Where do I find it?'

'Some say in metals, some say in rocks. Some say it's found in plants, or in your own body – even in your piss. Do not ask to find this.'

And he tore himself away from Hugh's grasp and went over to the woman, leaving the other man standing, holding the book aloft.

'But I will find it,' Hugh called after him, 'and when I do, you and every man in England will be my servant.'

Dudda looked back at him, remembering the purposeful Norman knight whose strength and courage had rescued him from his brother Ranulph's punishment. *What if he is right? What if he really can make gold?* He said something to Mildrythe, who squeezed into the hut. Moments later she came out, and gave something to Dudda, who came across to Hugh and handed him a small wooden box with inlaid decoration and a hinged lid. Opening the lid, Hugh saw the box was lined with silk padding, into which were set two little stone jars, one black and one white, both tightly sealed.

'Take it,' said Dudda. 'I don't need it, and I'm always afraid the boys might find it. It's my last souvenir of Egypt and of my master.'

Hugh looked at the jars curiously, then at Dudda. 'What are they?'

'Hydrochloric and nitric acid; together they make aqua regia. Mix four parts of this one, with one of this.' He pointed first at the black then at the white bottle. 'If what you make really is gold, the mixture will dissolve it. Then you will know. But take care, Hugh.'

'I will not spill them. I imagine they burn.'

'When mixed they are dangerous to lung and limb. But it is not only your body that is in peril.'

*

A day later Hugh de Bayeux was back in Berewic, in the shelter with the book and his equipment. Nothing would work without the philosopher's stone, and the book would not tell him where to find it. He would set men to find it. If it was anywhere near Berewic, it would be found. *What if I find it, and it does not work? What if it works, and I do not know? What if Dudda has tricked me, with his so-called aqua regia?*

There was only one way to know. Hugh found a small stone dish and took the two little jars out of their box. Prising the seals off with a knife, he poured a little of the colourless liquids from each into the dish, in the proportions Dudda had told him. The mixture began to give off fumes, and slowly turned a golden yellow. Hugh took off his wedding ring, and held it at arm's length over the dish, hesitating. Then he dropped it in.

*

It was midnight before he went into the hall house. Warming himself in front of the hearth, he noticed decorations had been put up for Christmas. One of Æadgytha's dogs came over and nuzzled him, but he pushed it away and went to his bed.

Stirring next to him, Æadgytha turned over. 'Where have you been?'

'In the Andredswald.'

'Do you not know what day this is?'

He remembered the decorations. 'Not Christmas Day?'

Æadgytha's eyes filled with tears. 'Two years ago on this day, we were married.' She turned away again, then lifted her head. 'What is that smell?'

'Acid. An experiment.'

Æadgytha turned over, and looked at him. She looked down at his hands, and saw his wedding ring was gone.

Sitting up, her face crumpled with sorrow; she could not speak. Hugh's face was blank. His mind was full of words and symbols, of diagrams and descriptions, and he could not be present in her presence, could not see her pain.

Æadgytha stood up. Taking off her wedding ring, she flung it at him. It hit him and bounced onto the floor.

'Take it! If you can be rid of yours so lightly, be rid of mine too!'

And she went into the hall and lay down by the hearth with her dogs.

Hugh scrabbled on the floor for the ring until he found it in a corner. It was worth something, and he might need to sell it if he was to find the philosopher's stone.

Under the Linden Tree

Winchester, Wessex, June 1046

Emma did not look up as her son approached. Seated in the shade of a linden tree, in the garden of the house where she was an exile in her own country, she made as if concentrating on a particularly delicate stitch in her sewing. Her hands, though gnarled with age, were strong and supple. The tree was in blossom; its sweet perfume hung in the air, while from time to time a gentle summer breeze shook a few yellowy white flowers onto her and the bench that encircled its base. The gown she wore was of simple yellows and browns; no embroidered silk for her girdle and circlet, only plain wool. The gentle hum of bees above her was an echo of the singing from the abbey next door, from where they had flown. Only when Edward was stood in front of her did she speak.

'I knew you would get tired of her and come back to me. Have you had enough of being dressed like a doll?' Now she looked up and saw Edward in his finery, his silk shirt and his marten fur robe, even for a casual visit to his mother. 'They say you look ridiculous.'

'They say I look like a king, with a king's presence.' Edward retorted. 'Something you did not concern yourself with, when

I first returned to this country. But then you never thought I should be King of England. Or take Edith as my queen.'

'You thought that after you married Hugh de Bayeux to a Godwin to gain your friend a manor in Sussex, you could marry into the Godwins yourself to keep a hold on the throne of England. Time will prove you wrong, Edward. Perhaps you should have married Æadgytha, instead of giving her to a Norman.'

'Edith is daughter to the earl and sister to Harold and the other Godwin brothers,' Edward retorted. 'She is far closer to the centre of the family's power than her cousin Æadgytha. And power is something you well understand.'

Emma withdrew the needle from her sewing, and stabbed the thumb and forefinger with it between them in Edward's direction.

'We women understand power, you can be sure. The power the powerless find for themselves, when men give them no choice. And I am sure your bride had less choice than Æadgytha when she took your ring in the winter snows last year. How pale they say she was, then; from cold, or fear? But she has found her power now.' Emma pushed the needle back into the fabric, and furrowed her brow. 'Is it true you have given her the treasury that you took from me?'

'Do I need to remind you, Mother, that you are no longer queen of England, and that Edith is?' Edward replied.

'Edith is a Godwin. Whatever she does, she will be scheming with her brothers to make you impotent. Speaking of which, it is not far short of eighteen months since you were wed. Perhaps you bring me good news?'

Emma saw her son's face tighten. He brushed the linden flowers from the bench beside her and sat down.

'There is time. She is young.'

'But you are not. And a king has only one task: to produce an heir to the throne.'

Emma looked down at her sewing and slowly began another stitch. She thought of what she had heard and seen of Edith; the convent-educated young woman, beautiful and clever, equally accomplished in the arts and sciences. Embroidery and astronomy.

'You know nothing of our marriage,' Edward went on. 'Perhaps the fault – if there is one – is not mine. Or perhaps I have other plans for an heir.'

Emma put down her sewing and turned to him.

'Do not play with England's future, Edward. It can only end in disaster.'

She saw the hardness in his eyes as he looked back at her. Sometimes she had longed for a son's love, unsullied by matters of state, free of the need to duck and weave to survive, and ensure survival for one's own. But she had not had it from Harthacnut, who returned only to die, or from Edward, who returned only to hate her for the death of Alfred. A thought struck her, and she fought the alarm rising in her.

'You cannot mean Wulfstan?'

Edward looked down at his hands, as he always did when thinking.

'I have choices, Mother; I will not make you party to them. And I told you, I will never love another woman.'

Emma struggled to her feet, unsteady on her stiff hips; Edward made no move to help her. She turned to look down at him.

'Listen to me. I do not care that you married against my advice. I do not care that you carry feelings for a woman you could never declare as your own, or that you have a son you can never name. I do not care that Edith was brought up with too much learning for her own good. You must make her pregnant, or I can find someone disposable who will. Or you must put her aside and take another wife.'

Now she saw Edward wringing his hands, as he always did when he was agitated or furious. He stood up and his height was overbearing; she felt his breath on her forehead as he spat his words out.

'No, I do not love Edith, not as I should a woman. But I have found in her a companion worthy of my admiration, and who has my interest at heart. In her beauty and her wisdom, she reminds me of a woman I knew in Normandy; in another life, they might have met and had much in common. I will not conspire against her, and I will not let you.'

Emma took a step back and looked him up and down.

'Oh Edward, if only you could see. There is so much more to being a king than dressing up, holding court and hunting. You are surrounded by forces that conspire against you, that want to use you to advance their cause. If you do not master them, they will master you. When that happens, do not think to come back here and beg for my advice; it will be too late.'

The wind stirred in the tree above them, and a little shower of linden blossom fell on them both. Edward brushed the petals off his robe.

'Well, you have never held back from giving your advice, even when I did not ask for it.'

He turned and began to stride away.

'Wait!' Emma called after him. 'You must have come for a reason – you have a charter for me to witness again?'

Edward stopped and turned back. He put his hands on his hips.

'Edith is witness to all my documents now. I have no need of you, Mother. If I came to tell you anything, it was that.'

Emma mastered her welling emotions. 'You will come again?'

Edward gave a little nod. 'Of course. Once, before you die.' He turned and was gone.

Emma put a hand on the trunk of the linden tree to steady herself. Slowly, awkwardly, she lowered herself onto the bench and picked up her sewing, blowing away the flowers that had fallen onto it. Pushing the needle through the cloth in front of her, she looked at the scene she was embroidering; a shepherd and shepherdess, with a lamb frolicking between them.

Die? When you have proved yourself a worthy king of England, I will die, Edward.

The Battle on the Plains

Forest of Valognes, Normandy, August 1047

It was a still, hot day. In a simple white dress and with a garland of flowers around her head, Estraya waited in the clearing in the forest where she lived with her mother and father. Gilbert was standing in front of her, fussing with the garland until she shooed him away. As he stepped back, he saw Samra coming out of the house. She too was dressed in white; she joined her daughter and embraced her. As their heads touched, the meeting of their dark hair took Gilbert back; back to the day they had looked at the book together when Felip had brought it from Cerisy. Only now Samra's hair was thinner, and there was no book. Samra stepped back, still holding Estraya by the shoulders, looking into her eyes, smiling. The girl smiled back and Gilbert felt tears rising; he had to turn away.

'It is time.'

Samra had spoken, and now she reached down to her ankle. Seeing her unstrapping the knife, Gilbert took a deep breath. *Mother to daughter. Fourteen generations, now.* And Samra was in front of Estraya, still smiling, taking one of her hands and putting the knife in its soft leather sheath into her palm.

'I am not ready.' Estraya looked wildly over to her father; as if he might stay this gift-giving.

Samra closed her daughter's hand over the knife. 'None of us ever feels ready.'

'I'm afraid. What if… what if what is written on it comes about?'

Estraya looked deeply troubled. Watching, Gilbert wanted to hug her to him, but he knew to bide where he was.

'The knife is its own master.' Samra's voice was quiet and kind. 'It will choose its time to act. We cannot say when.'

Estraya burst into tears. 'I don't want to kill anyone.'

Gently Samra took the knife and bobbed down to strap it to her daughter's ankle. Straightening, she took Estraya's hands in hers and looked into her eyes.

'Keep it with you always. Never use the knife in anger, or in jest. Do not seek out its foretelling; but do not fear its coming about. And if it does not, be the knife's keeper, for the one to follow you.' And she kissed her on the forehead, before moving away to sit on a log at the edge of the clearing. Eyes closed, head nodding slowly, she began to say a prayer in Ladino.

Now Gilbert did come over, and he pressed his daughter to him until the breath was squeezed out of her. Then he looked at her tear-stained face, and brushed away some hair that had caught there.

'Oh, my child. I think you do not belong to this world, and I fear for you.'

'What about the book? I don't have my mother's learning… the stars… the instruments… I will never be able to do that.'

'All who have held the book have brought to it what

they may. You are no different. The lore of the forest is your birthright; knowing its ways, and its creatures and its plants. I will make more beech tablets for you to write on. Only set down what you know and learn, and the book will be well served.'

'What I know, she has taught me.'

'No. It goes beyond that. You and I know that. Be true to yourself, is all.'

Estraya did not have time to answer. From beyond the trees a hunting horn sounded clearly, followed by the distant barking of dogs.

Gilbert turned in its direction, then back to Samra and Estraya. 'Go inside!'

Estraya looked puzzled. 'It must be Duke William!'

If William was here, he must be greeted and fed, and her father needed to rouse everyone and set them about their orders.

But Gilbert was frozen to the spot. 'Go – now!'

Samra got up and led the girl inside. Gilbert went over to the edge of the clearing and picked up a long-handled axe from a chopping block. He stood ready, gripping the axe two-handed as the sound of men, horses and dogs grew nearer. A horn blew again, very close. Gilbert tensed. Suddenly there was a noise behind him; a horseman had ridden into the clearing unseen and was bearing down. The rider came at him, reached out and knocked off Gilbert's cap before jumping off the horse to stand in front of him, laughing. And Wulfstan of Wessex threw out his arms and embraced Duke William's forest warden.

'Gilbert! No time to chop wood! We have ridden miles – we need food and drink!'

Stepping back from the embrace, Gilbert saw the man they had nursed from his accident; taller, broader. And with his blond hair and ready smile, handsome, now his last boyish looks had given way to true manhood.

But Gilbert knew that as a knight to William, it was not a life of mere hunting that had steeled Wulfstan. The year before, in the castle close by the Forest of Valognes, resentment among some of the Norman nobles had broken out into rebellion. Alerted by his jester, William, with Wulfstan and a few others loyal to him, had barely escaped in time, fleeing to the forest before taking the road along the coast looking to find safety. And from then Gilbert had heard no more. But he had remembered the words of Edward, now gone to be King of England, that one day someone close to his duke might be the one to strike at him. As he worked away in the forest, keeping the tracks open and the deer and boar ready for the hunt, he had wondered who might round the corner and demand his oath. And Gilbert always knew he could never serve a new master. As William of Normandy finally came into view, Gilbert threw down his axe and went to kneel before him, kissing the ringed finger that was held out.

'Gilbert…' William looked at the tear that had fallen onto his hand. 'I believe you thought me dead.'

'The man is not born that could best you, my duke.' Gilbert looked up. William too was changed; the power of the man standing before him was not just in the stature of his body but also in the gaze of his grey-green eyes, and it was hard, and more searching than ever. 'But I am glad to see it for myself.'

'A pity it has taken me until now to bring you my good

news. I have had many matters to settle since I left here; many men to put in their right place.'

Gilbert got to his feet. He knew too well what that meant. 'I am only sorry this thing happened here, or hereabouts.'

William nodded. 'Where the dog of ambition breeds with the bitch of resentment, treachery will be born.'

Wulfstan had been looking on in silence. Now he spoke. 'This must have had a beginning, Gilbert; our duke surprised at Valognes by those who knew where to find him. What do you know?'

Gilbert felt the eyes of every man in William's party on him. He looked at Wulfstan, then back at his duke.

'Am I suspected?'

William laughed. 'Your loyalty does you credit, Wulfstan, but you are wide of the mark. We came here to celebrate our victory and our deliverance. And where and what better than in the Forest of Valognes, on one of my warden's chases? We are eager for the hunt, Gilbert; let us be refreshed, and then about it.'

Gilbert bowed. 'Give me a little while to order things, my duke.' He turned away, smiling; but his heart was beating a little faster.

Wulfstan went over to the house and ducked in through the entrance. Inside, familiar things met his eyes: the table, the benches, the furnishings that had been around him when he had lain in that room more than two years before. Its quiet and its dark corners comforted him as they had done then; he closed his eyes. The smell of the fire, unlike any other he had known, tangy with the beech logs that Gilbert always liked to burn, took him back to the healing, after the pain. A noise woke him from his daydream. A girl in a white dress was moving past him towards the door. He caught her by the hand and she turned; in the swish of her soft, black hair, her dark eyes flashed.

Wulfstan gasped, startled by her beauty. 'Estraya!'

*

In the evening after the hunt, a great orb of a sun sank in the western sky, firing the thin layers of cloud above the trees into purple-red. William's party and Gilbert's household were outside, drawing closer around a fire now the feasting was done and the air cooled. William was relaxed, tired by the chase – which, as ever, he had thrown himself into with huge energy – and mellowed by the wine he was still drinking. As dusk fell, little by little people threw the last of their food scraps into the embers, or their bones to the dogs, and went to go to sleep. Finally only four remained: Gilbert, sitting with Estraya, across the fire from William and Wulfstan. Gilbert got up and threw more logs on the fire. As it blazed up anew, he spoke to William.

'Is it true that you have won a great battle, my duke?'

'The greatest of battles, my friend. We strangled the whelp of treachery at birth. But I am tired – let Wulfstan tell you the story of it.'

Wulfstan got to his feet.

'Well then, where do I begin? With Goles, coming into that room to alert us to the uprising? The scramble for clothes and weapons? Trying to find our horses in the dark? Waking others, not knowing if they would be friend or foe? Wondering if turning away would be followed by a blade in the back? I have never known fear like that.' As he spoke he paced around, from time to time pausing and turning to Gilbert and Estraya. Gilbert sensed his enjoyment of the moment, the strength that staying alive had given this young man; his centeredness and his self-assurance. 'But we got away. From here we made for the coast, avoiding any towns like Bayeux. We had to ford rivers and cross bays, skirt marshes and mudflats to make our way.'

'Easier to stay inland, surely?' Gilbert asked.

'Inland, attack can come from all sides.' William had spoken. 'Better to have the sea guard your flank.'

'Finally we reached Ryes,' Wulfstan went on. 'After that we had an escort from Hubert of Ryes's three sons, as far as Falaise and the duke's own lands and castle. We were safe, but not out of danger. The rebels would pursue us, we knew.'

'Who were the rebels?' Estraya asked, gripped by the tale.

William answered. 'Guy of Burgundy was their chief; that same cousin of mine. But he was put up to it by others – Ralph of Thury, Haimo, Grimoald and the Viscounts of the Cotentin and the Bessin; these western lands of mine that will still not bow to me.'

Gilbert drew breath sharply. *The Viscount of the Bessin – Ranulph de Bayeux, brother of Hugh, the book thief.*

'An army of twenty-five thousand they had between them,' said Wulfstan. 'We could count on not a third of that number. So we went to the French King. As Duke William is his vassal, he was bound to come to his aid. And he did, with ten thousand men. The rebels crossed the Orne to come after us, meeting on the plains south east of Caen. They wanted William dead. We left from Argences and joined with King Henri's force at Valmeray, and we rode to meet them at Val-ès-Dunes.'

The logs on the fire were blazing fully now, and in the dancing flames Wulfstan paced up and down, reliving every moment. The firelight glowed on his face and his blond hair, throwing his animated features into strong relief. Estraya sat on the ground, hugging her knees, watching him, spellbound. The strangest of feelings came over her, a pang inside that she had never felt before. It was a kind of terror, but exciting and exquisite as well. She wanted to crush it and at the same time to give herself to it.

Wulfstan continued. 'We were still outnumbered, and though not by many, we knew we had little choice but to stand firm. Then Ralph Taisson, one of the rebel side, came up from the south with his force.' He turned and spoke directly to Estraya. 'Imagine what that was like. Us in our mounted ranks, foot soldiers on either side, watching them get nearer and nearer across the plain. I can still smell the horses, taste the dust in my mouth as we waited, braced for an attack. But Taisson came on alone; he rode up to William, and struck him with his glove. "I vowed to strike you," he said, "and so I have. Now I will join you." His men were not many, but there were knights on horse among them. With that force, and with William and King Henri's skill, when battle was joined, we won more of the skirmishes. At one point Haimo unhorsed the French King, but before he could harm him was himself killed. Through the day we gained the upper hand, until the rebels broke and began to turn and flee; back towards the Orne.' He paused and took a drink. 'They started to cross the river but we came after them, cutting them down. Then panic set in; those not being hacked into the water flung themselves in to escape; but their armour weighed them down.' His voice softened suddenly and he stood staring into the fire. 'Unharmed or wounded, they all drowned. Their bodies joined the other dead in the river and were carried away…'

'So many bodies, they blocked the mill downstream at Barbillon.' William had stood up as he spoke this. 'Ranulph de Bayeux, Viscount of the Bessin, among them. I saw Wulfstan strike him down.'

'And the rest of the rebels?' Gilbert asked.

'Guy is fled to his castle at Brionne,' said William. 'We will besiege him there. The others are dead or exiled; some pardoned. But we will rein in our nobles. I will have the church declare a Truce of God, against which no man may rebel, and which will assure my order is kept.' He turned to Gilbert. 'By God, man, I will tame this Cotentin country, if it is the last thing I do. And now show me to my bed, Gilbert. I must sleep, for tomorrow I ride for Cerisy, to see how Felip is getting on with my abbey.'

As they went into the house, William stumbled in the dark. Gilbert put out an arm and he grabbed it.

'Too much of your filthy wine, Gilbert.'

'Not mine, my duke. Some of Felip's, from Cerisy.'

'Hah! My father endows Cerisy with his vineyards at Rouen, and Felip still thinks he knows better; he plants his own.'

'He's a southerner, my duke. They all think they know better when it comes to wine.'

William still had Gilbert's arm; even his half-grip was fierce. He turned and looked into his forest warden's eyes.

'I do not believe you betrayed me, my friend. But remember you are mine; one day I may ask a greater service of you yet.' He let go. 'Go back to your daughter. I can see now.'

*

In the light by the hearth fire Samra was sitting, rubbing on a long cylinder-shaped piece of wood. William went across and looked down.

'What is that?'

'An instrument I had Gilbert make for me. I have neglected it but today I am minded to take it up again.'

'And what does it do?'

'Brings closer the planets and the stars.'

William crouched down and ran a finger along the smooth wood. After a moment in silence, he looked at Samra.

'When Ranulph and Hugh de Bayeux used to come here before Hugh went to England, what did they talk about?'

Samra stopped rubbing, and looked at him. 'Ranulph said he would put your head on a spike above the gateway at Falaise Castle.' She saw his eyes narrow. 'And Hugh said he was master of the moon and the sun, and he would make gold out of lead.'

William laughed.

*

Outside, Wulfstan was still staring into the fire, lost in thought. After a while, he realised Estraya was standing a few feet away, looking at him intently.

'What is it like; to kill a man?' she asked.

Wulfstan shrugged. 'Nothing, if you have to do it.'

Estraya reached down to her ankle and pulled the knife from its sheath.

'I may have to kill someone, one day.' She showed it him.

He looked at the little knife in her palm.
'With that?'

A Slave

Meresham, Sussex, October 1047

It had been Cuthred's idea, and for that reason alone Eadric long mistrusted it. Three years on from his accident, Eadric walked with a limp from his shattered knee and his life was harder than ever. Working his fields and the demesne land was gruelling, and he barely had time to make his food and eat it. 'You need someone to help you,' said Cuthred. 'Buy a slave.' Slavery was a thing almost unknown in Normandy where Eadric had grown up, and frowned on by the Church and authorities. In the islands of Britain and the lands of the Scandinavians, it was normal; everyone bought slaves, including peasants of any means. Selling yourself was a last resort from starvation or poverty. Wars, raids and feuds supplied the market with fresh meat, and slavers from many lands knew they could bring their goods to England. 'I know a village on the coast where you can get one at a good price,' Cuthred had said. 'I have contacts there.' In the end, Eadric gave up his scruples and his mistrust.

A long half-day's ride from an early start brought Cuthred and Eadric to the place. Even in the late autumn sunshine, Meresham was dismal, huddled below the mass of crumbling cliffs on one side, the arc of the bay sweeping bleakly into the distance on the other. Once, it had had fishing boats and land behind it with a freshwater lake, until a savage storm broke through the shingle and left it unreachable from the sea and with salt-poisoned water. A few shabby houses and huts with leaking roofs and cracking walls were left to shelter the people who still lived there. Most had gone, but some of those that remained had begun to trade in slaves, brought to an unsteady landing nearby then herded at the point of a spear or sword to the village. There was no church, and no priest to care for the souls of the terrified men, women and children who stood roped together until paid for and led away.

As Cuthred and Eadric reached what might have been the middle of the village, a dog came up, barking, but no one came to see who they were, and it turned and scurried off after a short while. With a fat finger, Cuthred pointed Eadric towards one of the houses, but stayed on his horse. Slowly dismounting, Eadric went to the door and pushed it open. Inside he smelt cooking, dirt and sweat. As his eyes got used to the darkness, he could make out two human shapes, both squatting; one got up and came towards him. A woman not even twice his age, she was already old, with a lined face and deep-set, hard eyes. She looked curiously at him, then, without turning, called out harshly.

'Guðrun! Get up!'

Behind her, the second figure uncoiled from the floor and a girl stood, arms at her side. As Eadric moved towards her, she kept her head bowed, looking down. Even in the dim light he could see her hair was almost white-blonde, her skin fair.

'Tell me about her.'

'She was sold as a child into the Danelaw, the north

country, before coming here,' the old woman said. 'Before that, who knows? She speaks no English. I have kept her some eight years. Now she is sixteen, strong and well able to keep a house.'

Eadric circled round the girl, hesitating over what to do. He put his hands on her shoulders and gave her a little shake, to see how sturdy she might be. Still unsure, Eadric put a hand to her face and squeezed her chin so she showed her teeth, as if he were looking over a horse. The girl looked up in surprise and now he saw her face; flat features, cheeks slightly dimpled, and eyes of a deep, icy blue.

'How much?' Hearing the price the woman asked for, he held out a small leather bag. 'This is all I have.'

The woman looked at the money she tipped out into her hand and shook her head. She went out of the house and across to Cuthred, still on his horse, showing him the coins.

'For all the trouble I have taken, he offers me this!'

As Eadric came out of the house, he saw Cuthred searching in his pouch for something; at last, he took out some of his own money and threw it on the ground.

'There! And no more.'

The woman called the girl to come out, and set about picking up the coins. Guðrun appeared in the doorway. She steadied herself a moment against the doorpost, then set off towards Eadric and his horse. Each time she put her left leg down, her whole body swayed violently, so much that to steady herself she had to throw her right arm far out from her side. Looking down, Eadric saw her foot. Shoeless, it was turned in two directions, so that she both walked on the side of the foot, and the foot itself pointed in at its opposite, whose perfect straightness and movement made a cruel mockery of it. Sway, throw, steady; Guðrun made a slow and strenuous way across to Eadric, and then froze in fear as he lunged at her. Grabbing her by the neck, he threw the girl down in front of the woman as she picked up the last of the coins.

'A cripple! You have sold me a cripple!' He drew his *seax*.

The girl cowered away from him, terrified, but Eadric had made for the woman, who turned to run. Cuthred was off his horse in a moment and standing in front of Eadric, his own weapon drawn.

'No! There will be no blood shed here. You made an agreement, my friend, and you will keep to it. Now put the girl on your horse, and get up after her. We've a way to ride.'

Eadric looked from the man to the girl, still cowering; the woman was back in her house with the door bolted. He had been taken for a fool.

As they rode away, Cuthred said, 'A cripple for a cripple. That's good. And don't forget, I own part of her, until you pay me for it.' And he laughed.

Eadric said nothing. As they rode back, he turned things over in his mind; the hallmoot, his accident, now this. Darkness seeped into his soul and his eyes burned into the back of the man riding in front of him, so hard did he want Cuthred to suffer his hatred. Between his arms on the back of the horse, Guðrun jolted listlessly.

They reached Berewic at nearly dusk. As they rode slowly along, Eadric could see Guðrun looking around her, at the streets and the neat houses, at the stone church and the hall, turning her head this way and that. After Meresham, it must have seemed to her like some great city, with a cathedral and a palace. Once in Eadric's house he gave her bread, and waved her to a corner where she should sleep. In the morning, he woke to see her moving around, oddly graceful in her movements as she steered her limping body around the household objects Eadric never tidied away. Guðrun tidied, made food and mended, mostly without asking. Not that he spoke to her; he only pointed when he wanted something or put down the food or cloth or whatever he had brought back. When the hay was ready to make, she went to the fields with him, her halting progress bringing curious stares and some sniggers from the other villagers.

*

On Lammas Day Eadric returned from the fields and was washing his face and hands as normal. As he turned, face dripping, instead of the usual cloth, Guðrun was holding something in the palm of her hand. He looked more closely and saw a thimble made of silver and finely engraved. Picking it up, Eadric made out beautiful interlocking patterns and tiny writing around the rim in runes.

'If you need money to pay Cuthred back, you can sell this.'

After the months of silence between master and slave, Eadric was so startled to hear Guðrun talk, he made no reply. Instead, he turned the thimble over and over in his fingers. And when he did speak, it was almost to himself.

'I cannot read the writing.'

'Nor I. Something about love being stronger than iron, and a bond less easily broken. It should have been my dowry.'

Now he spoke to her. 'No one took it from you?'

All the while Guðrun had been looking steadily at him, but now she dropped her head. Her voice was distant but firm.

'I could keep it hidden; even when the men were with me.'

Above her, there was a quick intake of breath from Eadric.

'Did the woman not protect you?'

Looking down at her, the top of her head level with his chin, he saw the skin on her scalp, white beneath her ash-blonde hair. Her breath that came was out, not in, and it was a scornful snort.

'It was she who sold my maidenhead, and more than once.'

Eadric turned away and sat on a stool beside her, his still-wet face in his hands. He began to cry, then to shake with sobs. Body heaving, he took one hand away from his face and reached blindly for Guðrun's. She did not pull away, but looked down at him, puzzled. Eventually he looked up.

'Keep your thimble. I will handle Cuthred.'

An Offering

Cerisy, Normandy, December 1048

The first abbey church of Cerisy was full to overflowing. Black-garbed monks were packed in rows alongside the armed men of Duke William's household, and among these was Wulfstan of Wessex. Felip de Mazerolles stood beside Gilbert, his head barely at the forest warden's shoulder level. All eyes strained towards the altar, where Abbot Garin stood facing the crowd, looking down at William. On his knees, the duke was holding up a wooden casket inlaid with gold and silver, and studded with jewels. Taking the offering from him, Garin turned to the altar and bowed, before placing the casket in front of the cross. Still facing the altar, he stepped back, bowing three times as he did so, until at last he turned and placed his hands on William's lowered head. After a short blessing he held his hands up, palms outward, and the crowd burst into shouts and applause. St Vigor had come home to the abbey he had founded over five hundred years earlier.

*

Wulfstan had already pushed his way through the throng and gone outside. A steady drizzle was falling. He hurried down the hill away from the abbey buildings to a little farmstead by the river. Ducking under the eaves of a roughly thatched shelter open on all sides, he found it taken up by a pen made of hurdles lashed together. Sitting on a feed trough inside the pen, Estraya was scratching behind the ear of a large sow. It had its head in her lap, its eyes closed, and she was murmuring gently to it.

Wulfstan came up to the pen unseen behind her and whispered, 'If I put my head in your lap, will you scratch behind my ears?'

Estraya jumped and put her finger to her lips, but the animal stiffened, opened its eyes and moved away to the other side of the pen, snorting gruffly.

Estraya frowned. 'She will farrow soon. Then someone had better watch over her all the time, or she will roll on her piglets and kill them.'

Wulfstan looked at her as he leant over the hurdles. A year and more on from that night when she had listened spellbound to him, she was turning from girl to young woman. The elfin looks that had amused Wulfstan when she was smaller, were now singular features in a face striking for its dark beauty. He climbed the hurdle and sat next to her on the trough. Her heart gave a little leap.

'How do you come to be allowed here?' he asked. 'Are you not too tempting to these monks?'

She punched his arm. 'I came with my father, of course. He is honoured here for his work.'

'With your father, but not your mother.'

'Her God is not theirs.'

'I'm not sure your father's is. When I was recovering and he thought me asleep, I heard him praying for me to the old gods.'

Estraya smiled. 'He thinks we don't know, but we do.'

'And his master is so pious. William stops at every shrine, every chapel. It drives me mad sometimes.' He paused. 'And is your God their God?'

'Yes. Or, I think so… I don't know. The Cotentin is on the edge of the world; its past is not buried deep. Did you know St Vigor built the first Cerisy on the site of a Druid temple, peopled with gods the Gauls worshipped? Then the Vikings came and laid their gods over the land, wiping the saint away for a while.'

'Now Vigor is back – or at least, a bone from his right arm. William showed it to me in the casket.'

'Yes. And we make our feast days, like Christmas coming, when the Norse gods had theirs, and the Druids theirs before them.'

The pig had buried itself deep into the bracken on the floor of the pen and was snuffling happily. Estraya turned to Wulfstan.

'Are you content, buffing William's armour?'

'Yes.' He grinned. 'More than I ever thought I would be.'

'What is he like?'

'If I served a thousand other men, I would not find his equal.'

'And does he reward you?'

'I have no complaints.'

'But he could have given you land, after Val-ès-Dunes, taken from the rebels.'

Wulfstan shrugged. 'This will not be the last rebellion.

And besides, I will be thegn of a manor in England one day.'

'Is your brother not there now, and the eldest?'

'Ah, the peasant of Berewic. You saw Eadric when he came here. I doubt if he would have survived the first winter.'

'Perhaps he did. Perhaps he is thegn already. Perhaps he's killed the old thegn, and taken his place.'

Wulfstan had turned to Estraya, and now they were facing each other.

'Perhaps you are impudent, Estraya Abravanel. Perhaps someone should stop your mouth.'

'And who will do that, Wulfstan of Wessex?'

But Estraya was smiling and her dark eyes were shining. She inclined her head towards him a little, half closing her eyes, hoping he would respond. He half closed his eyes and moved his mouth towards hers.

As their lips touched and she closed her eyes fully, Estraya saw his face, horribly disfigured. One eye was open; and pouring from the empty socket of the other was not blood, but water.

Abruptly she pulled away and opened her eyes. They were wild with panic.

'Don't leave with William. Stay with us in the forest.'

Seeing the terror on her face, Wulfstan pulled back. He stood up.

'I must go. William will be looking for me.'

As he climbed the hurdle, Estraya put out an arm.

'Wait!' She was reaching down to her ankle. When she came back upright, Wulfstan saw in her palm the knife she had shown him on the night of the tale of Val-ès-Dunes. 'Take this; it will protect you.'

'This that your mother gave you?' He closed her hand over the knife, and gently pushed it away. 'You should not give away your family's treasure so lightly, Estraya.'

Abashed, the girl lowered her head. When she lifted it again, Wulfstan was gone.

*

At the top of the hill, a shape stepped out from the shadow of the abbey.

'Wulfstan!' a voice from the shape called urgently to him. In the drizzle and the growing dark, Wulfstan recognised the squat figure of Felip.

'I'm not surprised you left the ceremony early, Wulfstan,' said the monk as he approached. 'The woodsman's daughter is far more appealing than a bone in a casket.'

'To me, yes. Perhaps not to you.' He saw an eagerness in Felip's face. 'But you did not stop me to tell me this, I think.'

'True.' Felip hesitated. 'I wanted… The book – does Hugh still have it?'

'What book?'

Felip flicked back the hair that had fallen over one eye. 'A book Samra used to study – you must have seen it,' he said impatiently. 'Hugh de Bayeux took it from her when he went to England.'

'If you mean Samra's book, I know it. But I don't recall seeing Hugh with any book.'

Felip clasped his hands, brow furrowed in thought.

'Wait… it was kept in a wooden box; Hugh took the box also. Perhaps you saw this?'

Wulfstan shook his head. 'We came hurriedly to England.

Each of us had what few things we could bring. But who had what, I couldn't say.'

Felip sighed, pulling his scapular tightly round his neck against the wet. From the abbey, a bell began to toll.

'No matter. I must go to prayers.'

Wulfstan watched him go, wondering at the fierceness of his questioning.

I saw a box, he thought, *and it went everywhere with Hugh. I saw him with the book, and I saw the look he gave me as I came near him. Like the look you gave me now, Felip de Mazerolles.*

An Envoy

Cerisy, Normandy, October 1049

'Will you go on to the Forest of Valognes, my duke?' Felip asked William as they left the abbey church at Cerisy, the monk's stout frame waddling alongside the tall man of war. 'There will be hunting to be had, I am sure.'

His question went unanswered.

'And Gilbert would be glad to see you,' Felip added, as they reached the outside.

William stopped, breath steaming into the cold morning air. From behind the church, the sun had begun to climb into the sky above a horizon tinged with red. The first rays of sunshine lighting his well-fleshed face, he turned to the monk.

'The castle at Brionne has a stone keep, Felip, and the River Risle surrounds it on all sides. They said it could not be taken; Guy of Burgundy thought so, when he fled there after Val-ès-Dunes. But I waited, and besieged him there until he surrendered and came crawling out like a starving rat. So I came here to give thanks to St Vigor; bringing his relict here last year has pleased God.'

Felip bowed slightly. 'As will your generous endowment to Cerisy, my duke. God will favour you further, I am sure.'

William's face darkened. 'Only if God can sway the pope, in his council at Rheims. He has banned my marriage to Matilda.'

Felip looked uncomfortable. 'It is true that you and she are cousins, if far removed. Such things need to be considered.'

'Hah!' William retorted. 'An excuse. Matilda's father is the Count of Flanders, Felip. The count is an enemy of the emperor. And who is Pope Leo related to?'

'The emperor.'

'There you have it. But there is more than this. The council accuses our bishops of simony. The pope does not like it that the Hauteville Normans make inroads on lands he holds in south Italy as vassal states. And the thought of Flanders, allied to Normandy, makes the emperor uneasy.'

He walked on with his great bow-legged stride, Felip struggling to keep pace, until they reached the far end of the church, where the land sloped down to the river, and William's men-at-arms waited. William stood looking into the sun a while, then turned to Felip.

'Damn them all. I will be married to Matilda. And I will root these rebels out, wherever they hide and however long it takes. But hunting at Valognes will have to wait another day.'

Felip cleared his throat. 'I wonder, have you given thought to England, since Edward returned there?'

'Eight years since he left Normandy. I was a young man, then.' William paused, reflectively, then added, 'Why?'

'Flanders has become a refuge for all those who flee from English justice. Pirates, pretenders to the throne – Edward's own mother went there, and he bears Emma no love. He may also fear a Flanders allied to Normandy.'

The duke's grey-green eyes searched Felip's face

enquiringly. 'I bury you away in the Cotentin and you become a statesman, Felip? What is your interest in all this?'

'Edward was a friend to Normandy, and will always owe us a debt. His position is weak; he favours the Normans who went with him in the appointments he makes, and this enrages the Godwins. The Godwins are besides impatient that, married to one of their own, Edward has yet to produce an heir. He needs an ally.'

'Hugh de Bayeux was in England when Val-ès-Dunes happened,' William growled, 'out of my reach. I could not arraign him for his brother's treachery. And he was close to Edward; when he went with him to England, I thought he might be a link. I have heard no word from him.'

Felip came round to stand in front of the duke. 'I fear Hugh is lost to us. He is obsessed with an evil purpose he has found in a book.'

'To turn lead into gold? Samra hinted as much at Valognes. Then he is a fool, yes; evil, no.'

The monk brought his oval face closer to William's; he looked around them, as if he might be overheard, and lowered his voice.

'It goes further than mere alchemy, my duke. The book has a greater purpose; one that any prince in Christendom would quake to hear.'

'Then I will go to the forest, after all, and ask Samra to show me this book.'

'You will not find it. Just as I once took the book from her before she came to Normandy, Hugh stole the book from Samra, and took it with him to England. Yet he knows nothing of this greater purpose. I do, and so does Samra, for she is part of it. Send me to England; I will find Hugh.'

'I have half a dozen churchmen, more senior to you, that I could send to England on my behalf. Why would I send a mere monk?'

'Those are men you will need to petition the pope, once he is back in Rome, in favour of your marriage. Where I go and what I do, I can do unnoticed as a mere monk.'

With his searching gaze, William studied Felip, whose dark eyes had an intensity he had never seen before. *Hugh is not the only one obsessed.* The duke turned away a while in thought.

Normandy; too small to be a country, too big to be a dukedom. Everywhere I am beset, by jealous nobles within and ambitious ones without; and all the while I must own the King of France as my master. How I would love more breathing space, like the Hautevilles have got themselves in Italy. England – a kingdom with an ageing king… and without an heir. And I have some claim there, through Emma.

He turned back to Felip.

'News of Hugh, and cautious contact with Edward, would be useful to me. Cerisy is well underway; by next summer it will be able to manage without you for a time. I will let you go then – but be sure to bring back this book. I will see for myself, what is to fear in it.'

Felip watched William go, striding down the hill to rejoin his men at the river. Soon the sound of guttural laughter drifted up to him in the still, cold air. He walked on until he had reached the edge of the abbey buildings, where the monastery was still taking shape; he stepped over the lines pegged out for an infirmary.

Here, among piles of off-cut and discarded timber, he came across the huge trunk of an oak lying in the grass. The low sun was picking out the crevices in its bark, like furrows in a field. How pleased he and his monks had been to cut such a colossal tree from the surrounding woods, and to haul it up to the lumberyard for Gilbert's inspection. Felip walked to the butt end of the oak, pulled away an encroaching clematis, and stood looking at the star-shaped pattern of stained cracks that radiated from the heartwood. In his memory, Gilbert stood next to him, lips pursed. 'Shakes,' the forest warden had muttered, putting a hand on Felip's arm. 'It'll be no good. Sorry.'

I should tell Samra when I am going to England, thought Felip. He climbed up to sit on the trunk, damp with dew, and turned his face to the sun, closing his eyes. He savoured the rosy glow though his eyelids a while, then opened his eyes suddenly.

No. The book is as much mine as hers. It is my Latin that will bring the book alive, if it is to reach an audience. If one day I am to stand as she imagined herself, before a king and queen, sharing the knowledge it holds, it will be for the work I have done. But not in front of William; this brute of a man who thinks of nothing but castles and sieges. Edward, learned and wise as his brother was; he will be the one to hear me. I will take the book to him.

He got down from the trunk and turned to go; then stopped as he remembered the night under the dome in the observatory in Toledo.

What of the knife, and the foretelling?

For a moment Felip wrestled with the images on the star-dome, and the voice of Sophia. Then he put them out of his mind.

A sideshow; a distraction from the book that could see

it destroyed. And that a bloodline of kings could come from a woman in a forest; from Samra… impossible. Wulfstan is sniffing round her daughter, and he is a Wessex; but not of royal blood. The thought that this cocksure soldier might one day be a king… foolish.

Felip thought of Samra in the Forest of Valognes, the absence of the book like a rent in her being. He thought of Estraya, writing on beech strips, gathering knowledge meant go into a book that she might never see again. He thought of Gilbert, working away in his forest, strong, selfless and patient, as he had always been at Cerisy.

And he thought how he would betray them all.

A Man of Destiny

Berewic, Sussex, March 1050

Half his lifetime since he had stood with her at the moot tree, Harold Godwinson was seated beside his cousin in her hall house at Berewic. At twenty-one, Æadgytha was the striking woman she had promised to become even then, but she was troubled. There had been hard times in Berewic; after a few years of recovery, two bad harvests had followed. As he did from time to time, Harold had come to go hawking with Æadgytha, although this time it was a sport she felt ill at ease pursuing among the hungry folk of her manor. With the Godwin cousins that morning were Cuthred the reeve and Father Brenier the village priest, and they were discussing the prospects of the villagers.

'In a good year,' Cuthred was saying, 'a man might grow eight bushels of corn to the acre. Once he has given his due to you, my lady, and his tithe to you, Father, and the birds and mice have had their share, he has half that left, and of that a half is needed as seed corn. Yet he should still have enough to feed his family.'

'But not in a year such as last?' Æadgytha was looking at Brenier.

'People are already eating bread made from rye flour gone mouldy,' the priest replied. 'It makes their bodies burn and their minds prey to wanderings that can only be put there by the devil.'

'These years of want began when Edward brought over his Norman favourites,' Harold put in, and everyone looked at the earl's son, who had spoken with quiet authority. 'If I had my way, they would all be sent packing, including Hugh de Bayeux.'

The others knew too well that Hugh had spent his wife's money on the pursuit of making gold, and that she, not he, was the real thegn in Berewic, bearing the burden of her people's welfare. Neither Cuthred nor the priest dare say it, and Æadgytha looked abashed.

Father Brenier broke the silence. 'We will ride this out. I will draw from what is in the tithe barn. Let me go to the church and look at the record.'

'And I'll go to the fish traps,' said Cuthred. 'A good haul there will go a long way.'

*

An hour later, Harold and Æadgytha were stood under a tree at the edge of a wood above the valley. Released from her glove, Æadgytha's merlin was weaving across the field before them as her dogs snuffled through it. After a while a bird darted out from some tussocks; a partridge had broken cover. As it scurried along the ground, the merlin changed course to meet it. The partridge gathered speed and took off, stumpy wings whirring powerfully if ungracefully. With no hint of increasing speed, the falcon hurtled towards it, outstretched talons hitting its back with a thump the Godwin cousins could hear. In a puff of grey feathers, raptor and quarry met the ground, the dead partridge rolling over a few times as its killer landed on its feet, then stood eyeing it, head darting from side to side. Æadgytha went to her merlin, and proffered it a scrap of meat on her lure that it snatched and devoured as she bagged the partridge.

Harold caught up with her, his own peregrine still at glove, and she turned to him with a smile, gratified at the approval shining in his tawny eyes.

'Not much meat on a late winter fowl, but food for someone,' she said.

'Well done. You have trained your falcon well.'

'King Edward would be proud of me.'

Harold frowned at his cousin. 'I know you are loyal to Edward, but he was too long in Normandy to be an English king. And after five years he has given my sister no child.'

'Her five is better than my seven.'

Too late, Harold realised what he had said. 'I am sorry; I did not mean to pain you. Edward married you to a fool, and a dangerous one.'

Æadgytha shook her head sadly. 'When Hugh withheld from me at first, I thought it was in respect for my youth. Now if he is with me at all, he is like a caged animal; restless, and with his mind elsewhere. Yet I am a woman, Harold; I am alive, and in the here and now. What should I do?' She called her bird to glove and fastened the leash to its jesses.

Harold could see she was trying to stop the tears. 'I know what I would do,' he said gently.

She looked into the handsome face and shook her head. 'That is easy for you to say; you are a man. Besides, you have Edith; Edith Swan-neck, Edith the fair, Edith the fertile.'

Harold grinned bashfully. 'I am blessed in that, I know. And I would not flaunt my good fortune in your house.'

Æadgytha looked into his eyes. 'Cousin, I rejoice in your happiness; it is no reproach to me. Bring Edith here, please; and your children. I would be happy to see them.'

Harold nodded, smiling; then looked grave. 'But Edward's childlessness is no mere inconvenience. He becomes ever more pious; unworldly.'

'The Edward that came with us to hunt in the Ashdown was worldly enough.'

'Yet he grows older – and if he retreats into celibacy now, there will be no child; no successor for England's throne. And there is more. They say he means to promise the throne to William of Normandy.'

Æadgytha gasped. 'Duke William?'

'He has claim, distantly.'

'By that token, Eadric who holds a yardland from me has claim, if even more distantly. Could he be the next King of England?'

'Eadric the cripple? That is a step too far, I grant you, and one Edward could never make.' Harold smiled at the thought. Again, a shadow seemed to pass over him, and he continued in a sombre tone. 'Edward giving his Norman favourites land and positions in England is one thing. But the crown…'

'He blames the Godwins for Alfred's death, and hates our family for its power in the land,' said Æadgytha, 'but you cannot let him take England down this path. And if your father cannot see that, you must.'

Harold sighed. 'Edward's peace has been good for England. The country prospers; we are secure from our enemies. For this, many love him. And none would wish the dark days back, when the throne fell to the strongest or the most treacherous.'

Æadgytha raised herself up; tall and noble in her beauty, she seemed to Harold to radiate purpose.

'When I became thegn here,' Harold smiled to hear her call herself the thegn, not Hugh, 'I wanted nothing more than an easy life, and yet we have been beset by hardship. But it has given me resolve, and brought me closer to my people. Days of riches and quiet do not make a man, Harold. A man of destiny is forged in the heat of conflict, and suffering. You need to be such a man.'

'What should I do?'

'I know what I would do. Face up to Edward, and save England.'

*

Square and solid, the church was the only stone building in Berewic. In the late winter afternoon, the candles were lit and their light danced on the walls, decorated with saints and bible scenes, painted with brilliant colours. There were vivid greens from copper salts, red and yellow ochres from iron oxides, black from charcoal, and intense white from lime.

Hugh de Bayeux was standing at prayer in front of the rood screen when Father Brenier came in. As he came up beside him, Hugh turned and spoke to the priest.

'Do you come to pray with me, or for me?'

The bulk of the other man lowering over him, Brenier hesitated. He knew from Æadgytha that in this time of need

Hugh was more obsessed than ever with his experiments, and no nearer to success.

'What is it you have come to pray for?'

'That I might find what I seek.'

'Do the men of the village you have looking for the philosopher's stone, and who help you in your work, know what it is you seek?'

Hugh's eyes widened. 'How do you know what they do?'

'It troubles them; they come to confess to me.'

'They know that they will be well rewarded.'

'Berewic needs bread, not gold.'

Hugh stood up and nodded towards the rood screen.

'All the wealth you have behind there, Father, in plates and cups, in candlesticks and incense burners, would buy bread. Berewic belongs to me, as I am thegn here, and its church, with its wealth, belongs to me.'

'The church is playing its part, in helping the needy.'

Hugh stepped up to the screen and pulled on it with his hands, as if he would bring it down.

'What would you do, if I went through there and took some of its wealth, to carry on my work?'

Brenier was alarmed. He knew that he could not stop Hugh robbing the church. He began to move away, but Hugh grabbed him and pushed him up against the screen.

'Help me! I am on the edge of madness, I know, but I cannot stop what I have begun.'

As the candlelight flickered on Hugh's face, the priest saw the anguish in his deep-set eyes. The thegn's grip tightened on his neck.

'Take it!' Brenier gasped. 'Take whatever you want!'

'You fool! You think I came for your trinkets? You will

pray for my work, and for my success!' He threw the priest to the floor, and taking out some money, flung it at him. 'Here is coin for your trouble.' And he walked away.

'Wait!' Brenier called after him. 'I have something of yours.'

Hugh stopped and turned back. 'Who gave you this?' In the palm of his hand, Father Brenier was holding a wedding ring.

'The man you sold it to. He thought better of melting down the Lady Æadgytha's wedding ring, and he brought it to me.'

Hugh made to grab the ring, but the priest closed his hand over it. He saw Hugh put his hand on his sword hilt. Shaking with fear, but unwavering, Brenier went on.

'One day you will come to your senses, Hugh de Bayeux, and I will return this to you. And you will put it back on your wife's hand.'

For a moment Hugh looked at Father Brenier, his hand still on the sword hilt. Then he turned and strode out of the church.

Edward's Chaplain

Bosham, Sussex, June 1050

England.

Felip knew of it, of course – there were plenty of exchanges between Normandy and its northern neighbour; between traders, clerics and nobles. Yet a thrill ran through the monk as the boat he was being rowed in steadily approached England's coast, just like the smell exciting his nose – of silt, seaweed and salt.

Not that the approach to Bosham was exciting in itself; a low shoreline under the late afternoon sun, relieved occasionally by small clumps of oak and willow among muddy creeks and channels. The incoming tide was pushing hard up these, taking the boat swiftly with it, so that the rower needed to scull only gently, and mostly to correct a wandering course. As he peered past this man, Felip wondered how he knew which channel to take and where to steer through this maze, seated as he was with his back to their destination. He was more astonished still to see another man out on the mudflats, digging at a narrow gully leading back to a small, rounded basin that the incoming water was clearly meant to fill. Coated up to his thighs, this man looked as if he had emerged from the mud itself, his spadefuls of it flopping onto the wet mire around him as it shimmered in the sunlight.

The rower saw Felip staring. 'For the salt,' he said.

Felip nodded. He had heard of England's jewels and coin, and its fine metalwork in gold and silver. He had also heard of its bounty in salt, garnered from countless muddy shores such as this, where seawater trapped in shallow pools at high tide evaporated to leave a briny deposit. And salt was wealth indeed.

At last, they rounded a bend and there it was. Hugging the shoreline at the head of a creek, at first sight Bosham looked as reluctant as the crouching clumps of trees to rise above its horizon; low houses, in front of small boats pulled up on some shingle, in browns and greys like the surrounding landscape. The boat moved further round, and gradually Felip could see larger structures; a manor house, and behind a church, the buildings of the community of priests that King Edward had granted with the church to Osbern, his Norman chaplain and cousin. With this grant went the church and lands in the west of the manor that rivalled in value those of its owner in the east, the great Earl Godwin, in ploughlands, meadows, mills, woods, fisheries and saltworks.

*

Felip was surprised to meet such a young man. At twenty-three, Osbern was the age the monk had been in the early days of the foundation of Cerisy, and he reminded him of his younger self; energetic and self-assured. The handshake Osbern had given him was firm; the grey eyes beneath the sandy coloured hair were keen and searching.

'You are just in time,' was the first thing Osbern said to him as he met him on the foreshore, 'we will go directly to prayers. Come!' And he turned and marched off in the direction of the church. Then he stopped and came back. 'Do you need me to speak French?' Continuing in French, Osbern added, 'When I was growing up in Normandy, the fame of Felip the scholar reached me. The man who spoke Latin, Greek, Hebrew and Arabic. Not English?'

'I did learn English,' Felip replied. 'But learning, and being among a people speaking it, are two different things.'

Osbern smiled. 'The English are a bastard race. They have borrowed their tongue from Britons, Romans, Saxons, Vikings, and they treat it with little respect. You will adapt to what you hear in Sussex. Then if you go into Kent, or Wessex, you will have to learn again.' Putting an arm round Felip's shoulders, he added kindly, 'But we can speak English tomorrow.'

There were to be more surprises for Felip that day. That the sun stayed in the sky noticeably later even than in Normandy, and certainly later than in the Languedoc or Spain. That the service he attended with Osbern in the church was a celebration, that year being four hundred years since an Irish priest called Dicul and a few companions had settled at Bosham. By the time St Wilfrid had come to convert the South Saxons thirty years later, there was already, Osbern said, a small Celtic monastery at Bosham with five or six brethren; the six priests around them were their descendants in the faith. And the greatest surprise – that once the six had later eaten with Osbern and Felip, they said their goodbyes and retired to their own houses nearby.

As the door closed on the last of these, and the candle on

the wall nearby guttered, Osbern turned to Felip to refill his cup with mead.

'You are intrigued. But we are not a monastery like yours at Cerisy, Felip; just a community of priests who share the duties in our church and draw from the same funds to support us. I am their head, their dean; but that is all. They have taken no vows of silence, or chastity. Tomorrow they will be about their work in the parishes that belong with the lands Edward granted me, visiting the poor and the sick and upholding the word of God, like any other village priest.'

'I wonder, does England have yet more to astonish me?'

'Oh, plenty,' Osbern replied. 'England has been ravaged by invaders for centuries. It absorbs them, like it does their speech. In time, the invaders become English – they may keep some words and customs, but they are English, and all that goes with it.'

'And what is that?' asked Felip.

Osbern leant back in his chair to think a while. 'I could take you from here to a house where a man has a sick wife and a crippled child. His fingers are coarse and stiff from the damp that hangs around him. This man has a workbench, and on it, under the light of a cheap candle, he crafts the most exquisite jewellery you will ever see; in gold and silver, inlaid with precious stones. The delicacy of it, the intricacy, is perfection in miniature, and humbling to behold. England is full of such contradictions, Felip. It upholds men's freedoms, and relies on slavery for its meanest tasks. Its people are surly and quick to anger, yet they bear enormous hardship with calm and humour. It is on the edge of the world, yet the knowledge of the world comes to it. Its cathedrals and monasteries are ramshackle, and within them the greatest books are being written and copied. Contradictory, irritating, and ramshackle; yet there is much to love about England.'

'And is the faith strong? St Vigor founded my abbey a good hundred years before your Dicul came here, but even now the old gods have some pull on those living in the deepest Cotentin.'

'England is long settled and farmed; it has few remote places – the woods of the Andredswald that lie to the north of here are an exception. For many years it was England that sent men who would become saints out to other lands, to be a light in their darkness. Now tell me,' he added quickly, 'what brings one of the Brothers to England?'

'Indeed,' Felip replied, 'it is these cathedrals and monasteries, and their learning, that have enticed me. I shall travel in search of them.'

'Then you should go to Canterbury, Felip, that great centre of the faith where St Augustine established his church. Or to Winchester, which has three foundations to its name, and where our king was crowned.'

'King Edward resides there?'

'From time to time. He travels much and is also often at Thorney, near London, where he is having the abbey rebuilt, and a new palace built for himself. Do you seek him?'

'I...' Felip hedged, 'I have heard much of his piety and his good works. Just to get sight of him would be a gladness.'

'Indeed. But you should take care. These are troubled times, and another Norman thronging around Edward will not please all the English.'

'I am from the Languedoc.'

'They will not make the distinction.'

'Will the protection of my monk's habit not be enough?'

Osbern leant in, as if someone might be listening. 'There is a power in this land,' he said softly, 'and its seat is just east of us here. Earl Godwin and his sons rule England, many say, and they are a vicious and lawless family. Only last year, Swein, the eldest son, murdered his own cousin here. He was outlawed; declared a *nithing*, and driven abroad for the second time – the first being for abducting an abbess; a dreadful crime! But it is common knowledge he will be pardoned sooner or later, by some bishop the Godwins have under their sway.'

Felip nodded. 'We in Normandy know of the Godwins. You are too young to remember when Edward and his brother tried to return here, and the Godwins betrayed them, leaving Alfred dead. Yet Edward depends on them, does he not?'

'For now.'

Osbern looked away, and Felip sensed he was holding back from saying more on this. He changed the subject.

'Will you ever go back; to Normandy?'

'My family served the dukes of Normandy. My father was his steward, and he was murdered in Duke William's bed, protecting him from assassins when William was a boy. I was barely a man when I came here with King Edward and his party. But I consider myself now to be English, and I serve Edward. I will not go back.'

'Do you recall a man called Hugh de Bayeux in Edward's party?' Felip said. 'And two young men of about your age – brothers, called Wulfstan and Eadric?'

'I remember them from the boats, though afterwards we went separate ways. Though I was here two years later, when Wulfstan passed through Bosham, on his way back to Normandy,' Osbern added.

Felip looked intently at Osbern. 'Did he say what became of the others?'

'Oh yes, for he was angered. Edward had given Hugh de Bayeux a manor, and sent Wulfstan to serve Duke William.'

Felip felt his stomach tighten. 'Do you recollect what this manor was called?'

But Edward's chaplain only shrugged. 'I knew of it. But the name escapes me now.'

Felip's shoulders dropped with disappointment. He stared into his cup. Then a thought struck him.

'Could it have been… Berewic?'

'Berewic – yes, that was it. It is perhaps two days' journey from here to the east, less if you can go by ship. But how do you know Berewic?'

Now it was Felip that shrugged. 'I probably heard one of them mention it, when I knew them in Normandy.' He got to his feet. 'It is late, and I should like to find my bed.'

He slept very little. *Berewic, and the book, are two days away. But first, to find Edward, and prepare the ground with him.*

A Contract

Forest of Valognes, Normandy, July 1050

Quietly, Gilbert came up to the side of the pen and stood looking through the slats. In the shade under the low branches of the trees, his daughter was sitting with a young fallow doe, its dappled coat blending perfectly with the leaf shadows from above. To this sanctuary, away from the main activity of the forest clearing but close enough to deter wolves, the doe had been brought after being found in a snare earlier that year. When Estraya saw her father, and pulled her arms from around the animal's neck, the scars left by the withies as it had struggled desperately to escape were still clear. Slowly, she got to her feet and came across to the gate in the high fence. Gilbert opened it for her and she stepped through.

'It cannot be long now,' she said to him, looking back through the slats.

Her father studied the doe's swollen belly. 'Days,' he said, 'if that. This will be her first fawn, too.'

'She will not be frightened, at least, to be alone, and she will be safe here.'

Estraya knew that a fallow doe always separates from the herd before giving birth, and finds a quiet place to have her fawn. The pen would be quiet enough, but they would need to leave her to it, and not intervene.

'She has known enough fear in her life,' Gilbert said, 'in the snare with the men around her, waiting to get near with their knives. We were just in time.'

'Do you not hate them; people who could do this?'

Gilbert put a hand on her arm. 'They have to feed their families too. It's part of the way of things. Just as the doe will have to take her fawn and go back to the herd.'

Estraya looked at him imploringly. 'Can we not keep her? I would so like to see her raise her fawn.'

'You know we can't. It's not fair to either of them.'

His daughter's eyes filled with tears, and she shook her head. 'But if she goes back, one day you may hunt her, or her fawn when it is grown.'

Gilbert pulled her into his arms and held her in his strong embrace. 'We might; that is true.'

Estraya looked up at him through her tears. 'I don't understand why you care for these creatures and then kill them.'

Gilbert frowned. 'It's hard to explain, I know. But we are like any farmers or herdsmen here in the forest. The animals around us are in our care, and if we find any sick or injured, we tend them as we would our own children; we grieve if they die. But we need them for the hunt, and the hunt provides for us, those that come here, and many others besides. In their deaths, we have fully valued their lives, and they've returned to us what we have given them; that is the contract that we have with them, and we honour them for it.' His daughter buried her face in his chest, and he felt her body shaking against his. 'But listen,' he went on, 'we will know this doe, as we go about the forest. If we come across her, I'll take you to see her. I promise. And if I can make sure she and her offspring are spared, I will.'

Estraya pulled out of his grasp, until he was just holding her by the arms. She looked up at him. 'Thank you.'

'But we should leave her now, and not come back until she has fawned.'

Estraya nodded. 'Just let me stay here one moment longer, to look at her.'

Gilbert put a hand to her face and stroked her cheek gently. 'One moment; no more. She needs to be alone.'

He turned and began to move quietly away from the pen.

'You do not need to worry for her future,' his daughter called after him. 'She will find me, when she needs me.'

*

Outside the house, Samra was sitting in the sun, eyes closed, recalling, as she often did in the summer heat of Normandy, the burning skies of Spain, and imagining herself back there, among the scented gardens and their flowing waters. As Gilbert hurried past, she opened her eyes and put a hand out to catch his.

'What is it?'

He stopped, and told her about Estraya and the fallow doe.

Samra listened. 'Sit down a moment.'

As he sat on the bench beside her, Samra took his hand between both of hers and gave it a squeeze.

'Our daughter misses Wulfstan, my love, when he is not here. She has poured her longing into this animal, to compensate.'

Gilbert sighed. 'I know. But she's always wanted to tend every creature she has found, or that I've brought back here. Some huntsman's daughter she is; I'd be better off showing Duke William a menagerie of animals in pens when he comes.'

'You are thinking a son would not have so disappointed you.'

Gilbert turned and now took both her hands in his, looking at her intently.

'No! No, not at all. It was meant kindly, what I said. I would not trade Estraya for all the sons in the world. And I know she was meant to follow you, for the knife, and its purpose. For that, and for everything she is, I hold her dear. But I worry about her, is all. That for her otherness, she may one day come to harm.'

Samra put her arms round Gilbert, and held him to her a while before letting go and holding him by the shoulders, looking into his light blue eyes. She kissed his forehead.

'You are a good man, Gilbert; I love you for it. But something else troubles you, and has done since you returned from Lessay. I wish you would not keep it from me.'

Gilbert looked startled a moment, then looked away. He nodded. 'You are right, my love, as always. But I didn't want to bring you unwelcome news.'

'Tell me.'

Taking her hands in his again, Gilbert looked at Samra. 'There were monks at Lessay, from Cerisy. Of course, I asked after Felip.'

'What did they say?'

'Gone to England, a month ago.'

'Did he leave any word? Any message for me?'

'None.'

'Then he is gone for the book. He wants it for himself. I was always afraid of this.'

'Gone to bring it back, surely?'

Samra shook her head. 'No, he will not do that. Thank God I did not tell him about Wulfstan.'

'Wulfstan? What about Wulfstan?'

Samra put a finger to his lips. 'Now there is something I must keep from you, Gilbert. For I have cause to worry about Wulfstan, as you do about our daughter.'

A Bargain

Thorney, London, July 1050

Once again, Felip had been rowed to his destination, only this time it had been but a short distance up the Thames from the teeming wharfs of London, where after coming from Bosham he had been staying a while at the Cathedral Church of St Paul. From this place, already rebuilt for nearly a century after the Viking invasions, the oarsman had taken him to a building site, for the new Abbey of St Peter was the creation of King Edward, and it was not yet ten years in the making. So he had alighted amid familiar scenes; masonry and timber, pulleys and wheels, forges and sawpits, were all part of the work still going on at Cerisy in his absence.

On the quay, feeling both anxious and eager at the message from Edward that had summoned him to the little island where the River Tyburn joins the Thames, Felip waited. Across the Thames he could see marshlands, intermingled with fertile riverside fields growing crops destined for the hungry mouths of the city; there were boats on the river bringing goods from further upstream for its needs and its luxuries. Above where the broad Thames disappeared from sight into the west, a bank of black cloud was looming. He heard a roll of thunder. Behind him, voices were calling urgently for work to be hurried or protected in the face of the approaching storm.

A courtier appeared and ushered Felip quickly through the building site, the monk attracting no attention in his familiar Benedictine habit. He saw with some surprise that the grand structures of the abbey taking shape around him gave way at last to a crude group of buildings around a hall, all set rather awkwardly on a piece of rough ground. Clearly his palace was not Edward's priority on the island.

*

Meeting England's king in his private apartment, with a table set out with refreshments, Felip was struck, as were all who met the king for the first time, by Edward's cornflower-blue eyes, his long, milky-white hair, and his thin hands with their delicate skin. Yet when they clasped together around one of his, the hands were warm and strong, and they held it for some time while he spoke.

'Felip! At last! I have chided myself so many times since I came to England that I never visited you at Cerisy, though its founding and your work on it have been an inspiration to me here. If this man can carve an abbey out of a wilderness, I have told many, then building one on an island a stone's throw from London should not defeat me.'

Felip rubbed his backside ruefully. 'A little more than a stone's throw, my lord.'

'Of course – you have had a journey, and I am forgetting myself. Please; be seated, and be nourished.'

Edward waved urgently at a servant standing by the door,

who came to the table and poured wine into a cup among the bowls of sweetmeats that were set out. Felip sat and began to eat and drink, noticing that Edward did not; rather he took water, which he poured himself, before sitting at the other side of the table.

Feeling Edward's gaze on him after a while, Felip paused and cleared his throat. A flash of lightning lit the dark outside, followed by a thunderclap. Another servant began to close the shutters.

'I am greatly honoured by your summons, my lord, though I feel a mere monk does not deserve a personal audience with a king.'

'Nonsense. William has trusted you with a great project in the Cotentin, and he is a good judge of men. How is the young duke?'

Felip remembered that William would have been fourteen when Edward left Normandy.

'Older, my lord.'

Edward smiled. 'As am I. But I remember how William and I used to hunt together when we were younger. And the Normans know how to hunt. Tell me, does Gilbert still run the Forest of Valognes for William?'

'He does indeed.'

'And Samra – she lives, I hope? I know her health suffered, in the north.'

'I have not seen her for some while, but I believe so.'

'Good…' Edward paused, as if thinking. It was so dark now, that one servant began to light candles, while the other put logs on the fire embers in the centre hearth. 'And Wulfstan,' Edward added suddenly, 'he is in William's service?'

'Ever at his side, my lord; they have put down rebellion together.'

'Wulfstan has not been hurt, I hope?'

Felip smiled. 'Only when hunting.'

Edward laughed. Again, he seemed to be thinking, before he went on. 'I should like to make myself known to William. Did he have any words for me?'

'Only that he too would like to make himself known to you. Although I would embellish if I said he sought me out to bring you this message. I asked to come here.'

Edward nodded. 'For what reason?'

Felip took a breath. He looked at Edward, whose face was now lit by the candlelight, and the flames that were beginning to rise quickly from the fire. The king's eyes were fixed keenly on him, as they had been the whole time. He took his chance.

'Hugh de Bayeux, who you brought here with you, and installed in Berewic as thegn, stole a book from me. I would have it back.'

Edward laughed, a silvery peal of laughter surprising from a man. 'A book? We have thousands of books in England. Our monasteries are full of them. Choose which you will, and I will give you it for a replacement.'

Felip leant across the table to Edward. 'This book has centuries of knowledge; it is the work of great scholars of many faiths. Knowledge that would light the way of a wise ruler to the glory of God, and benefit the lives of his subjects. It is not to be replaced.'

Edward looked back at him. Another crash of thunder sounded. 'You are one of the scholars?'

"The latest, and the least. The book began its life in Moorish Spain, written in Arabic. I have been translating parts of it into Latin. But I have much work to do. And, the book needs a place of safety.' He looked around. 'Imagine if it were to be the first book in your new abbey.'

Nodding slowly, Edward took a drink. 'I will make a bargain with you. Stay here a while, and help me build this Abbey of St Peter; my West Minster, just as St Paul's has been my East Minster. It will be my burial place, and the greatest cathedral in England. But it proceeds slowly. It needs your hand to guide it and to urge it on. When you have done this, you may recover your book.'

Felip swallowed hard. He had imagined a refusal but had not been expecting such an offer, or delay in finding Berewic and the book. Outside, the rain had started; he could hear it on the roof, getting louder by the minute.

'A while, my lord… how long might that be?'

Leaning back in his chair, Edward ruffled his long hair.

'Let's see… I was thinking ten years, perhaps fifteen?'

Now the lightning flashes were coming more rapidly, visible even through the closed shutters. Thunder rolled again, and the rain drummed so furiously on the roof above them that Felip wondered if he had heard right. He stood up.

'My lord, I cannot sustain such a wait. This book has become my life's work; I have poured body and soul into it, and risked my life for it. Every day it is with that – begging your pardon – that thuggish knight you have seen fit to grant an English manor to, is a day I fear it runs closer to its loss forever.'

He dropped to his chair again and took a deep draught of wine. *Let it numb me, as I am rowed back to London empty-handed.*

Edward looked at him, open-mouthed. Then he jumped

to his feet, banged the table with a fist, and broke into peals of laughter that sounded over the rain, like one music over another.

'Oh, Felip, your face – hah! Oh God, the look on your face!'

He slapped his thigh and turned away to try to stop laughing, doubling up before mastering himself at last and turning back. He slumped into his chair, still shaking, breathing heavily. Felip stared at him.

'Forgive me,' Edward went on. 'I could not resist the jest. Give me a year, Felip – say a year and a month, for it will take you the month to get to know this place and its people. If I am pleased with your work after this, go get the book and bring it here. We will treasure it.'

Felip closed his eyes. *Thank God.*

A Serving Girl

Gloucester, Wessex, August 1051

'Come!'

At the door, Beornwyn hesitated. To be summoned to the king's private chamber at such a late hour could mean only one thing, her fellows in the kitchen had said. *We saw him, looking at you. There must be a fire in the royal hearth yet. Better get along.*

As Beornwyn paused, the door was opened and Edward of Wessex stood before her. She was shocked to see him in a simple nightshirt; the ermine and gold that the queen was careful to dress him in at any occasion, even the feast they had enjoyed that evening after the hunt, seemed as much a part of him as Edith's presence beside him. Looking beyond Edward into the little room, Beornwyn almost expected to see Edith waiting; but he was alone.

Edward took her hand and drew her into the chamber. As she looked around in awe at the rich furnishings, the bed with its fine covers, the tapestries on the wall with hunting scenes, he looked steadfastly at her.

'When you were in the hall, you were so like her,' he murmured. 'The fair hair, the blue eyes, the way you moved.

A Serving Girl

Serving at the other table, as you bent over to fill someone's cup, I saw you sideways on and I wanted to call out, "My love; is it you?" And yet I did not want to beckon you, to break the spell.'

A brush of his hand on her cheek brought Beornwyn back to look at him, gaping. *What is he talking about?*

The king laughed. 'You look amazed. Do not worry. The spell is broken, now I see you close up. You are not so like her, in truth. But for a moment…'

'My lord, I…' the girl stammered, 'I… what do you want of me?'

Edward took her by the hand and led her to the bed. He sat her down, and pulled up a stool to sit opposite, still smiling.

'Nothing that you are imagining,' he said gently. 'I am beyond all that; and besides, I would not sully her memory.'

'Whose memory?'

By now Beornwyn had grasped that he had not been talking about his queen, although the rumours about their lack of intimacy should have told her this already.

He shook his head, and for a moment he looked away, seeming lost in thought. Then he looked back.

'How old are you?'

'Seventeen. And a half.'

'Younger than her, by a little. And I was older than her, though not by much. Not married?'

'Was. He died.'

'Did you love him?'

'No.'

Beornwyn surprised herself to say this; yet there was something about the man, with his long, milky-white hair and his delicate features that eased her confession – and made her realise that she was listening to his.

'Then you will never have known what it is to love; to see someone, as I saw you in that hall, and to know in an instant that now and forever, this person will be the one thing that binds you to life. And to have that love returned, freely, without question, over and over; never asking if tomorrow might be the day it must end.'

'Did it? End?'

Edward's gaze dropped to the floor and she saw him wring his long, thin hands in distress. Faltering, he spoke slowly, without looking up.

'I was a prince. A throne and a kingdom were mine, if I wanted them. The here and now that we enjoyed, I was told, could not be the forever. When a child was born, it was taken away. She was… sent away.'

'You never saw her again?'

'She died. And with her, my ambition and the love I could have for any other woman died too.'

Moved by his sorrow, Beornwyn leant towards Edward and took his hands in hers.

'But you became a king. And a good king, too.'

He looked up, smiling, but she could see his tears.

'You are kind.' He paused. 'Will you pray with me?'

Before she could answer, Edward was on his knees, hands clasped. Awkwardly, she got down beside him, putting her hands together and watching as he prayed silently. Suddenly he collapsed in sobs, his body slumped and shoulders heaving, as he gave way to overwhelming anguish.

'She died from grief. And I was the cause.'

Beornwyn looked at him, aghast. Beside her, her ruler

and the most powerful man in the land was a wreck of misery, and she did not know what to do. Frantically, she searched her memory and found an image of her younger brother, distraught at the death of a sheep. Putting her arms round Edward, she pulled him to her body and held him, rocking the king gently, stroking the back of his head.

'There…' she soothed. 'Don't cry. We'll get you another one.'

Abruptly, Edward pulled away and got to his feet, glaring down at her.

'What? Do you mock me?'

'No! I'm sorry; I meant to say—'

'Get out!' The King's face was a mask of fury. 'You are nothing but a whore – sent to tempt me in my hour of weakness! A whore!'

Beornwyn scrambled clumsily to her feet, knocking over the stool. As she righted it, a thought occurred to her.

'The child – do you know what became of it?'

For a moment she thought the king was so angry he might hit her, as he stood in front of her, body swaying, fists clenched.

'Leave me! Get out, damn you!'

As Beornwyn fled from the chamber, Edward grabbed the stool and hurled it after her; it crashed against the doorpost and fell to the floor in pieces. Flinging himself on the bed, Edward buried his face in the covers, weeping.

'Oh, Wulfstan! Wulfstan!'

The Bridge

London, England, September 1051

Felip held up his hand and the oarsman stopped. The incoming tide and the outflowing Thames were almost in balance, and the rower needed only to hold the oars steady to keep the little boat in position in the water. Ahead of them, a pontoon of boats larger than theirs was lashed together, preventing any vessel from passing between the piles supporting the London Bridge. Above and beyond their boat, the wooden bridge – the only river crossing in London – was not busy, as it usually was, with the traffic of carts and oxen, of traders and merchants on foot or on horseback. On the north and south sides, the bridge was thronged with men. Men armed; men carrying the banners of the houses of Wessex on the London side, and of Godwin on the Southwark side. The space between them was empty, save for the occasional messenger scurrying across from one side to the other and back.

'Put me down,' said Felip.

The oarsman grunted. He had not wanted to come anywhere near the bridge; only the ring with the seal of King Edward that Felip wore had carried enough weight to make him do that. Like everyone at Thorney, he had heard about the growing confrontation between King Edward and Earl Godwin. A confrontation that had begun a month before, when a fight broke out between the citizens of Dover and the retinue of Eustace of Boulogne, returning from a visit to Edward, his brother-in-law. A fight that left some two score dead between both sides, and the king with an opportunity – for Dover was in Earl Godwin's country, and Edward had ordered the earl to devastate the town as punishment. He had refused, and the Godwins mustered their family's might from around England. Their forces came to Gloucester; but so did Edward's, and as the two sides faced each other, it had seemed there must be war between the king and England's most powerful family. But wiser counsel had prevailed; Edward did not press an attack, and the earl felt sure enough to come to London to face any charges against him in front of the *witan*.

All this was a distraction to Felip. He had served his year and a month helping with the work on Edward's abbey at Thorney, and he was anxious to leave. But Edward had been absent in Gloucester and when he had returned, it was to take up position to meet Earl Godwin in London itself. Well, if Edward would not come to him, he must find Edward. Felip scanned the north bank for a place to land.

The oarsman grunted again. 'Which side?'

'The king's, of course. Which damned side do you think?'

The man shrugged and began to row. Like many English who had listened to the story of the stand-off between king and noble, his instinct was to side with the Godwins. Too many foreigners had been given preference at Edward's court, or appointed to other positions. In March that year, a perfectly good Englishman had been overlooked for Archbishop of

Canterbury; a relative of, and supported by, Earl Godwin, who in this was only backing up the wishes of the monks of Canterbury themselves. Edward had overruled them all, and appointed Robert of Jumièges – his friend and mentor from his days in Normandy. But the oarsman also knew what everyone else did by now – that after the events at Gloucester, Edward had called out the *fyrd*, giving him a superior armed force and making the Godwins' support melt away, as men had to choose between king and rebel. As Godwin, Harold and his other sons made their way to Southwark, they had found Edward on the other side of the bridge holding the hostages he had demanded. The throng on the Southwark side was a Godwin show of strength, but now it was a show only.

Felip's ring, when he landed, served to take him through the crowd and to Edward's temporary headquarters in the small tollhouse a few yards back from the bridge. As he entered, the smell of the place reached his nose at once; stale food and sweat. A messenger brushed past him; he watched as the man began to hurry across the bridge, turning now and then to look uneasily behind him. Edward turned as Felip came in; to the monk, he looked to have the purpose of a much younger man, with bright eyes and a face that could have been set with anger, eagerness or both.

Felip bowed. 'My lord.'

He would have been less formal at Thorney, but the courtiers and soldiers around Edward were glaring at the monk who had dared to intrude on their King's plans and negotiations.

'Felip!' Edward embraced him, then turned to the others. 'See how he comes through thick and thin, to bring me news of my abbey?' Turning back to Felip, he asked, 'How does my West Minster proceed?'

'In truth, my lord, there has not been much work done these past weeks.'

'How so?'

'Many said I would find a new master when I came here to London.' Felip hesitated. 'Some even wished for it.'

There was an outcry from those behind Edward, and they pushed forwards, one reaching past the king to try and grab Felip. Edward shoved this man aside.

'Enough! He speaks only as he finds. Go on, Felip.'

'The Godwins are against any project of yours, my lord, as you are against any of theirs. It was likely that if they took power, the new abbey at Thorney would be cancelled.'

Edward nodded slowly. 'But as you see, Felip, I am still king here. Do you know what message that man you saw leaving here just now was taking?'

Felip shook his head.

'Godwin sent a message to me, suing for peace. "You may hope for my peace when you give me back my brother alive" was my counter,' said Edward grimly.

'But, my lord,' Felip said quickly, 'your brother lies buried with the monks at Ely. None can bring him back; not even the great Earl Godwin.'

Edward spread his long, thin hands. 'Indeed. The earl has gambled, and lost.'

Smiling, he turned back to those around him, who were muttering approvingly. Felip stared at him, open-mouthed.

'You think because you have won a battle, the war is over? You are a fool.'

Edward turned back, and the smile was gone. Behind

him, all were speechless with shock. *He called Edward a fool?*

'If you back the Godwins into a corner,' Felip went on, 'you will give them no choice but to fight you.'

Edward's eyes narrowed. 'Not if they are exiled. And I will exile them. The writs are being drafted even now.'

Felip gasped, and shook his head. 'Even worse. I have seen the Godwins; I have been in their manor at Bosham, watched them preening, heard them boast openly of being England's kings one day, one way or another. Exiled, they will lick their wounds. They will gather forces, and support. They will be back, and Englishmen who fear foreign domination will rally to them. You will rue this day, Edward.'

Uproar broke out behind Edward, with everyone shouting at once. Two men pushed past the king and seized Felip by the arms, dragging him to the ground. Blows rained on his face and body, until Edward's voice could be heard shouting above the din, and others pulled the men attacking Felip away.

'Silence!' Edward roared. 'Listen! The messenger has returned. The Godwins are leaving. It is over.' He looked down at Felip. 'I am King of England, and I will do as I please.'

Shouting filled the tollhouse again, but this time it was the sound of triumph. Men applauded, embraced each other and rushed outside onto the bridge to see what everyone else watching was seeing. Not a single Godwin banner was flying on the Southwark side of the bridge.

Slowly, Felip got to his feet, wiping the blood from a cut lip. Now the room was empty of everyone but England's king, he could see a table in a corner, with some documents on it, and food and drink. Edward had gone over to it, and was pouring himself a cup of wine. Felip stood behind him, brushing the dirt of the floor from his monk's habit. Edward poured another cup of wine, and turned back to offer it to the monk. Felip took it, but did not drink.

'You are wrong about the Godwins,' Edward said. 'I will stamp out this nest of vipers. As well as banishing the Godwin men, I will send my queen away, their kinswoman; they will not come by the throne through our loins, either.'

Felip raised his eyebrows, but said nothing, and took a drink. Edward was speaking again.

'After that, I need to consider who will succeed me. There is a nephew in exile on the continent, but who knows where. And he would still be a foreign king, in a land he does not know, at the mercy of the Godwins.' He paused, and at once his eyes filled with tears. 'If only I could name my son.'

Felip stared at him. 'You have a son? Who?'

Edward looked around the room, and leant in closer to Felip. 'Whose interest did I always have, in Normandy? Who have I sought to shield, from the nest of vipers, by sending him back there, to be protected by the man who I will name as my heir?'

'Wulfstan,' Felip gasped. 'Wulfstan – and you will make Duke William the next King of England. Why? And why not acknowledge Wulfstan?'

'William is kin to me, through my mother. He will rule with a rod of iron; he will obliterate the Godwins, if they oppose him. I cannot admit Wulfstan as my son – and you must never tell him, or anyone.' He grabbed the monk by the neck and pulled him close. 'I should not have told you. If you ever reveal this, I will have you killed.'

Feeling the grip on his throat, the blue royal eyes burning into his, Felip had a moment of panic, wondering if he was really hearing Edward, or still lying on the floor in a daze from the blows earlier. He thought on the stories he had heard in his time at Thorney; that Edward had been behind the sudden death of his predecessor Harthacnut. Felip dropped his cup, struggling to speak.

'I swear, I will never reveal it!'

Edward let him go. 'Then we are done here. Now I must clear up this mess. Go back to Thorney, and to my abbey.' He turned back to the table and drank from his cup.

Behind him, breathing heavily, Felip spoke slowly.

'I have served you as you wished, Edward King of England, and for the year and the month you demanded. I came here to ask to be released; and for help to regain the book you know I seek, that Hugh de Bayeux has in his possession.'

Edward turned again to Felip. 'If Hugh has property of yours, of course you must ask him for it. He is bound to give you it.'

'Thank you, my lord. You know what this book is, and what it means to the world. I said I would bring it to you, for your new abbey. I doubt Hugh will resist a few of the king's men, when we come to Berewic.'

But Edward was shaking his head; his long, white hair shook with it.

'I cannot spare men-at-arms at a time like this. I have more important things to think about.'

'My lord, Hugh will not easily let the book go. You have to help me in this!'

Edward's mouth fell open and his eyes widened.

'You come here and preach to me in front of your betters on how I should rule, and then demand my services for an errand? I cannot help you, you impudent monk. Damn you

– and damn your book!' he roared at Felip. 'Get out of my sight! If I ever see you again, or your book, I will have you both burned!'

Edward drained his cup, and slammed it on the table as Felip fled from the tollhouse.

Once outside, Felip headed across the now-empty bridge towards Southwark. On the other side, a burly soldier barred his way; Felip looked down to see a sword at his chest. Beyond this man, Felip could see a jostling throng, shouting and shoving to get down to the riverside, where boats were cramming the water's edge. Some of the men were falling in the water in their panic to get into the boats, with others throwing their weapons into them before clambering in.

'Who do you seek, monk?'

Felip looked down from the bridge at the disorder below.

'How can the Godwins be so easily overthrown? Have they nothing to bargain with?'

The soldier shook his head. 'Edward holds hostages against their return; two boys, Wulfnoth, youngest brother to Harold, and Hakon, the son of his brother Swein, by the Abbess of Leominster, they say.'

'Where are they going?'

'To Thorney,' the man answered, 'to gather such things as the earl has there at Edward's palace. Then to Bosham; after that, who cares?' He looked down at the river. 'But they need to hurry; the tide won't favour them for long to go upstream.'

'Then let me go with them. I have my possessions at Thorney too, and a refuge in Bosham that I need.'

The man looked at him, frowning; then put down his sword. Felip went to move past him, but the soldier moved across to block him. He held out a hand, palm upwards.

Felip pulled a purse from his tunic and dropped two coins from it into the palm.

The man grunted. 'If you weren't a Norman, and so in the king's good grace, I wouldn't let you go for so little.'

Pushing past him, Felip hurried on, calling back over his shoulder, 'I am from the Languedoc!'

*

In the tollhouse, Edward took a while to regain himself, eating and drinking from the table. Outside, there was noise – carts and horses beginning to cross the bridge again, and people running, cheering and shouting. From somewhere near, he heard a scream and a splash: a Godwin supporter, or suspected supporter, no doubt meeting his end in the Thames.

Inside, all was still. A shaft of sunlight came in through a window. From under the table, Edward heard a noise; he could not mistake the scraping of feet on the ground. Slowly, carefully, he lifted the cloth on the table, which hung to the floor. Blinking in the light, two pairs of eyes were looking up at him. They belonged to two children, boys of about eight and four years of age; well dressed and terrified.

'You can come out, boys,' Edward said. 'You are safe, but you belong to me now.'

A Parting

Forest of Valognes, Normandy, October 1051

Throw a stone into a pool and the ripples will spread far and wide, reaching shores distant in time and space. When the ripples from the Godwins' downfall reached William in Normandy, he decided he should prepare to visit King Edward. And he would take with him his trusted friend, Wulfstan of Wessex. Before he could leave, Wulfstan needed to pay a visit of his own; to the Forest of Valognes, and the clearing where William's forest warden lived with his daughter and her mother.

A week of unseasonal hot weather had left the forest suffused with a golden haze that hung in the very trees. In the sunshine, Estraya and Wulfstan had taken the path up through the pines and beeches, then followed it down to the marshland. Estraya began to skim stones across the water in front of her. Then she turned to Wulfstan.

'Why? Can Duke William not take another man?'

'I speak English; he doesn't.'

'I have hardly seen you since Val-ès-Dunes.'

'Nonsense! I have come here often; as often as I might.'

Wulfstan was in turmoil. He did not want to leave Estraya,

but he knew he could not refuse William. 'We won't be leaving yet; perhaps not till Christmas, when William has settled things with the Count of Anjou.'

'The Count of Anjou? My father told me he was put down by the King of France and excommunicated years ago, for seizing the Bishop of Le Mans.'

'He was. William rode at the king's side then, and I at his. But the count never let the bishop go, and lately he was invited into Maine, which borders on Normandy, as its new ruler. From Maine he invaded us, and took Alençon. Now William is laying siege to Domfront, in Maine.'

Estraya shook her head. 'I do not understand the world of men. One moves here, another moves there – like a game of chess, but with blood, and death.' She picked up another stone, and gave Wulfstan a mischievous smile. 'Should the pawn not be at the knight's side, just now, to help free the bishop, and the castle?' She poked him in the ribs with the stone in her hand.

Wulfstan looked puzzled. 'Pawn… you mean me? I am charged with the preparations for the visit to England; the ships, men and provisions, sending envoys, and so on. It's important work.'

Estraya turned away, and threw the stone. 'Well; don't let me keep you from your important work.'

Wulfstan looked abashed. 'I might be able to come again, before I go.'

'William will not let you come here again. You know that.'

'But I will not be away for long.'

Estraya shook her head and looked across the water, as if searching for something. 'You will meet another woman, and you will stay.'

Angrily, Wulfstan pulled her round to face him. 'Never! You are all I care for in this world.'

'More than William?' She was smiling impishly.

'This much more.' He pulled her into his arms and kissed her, long and hard. But he was looking over her shoulder, at the path back up through the trees.

'William loves you. You are like a brother to him. So you will go.'

Wulfstan looked at her, elfin-featured, dark eyes shining; and he wanted to fall into her very being.

'And you would keep me here, spirit woman of the forest, with your charms.'

Estraya laughed. Pulling out of his arms she went up to the water's edge. 'Let's go in.' In seconds she was out of her clothes and stepping in to the water.

As he watched her, Wulfstan saw the knife was still strapped to her ankle. He came to the water's edge and hesitated.

'I can't swim.'

'It's not deep – you can stand.' Already she was up to her thighs in the shallows.

Wulfstan undressed and waded awkwardly into the water, feeling mud and dead reeds under his feet. He stood beside Estraya, aware of his bright white skin next to her brown body. She went further out, threw herself full length and swam away from him, then turned, waving.

'See! I can still stand, here.'

Wulfstan took a couple of steps and put his foot on a log, nearly falling over, then retreated into shallow water. Estraya laughed and swam back, crouching in the water in front of him. She reached out a hand and traced a finger along the livid scar on his leg where the bone had been reset, smiling, as if remembering her younger self nursing him. The tenderness of her touch felt to him like the brush of a butterfly wing.

Suddenly, she pushed herself upright and jumped into his arms. As she wrapped her legs round his waist and her arms round his neck, she closed her mouth on his, and Wulfstan slowly fell backwards into the water. He came up spluttering, to see her astride him, laughing, rivulets of water running down her face and body, leaves and bits of reed stuck to her breasts and belly. Looking into the depths of her eyes, Wulfstan saw what Gilbert had seen in Samra that day in the square in Rouen – echoes of a distant land, under other skies. And like Gilbert, he felt himself taken up into something he did not understand, yet knew he would become a part of.

'Do not look to the path that will take you away from here, my love,' Estraya whispered softly, 'or think on tomorrow, taking you away from me. Be in the here and now; this is our time and place, and together we will take it.'

Wulfstan reached up, and pulled her body down towards his.

*

In the warm, shallow water, Estraya raised herself from Wulfstan's now dozing body, and looked into his face. How much he must have seen, in his young life, compared to her. The thrill of the chase; the terror of combat. Nobles and soldiers, servants and envoys, all passing before the guileless blue eyes, closed inches from her own. And she, eighteen years in a world bounded by no more than a few miles of trees, grass, rocks, streams and marshes, yet bearing a burden as great as any duke or king, passed down to her through the centuries. No great battle sword with glinting edge and bejewelled hilt; just a plain little knife, with three lines on its blade. Estraya brushed Wulfstan's lips with hers; the passion of not long ago replaced with the gentlest touch. Unbidden, a thought came to her.

What if Wulfstan's is the life I am meant to take?

The very shock of it seemed to still the landscape around her. The trees stopped their soughing, the ripples over the water behind her froze; the sun that had been warm on her naked body suddenly chilled. Slowly, she reached to her ankle for the knife in its sheath.

If I kill Wulfstan now, we will be together forever. He will never leave me, and the horror I foresaw in the pigpen will never happen.

Feeling her movement, Wulfstan stirred a little in his sleep. Trembling, Estraya brought the knife up to his chest. Behind Wulfstan's head, a lizard ran across the sand. It stopped a moment and fixed her with an unblinking eye before scuttling off. She took a deep breath and gently pressed the knife to the flesh where she knew his heart must be, seeing it indent slightly. A noise made her look up. In the trees beyond the water was a deer; a fallow doe, with scars on its neck. It stood looking at her with an intensity that belied its dark, animal eyes. Estraya looked down at her hand with the knife, and pulled it back; when she looked up, the doe was gone. Instantly, the sun was warm again on her back, and the wind played again in the trees and over the water.

'What's this?'

Estraya startled, to see Wulfstan wide awake and looking down at her hand with the knife by his chest.

'We should make a pact,' she said, half laughing with relief. 'You and I, together, always. Just a little cut on each of us, then mingle our blood.'

'All right.' Wulfstan sounded bemused. 'But not there.'

*

Next morning, Wulfstan was standing in the clearing by his horse, pulling the straps tight on the saddle, Estraya next to him. Gilbert and Samra were watching from the doorway of the house beyond.

Wulfstan finished the straps, and buried his face in the horse's neck, then turned to Estraya. 'I cannot go. I cannot leave you.'

She put her finger to his lips. 'You must go.'

Estraya reached up and kissed him, then turned away and ran towards Gilbert and Samra and the house. Wulfstan got on his horse, watching her go.

As Estraya went past, Samra put her arm out to stop her. Her daughter turned to look at her, and Samra could see the tears in her eyes.

'You know he would stay, for you,' she said.

Estraya shook her head. 'You know he cannot.' She pulled herself away and went inside.

Wulfstan rode away, unable to look back.

'May Magni be with you,' said Gilbert under his breath. 'God of strength, son of Thor.'

Samra went inside and found her daughter on the bed where they had tended the injured Wulfstan, sobbing. She lay down at her back, and put an arm across her, tucking the hand under, and gently stroking her hair with the other hand.

A Parting

'Wulfstan loves your hair, above all,' she murmured.

Estraya turned to her, wiping tears from her face.

'He has told you this?'

'More than once.'

'I always envied you yours, so dark and thick.'

Estraya took a length of her hair and laid it next to her mother's, which was now beginning to show some grey.

'He will come back, won't he?' she said suddenly.

'It is only a visit.'

'Last night I had a dream. Wulfstan was in a river, fighting with another man.'

In an instant, Samra was taken back to the day Alfred had come to the forest to tell her about Wulfstan, and the image that came unbidden as he did so. *In a village, in a river, two men fighting.* So Estraya could not see her face, she rolled on to her back. Taking her daughter's hand, she gave it a squeeze.

'It was just a dream.'

Estraya propped herself on an elbow and looked down at her mother.

'Wulfstan had the knife.'

An Arrival

Berewic, Sussex, November 1051

Guðrun pushed at the gate, but it would not move any further. Looking over the top bar, she could see it was stopped on the other side by a wooden peg hammered into the ground. She tried to lean over to pull it out, but could not reach. After her four years in the village, the stares and sniggers had died down, but not the occasional act of cruelty towards her. When open wide, the gate was no obstacle to her walk with the flung-out arm and swaying body; but part open like this, she would have to shuffle sideways through it, slowly and awkwardly, knowing someone was watching, and enjoying her distress.

Guðrun began to make crab-like movements through the gate, dragging her left foot after her, pressing back against the bars for more support. The sloping ground was rutted and churned from the passage of carts and animals, and wet from the rain. Guðrun felt herself slipping as she tried to inch sideways. With no choice now but to push hard into the ground with her turned-over left foot, spasms of pain were shooting up her leg. She moved the weight back to her right leg, but it slipped from under her, and she crashed to the ground, landing heavily on her side, before turning over face-down in the cold mud. In her distress, she did not make a sound; she would not give her watcher that pleasure.

Guðrun was still trying to grab on to the bars of the gate to pull herself up when she became aware of someone beside her. Turning her head with difficulty, she saw a man wearing a heavy, dark tunic, whose hair was shaved in the middle to leave a ring around his head. As he leant down to her, his hair flopped over one eye.

'Let me help you,' he said in an accent she could not place, but was not unlike that of her lord, Hugh de Bayeux.

The man was still trying to pull her upright when she heard Eadric calling from across the field.

'Guðrun!'

In a moment, he was at her side, shoving the other man out of the way, and getting his strong arms under her armpits to lift her to her feet. She stood holding on to the gate, breathing heavily, plastered in mud. Eadric turned on the man.

'What have you done! Is it not enough that everyone in Berewic mocks Guðrun, without a monk coming to chastise her? She is not the devil's work, whatever you see on her body.'

'I saw her from the road as I was coming into the village,' the man replied. 'If I took her for anything, it was a sheep caught in the gate, not a woman, under all that mud. But what I found when I came to help was one of God's creatures.'

Guðrun saw Eadric's shoulders relax, and his voice had softened when he spoke again.

'Then you have my thanks. And you are welcome to my home and hearth, if you are newly arrived here, unless you have somewhere else to go today. But first we must fetch our cow from the common, so that she is inside this night.'

Once the animal was collected, the three made their strange progress back to Eadric's house; he limping on one side of the monk, Guðrun with her laboured walk on the other, the little red-brown cow ahead of her. A conversation passed back and forth across Felip that he struggled to follow, and not just in speech – Osbern was right about the English – but in setting. The cow was in calf, but later than she should be, thanks to someone called Cuthred not letting them have access to a bull sooner. So the calf would be born into the summer, when the fresh grass to feed its mother had been hayed. It was a world away from Felip's life of church and cloister, book and bell, and timber and tape measure. And when Guðrun and Eadric spoke the name of the reeve of Berewic, there was an added chill in the November air.

Inside the house, Guðrun washed her face, then went behind the rough blanket that screened off her corner to change from her filthy clothes. On the other side, Eadric was feeding the fire; she could hear logs beginning to crackle in the hearth, see and smell the smoke as it rose to the roof hole. Eadric was speaking.

'I doubt Guðrun has seen a monk before. She had been eight years a slave when I bought her, kept in one room.'

'She is very fair – a Dane perhaps?' The monk had spoken.

'That may be. I do not know her full story.'

Guðrun tried not to remember. The village. Men coming. Her father, dead on the floor. Her brother dragged away, furious and helpless. The violence done to her mother, that she only later fully understood. Letting her dirty underdress fall to the floor, she shuddered.

'You have handfasted her, now?' the monk went on. 'Taken her to wife?'

'No.' Eadric sounded a little put out. 'Though I do not call her slave. She is worth more than that.'

'Indeed. I thought perhaps from the gentleness that you showed her, and her response, that there must be more between you.'

Behind the blanket, Guðrun looked down at her body, with its white, white skin. Cupping her hands under her breasts, she lifted them a little.

'She is strong, and capable,' Eadric was saying. 'And she reminds me of what has been done to me here, in the unkindness done to her, and her crippled state.'

Beyond her belly, on the floor, Guðrun could see her foot, turned and twisted. Quickly, she began to put on clean clothes. When she came out into the room, she saw Eadric and the monk seated at the trestle table. Eadric smiled at her.

'Good. Now you must go to the river and wash your clothes, before it gets dark. But first, fetch us bread and ale.'

Busying herself fetching a jug and two cups, then bread on a board with a knife, Guðrun made her swaying movements around the room, deftly avoiding fire and furniture. When she had cut two slices of bread, she stood with her hands on the table, watching Eadric pouring the ale. He paused, jug in hand, and looked up at her.

'Was there something else?'

She stared at him, ice-blue eyes fixed on his grey. *Say it now. Say you will handfast me*, she wanted to blurt out. But she shook her head and turned away. Grabbing the bundle of dirty clothes, she hurried from the house.

Eadric finished pouring and took a drink. He looked at the monk, who seemed familiar to him in a way he could not place.

'What brings a Benedictine to Berewic? You are a long

way from any abbey, and certainly a long way from your own, to judge from your accent.'

'True.' The monk finished a mouthful of bread, and continued, 'My own abbey is in Normandy. Lately I have been at the king's new abbey at Thorney. But we had a falling out at the time the Godwins were fleeing, and I came with them to Bosham, then here. They charged me to bring news of the family to one of their kin – the Lady Æadgytha.'

Eadric took a piece of bread and began to pull it apart.

'We had heard the Godwins were overturned,' he said slowly. 'Æadgytha has been troubled by this news. But the Godwins fled, you say? Where?'

'Edward has banished the whole family, and they are gone into exile; the earl to Flanders and Harold to Ireland. For good measure, Edward has confined his wife – Harold's sister – to a nunnery. It may be that Edward's vengeful gaze falls on your Æadgytha too.'

'She is married to a Norman, one of Edward's favourites that he made thegn, and gave Berewic as his manor. She should be safe. But she will be distressed to hear all this.'

'The Norman – is he Hugh de Bayeux?'

'Yes. You know him?'

'Knew him, in Normandy. What is his standing, in his manor?'

Thoughtfully, Eadric chewed on a piece of bread before speaking.

'He does not concern himself with Berewic, or its people. He pursues an obsession that costs greatly and brings nothing in return. And he and his wife are childless.'

The monk nodded. 'This obsession – is it to make gold from lead?'

Startled, Eadric answered, 'I am a peasant. I know nothing of what he does. And he pays the villagers who help him enough to buy their silence.'

Opposite him, he saw the monk take a drink. The monk stared into his cup a while before he said, 'Have you ever seen Hugh with a book?'

Eadric shook his head. 'A book, no. But what kind of book?'

The monk leant across the table, as if confiding in him.

'My book. A book of great power, and value. I used to study it in Normandy, where it was kept hidden by a woman, who also knew some of its secrets. But Hugh de Bayeux took it from her and brought it here. He is using it to pursue his obsession.'

Suddenly, Eadric realised. *The Forest of Valognes, where Wulfstan and I were taken as boys. Samra used to study in a book and write in it. You are Felip de Mazerolles, the monk that I remember seeing at Valognes, when both of you were with the book; but it was Samra's book.* He looked at Felip, who was again staring into his cup.

'So this is not so much about bringing Ædgytha news. You are here to regain… your book?'

'Yes. Can you help me?'

Eadric thought quickly. *The Godwins are gone, and Ædgytha must beware Edward now. But Berewic still belongs to Hugh. Anything that undermines him brings closer a day when I might regain my manor. Losing the book might be such a thing.*

'Yes. You may stay in my house as long as you need. But you will need to tread carefully; Hugh is a man of quick temper, and great strength. If the book is part of his obsession, and you come close to it, he will strike out.'

The monk smiled and reached across the table with a hand.

'I am Felip de Mazerolles, and I am already in your debt.'

'And I am Eadric,' Eadric replied, shaking the hand offered him.

'I knew an Eadric once, in Normandy. He would be about your age now. He was of the house of Wessex, with a claim, it was said, on Berewic.'

Eadric smiled. 'Eadric is a common name. The man you see is a *gebur*, with just thirty acres to his name in Berewic, tied to his lord's manor, and owns only what you see in this house around you.'

'And a slave,' Felip added.

The door opened, and in a rush of icy air, Guðrun was standing in the doorway, holding a wet bundle. She looked cold and wearied.

Eadric jumped to his feet, helping her into the house.

'Get these clothes round the fire,' he said, 'and warm yourself. I will bring food for you. Felip is staying with us a while.'

Guðrun nodded, and began to arrange the clean clothes on the hearthstones on the other side of the fire. Eadric threw more logs on the fire, and as the wood crackled and the flames rose between him and Guðrun, he turned back to Felip.

'No slave,' he said.

News

Berewic, Sussex, November 1051

'All of them?'

Æadgytha's face showed her dismay. She motioned the monk who had come from Normandy to sit down, then herself sat at the long table on the raised dais in the hall house. Around her, the space was hushed; the furnishings on the walls hung silent, as if they too had heard the news with a heavy heart. Even the fire in the hearth seemed to burn without any sound. Regaining herself, she went on.

'We had heard they were faced down at Southwark and scattered to their lands. But banished? Fled from England? All the Godwins?' Æadgytha put her head in her hands.

'I was at Bosham myself, when the earl left for Flanders with his wife and two of his sons, Swein and Tostig,' Felip said. 'Two other sons, Harold and Leofwine, fled west, making for Ireland. Wulfnoth is hostage to Edward against the Godwins' return, with Swein's son Hakon.'

Æadgytha looked up. 'And Edith?'

'Edward has sent his wife to the nunnery at Wilton.'

'The place of her childhood.' Æadgytha nodded. 'My poor cousin, obliged to marry a man she did not know, or care for.

Edith is an educated and cultured woman – she speaks four languages, Felip de Mazerolles; can you better that, for all the travels and learning you have just told me about?'

'Well, in fact…' Felip began.

'At least she is safe at Wilton. I will visit her there.'

She saw Felip's eyes widen.

'I would advise caution, my lady,' the monk said hesitantly, 'until Edward regains his calm. He has a lust to destroy the Godwins, and being buried away here at Berewic will not save you.'

Æadgytha smiled. 'You find my manor small and uninteresting, Felip. Yet Edward has been here; he and I have been hunting together. We know each other; it was he who gave me as wife to Hugh de Bayeux. Hugh is his friend. I do not fear Edward, or his wrath. But I will wait a while.'

Felip looked around him. 'What you have here is solidly built and well-ordered, my lady. If Cerisy is as thriving when it is completed, I will be satisfied.'

'You are kind, Felip. I have built on what my father achieved here, and there have been hard times to endure. Yet I can admit to some pride for myself. Is that a sin, in the mere wife of a thegn?'

'Not at all, though…' Again the monk was hesitating; Æadgytha wondered what was to follow. 'I have known Hugh a long time – almost twenty years.'

'Twenty years?' Æadgytha tried to imagine. 'Hugh must have been a boy!'

'A young man, and I was not much older.'

'What was he like?'

'Strong. Brave. Determined.'

'Determined how?'

'If Hugh de Bayeux had a purpose, he would not swerve from it.'

Æadgytha felt on her finger where the wedding ring should have been.

'Then, as now.'

If only I were part of his purpose. What has he been told, this Benedictine? Does he judge me, in my childlessness, and my failure to keep my husband grounded in his manor?

Æadgytha saw Felip shuffling in his chair. The hair had flopped over one eye, and he brushed it back with a nervous flick.

'Tell me what is on your mind,' she said.

'Does Hugh have a book? It may be wrapped in a cloth and kept in a box.'

Felip was looking at her, and she saw a light in his eyes. The same light Hugh had whenever he was near the book; in the eyes that, the rest of the time, were dead.

'Yes, though he does not let me see it. You know this book?'

Felip let out a long sigh. 'It is mine. Hugh took it from me in Normandy.'

'And you have come to take it back.'

'I know what he uses the book for, what his purpose is. He will not succeed.' There was a hardness in the monk's voice as he went on. 'The book has a greater purpose. It must be restored to that purpose, and to me.'

Æadgytha nodded. 'If it brought Hugh back to the world, and to me, I would help you. But I fear you would unleash a fury in him that would destroy us all. You cannot know what he would do to pursue his goal.'

'I think I can. But… is the book here?' Again, she saw a flash of light in his eyes.

'He keeps it in our chamber.' Æadgytha stood up and nodded towards the door on the far side of the hall. 'But I do not know if it is there now, or if Hugh has taken it for one of his experiments.'

'May I look?' Felip's voice was shaking. He was already on his feet.

Alarm flooded through Æadgytha. *I should stop him.*

'Wait. Let me see if it is there. Hugh hides it away; you will not know where you might find it.'

Heart racing, she made to go to the door to the chamber. *Is this happening? Am I letting the book go? What will become of me if I do?* Felip was following her.

There was a noise behind her. She and Felip turned at the same time.

Hugh de Bayeux burst in through the door to the hall house, dishevelled, wild-eyed and breathing heavily. A dog followed him in, as filthy as he was, and flung itself down by the hearth. Æadgytha glanced at Felip; she was used to her husband's appearance but she could see the monk's astonishment as he moved to stand behind her.

Yet there was something different, this time; Hugh had news, she could tell.

Is Felip wrong? Has Hugh succeeded?

Throwing himself on a chair at the table, Hugh looked up at her.

'A messenger is here. William is coming from Normandy. Edward cannot receive him in London – he has gone to be with his mother at Winchester. So Duke William will come to Berewic first.'

With difficulty, Æadgytha recovered herself.

'Then we must make ready. The hall must be cleared out

and food brought in. And Duke William likes to hunt, does he not?'

'There is no hurry,' Hugh said. 'He has yet to leave Normandy.'

But he was looking past her, at Felip, who was standing open-mouthed, looking at him.

'Felip de Mazerolles. Why has it taken you so long to come here?'

Felip bowed slightly. 'I bring a message from the Godwin family to one of their own.'

A servant came in, and Hugh ordered food and wine to be brought.

'The Godwins? How did you get mixed up with them?'

'I seemed to incur Edward's rage at the same time as they did.'

Hugh put his feet on the table and leant back in his chair, arms behind his head.

'Well, deliver your message. We will not keep you; I am sure you are needed in Normandy. How goes that abbey of yours?'

'It makes progress, I hope. I have not seen it for almost two years.'

Æadgytha looked uneasily from her husband to the monk and back. 'Felip has been helping with the abbey at Thorney, Edward's West Minster,' she said. 'We should go and see it, perhaps.'

The servant returned, and placed food and a flagon of wine on the table, with three cups. Taking his feet off the table, Hugh began to eat noisily; he motioned to Æadgytha and Felip to join him, but both declined.

'I am too busy here to go to Thorney,' Hugh said, between mouthfuls of food. 'So, what is your news of the Godwins?'

Felip said again what he had told Æadgytha; the names and their destinations, adding only that he thought he had been told Ireland, but he was not sure.

'You know why they went to Ireland?' Hugh asked, pouring a cup of wine and taking a drink. 'Slaves. The Godwins do a great trade with Ireland in slaves. It makes them very, very rich. Æadgytha's family's wealth is founded on trading in humans, like cattle.' He jabbed a finger at her. 'Isn't that right?'

Æadgytha looked uncomfortable. She began to say something, but Hugh cut across her.

'It is no matter now. Æadgytha may be the only Godwin left in England, save for Harold's bastards. And if Duke William is in England, it can mean only one thing.'

'What is that?' Felip asked.

'That it is true; Edward means to make William the next King of England.' He drained his cup and got up from the table. 'Now I must go; I have work to do before it gets dark.' He came over to Felip and stood before him, his bulk looming over the squat figure of the monk. 'You may stay with us this night, if you have nowhere else. We can see you on your way in the morning.'

Æadgytha could not mistake the threat in Hugh's voice. 'Felip is lodged in the village,' she said quickly.

Hugh de Bayeux paused, still looking down at Felip. Then he whistled for his dog, turned, and strode from the hall.

Æadgytha looked at Felip; he was clearly shaken. 'You need to be wary,' she said to him. 'Hugh will not brook your presence in Berewic.'

The monk shook his head. 'It is more than that. I promised Duke William before I came here that I would be an emissary for him with Edward and bring him news of Hugh. And that I would bring the book back to him. If he thinks I have failed him, he will not tolerate it.'

Pouring a cup of wine, Æadgytha brought it to him. 'Then you must leave, as Hugh believes you will, tomorrow.'

Felip drank a little, and shook his head. 'I cannot. I am so close to the book.' He glanced across to the door of the chamber. 'I need only one opportunity. Help me; please.'

Æadgytha put her hand to her forehead. She knew the risk; what would Hugh do, if he were parted from the book? Yet if he were rid of it, and its hold over him could be broken… Dropping her hand from her face, she took Felip's free hand with it.

'Gather your things from wherever you are staying. Tell them you are leaving Berewic. Then meet me at the church. The priest knows how destructive Hugh's obsession is for all of us here. He will hide you.'

'Thank you… thank you!' Felip kissed her hand. 'And then?'

'When William is here,' Æadgytha said firmly, 'we will all be engrossed. At some time or other, Hugh will have to look away from the book. When he does, I will tell you.' She took the cup from him, and drank deeply from it. 'And then, God help us.'

*

It did not take Felip long to take his leave of Eadric and Guðrun. Eadric was sorry to see him go, he said; Felip sensed the woman was not so unhappy. As he headed to the church, his way taking him close to the paddock where Hugh and

Æadgytha's horses were kept, he saw Hugh talking to a young man who was feeding another horse. From his livery, Felip realised this must be Duke William's messenger. Felip paused, keeping out of sight. Hugh's manner with the man was animated, even overbearing; several times he jabbed at him with his finger. Then Hugh gave him something, patted him on the back and strode off, his dog following close behind.

The Butcher of Alençon

Rouen, Normandy, December 1051

Gilbert and Samra were in Rouen, making their way up a long staircase, at the top of which armed men stood guard in front of a large studded door. These men looked at the couple questioningly; the warden from the forest, craggy and weather-beaten, and the woman with him, tall, dark and angular. At a voice from beyond the door, the men-at-arms made way, and Gilbert and Samra passed into a large room with a high ceiling. The same splays of weapons and rich tapestries with scenes of battle and hunting which had greeted Wulfstan on the day he pledged himself to William were on the walls. A powerfully built man with a full face, at twenty-four much younger than them, rose from a high-backed chair and came swiftly towards them. This man, who Samra had last seen in the year of his victory at Val-ès-Dunes, embraced Gilbert, and in the look William of Normandy gave her while his forest warden was in his grasp, Samra remembered what Gilbert had told her before they left the Forest of Valognes.

He has suffered another rebellion, another invasion. Be cautious; it will have damaged him.

'Gilbert! You have come quickly, and I am grateful to you.'

William looked again at Samra. 'At least you had a companion on your journey. I hope you were both rested last night and fed this morning?'

'Thank you, my duke,' Gilbert replied, 'we have had comforts in your palace we are not used to in our forest. And thank you, that you made Samra welcome to come with me. She'll be able to make visits in the town.'

'Of course. I understand that she wants to be with her own people when she can.' Now William addressed Samra. 'You will find, I hope, that the Jews prosper under my rule. As long as they do not incite uprising, or join in it, or act against any Christian, they will have my benevolence.'

Samra nodded. 'I have heard it is so.'

If William was expecting an expression of gratitude, it did not follow, and Gilbert felt obliged to fill the silence that hung between them all.

'News of your victory at Alençon is on everyone's lips, my duke. I share in their relief that the siege is ended, and that the townspeople there have thought better of declaring for Anjou.'

'Alençon submitted, and Domfront followed soon after. Two victories for the price of one, Gilbert. Worth a celebration, eh?'

Gilbert nodded. 'I came at your summons, my duke. What would you have me do? Escort you to the Forest of Valognes? It's ready for you.'

'Of course it is, of course it is.' William patted his warden's arm. 'No, Gilbert; I thought to rejoice in my victory with a hunt at the Forest of Lyons.' His face darkened. 'But when I got there, all was disorder. The man I had placed in charge, nephew of the man who replaced you, was too much in his cups to bother himself with my hunting grounds. We got less than a day's chase, and barely any game to show for that.'

Gilbert's mouth had fallen open but he was wordless; clearly, he could not conceive of such neglect. Samra, however, was occupied with another thought.

Is he going to move us back to Lyons?

'That man is no longer in charge,' William went on, 'another is. But he is young, and though willing, he needs a guiding hand. Take a few days, go to the Forest of Lyons, and give what help and learning you can. For the man who made the Forest of Valognes and helped build Cerisy, it should not be too much work.'

Gilbert bowed. 'You do me a great honour, my duke. Of course I will go.' He hesitated. 'Indeed, if I am to make the most of my time, I should leave shortly.'

'I expected as much. All is ready for you; go as soon as you like. Samra may stay here, while you are away. I am a simple man, and no philosopher, but there are many things she and I can talk about.'

Holding out the hand with his ring, William gave Samra the look he had given her when he was embracing Gilbert, and again it made her uneasy. But Gilbert broke into a broad smile, as he rose from kissing the ring.

'Give me a few days, my duke. Then Lyons will be as it was.'

Clasping Samra in his arms, he spoke in her ear.

'Enjoy the comforts of this place, my love, and the town. All too soon we'll be heading back to Valognes, and the draughts and the snow. You will be all right.' It was almost a question.

'Yes, yes. Just go.'

Samra was half laughing, and pushing him away, but there was sorrow in her eyes. Since Gilbert's time in Cerisy, she had become unhappy at his absences, of any length, although she would never have told him this. He turned, and his long stride took him from the room. In the silence that closed after him, Samra felt a nameless panic sweep over her. But William was speaking, and she turned to him.

'Sit, please.' He motioned her to a chair near his own and sat himself in his, looking at her. 'Who will you visit today?'

She felt a relief to focus on something mundane.

'Well, there are many in the quarter who were good to me when first I came to – came back to – Rouen, after I went with Gilbert to the Forest of Lyons. But one woman was – is – dear to me above all the others. She understood what I had lost.'

'The book?'

Samra was startled. *What does he know of the book?*

As if he had heard her thought, William went on, 'Felip told me about it. Hugh de Bayeux stole it from you and took it to England with him.'

'Yes.' She dropped her head and her voice was a whisper. 'And there it remains.'

William got to his feet, and paced a little into the room, before turning back to Samra.

'Felip told me I should fear the book, as should any ruler in Christendom. Why?' His voice was hard, and his grey-green eyes were searching as he looked down at her.

Samra shuffled a little in her chair. Thoughts raced through her mind. *Could he be part of this story? Surely, that is impossible…*

'Imagine,' she said, 'if the power that you wield, the power that has you race from border to border in your own lands, in constant fear of attack and insurgence, was of a different kind.'

'Go on.'

'If it was the power to bring to peoples' lives the blessings of knowledge; the whole world and its materials at your service, to do good.'

'The knowledge of the scientists?'

'Yes. And if realising this knowledge existed at the service of all, all bowed to it, and gave up their own allegiances, and squabbles.'

'No kings?'

'None but that rule through the power of knowledge alone.'

'Does God have no part in this?'

'It is all for God. But there can be no intermediaries. Man, science, God; that is the new trinity.'

William nodded slowly. 'Well, I will see for myself, when Felip brings me the book.'

Samra looked at him in astonishment. 'Felip? Felip said he will bring you the book?'

'I charged him with this task while he is in England.'

Samra laughed; a laugh of disbelief but also of relief, that this soldier and ruler of a dukedom could be so taken in. He was indeed a simple man.

'Felip is deceiving you; he will not bring you the book. He wants it for himself. It has done to him what it does to all who spend too long with it; taken over his soul. His purpose is to use it for his own ends.'

William moved to her chair and leant over her.

'I abide you, for the love I have for my forest warden,' he

said calmly. 'And I tolerate your learning, like that of all who claim science as theirs, for what it might one day do for me. In three days I will go to England, and Felip will deliver me the book; or I will find it for myself. But Felip should not thwart me, nor should you make me uncertain in my faith.' He straightened, and motioned to the door. 'Now, go and find your people. I will expect you here at nightfall. We will talk more tomorrow.'

*

The same day, Samra walked through a frosty Rouen on her way to the Jewish quarter. She remembered herself from nearly twenty years before, being pushed on through the streets and the alleys with their houses crowding in, by the captain who believed that she had nearly wrecked his ship. She remembered not the cold, grey sky that was above her now, but the summer sun burning on her back where the pole was tied across it, and to her arms at the wrists, so that she staggered under its burden, felt it chafing her flesh. She remembered the stares and the jeers of the onlookers, and the gathering number of townsfolk who had followed captive and captor into the market place.

Suddenly here she was, in the market square itself. The centre was empty; only a few people crossing to go to or from one stall or another round the outside. She heard the calls of the traders as they presented their goods, the meat and the leather, the cloth and the metalwork, and smelt the same smells she had then. The space seemed to her too small to have held the throng it did that July day, when she had been brought here to be sold.

Samra shuddered; she felt that eyes must be on her now as then, in the otherness of her race. But no one paid her any heed. Moving to the centre of the square, she stood on the spot where she had stood that day, and saw again in her mind's eye the tall man, pushing his way through the mob towards her and to the foot of the platform. She recalled looking up, dizzy from pain and thirst, and seeing him pay Jaco, then mount the platform steps and come towards her. Recalled looking into his blue eyes; eyes that had looked straight back into hers, pitying and curious at the same time.

You and I will be connected, in this story, a voice in her head had spoken. *As the chapters unfold; now and forever connected.*

Samra remembered the cutting free, the bread and water, the descent into the baying crowd. And Felip – suddenly Felip had been there, her betrayer at the mountain pass in Spain. A flicker of hatred went through her now as she thought of him, in England with the book. Then she felt a spasm of shame at this feeling.

Felip is not to blame; if he has fallen prey to the power of the book, he will pay, as I did. And Felip is part of this story, too. Nothing happens but for a purpose.

*

A short while later, Samra was knocking on the door of a small house on the right bank of the River Seine. The servant who answered showed her into a darkened room, and a woman stepped out of the shadow towards her. When Samra had first met her on her visits to Rouen from the Forest of Lyons, Miriam Bonafoy had been, like her, a woman in her early twenties, with a young child. They had both been surprised, then, how different they looked – Samra tall, dark, angular, and Miriam short, with fairish hair and rounded face and figure. Only their dark, dark eyes had connected them. Now, the woman who greeted her had hair flecked with grey, and moved slowly as she held out her arms to take Samra's hands in hers.

'Samra! How long has it been?'

'Over fifteen years since I came to tell you I was moving to the Forest of Valognes.'

'How sad I was that you were leaving, and how anxious you were, to be uprooting yourself to go into the wilds of the Cotentin. But you are well? You have thrived? Is Gilbert still the duke's forest warden? Your daughter – what was she called? Did you have other children?'

'So many questions!' Samra laughed, and the years seemed to roll back, to when they were sat in that room, talking about family, and reading together. 'Estraya is our only child, and Gilbert is still warden at Valognes.' The servant returned with wine and lit candles before leaving them. Miriam bade Samra sit at a table with her, where she poured wine into two cups. 'And you,' Samra went on, 'how many children?'

'Five. Three lived; two sons, though one has poor health. Our daughter is soon to be married.'

Samra looked around her, as if to see signs of childish things in the room still, as the candlelight grew stronger and the dark corners came into view. But among the sturdy, dark furniture and on the walls were only the trappings of wealth – gold and silver ornaments and beautifully embroidered hangings, here and there the glint of a jewel, and, centre on a wall, a bronze mirror dimly reflecting her image. It was wealth that was careful to hide itself at home, not to flaunt itself on the streets. Where the children of Israel mixed with the descendants of the Vikings, tolerance went only so far, and smouldering resentment was easily fanned into the flame of vicious hatred. Only twenty-five years before she had come to Normandy, Samra knew, that flame had consumed many of Rouen's Jews; Miriam's own grandmother was among the women who had thrown themselves into the river to escape the violence of the mob, and drowned. She drank from her cup, and saw that Miriam was looking at her.

'You have been through much, I can tell,' said her friend.

'The forest is not an easy place.' Samra looked at her hands, and at her twisted fingers. 'Though Gilbert has made it as comfortable as he can. And Estraya loves it; she is rooted in it like a tree.'

'I meant in other ways. The book – the monk never gave it back to you?'

'He did. Then another man took it, and I am ten years without it again.'

Miriam reached across the table and took her hand.

'I am sorry. I know what it meant to you. But the knife?'

Samra's face brightened. 'Estraya has it. She is its keeper now. Perhaps my work is done.'

'You do not believe that, I can tell. The purpose you told me the book has… though it terrified me, you will see it through.'

Samra nodded, and at once a terrible anguish came over her, a fusion of sadness and tiredness. She thought of what had happened in the past, of her age now, and of what lay ahead. Images floated in her mind: the mountain pass, the transit of Venus, Wulfstan leaving for England. And faces: Felip, Edward, Hugh de Bayeux, Estraya. Now Miriam was in front of her, and Samra was sobbing in her arms.

'I do not have the strength to go on. Let me stay here, among my own people.'

Miriam held her for a while, rocking her gently.

'Oh, my dear. My dear… of course you will go on.' Letting go, she held Samra now by the arms, and looked into her friend's tear-stained face. 'You are an Abravanel. And what would Gilbert do without you?'

Samra thought of Gilbert, probably now rattling along to Lyons in a cart like the one he had taken her there in, and smiled.

'I don't know.'

Miriam sat again at the table and took a drink. 'Then you must think how you will get the book back.'

Samra shook her head. 'The book is in England, and Felip – the monk – has gone after it, though I doubt he will bring it back to William.'

'Duke William? The duke knows of the book?'

'Felip told him of it, and William commanded Felip to bring the book to him.'

'Let us hope your Felip did not tell the duke too much of the book's purpose.'

With a pang of alarm, Samra recalled her meeting with William earlier that day. 'What he did not tell, I fear I have.'

Miriam looked horrified. 'William knows? Knows about the ruler, and the foretelling?'

'About the ruler; not about the knife or my part in the story. And I believe I know what that part is now.'

Miriam leant across the table and whispered, 'Tell me.'

Samra shook her head. 'It is only a feeling. And, friend as you are, I cannot tell you, any more than I could tell William.'

Taking her hands, Miriam said firmly, 'To have told the

duke even what you did… he is dangerous. At least he is here, and the book is in England.'

'William is going to England. He means to see the book for himself. But dangerous? In the defence of his country, he has had to be strong; he is loved for this. He is a good friend to Gilbert and a pious Christian. What I told him of the book unsettled him, but I cannot think he would harm us.'

'Harm? Let me tell you what harm this duke is capable of.' Samra looked at her friend and saw that her eyes were full of distress. 'You have heard of his triumph at Alençon?' Miriam went on. Samra nodded. 'When he reached Alençon, it was dawn. The gates of the town were closed to him, of course, and he turned to the fortress. As he began his siege of it, the defenders shouted insults from the walls at him. Then they beat on the hides that protect the tops of the towers, and called him a pelterer.'

Samra frowned. 'I don't understand. Why would they call him that?'

'His mother's family, who had been undertakers in Falaise, would have worked with animal skins. Some say – though few dare say it – they may even have been Jews. At any rate, the slur on the duke was great. He said nothing, but had his men mount the siege twice as quickly. The fortress soon fell to them, and William ordered that thirty-two of the defenders be taken in front of the town gates. As the townsfolk watched from the walls, the hands and feet of these men were cut off. Alençon surrendered at once. This is your beloved duke.'

Samra gasped and pulled a hand free of Miriam's to put it to her mouth. 'And Domfront followed. They knew what he would do to them.' She felt her friend's hand tightening its grip on her other hand.

'When does William go to England?' Miriam asked her.

'In three days.'

'You must not go back to the duke's palace before he leaves,' Miriam said urgently. 'Stay with us.'

'What if he searches for me here?'

'Then we will find other houses where you can hide, and if Gilbert comes back from Lyons meanwhile, we will intercept him, so you and he can return to Valognes together.'

Samra nodded. 'You should not put yourselves in danger.'

'It is nothing. Just pray that the butcher of Alençon does not find your book while he is in England.'

A Feast, a Thief, and a Pledge

Berewic, Sussex, December 1051

William had come to Berewic; his ship was tied at the quay, as once the ship of Harold had been, and that of Earl Godwin before him. Taking advantage of the banishment of the Godwins, the Duke of Normandy had sent word to King Edward, who had invited him to England; but now Edward was gone to Winchester to be with his mother Emma in her final days, for Ethelred's widow, who had once astonished England by marrying his victorious enemy, was dying. So William, her great-nephew and head of the family which had sheltered Edward and the other English exiles in Normandy, was now in the hall house of a Godwin – Æadgytha, whose father had murdered one of those exiles when he came back to English soil with Edward's brother. But that was long ago. Now the Godwins were diminished, the Norman faction was in charge, and William was visiting a Norman that Edward himself had installed at Berewic; Hugh de Bayeux, his old hunting partner, married to Æadgytha – and Hugh had the book.

The hall house was decked out for Christmas, and the hearth was piled with blazing logs. The flames roared upward, and the hot air and smoke flew out through the roof hole into the cold night air. Cauldrons suspended over the fire from the rafters bubbled and steamed. Hugh and Æadgytha sat together on chairs behind the table on the raised dais along one of the long walls. William sat with Wulfstan, who was beside Æadgytha, while beside Hugh sat the leading men of the village, including Cuthred the reeve and Father Brenier the priest. Along the long wall on the other side of the hearth, the freemen of Berewic, including the jurors from the hallmoot, sat on benches on one side of a trestle table, opposite William's men, among whom Eadric had been given a seat. In the warm, smoky room the ale and mead flowed, stew was ladled from the cauldrons, and bread was broken on the tables.

*

In the crypt of the church, Felip pulled on a piece of bread Father Brenier had left him and shivered. For a week he had stayed hidden, crammed into a space beside the tomb that held Æadgytha's father, Sighere. William and some of his party had come in to the church to pray every day and Felip had feared discovery; but no one came down into the gloom of the crypt, lit as it was by only three small windows at ground level on the north, east and south sides. Now he was counting the hours on a candle Æadgytha had brought him, waiting until he could make his move. The candle was set on the tomb, and as he watched it burn down, he reflected on the man lying within; the Godwin who had killed Rædmund the old Thegn of Berewic on the day that Alfred had been taken captive. He remembered the shock that went through Normandy when the news reached them; the disaster of the failed return of the Wessex, and the treachery of the Godwins. And now a Godwin was hiding him in the church, and when Æadgytha had come to bring the candle that day, it was to tell him this night would be his chance at last to take the book, and to give him all the help she could.

'Hugh will be with me in the hall house, feasting with William and the others who are invited. I will leave the shutter open on a window to our chamber. When you find the book, take it to the paddock by the hall house. Take Hugh's black stallion; it is strong and fast, and the loss of it will slow him down if he is pursuing you. But be hasty in everything you do; the sooner you escape Berewic, the better,' she had said.

At last the candle reached the mark. Felip swallowed the last piece of bread, and made his way out of the crypt.

*

In the hall house, William was breaking his bread. He turned to Wulfstan.

'What do you see?'

Wulfstan looked around. 'A feast.'

William shook his head. 'If you are to handle men, you need to observe them, Wulfstan. Observe and understand. Then you will know what to expect of them, how to manage them.'

'And what do you see?'

William looked past him to Æadgytha. Hearing but not understanding the French they were talking, she smiled at him, then looked away.

'I see a woman who is beautiful yet unloved. I see her

strong for the sake of her people, to whom she is the real lord here. I see her fearful of the future, yet determined to keep what is hers. I see her, like me, taking in the people in the room around her; seeing who talks to who, and how. Now she is looking at a man she gave land to here, who is looking at his brother beside me, who he last saw eight years ago. Another man at our table, who serves that woman as her reeve in Berewic, is looking at the first man, who he despises. And I see another man at our table; he also had a brother, and the man beside me killed him. Yet I cannot tell how that sits with him, for this man that I chased the deer with as a boy in Normandy is the ghost of a man who now chases shadows here in Sussex. Change places with Hugh, Wulfstan; I will talk to him, if I can.'

Wulfstan leant back and spoke to Hugh, who rose, and they swapped seats so Wulfstan was now on the other side of Æadgytha. As he took his seat she levelled her gaze at him, and her hazel eyes looked into his; the frightened but determined girl he had confronted in this very hall replaced by a woman of flawless serenity and authority. She smiled at him and suddenly his English deserted him, leaving him speechless.

'What a difference eight years can make, Wulfstan.'

Her voice was calm and soothing, and he reddened a little to recall how he had spoken to her then. Æadgytha smiled all the more. Wulfstan thought of his Estraya, back in the forest, a girl lively and mischievous, appealing. But this was a woman, poised and graceful, achingly attractive.

*

William was talking to Hugh.

'What can so occupy a man in an English manor that he goes ten years with no word to a friend?'

Hugh stared at the table in front of him, toying with his knife. 'Is it only ten? It feels like fifty in this place.'

'And if you make gold, will God give you fifty years more life? Or a child?'

Hugh looked at him. 'The gold is only a means to an end. It will unlock the secret to so much more; to immortality itself, perhaps.'

'Is that what your book tells you?'

'Who told you about the book? Samra?'

'A little. And Felip. Both of them, just a little. But Felip said also that the book has a purpose that I and any ruler should fear.'

'Felip!' Hugh scoffed. 'Felip is a scoundrel and a Cabbalist. He came here days ago, looking for the book. I sent him packing.' William's searching gaze did not waver, forcing Hugh to continue as he fiddled with the knife in front of him. 'The book is a curiosity. A collection of haphazard thoughts, and so-called secret knowledge. I test my Arabic here by reading it.'

'So your goal is not gold, or immortality?'

'Someone once told me that the path is the goal. Let me amuse myself on the path, my duke, I beg you.'

William leant in towards him. 'Bring me the book, Hugh. I will see for myself.'

*

Felip opened the shutter, and eased himself through the window into the chamber. On the other side of the wall, he could hear the hubbub of voices as the feasters ate their way through the food and drank their way through the drink. The smell was reaching him as well; his stomach yearned for the good things it came from. He gritted his teeth, opened the shutter wide to let in the moonlight, and began his search for the box with the book.

*

At the table in the hall, Wulfstan managed to speak to Æadgytha at last.

'Berewic is a tribute to your lordship. I doubt it could have prospered without you.'

'There have been hard times. I hope they are behind us. But it must be strange to you, to be in the place you and your brother so wanted to claim for your own.'

'As hard as it must be for you, to be in the presence of the man who claims England for his own.'

Æadgytha looked across the room. 'You should talk to your brother.'

*

In the chamber, Felip was trembling. The book was there; he knew it. He could almost smell the leather and the parchment, almost feel the pages between his fingers, with their script and their diagrams.

But where is it?

He felt along a shelf on a wall; some trinkets, but no

book. The shelf would have been too narrow, in any case. There was a chest and a table with some of Æadgytha's things on it; a comb, and a brooch or two, but no book. Felip opened the chest to find it full of clothes. He rummaged in it until at the very bottom he found a blue gown, discoloured and fraying. *It must have been Æadgytha's wedding gown.* Breathing heavily, Felip sat on the bed. A knock on the wall between the chamber and the hall made him jump. *If Hugh decided to come in here now, Æadgytha could not stop him.* Moving his feet back to stand up, Felip felt his heel kick wood. He reached down and pulled out a box. When he picked it up and opened the lid, in a shaft of moonlight he saw a cloth, decorated with a moon and stars.

*

Wulfstan rose and went across the hall to where Eadric was seated. As he came up behind him, Eadric got to his feet, and the two exchanged a cold embrace. Eadric felt the bulk of the man he was holding, his strong frame and well-rounded upper body. Wulfstan felt Eadric lean and sinewy in his arms, slim but strong for all that. Soldier and farmer embracing.

They looked at each other a moment before Eadric spoke. 'You look well, brother.' He nodded in William's direction. 'Being servant to another man clearly suits you.'

'Working another man's land must suit you likewise. I hear you prosper.'

'I do well enough, at last. It has not always been easy. I cannot count on any man to feed me, as you might.'

Ignoring the jibe, Wulfstan shrugged. 'I am well looked after, though God knows I have to work for it. William is beset by rebellious nobles, throwing up castles and holding out in them. But tell me, do you hunger after Æadgytha's manor still?'

Eadric's voice was cold. 'I am a patient man, as you know. Eight years is not long in our handlings with Berewic and the Godwins.'

Wulfstan changed the subject. 'I saw you in your fields today, with your slave. I could hardly mistake her.'

He took a step back and mimicked her gait; the hobble and the arm thrown out. Eadric's eyes narrowed to slits.

'I am slave to no man; nor is Guðrun. Now if you do not mind, brother, I have done with the favour that allowed me to eat in this place. And no doubt you need to get back to your master.'

He turned and limped away. Watching the exchange from the other side of the hearth, Cuthred smirked.

Hugh de Bayeux had left the hall, leaving an empty seat between William and Æadgytha. As he turned to come back, Wulfstan saw his duke lean across and take Æadgytha's hand and hold it, as if to comfort her. Wulfstan stopped. Æadgytha looked surprised, but did not pull her hand away.

*

Outside, under the full moon in a clear night sky, Hugh was talking to the man whose message had called him from the hall. In his hand the man was holding a large piece of something like stone, a deep red colour.

'Where did you come by this?' asked Hugh, taking the fragment and noting that it felt heavy, like a metal.

'In the valley in the woods, where the Romans made their iron. In the stream there is much waste and black stone, and then a few pieces of this.' The man lightly held a knife close to the stone and the blade clunked onto it. 'See how metal moves towards it.'

'Then it can only be the philosopher's stone.'

Hugh held the object up and in the moonlight it glinted a dark, steely red. In the bright, cold air, his breath fell on it like steam.

'The red stone, to create gold. Now our work can begin. Go and tell the others to be ready tomorrow – early. Then get some sleep.'

As the man left him, Hugh turned to go back to the hall house. He would be expected to rejoin the feast, but he too needed to sleep. Yet he could not go to his chamber without going through the hall. Unless… There was a shutter open, he had noticed, as he came past to meet the man. Æadgytha must have left it open; he had meant to tell her. As he reached the outside wall of the chamber, Hugh saw the shutter was open wider than he recalled. He made to climb through the window opening, then paused.

I will not sleep. I have to see where this philosopher's stone is to be found.

*

Eadric had passed Hugh and the man on his way home. He had been surprised when the monk announced he was leaving; he had enjoyed his company, and his conversation. Yet he was glad, too, that the house was his and Guðrun's again.

Not expecting him so early, Guðrun was dozing in his bed. As he came in, she threw off the covers and made to get out and go back to her corner. Eadric held up a hand.

'No; stay.' A command, but gentle.

Slowly she sank back. Eadric sat on the end of the bed where a shaft of moonlight fell. In it he could see her left leg, and the twisted foot that ended it. Guðrun moved it back into the shadows, but Eadric reached for the foot and pulled it towards him.

'When I see you move, I am watching you dance.' And he bent over and began to kiss her ankle, and then her foot, and then the sole of the foot as it turned in on itself. 'For this alone I would love you.'

Guðrun raised herself on the bed until she was sitting. 'I get in your bed when I can. I like to dream.'

'And what do you dream?' he asked softly, raising his head again and looking into the darkness where her voice had come from.

'Of this moment.'

'Stronger than iron, and a bond less easily broken,' Eadric murmured.

Suddenly Guðrun was kneeling in front of him in the moonlight, and the unfastened underdress was falling from her shoulders.

He put his arms under hers and lifted her towards him, feeling her body press against his.

'I dream too.'

'And what do you dream?' she whispered in his ear.

'Of the love of a good woman, and children to follow me here.'

Guðrun knelt astride him and pressed her forehead to his. 'The first you have. As to the second…'

And she closed her mouth on his, and let the weight of her body pull them both over on the bed.

*

In the paddock by the hall house, Felip stood, gasping. Too stout to easily run as fast as he had to get there, he needed to calm himself before he tried to mount a horse. In his hands, the box with the book felt warm, familiar. He scanned the line of horses; Hugh's was at the far end, dark, and a little taller than the others. Slowly he went to it, put the box on the ground, and stood stroking its nose a while, talking soothingly under his breath. It snorted a little and he could see its eye, bright in the moonlight. Carefully, he untied it.

Holding the reins with one hand, Felip picked up the box with the other, then realised he should have asked Æadgytha for a bag for the saddle. How could he get on a horse holding the box? Cursing his stupidity, he tried to think.

If I balance the book on the saddle, as I climb up? No; it will fall off. If I put the box on a fence post, mount the horse, then pick the box up from the post? He tried to imagine making this move, with a lively horse that did not know him, and foresaw disaster. *Once I am on this horse, all I will be able to do is ride.*

Tying the horse up again, Felip put the box down, opened it and took out the book in its cloth. He was trying to put it under his tunic when he heard a voice behind him.

'A late hour to go for a ride, Felip.'

Felip turned, and froze. Hugh de Bayeux was standing a few yards away. He turned towards the horse, trying to hide what he was doing, but now Hugh was beside him. Slowly, Hugh reached down and pulled Felip's hands away from his tunic, with the book. Felip heard the hiss of the thegn's breath in the cold air.

'A thief. A thief in our midst. I should call out the

villagers; I should have you thrown in the prison cage, Felip de Mazerolles.'

'This is not your book, Hugh de Bayeux; nor ever was.'

'You believe it is yours? Remember, I was there that day in Spain, when you took the book from its owner, Felip. I saw how you coveted it, even then, for all your talk of safe-keeping.'

'Then we are both thieves.' Felip held the book up. 'Between us, we should return the book to Samra.'

'No.' Hugh was shaking his head. 'I have come too far to abandon my quest, and I am so close to success.'

Felip felt an anger sweep through him at the unyielding man in front of him. 'It is madness! How many men do you think have tried to make gold, and come away with nothing but their souls lost to damnation?'

'Many enough; but not too many for another man to try.'

In that instant, as he looked into the deadness in Hugh's blue-grey eyes, Felip saw himself reflected as another man, craving and obsessed, bent on a purpose from which he would cast aside all who tried to stop him. And he saw, too, Samra in the Forest of Valognes, honourable and wise, grieving for the loss of the book, a loss he had tried to make permanent in his deception. If Hugh de Bayeux was a madman and a thief, then he, Felip de Mazerolles, was no better. He shook his head sadly.

'Oh, Hugh. Why should you be any different?'

'Because it takes only one man to succeed. I am that man, and those that follow me will know my name. And when they find you dead here tomorrow, you will be only another Norman, who the English hate so much.'

Too late, Felip saw the hand that came towards him,

and the blade of a knife in the moonlight. He tried to move the book between them but felt the sting of the blade in his stomach. As he fell to his knees, Hugh pulled the book from his hands. Dimly, Felip saw him put it in its box, rise, and walk away. He pitched on his face in the grass.

'Languedoc!' Felip called after Hugh faintly. 'I am from the Languedoc.'

Blackness swept over him.

*

Cuthred was making his way home when he heard the horses in the paddock. Something was making then restless. He went to the fence and looked along the line of horses; on the ground at the far end, he could see a black shape. Probably a badger, foraging for food among the horses – one must have startled, and kicked out at it. It happened from time to time; badgers were persistent scavengers. If it were dead, he would take it to his sister, a midwife who lived with Cuthred with her son; it would be useful to her for many kinds of medicine. If alive, he would find some way to dispatch it first, but he would need to be careful of the powerful jaws. But when Cuthred drew nearer, he saw it was not a badger; it was a man, and closer still, he recognised the monk who had appeared a little while ago in Berewic, and had recently vanished just as quickly. He recalled this monk had stayed with Eadric, where, no doubt, he had had his ear filled with poison about the village reeve.

The monk was lying face down with his head turned to the side, showing his face, ghostly white in the cold moonlight. Turning him over, Cuthred saw the dark stain on his habit and the wet pool on the ground. He ran home as fast as he could on his short legs, and called for his sister and her son, a young man called Botulf. Between them, they carried the monk home. The midwife was used to rent bodies and blood, and did not qualm as she quickly examined the monk, once his sodden clothes were pulled away. He was lucky, she announced, for the blow had been deflected into his side and missed any vital organs. But he had lost a lot of blood, and would need stitches, and a long period of care. Happily, Cuthred noted, from the purse at his belt, it looked as if the monk had the money to pay for it. They all agreed it best not to tell anyone about their patient.

*

When Hugh reached the hall house, he climbed in through the window with the open shutter. He pulled back a heavy chest that stood over a storage pit in the floor he had made years ago; to take the gold, when he made it. Lifting the boards from over the pit, he placed the box with the book inside, replaced the boards, and heaved the chest back over the pit. He would not need to look at the book again. Everything he wanted from it he knew by heart. Now filled with a purpose he had not known for a long time, he lay down on the bed on his back, with the images from the book dancing in patterns on the roof over his head. Sulphur, mercury; lead. Charcoal, fire; gold. Much later, when Æadgytha came in, she found him awake, fully clothed. She looked down at him in surprise.

'Where did you go so suddenly?'

Hugh raised himself onto his elbows.

'It is time,' he said, taking her hand.

*

In the dawn, Hugh was gone; he had met his men to go to the valley in the woods. He was surprised not to find a body by his horse, only a red stain in the grass. As he fetched water from the trough to wash the blood away, he pondered. Perhaps the monk had survived, or perhaps someone had robbed the body, and Felip was now in a village cesspit. It did not matter either way.

*

In Hugh's absence, Æadgytha took William and Wulfstan hunting. As they rode along the valley and up through the woods, a hoar frost clung to the grass and trees, white as the breath their horses gave out into the cold air. A red winter sun hovered above the horizon as if reluctant to climb any further into the sky. They put up little game, but William did not seem worried. He could tell this was not the Forest of Valognes. Through Wulfstan, he asked Æadgytha why there were no rabbits. She laughed. 'No rabbits in England,' she said, 'you should have brought some.' Æadgytha told him he should come for longer next time, and they would take hawks, go to Ashdown, and hunt properly. 'If Edward has promised you the crown, you must plan to return?' Repeating this in French to William, Wulfstan raised a chuckle from his master.

At midday they pulled up their horses in a clearing small enough to provide shelter, large enough to let in the winter sunshine. Wulfstan and William dismounted; Æadgytha made to do the same, but William lifted her from her horse as easily as if she were a child and leant her back against the trunk of a tree, facing the sun. He left his hands on her hips a while, and kept his gaze steadily into her eyes in that way he had of looking into someone's soul. Friend or foe, you would not keep any intention from Duke William.

Abruptly he let go and turned away, said something, walked to the other side of the clearing and vanished into the trees. Wulfstan and Æadgytha watched him as he marched off; his tall, stocky frame and his bow-legged gait.

'He needs to shit,' said Wulfstan.

He leant back against an oak tree beside Æadgytha. They both closed their eyes a while in silence, letting the weak sun warm them.

Æadgytha spoke first. 'So when William is done here, he will go to Edward. Then he will return to Normandy, with an oath for the crown of England, and two of my kinsmen pledged hostage for it. Everything he came for.'

Wulfstan had picked up a handful of acorns, and began to turn them in his palm. 'Perhaps. Edward is a strange ruler, strong in some ways, weak in others. He may yet change his mind. And you Godwins are like quicksand to him – you bear him up one moment, and swallow him the next.'

'Edward had only to father a child with my cousin, and we would not be speaking of any of this.'

'Again, perhaps. But I tell you this,' Wulfstan threw an acorn at the trunk of a birch tree opposite them, 'for William, England is his; his by lineage,' another acorn, 'his by right,' another acorn, 'and his by promise.' Another acorn flew off the trunk. 'And he will pay any price to keep what is his. That is his pledge.'

'I married a Norman knight I did not love to keep what is mine. And had someone who would dispute me for it work my demesne, and his brother sent to serve as a knight to William.'

'That was always meant for me.'

Both were silent again, buried in their memories of the people they had been on that day eight years ago. The girl of fourteen, afraid yet ready to defy her king to keep the manor a previous king had granted to her father. The young man of fifteen, angry and ready too to defy Edward to regain it. And now William, king in waiting, was in the trees, shitting on his future kingdom. A single magpie flew from the trees behind them and landed in the clearing, calling harshly. William reappeared on the other side, still pulling up his trousers, grinning.

Looking across at him, Ædgytha asked Wulfstan, 'What is he like, as a master and a man?'

'He has no equal. He trusts totally in his own strength and the loyalty of his friends. He will fight to the death for those who are with him. Those who oppose him, he will crush with no mercy.'

Wulfstan dropped the final acorn onto the ground, and pressed it into the cold soil with his foot.

'You may yet lose what is yours – you have no heir.'

Ædgytha pulled her lips tight. 'I have prayed to Our Lady often that she may send me a miracle.'

'Who knows.' Wulfstan turned to face her. 'Miracles can happen.'

*

When the hunting party returned, Hugh was waiting. 'Felip de Mazerolles has stolen the book from me,' he declared.

William nodded, but said nothing; the book was on its way to him, he was sure. Wulfstan shrugged, but said nothing; in the struggle for Samra's book, Felip had won, for now. Æadgytha felt the thrill of a plan achieved, but said nothing. But afterwards, she noted that her husband's lust for gold was greater than ever, and she despaired.

Assassin

Rouen, Normandy, December 1051

Jaco drained the last of his cup and went out into the cold. Pulling his tunic tighter around him, he looked up at the grey sky above the rooftops; a few flakes of snow were falling. He had been no more welcome in the alehouse just now than he had been when he landed in Rouen nearly twenty years ago. He made his way through the narrow streets, remembering the hot July day when he had been hurrying in the other direction, back to his ship with a fistful of coins from the sale of a slave.

He relived the panic he had felt when he reached the quay and the *Tita* was not there. He remembered running up and down, frantically searching; had he mistaken where his ship's berth was? He remembered stopping, drenched in sweat, as a small crowd gathered round, and seeing the angry faces as they told him, 'We have heard how the devil woman brought bad luck to us all in the storm that damaged our town, and how it nearly cost you your ship. Well, no one wants a captain who brings bad luck; they have left, with their curse on you, and our curse is on you too, Jew.' Jaco had run from them, to the Jewish quarter he was headed for now, to find refuge among his own; but they too had spurned him. 'A man who trades in his own people is not one of us. Our doors are barred to you; be gone.' So Jaco had scurried away through the town like a rat, to hide where he could, with nothing but the clothes on his back and the price of Samra's sale to keep him. And the man who swore he would have no master worked where he could and begged where he could not. He worked for any who would have him, doing anything they bid him, however dirty, dangerous or desperate.

Jaco stopped. He had reached the house he had been sent to.

*

At the same moment, Gilbert reached the town square. Just as he had all those years ago, he had left a man minding a horse and cart with promise of payment if he waited a while, and he had come to the place where his life had taken a new course.

Everyone comes into and leaves your life to set you on or change you from a path.

Now the market place was busy, but not packed as it had been then, with an eager and curious crowd. Yet as he walked to the centre of the square, people still turned to look at him, the tall, squarely built man of the forest, out of place among the squat townspeople.

Gilbert stood in the centre of the square, where the platform would have been. He saw himself, a man of twenty-six whose only world had been the Forest of Lyons, advancing towards a woman who he knew from sight belonged to another world, exotic and unfamiliar. Like the other onlookers, he had felt curiosity; unlike them, he had felt no hostility – only compassion. In his mind, Gilbert pieced together the fragments Samra had told him – gradually and painfully – of the time that had led up to that point. Of a purpose, of a journey of hope; of betrayal, of capture, of near rape and near death. He thought of Samra's life after they had come together – the joy of Estraya's birth, the return of the book, the disc on the whitewashed wall tracking Venus, vindicating her science. Of the crippling Normandy winters, Samra's despair at the loss of the book, and her watching Wulfstan leave them, trying to comfort Estraya in her desolation.

Did I do enough for Samra? Too busy with my forest and Cerisy; too eager to please Duke William. Yet what would I be without her?

As they passed by across the square, people were making sidelong looks at the tall man who was staring into the distance, body swaying slightly, wiping tears from his eyes with the back of his hand.

'I knew I would find you here,' said a voice behind him.

Gilbert turned to see Samra standing, smiling. She took his hands in hers, and kissed them.

'How did you know?' he asked, smiling too, noticing – as he always did when he had been away from her – that her beauty seemed added to, not lessened, by the lines on her face and the grey in her hair.

'You would not have had time before you left. But when you came back, you were bound to come here, as I did. To remember.'

Gilbert squeezed her hands. Suddenly he broke into sobs, shoulders heaving.

'Oh, Samra. I am sorry. So sorry.'

'No. No, no, no...' She took him in her arms and pulled his head down to her shoulder. 'You have nothing to be sorry for.'

His voice on her shoulder was muffled. 'For everything I have not done, and not been for you.'

'But for you, I would be dead.'

He lifted his head and looked down at her. 'I took you from your world and imprisoned you in a cage. I have not understood you, and what you need. I wouldn't blame you if you stayed here.'

'Stayed here?' Samra shook her head. 'A few days ago, in a moment of despair, I was ready to do that. But listen to me, Gilbert, forest warden to the dukes of Normandy. The forest you took me to has been my sanctuary. I would not exchange you and your cage for any palace – or for any observatory or laboratory.'

'I have seen you suffer in body and mind.'

'Yes, in both. But neither has been your fault.'

Samra was still holding Gilbert, but now she pulled free and reached into her clothing.

'As I came down the steps that day here, one of the coins you had thrown to the slaver was trapped between the planks.' She reached out a hand and Gilbert saw a small silver coin in her palm. 'This one.'

Gilbert took the coin and turned it in his own hand. As his breath steamed on it in the cold air, he saw how it shone from careful polishing.

'As I picked it up, I had in mind, I would gather enough coins to one day pay you back. I don't know how I would have done that – I thought I was going to be your slave, with nothing.'

'My slave?' Gilbert laughed at the thought. 'Come to think of it, I have been waiting to be paid back. So far, all I've had is one child. And now this.' He grinned and held the coin up between finger and thumb.

Samra was laughing, and crying too. Laughing and crying together. Suddenly they were hugging each other, in a moment of union as intense as it was affirming.

Gilbert pulled free, put the coin in her palm and closed her hand over it.

'No. Keep it. One day, you'll put it to a good use.' He paused. 'Just tell me one thing… something I've never asked.'

'Yes?'

'The storm that brought you here – was it your doing?'

Samra smiled and shook her head. 'The only witchcraft on that ship was the power of coincidence. And yet it was meant to be, was it not?'

'Nothing happens but for a purpose,' said Gilbert.

They stood a while, facing each other. Suddenly Samra began to look round her, scanning the faces of the other people in the market place.

'Where were you headed before you came here?' she asked Gilbert.

He heard the unease in her voice.

'To William's palace, of course, where I thought to find you.'

'We must not return there. Come with me now, to where I am staying, in the Jewish quarter. Tomorrow, early, we will leave for the Forest of Valognes.'

'But the duke's man who took me to Lyons in his horse and cart is waiting for me. William will be expecting me.'

'William has left for England. And I feel no safer with him gone than with him here.'

Gilbert wanted to ask her what she meant, but already she was turning to go.

*

Samra reached out to knock on the door of Miriam's house and noticed it was slightly ajar. She pushed at it but something behind the door was stopping it from opening. She turned to Gilbert beside her.

'Let me,' he said, and put his shoulder to the door to give it a shove.

As he pushed the door further open and the obstacle behind moved with it, Samra saw Gilbert looking at the smear of blood it was leaving on the floor. She looked at him, wild-eyed with alarm.

'Is there another way into the house?' Gilbert said to her urgently, pulling the door back until it was nearly shut again.

Samra remembered where Miriam had shown her she could make a quick escape, if anyone came looking for her.

'Around the side.' She pointed. 'It leads to a back passage where the cesspits are.' Gilbert turned to go and she caught his arm. 'I'm afraid.'

'Wait here,' he said. 'Do not go inside.'

Gilbert vanished round the corner of the house, leaving Samra on the doorstep. More snow was falling and she shivered. She pushed the door a little way and tried to listen inside. Pushing again, she found she could squeeze through the gap and into the house. Behind the door was the body of Miriam's servant, face down in a pool of blood. Biting the back of her hand to suppress a cry, Samra listened. Faintly, she heard a voice she recognised as Miriam's. Advancing a little in the direction it had come from, Samra listened again; the voice was coming from the same room she had been shown into when she had first come to the house, and where she had spent the evenings since talking with her friend. Without thinking, she went to open the door into the room and heard a man's voice from inside. With her hand on the latch, she hesitated.

I know that voice.

She pushed the door open and stepped inside. Across the darkened room was the captain of the ship who had brought her to Rouen; grey was now showing in his hair, but she recognised his sea-green eyes at once. He was standing behind Miriam, one hand gripping her arm, the other with a knife at her throat. Both were staring at the doorway Samra had just come through. When he saw her, Jaco let out a cry.

'You!'

But as Samra took a step forwards, he pressed the knife into Miriam's throat. Miriam's eyes bulged with terror. Samra stopped.

'My friend has nothing to do with this. Let her go.'

'Gladly,' Jaco replied, 'for it was not her I was sent to find. Though when they told me to come here and wait for a woman to return, I had no idea it would be you. Now I fear more devilment from you. Keep your distance.'

'Who sent you?'

'The man did not say where his order came from. His money was enough for me.'

Behind Jaco, Gilbert had appeared in the shadows. He put a finger to his lips, then made a motion with his hand to his mouth. *Keep talking.*

'Did you not think I would run, when I saw an open door, and the servant's body?' Samra went on.

'It had to be open, to let you in. And curiosity always gets the better of people.'

Gilbert was inching his large frame across the floor, making for where Jaco was standing behind Miriam. Samra watched as he slowly drew his hunting knife.

'I will walk forwards,' Samra said to Jaco, 'and you will let her walk towards me. When we pass each other, she will be exchanged for me.'

'Samra, no!' Miriam cried out, but her cry was stifled by the blade pressing again at her throat.

'No tricks?' said Jaco. 'No devilry?'

Samra shook her head, but she was trembling inside. Gilbert had almost reached Jaco's back. Suddenly Jaco threw Miriam aside and spun round to face Gilbert, the knife in his outstretched hand.

'A wealthy household,' he said, 'able to afford a bronze mirror.'

Miriam had run to Samra and both were holding each other, watching the two men. With his own knife, Gilbert was facing Jaco uncertainly. The other man was smaller and not as strong, but clearly used to a fight. His wiry body was half crouching in front of him.

'I paid you off once,' growled Gilbert. 'I'll not do it again.'

Jaco straightened, the light of recognition in his face. He laughed.

'Are you here, too? What did I say to you before, woodsman? "Go home, this is no place for you."'

'Oh, but it was my place. And it is now.'

He made a lunge at Jaco that the other man dodged easily, but it allowed him to put himself between Jaco and the two women.

'You can leave here alive,' Gilbert went on, 'but you must go now.'

'Not without what I came for,' Jaco said, looking past him at Samra.

'Whatever you were going to be paid, I can pay more,' Miriam, who was now shielding Samra, cut in. 'Name your price.'

'I have been paid – half my price. And the other half when I come back with the news of her death.' He pointed at Samra.

'Then I will double it. Please!' Miriam pleaded. 'Just go!'

For a moment they all stood, Gilbert fixed on Jaco, who was half watching him and half watching Samra, who was behind Miriam. Then before Gilbert and Miriam could stop her, Samra pushed past them both, and put herself between the two men. Facing Jaco, she spoke to him in Ladino.

'You know you cannot do me harm. Remember what happened on the ship.'

Behind her, Gilbert had frozen. Miriam was white with shock. In Samra's mind, planets and stars were wheeling in the cosmos above her head, conjunctions and eclipses coming and going in a fraction of a second, with every angle and every shaft of light bearing down on her, rooted to the spot in a small room in a town in Normandy. She held out her hand for Jaco's knife.

Oh, Sophia. If I am wrong, it is all over.

Jaco was staring at her; she saw his eyes widening and emotion moving across his face as he wrestled with his choice. In that instant, she saw not the slaver, the captain of his own destiny, but the man who had cowered in the alleys of Rouen like an animal, living from day to day with the curses of all others heaped upon him. What had befallen him might befall any of their race, once the tolerance of their fellow men was taken away.

'Are you not a brother?' she went on. 'One of the Sephardim?'

Jaco's voice was a hoarse whisper. 'You know I am.'

From behind Samra, Gilbert saw Jaco's arm with the knife move. He heard a voice call out 'God, no!' and realised it was his own. Miriam screamed.

Jaco took the blade of his knife with his other hand, and held the handle out to Samra. Slowly, she reached for it. Behind her, she could hear Gilbert exhale. Jaco looked around him wildly, as if fearing sudden attack from any of them. Then he pushed past Miriam, whose body was swaying unsteadily, to the door of the room.

'Wait!' Samra called to him. He turned in the doorway. 'If you need sanctuary, come to the Forest of Valognes.'

Jaco looked at her a moment, then ran from the house.

The Trap is Set

Berewic, Sussex, December 1051

As they walked from Eadric's fields up the path through the vegetable garden to his house, Wulfstan put an arm around the older man's shoulder, and this time it was done warmly.

'I am impressed, Eadric.'

'I see to my ditches, I plant the quicks for my hedges,' Eadric replied. 'I see my land is fertile, drained and well protected, that my stock is well cared for. No farmer can do more.'

At the door, Wulfstan paused and looked at Eadric. 'And I am grateful you thought to ask me here. After that night in the hall, I feared we might be parting on bad terms.'

'Blood is thicker than water.'

Eadric motioned Wulfstan to go inside. Guðrun was serving food as he entered. Wulfstan looked around him at the clean, comfortable room. There was a trestle table covered with a linen cloth, and three stools. In one corner was a wooden chest and in another, a loom. An embroidered curtain screened off another corner, which, from its shape, must have had a bed. As he sat down, he observed the table was set with bowls and cups for three, and that Guðrun sat with them after she had served. Wulfstan knew he was an honoured guest because there was meat in the pottage, if only a little. They ate in silence a while, then Eadric paused and toyed with a piece of bread in front of him before beginning to speak.

'We have each made the best of what we have. But I have had little choice in what I do here, whereas you…'

Wulfstan stopped eating and looked up. 'How do you mean?'

'You come here at a time when England's fate hangs in the balance, when her crown has been pledged to the foreign lord you serve. And yet you are English; a Wessex.'

'We Wessex owe much to the Norman dukes.'

'We do not owe them England. Where would you stand if Edward died tomorrow and William pressed his claim?'

Wulfstan looked uncomfortable. 'I was sworn to serve William, by our father. Edward fulfilled the vow for him when he came here with us, those years ago. Would you have me break that oath?'

Eadric leant over the table towards Wulfstan and lowered his voice. 'Many say the Godwins are England's future, not William.'

'The Godwins!' Wulfstan started back in disbelief, pushing his stool away from the table. 'I should help our enemies now?'

'I have seen the Godwins serve England well. I know now that this is their purpose above all. They are fine soldiers and able statesmen. And Edward has banished them out of spite for what happened to Alfred. England cannot be governed from spite, brother.'

Wulfstan nodded. 'I have looked at Æadgytha often since I came here. I have reminded myself that her father killed ours. And yet she is so admirable, so noble, so…' He trailed off into a sigh.

Eadric's eyes narrowed. *He has more than admiration for her. This is good.*

'Whatever we feel about our rights here, Wulfstan, do you want to see Norman soldiers' boots tramping through Berewic? You need to choose; are you Norman or English?'

'Stay in England?' Wulfstan dropped his head and looked at his hands. 'William will never allow it; let alone King Edward.'

'I will square it with William. And if he agrees, Edward will agree also.'

*

Outside the hall house, William of Normandy's party was preparing to leave, gathering equipment and saddling horses. Inside, William was alone, seated before the hearth. He looked up as Eadric limped over; the man who had left Normandy ten years before as little more than a boy. As he too had been – if William of Normandy was ever just a boy.

Eadric gave William a little bow and looked around. 'Where is Æadgytha, my lord?'

'In her chamber, asleep. Where is Wulfstan?' William asked.

'He bides at my house. And I would have him stay there.'
William raised his eyebrows.

'If I may speak frankly… We both know the power the Godwins have in England,' Eadric went on. 'They may be cast down, but they will be agitating even now to come back, and they will make Edward change his mind on the succession.'

'And if they do, I will take hostages against that. Edward has agreed; Wulfnoth, brother to Harold, and Hakon, Harold's nephew.'

'If – when – the Godwins return, there will be turmoil. They will not allow their kin to be easily spirited away. You need someone here you can trust, to deliver the hostages.'

'Wulfstan.' William looked into Eadric's cold grey eyes. 'Why does he not come to ask me himself?'

'He fears your anger, my lord. That you would refuse.'

William got up and took a step towards the fire in the hearth, staring into the flames. 'He is right. I would have him with me.' He turned to Eadric. 'What do you gain from this?'

Eadric stepped closer and lowered his voice. 'You know the Godwins took this manor from us, when we were exiled with the other Wessex. You know our father Rædmund died at their hands. When you are master of England, give me Berewic.'

William looked at Eadric's thin face, with its hard eyes. *You are a serpent. But you may be useful to me.* He bent down, picked up a log and threw it onto the fire.

Discomfited by his silence, Eadric pressed his face into William's. 'It is my right!' he spluttered.

William put a hand on the other man's chest and pushed him away. It was a slight movement, but so powerful that Eadric fell back onto the floor.

'Do not speak to me of your right. If I give you Berewic, you will do me service for it, just as you do service now for your little patch of dirt.' He glared down at Eadric, who tried to shuffle away on his back. 'Now go, and tell Wulfstan to stay indoors when we depart. It will break me to leave without him.'

*

Wulfstan sat watching as Guðrun cleared away. He looked at her white-blonde hair, fair skin and rather plain face with its icy blue eyes. *Not like my dark Estraya at all.* A pang of anguish ran through him. *Estraya!* He got to his feet and went to the door. He paused, Guðrun looking at him in surprise. Then Wulfstan turned back. *Estraya will not be expecting me so soon. And Eadric will be wrong; the Godwins will not return, and I will be back in Normandy within the year.*

He sat down again and found he was looking at some shelves on the wall. On one of them was a silver thimble, beautifully engraved.

Wulfstan picked the thimble up and saw the writing on the rim. He held it up to Guðrun.

'What does it say?'

Fifteen

Rougemont, Normandy, January 1052

Dawn had been breaking when Estraya left the clearing with its little group of houses in the Forest of Valognes. Around her all had been quiet; not a dog barking, not a wisp of smoke from a roof hole, no one moving outside. In a couple of days it would be Epiphany, the end of the period of no work that had begun on Christmas Eve, and by this time of day there would be activity everywhere. She had chosen her time well to slip away unseen. In the house she had left the knife, in its sheath next to where she slept.

A strong cloak around her shoulders and some food in a pouch at her belt was enough; Estraya was a child of the forest and it held no fear for her. For a while her path had taken her along the way where Felip had once carried her on the back of his horse as he came through the snow on one of his visits to the forest. But Felip, like the book, was gone to England, and neither might be seen again.

Estraya pulled her cloak tightly to her neck and walked on. In a short while her path crossed a stream, and she turned to follow its course, gradually downhill and gradually getting bigger and wider. She knew she needed to

FIFTEEN

press on; half a day's ride on a horse to her destination was a day's walk, and the days were short. Eyes darting between the path ahead and the ground at her feet, she moved surefooted and silently, as she had learnt to from when she could first walk. Around her groups of trees came and went, small and large, all quietly enduring the wintertime, standing over their last year's leaves; crisp brown oak, soft dark ash and crinkled golden chestnut. Alders gripped the edge of the stream, which was slowly becoming a little river, teetering on the banks with their roots dipped in the icy water. Grass was at her feet, with patches of shrubs she had to steer round and stones and roots ready to catch her if she lost concentration. Then the path went up a little hill, at the top of which large rocks were interspersed with clumps of heather and bilberry.

Pausing to look down at the river, Estraya sat on a rock and beheld a landscape as familiar to her as the inside of the house she called home. She felt it not lifeless in the winter cold, but breathing gently, holding itself ready for the spring that would follow. Three hundred and twenty years ago, the girl who was her forbear had played on the roof of her father's house in Spain and he had crafted the knife for her. Spring had followed every year since, as it had in every year in the world before that. A few bilberries still clung to a bush at her side, black and wizened. Pulling them off and into her mouth, Estraya felt a surge of juicy acidity through her body that made her quiver; the bushes around her and the trees beyond the river seemed to tremble in response. She stood up and felt her legs rooted in the soil, so much like the trunks of the trees she could see that she cried out in amazement. Again, the landscape around her responded; a sensation hardly to be noticed, but there.

They know I am here, and they are telling each other.

*

In the house in the clearing, Gilbert was looking at Estraya's empty bed. As Samra came up beside him, he showed her the knife in his palm.

'I didn't notice this before. And she is nowhere outside.'

Samra tried not to sound concerned. 'She must be round about, somewhere in the forest.'

Gilbert shook his head. 'I have searched in all the usual places.'

'I worry for her.' Samra looked down at the knife. 'She has not been herself since Wulfstan left.'

'Do not fear, my love. She knows the forest and its ways.' Gilbert closed his hand over the knife. 'But I will saddle a horse and go and look for her.'

Samra nodded. 'Take food, and blankets. But hurry – there is not much of the day left.'

*

The little river Estraya had been following turned sharply through some low hills and into a narrow valley, and the track she had been on was cut off by the bend in the river, becoming a narrow way up through the trees. Pushing herself uphill, Estraya left the river behind and below her, remembering how as a child her father used to bring her on his horse up the steep slope at a canter, pressed back into his stomach, her short legs lifting in the air, both of them hooting in delight. The track levelled out and Estraya turned onto a path to her right, following it through the trees until it opened out onto one of three narrow terraces overlooking the river. Below her, on the second and largest terrace were some low, ruined walls, and below that on the third terrace stood a few old fruit trees. She had reached Rougemont.

From this highest terrace she could see how it stood at the end of a narrow bluff, with the river on three sides and the thick woods behind giving it natural shelter and protection. Under a weak afternoon sun, the river sparkled far below her, hurrying around the bend before settling into a deep pool. A flock of crows was heading across the river to their roost in the trees behind her, charred scraps of cloth against a milky sky. Beyond the river, the woods unfolded into the distance.

She made her way down a steep slope to the ruined walls, passing among large stones still sitting perfectly on each other, with many more strewn at random in the long grass. Sitting on a fallen stone, Estraya took a little bread from her pouch and began to chew on it, looking around her at the other stones. Her father had told her how Rougemont was once a castle, destroyed in a Viking raid long ago, probably at the same time as the first Cerisy, and never rebuilt. Finishing what she had eaten, she half ran, half scrambled down a steep little path to the lower terrace, and pulled a shrivelled apple from a tree. She took a bite, recalling her first visit with Gilbert, when he had fooled her by saying how sweet and tasty the apples were, and had laughed at her as she spat out the bitter flesh of this wild descendant of the original orchard, screwing up her face and squealing. Smiling, she ate the apple whole, before taking a narrow, crumbling path down to a bank of sand by the river. Crouching to drink from a little spring that issued from the base of the terraced hillside and flowed to the river, she swilled the crisp, cold water round her mouth, savouring the apple taste it released, before swallowing. She drank again, and looked up. In a clearing sky the sun had come out fully, bathing her and the terraces above in vermillion light as it sank gently towards the horizon.

Estraya turned to sit on the sand facing the river and the sun, closing her eyes and letting her cloak fold round her until it touched the ground. Her eyelids flooded into crimson, and the quietly moving water of the river as it slowed into the deep pool became her breathing. Her nose savoured the air around her, bringing alive the elements she knew from pages of the book: wood, water, iron and earth. Beneath her, the world murmured a little, and the trees beyond the river whispered to the sky and the departing sun. A surge of joy, so intense it made her clench, filled her body.

Here. Now. All that I could ever want to be. Me. This. All one; connected, indivisible.

When she finally opened her eyes, the sun was disappearing behind the trees, leaving a sky clear save for a fiery red rim on the edge of the world. Looking behind her, she saw the vermillion light rapidly diminishing up the hillside. At the top of the bluff, the crows in the trees took to the air, wheeling and calling out harshly.

Something has startled them.

Quickly, Estraya clambered back to the third terrace with the fruit trees, then to the second with the ruins. In the fading light, the stones were becoming formless black shapes in the grass, but she knew what she was looking for. Between two sets of standing stones, a few steps were set

FIFTEEN

into the ground; she ran towards them, and flung herself at where they vanished into darkness below. Inside, the hole opened up into what must once have been a cellar, large and accommodating. Estraya pressed herself against the far wall and waited.

*

Gilbert cursed as he ducked under the branches over the path to the bluff. Next time, he would bring something to lop them with. Reaching the first terrace he stopped and dismounted, leading his horse carefully down the slope to the second. The light was fading; stars were appearing in the sky, and a half-moon was rising. Once among the stones, he found one to tether the horse to and began to move slowly through a jumbled landscape that in full daylight he would have crossed easily. Stubbing a foot on a stone low in the grass, he cursed again. Then he saw it; the two standing stones with the steps between. Quietly he approached the shadow between the stones, and peered down the steps.

'Estraya?'

No answer. He was about to call again, when a dark shape in a cloak flew at him from the blackness below. And Gilbert hugged his daughter to him, as if he would never let her go. Finally Estraya pulled out of his arms, and looked at him, hands on hips, dark eyes shining.

'How did you know I was here?'

'You always used to say you would come and live here when you grew up.' He paused. 'I think you've grown up.'

'I was all right, you know. I have food with me. And a warm cloak.'

Her father laughed. 'I gathered some dry wood on my way here – in one of the bags on the horse.' He unfastened a large pouch slung at his back and handed it to her. 'Get a fire going – I'll go back to the trees up top and get more wood while I can still see.' He walked away, calling over his shoulder, 'There's food and blankets in the other bags.'

Estraya went to the horse and pulled a handful of twigs and small wood from a bag. Between the standing stones, she sat and took some things from the pouch Gilbert had given her; a flat piece of wood with a small dip in the middle that she held down with her feet, a short piece of stick with a sharp end, and a second, longer and thinner stick with a cord attached between both ends like a bow. She put a lump of moss from the pouch into the dip of the flat piece of wood on the ground. Wrapping the bowstring around the smaller stick, Estraya pushed the sharp end of this down into the dip, and began to pull it back and forth with the bow, so the stick spun quickly in the dip with the moss around it. After a few long strokes, smoke rose from the moss; Estraya cupped it into her hands and waved it back and forth, before putting it on the ground and adding small twigs to the flames that had started. She fetched the rest of the twigs and wood from the bag, and added them slowly to the fire.

*

Under the light of the moon, now high in the sky, Gilbert was sat with his back against a standing stone, Estraya in the crook of his arm with her head on his shoulder, blankets under and over them. Beside them, the last of the wood on the fire crackled and wisps of smoke rose, to disappear into

FIFTEEN

the dark. Tethered to the other stone, the horse was on its side, asleep.

Gilbert pointed with his free arm at a larger, brighter light among the array of stars above them.

'Do you remember that day in the shelter, with the lens tube? You must be the only child to have ever held Venus in her hand.'

'I realised then what the book could do,' Estraya answered. 'But I remember the sadness that settled on my mother after Hugh de Bayeux wrested it from her. It was the refrain of my girlhood.'

'Samra has endured much in that loss.'

'And I admire her for her forbearance, as much as I love her for what she has been for me. I loved the book too.' Estraya paused. 'I'm sorry, I could never tell her this. But I resent the power it has had, over all our lives.'

Gilbert sighed. 'I don't blame you. I often wonder myself what it has all been for. The book and the knife.'

'The knife is too great a burden. That's why I left it.'

'Again, I understand. But they are intertwined, the book and the knife. And you're its keeper, and the bearer of the foretelling. Until you fulfil it, or pass it to the next generation.'

'I don't want to fulfil it. And I don't want to hand the knife to a daughter of mine and tell her she might kill someone one day. What does the foretelling mean? What has it to do with the book?'

Gilbert shook his head. 'I don't know the answer to that. But we are all part of something. I feel that.'

Estraya turned her face to look up at him. 'I nearly killed Wulfstan.'

'When?'

'The day we went to the marshland. Before Wulfstan left.'
'It must have been an accident.'
'No. I wanted to kill him.' She felt his body tense.
'You love Wulfstan.'

Estraya turned and got onto her knees beside her father, taking his hands in hers.

'I love him so much, I could not bear to part with him. Could not bear the thought that he might be lost to me. Dead, he would be mine forever.'

Looking into his face, she saw the strong jaw moving as he wrestled with what she had told him, his light blue eyes looking into hers, up at the stars, and back at her again.

'You are lucky,' she went on, 'if you have never known what it is to love someone so much, that in being with them you can only count the hours until you have to part again. That being apart from them is like half of you has been torn away and you dread never getting it back. When a word from someone can make you the happiest creature on earth, or the most miserable.' As she spoke, the emotions heaved in Estraya again; she felt the ecstasy and the agony, the nothing between, of her love. 'I resent Wulfstan, like the book, for the power he has over me; that power I first felt when he stood by a fire like this and told us about the battle at Val-ès-Dunes. And I hate myself for it.'

In the firelight, her tears flowed like bands of blood down her face. She felt Gilbert grip her hands, interlocking his fingers with hers, then saw him relax and smile.

'But you didn't kill him. It was not written that you should.'

'No.' Seeing the kindness in his eyes, Estraya felt relief; the same relief she had felt at the water's edge, when she pulled the knife away from Wulfstan's chest. 'I will never kill anyone.'

FIFTEEN

'So you came here.'

'Yes. And now I understand what I am. I am the stars, and the sky. I am the forest, and the river. I am the earth and the air, the wood and the water. I carry the knife, but its foretelling will not come about through me.'

Gilbert took this in for a while, before asking, 'And now you are here?'

Estraya sat down again and buried into her father's arms, pulling the blankets over them. 'I could live here. There is shelter; there are fish in the river, wild plants, fruits. I can set snares. Everything you have taught me.'

'And the wolves and bears and wild boar I taught you about?'

'Let me see... Wolves come at night, and a good fire keeps them away. Bears avoid you, if you avoid them. Boar are dangerous only if you come between a mother and her young.'

Gilbert laughed, recognising his voice in the list she recounted, and hearing hers, brighter again. But he stopped suddenly.

'And when your child is born?'

Estraya took a breath and held it. *How does he know?*

As if in answer, her father went on, 'I am with living creatures, my love, day in and day out. You think I don't know when one of them is pregnant?'

She breathed again. 'Does my mother know? Will she be angry?'

'I haven't asked Samra if she knows. She is wise in many things, and angry at few. Your loving Wulfstan is not one of them. You will tell her when we go back. And please, take this again.' From inside his tunic, Gilbert pulled out the knife in its sheath. 'It's a stupid little thing and I'm afraid of losing it.'

Estraya giggled. Under the blankets, she tied the knife to her, and snuggled once more to her father's chest.

'Tell me about how you and Mother met.'

'I have, many times.'

'I know, but I love the story.'

So Gilbert told her again about the market place and the crowd, and the dark woman on the platform, and the knife. About the journey back to Lyons, and the cart, and the star-naming, the star-falling, and the star-daughter born to them after.

In his arms, the star-daughter was asleep, the life quickening in her belly, the knife at her ankle; the fourteenth generation of daughters to carry it.

And now there would be a fifteenth.

The Charcoal Burners

Andredswald, Sussex, March 1052

Dudda closed his eyes, and turned his face to the sun. It was not the lingering, sultry days of summer that made him think of his youth in Egypt, but a day like this. A day when, after the long nights and the cold that seeped into the very ground of the woodland, the whole earth seemed to relax under the first warmth of the year. A day when the trees lifted their heads, and the green spears of leaves on the woodland floor began to fulfil their promise of the swathes of bluebells that would come in a month or two.

So Dudda began to dream, to think himself back in Cairo, among the turbaned men and the veiled women thronging the streets, and the drovers whipping braying donkeys down impossibly narrow alleys to the souks, where stalls were heaped with goods from across the world, with cumin and cucumbers, with silks and swords, and everywhere smelt of spices and foul drains. The big man saw his younger self, dodging people and animals, hurrying to knock on a door in a wall, where in a tiny room on an array of narrow shelves, jar after jar held the wonders of the world. Here was a vivid yellow substance that clung to the glass and threated to corrode anything it touched, there the embryo of some unknown ghastly creature, trapped forever in an oily liquid, staring sightlessly out. An old man, who seemed to have fused into the wall against which he sat, emerging from the shadow, holding out a hand for the coins that would make him reach for a particular jar, then watching Dudda bolt through the door with whatever his astrologer and alchemist master had charged him to buy. This he needed to keep hidden under his robe as he dashed back through the streets, to the workshop crammed with contraptions to boil, distil and separate, and the tables laden with minerals, plants, animal parts and other substances ordinary men would not dare to ask about. And his master, eyes lighting with anticipation, grasping whatever Dudda had brought him, turning at once to his bench and pestle and mortar, adding the new material, and resuming the work that would bring him closer to the intangible secrets of the universe.

In front of Dudda, a twig snapped. He opened his eyes to see a man standing before him, with a bag over his shoulder. A man whose hair was unkempt, whose clothes were shabby and whose boots were filthy. A man Dudda would not have taken for the well turned-out knight he had first met years before in Normandy, but for the light blue-grey eyes fixed intently on him.

'What brings you to the woods again, Hugh de Bayeux? Have you given up your quest? Or have you come to show me the gold you've made?'

'Neither. But I will have gold, soon, and you will help me.'

'I have nothing to tell you this time, and nothing to give you either.'

'Oh, but you have. You are surrounded by it.' Hugh

looked across the clearing at the turf-covered pile, as the smoke seeping from it into the sunlight wafted across them both. He wiped a hand across his eyes. 'I wonder you can live in such a place... Dudda, do you call yourself?'

'I do. And I do not notice any more the smoke and the smell. It becomes a part of you when you live with something for so long; it gets into you, body and soul – as you must know, Hugh. Now tell me what you came for and we can be done.'

'Charcoal.'

'Well, charcoal I have, that's true. How much do you want?'

'All of it. Everything you have made this winter. I have horses and carts waiting.'

Dudda smiled. 'Our whole winter burn? And what about the smiths and the metalworkers and the glass blowers hereabouts? What are they to do, when I tell them there's nothing for them this spring?'

'Do what anyone would do; go elsewhere.'

Dudda shook his head. 'I cannot give you so much, and you cannot pay me enough for it.'

In answer, Hugh took the bag from his shoulder, and tipped it out onto the woodland floor. Among the brown twigs, and the green spears of the bluebell leaves, Dudda saw silver and gold; plates and cups, candlesticks and incense burners. He looked at Hugh.

'If you came by this how I think you have, Hugh de Bayeux, I cannot take it. And what use is a silver platter to me here? Now go.'

He turned away and began to walk towards the charcoal mound. Behind him, he heard a scream. Turning round, he saw Mildrythe running into the clearing, a look of wild terror on her face. She stopped, chest heaving from her effort, and pointed behind her into the trees. Two men emerged together into the clearing, slowly pushing two young men they held gripped tightly; Mildrythe's twin sons.

Dudda moved with a speed hard to believe in a man so colossal. He propelled himself across the clearing towards the two men, his great arms and legs moving like those of a large beast. As the men saw him, they froze, holding their charges in front of them like shields. But Dudda was bearing down on them, arms outstretched, hands making two great fists aimed at their heads. They let go of the twins and ran. Both twins headed across the clearing towards Mildrythe, but Hugh grabbed one as he went past, and pulled the young man back against his body, putting an arm around his chest. The other twin stopped and stared at his brother, seeing the knife Hugh had pulled out and held to his throat. Dudda made to move towards Hugh, but halted on seeing the blade pressing against the flesh of the young man's neck. Mildrythe was motionless, hands to her mouth, eyes filled with fear.

'Enough!' Hugh looked round at the others. 'If you want him to live, I will leave with what I came for.'

Dudda relaxed his body, and put his hands on his hips. He looked at Hugh and laughed. Bellows of laughter came from his giant frame and his dark curly hair shook.

'Oh, Hugh,' he said at last, 'you do not know how many times I've wanted to stand where you are now, with a knife at that boy's throat, or at his brother's, or both of them.'

Dudda laughed again, and wiped a tear from his eye. Hugh stared at him in disbelief. Behind him, Mildrythe was open-mouthed.

'I don't think there are two more senseless, worthless boys in the whole of the Andredswald,' Dudda went on. 'I curse every day that I am lumbered with them. But their father stupidly got himself killed, and they are in my charge now, God help me. They can't carry out any task without dawdling, missing something, or squabbling. If it was up to me, I would let you do your worst – no, I would help you; really, I would. Yet they are Mildrythe's sons, and I cannot let them be taken from their mother, for she loves them, as mothers love their children in spite of everything. I admire her for it.'

Dudda turned to look at Mildrythe, who was still speechless. Then he turned back to Hugh.

'So take your charcoal; I will not try to stop you. And take the church's treasures back with you. You can damn yourself if you like, but I won't.'

Hugh smiled. 'I will repay you in gold, when I have it.'

'That you will not,' Dudda said quickly. 'But you can repay me; set apart some land in Berewic, enough to live from, and build me a house on it. I'll not want to be in a hut in the Andredswald when I am old bones.'

As Hugh went to find his two men, Mildrythe came up to Dudda, who took her in his arms. In his bear-like embrace she turned her face up at him, with a look that was part loving, part furious.

'What will we do for money now?' she asked.

'I have some put aside, if I can find where I buried it.'

One of the twins was looking at the red mark on his brother's neck where the knife had pressed. He put a finger to it.

'He said we were stupid.'

His brother swatted the hand away.

'Senseless, is what he said. You're stupid.'
'He should have stuck that knife in you.'
He poked his brother, who poked him back.
'In you, you mean.'
'In you.' Poke.
'In you.' Poke.
Dudda looked at Mildrythe, and sighed.

Ælfwyn

Berewic, Sussex, May 1052

Æadgytha awoke suddenly, snatching at fragments of the dream she had been having – the same dream she had had before, but this time more vivid than ever, and closer to an ending. As often now, Hugh was absent from their chamber, busy with his work. Æadgytha sat up, shivering in the cold air, and, taking a cloak, went through into the hall house. There was still wine on the table. Taking the flagon, she drank straight from it, gulping thirstily. Two servants were asleep by the fire and she went to lie between them, with her back to the warm hearthstones. After a while she began to doze. Turning over, she watched the last flames licking up from the embers, feeling her eyelids closing.

The light of the flames was changing to another light – the sparkle of sun on water. Once again, Æadgytha was in her dreamscape, once again looking down on Berewic as her falcon might have done. A great crowd of villagers was on the riverbank, waving and shouting as they watched two men in the river below them. The men were fighting, as they had in Æadgytha's dream before, and still she could not see their faces, however hard she strained from above to do so.

Why am I not down there? Why am I not among my people?

Now the scene was changing, and people were streaming down the bank towards the two men, as if the whole village were on the move and itself a river, pouring into the river below it. This Æadgytha had also seen before in the dream, but now something was different. There was a flash of light on an object – something that flew from the two men in the river, high into the air, and the arc of whose flight took it to the mill pond beyond, where it dropped into the water, twirling and shimmering as it began to sink to the bottom. Now a lone figure had detached itself from the crowd and was moving away; moving at speed towards the mill pond in a straight line, contrasting with the random movement of the people at the river. Æadgytha strained again, trying to force her floating dream-body closer to the ground to see this single being on its unwavering path.

Someone in the crowd called out, and as Æadgytha got agonisingly just a little lower and nearer to the figure, it turned. *There!* For a moment she saw a girl; a girl with flaming hair and fierce green eyes, who looked back for a moment before turning away again. In her dream, Æadgytha was trying to call to her, in words that would not leave her mouth.

Stop! Speak to me. What has happened? Where am I in this?

Now the girl was looking desperately towards the mill pond to see where the object had gone, shielding her eyes from the sun with a hand.

I can see it – I know where it is. Follow; follow me!

Æadgytha was moving above the girl and just beyond, praying she could lead her on. And the girl went on, hesitantly at first, then with more certainty, until at last she reached the edge of the pond and threw herself in.

'Ælfwyn!'

The voice had called again. It was Hugh de Bayeux.

Æadgytha was awake, trembling with excitement and fear.

Ælfwyn! You are mine – and you are in danger. God help you, for I cannot.

Birth

Forest of Valognes, Normandy, July 1052

In the night, Estraya was awake.

Lit by the full moon through the windows around the room that Gilbert had made for her within the main house, she saw familiar things. Tables strewn with rocks and minerals, some whole, some crushed and in little bowls and jars; a pestle and mortar held a pale yellow powder awaiting testing or transfer. Plants occupied other tables or were hanging in bunches from beams; drying slowly, they scented the air, like a northern echo of the Spanish gardens of her mother's memory. Among the hanging plants and on the walls, animal skins were stretched to dry in their turn; here the stripes of a boar piglet skin, there the spots of a fallow deer hide, catching the moonlight. It was a space Estraya needed, not just for her work and her collections; very soon it would be needed for her and her baby.

Heavily, she got up from her bed and went to the door, listening. Around the clearing, a warm wind was blowing softly in the treetops. Above her, the sky was scattered with stars, so bright and so close that they seemed to weigh on the earth itself. Extending a forefinger towards the cluster of stars in the Great Bear, Estraya began to move it around the sky; *Kochab – Dubhe – Alioth – Alkaid…* silently naming them, as Samra had taught her.

As with most nights now, Estraya needed to pee; but as she went over to the trees, she knew it was not this that had woken her. Above the sound of her piss on the leaves, she began to hear a breathing, heavy and frequent; the panting of an animal. Getting to her feet, she followed the sound to the pen set back from the forest clearing, and quietly stepped inside through the open gate. Lying on the other side under the trees, the scars on its neck visible in the moonlight, was the fallow doe from two years ago. It was on its side and Estraya could see its swollen belly, heaving in time to the panting, which from this close was a pained snort, flaring in the animal's nostrils. The doe lifted its head and turned it to her as Estraya drew closer, but did not try to move.

You did not come back last year; this must be your second fawn… why are you back now? Are you troubled?

Gradually, Estraya came up beside the doe and knelt behind it. Among the bloody fluid in the leaves, under its tail she could see a hoof protruding.

One hoof… where is the other?

Remembering how one of the cows they kept had presented its calf like this, Estraya put a hand gently on the doe's back. It twitched but otherwise stayed still and turned its head away, laying it on the ground again. Slowly, Estraya reached for the deer's opening and put her fingers inside. Feeling around the fawn's head and the shank of its protruding leg, she found the other leg, bent back beyond the birth canal. The weight and size of her own belly hindering her, Estraya adjusted her position on her knees and reached in with her hand, trying to move the bent leg to the opening.

There was a noise at the gate to the pen and she looked up to see her mother standing, watching; the concern on Samra's face was clear, even in the pale moonlight. Estraya put a finger to her lips, and waved her mother away.

She will trust only me.

The leg was hard to move in any direction, and as she wrestled with it, Estraya knew the pain she must be causing the animal. Yet it remained still, only grunting at a harder push or pull. Feeling the strength begin to ebb from her own body in the heat of the night, Estraya began to despair; the doe would die if it could not give birth. With the back of her other hand, she wiped away sweat, and tears.

The doe turned its head to her again, and as their eyes met, for a moment its panting stopped. It raised its rear a little, and in that instant Estraya's hand on the leg was pulled into the opening with it. Suddenly, there were two legs, and the start of a head. Estraya shuffled back in the leaves, the doe began to push, and the fawn slithered into the world, snorting, flanks heaving like bellows.

Now Estraya cried. She wept with joy and relief, laughing as the fawn struggled to get to its feet, failing hopelessly. The doe turned and began to lick up the afterbirth, then the fawn, clearing the mucus around its nose and eyes. Soon the doe was on its feet, licking hard from head to foot, the fawn shaking its head and flapping its oversized ears, still making attempts to get to its legs. Soon it would be able to stand, and to suckle.

Estraya felt wetness on the ground beneath her. Putting a hand between her legs, she gave a look of panic to her mother at the gate of the pen. Samra smiled and motioned her to come. Estraya struggled to her feet and made her way laboriously across the pen, feeling an immense heaviness in her body through her legs and into the ground. Samra hugged her daughter to her, then put an arm through hers to help her through the gate. As Samra made to close it behind her, Estraya stopped her.

'She will need to take her fawn away,' she whispered.

Samra nodded. 'Did you see – was it a doe, or a buck?'

'A buck – and a big fawn. One day, he will be king of the forest. And he will remember me.' Her dark eyes were shining, her face lit with joy. Suddenly a flash of pain shot across Estraya's face. 'I am tired. I need to go inside.'

'You will be tired, before another night is through,' her mother said. 'And you will have a birth of your own.'

*

In the morning, Samra crept out of Estraya's room with a bowl of water. Standing it on a table, she went over to a chest, passing Gilbert, who was snoring by the hearth. She opened a drawer in the chest and took out the coin she had picked up from the platform in Rouen the day she was sold and which she had later shown to Gilbert. Returning to the table, Samra said a prayer in Ladino, looking into the water in the bowl, which was cloudy and pink. Then, as the Sephardim do when a baby is born, she threw a silver coin into her grandchild's first bath water.

In her room, Estraya was sleeping, her child beside her. She had given birth to a boy. In the fifteenth generation, the line of daughters was broken.

The knife would pass to a son.

Fields of Gold

Berewic, Sussex, July 1052

There was one evening of the year when the sun setting in the west shone directly into Eadric's farmhouse and along the full length of the table where he and Guðrun would sit. This was that evening, and Eadric had come to the door to look.

The orb of the sun was beating a glowing path across his yardland that stretched away over the valley to the river. That part of his thirty acres in front of him, of plough and meadow, of rough grazing and withy beds, was suffused in warm light. The breeze through the barley, almost ready for the sickle, was spinning golden ripples, above which a haze of insects danced, and the swallows chased and turned. From just below him, Guðrun was making her way up the path through the vegetable garden, holding a basket in the crook of an arm. The difficulty that her club foot gave her movement was added to by her heavy body. As she grew nearer, Guðrun looked up and smiled.

Eadric felt the breath being pulled from his body by a huge pang of joy; an ecstasy that grabbed him as if he had been waiting his whole life for this moment. He looked at

Guðrun, radiant and fruitful, and beyond her at his crops, standing perfect in the setting sun, just as ripe with promise. And he knew that however high he rose, whatever wealth he gained, he would never again know such a moment of utter fulfilment. Even as he grasped the instant now, as the breath shuddered back into his lungs, in doing so it was lost forever; like a child grabbing at a perfect flower and seeing the petals fall into the dust.

Guðrun met him at the door. Reaching to kiss him, she turned and gazed with him across at the red globe of the sun now quickly dropping to the horizon. He pulled her close to him, and Guðrun leant back into his arms, taking his hands in hers and gently running them over her swollen belly and up under her heavy breasts. Turning her face up to his, she saw the tears in his eyes. The sun disappeared, and almost at once it was colder.

The Secret

Forest of Valognes, Normandy, August 1052

Taking her baby and a clean dress with her, Estraya followed the path that led uphill through the pine and beech trees and past the rocky outcrop, and down to the edge of the trees and the marshland.

She lay the child down in the warm stones at the edge of the marsh, then undressed, picked the child up and stepped into the water. As she waded into the shallows, the warm water advancing up her body felt like a balm. At last she reached a place deep enough to squat; holding the baby in the crook of an arm, she splashed water over herself and rubbed between her legs, laughing with relief as the smell from her body was carried away. Among the Sephardim, after the birth of a child, a mother may not uncover herself or change her clothes for thirty days.

As the water splashed him, her baby laughed too, wriggling and giggling in her arm. Estraya held him in the water a little way, and watched as he kicked. Her son was already as dark as her, with dark eyes, and dark hair showing on his head in the afternoon sun.

You will swim, my little one; water will be your world, and the trees above you.

In that instant she saw not the warm shallows of the marsh around her, but the bend of a river below a steep bluff, with deep, deep water. Two young people, boy and girl, were diving into the water; he dark of skin and hair, she fair of skin and red-haired. As shafts of sunlight cut through the water, light danced on an object twirling and sinking into it; a knife, light flashing on its blade. And the boy and girl dived at the same time, but the red-haired girl reached the knife in the water first.

*

When Estraya came back to the clearing in the forest, her mother and father were sitting in the shade on a tree stump; the 'manor' that Gilbert had given to Wulfstan and Eadric. Gilbert watched his daughter, darkly beautiful and graceful, talking softly to the baby she held to her breast in one arm, a dirty dress over the other, as she went over to a fire he had lit in the clearing. In the clean white dress she wore now, she reminded him movingly of the girl to whom five years ago Samra had given the knife now at her ankle. Estraya turned and looked at him, then threw the dress on the fire.

'His name will be Ralf,' she said. 'When Wulfstan returns, I will tell him.'

Gilbert looked at Samra. They both knew what their daughter knew; that Duke William had returned months ago from England, without Wulfstan. He got to his feet. Putting out his arms, Gilbert kissed Estraya lightly on the forehead as she passed him her baby.

'Sit down, my love,' he said. 'Your mother has something to tell us.'

Samra stood up and turned to Estraya as she sat on the stump, hugging her knees. Standing beside Samra, Gilbert rocked his sleeping grandson.

'Before I gave you the knife, my child,' Samra began, 'I spoke of the generations through which it had passed from mother to daughter. I could never have imagined this would change; but with the birth of your – of Ralf – it has. He will be the next keeper of the knife.'

'There may be a daughter yet,' Estraya said, 'when Wulfstan comes back.'

'He will not come back. In your heart, you know that.'

Estraya buried her face in her knees, and her mother sat down and put an arm round her, holding her against her shoulder.

'I am sorry,' Samra said gently.

Gilbert watched as Estraya's shoulders heaved. He could hear her muffled sobs and fought back his own distress. After a while she looked up, face tear-stained and crumpled.

'I know.' Estraya stood up, smoothed down her dress and wiped her face with the back of a hand. 'And I know that Ralf has a destiny; he and the knife. This is what you are going to tell us.'

Samra looked up at her. 'Yes.'

In a few minutes, it was told. Gilbert listened intently, trying to picture the scene beneath the observatory. The three friends around the table, listening to Sophia, and hearing about the ruler whose power would come from the book, the knife and from Samra. *The ruler I speak of will come from your bloodline.* He looked down at Ralf, tiny and unaware in his great, strong arms.

'We live here in the forest,' he said, turning to Samra. 'How will any that are born here sit on a throne?'

'Many times after that day, I said the same to myself,' Samra replied, 'until Alfred confided in me before he went to England, and wrote his secret in the book.' She looked up at her daughter. 'Ralf is Edward of Wessex's grandson.'

Gilbert felt a surge of astonishment, and panic. He barely noticed as Estraya came to take her child back. She held the boy aloft, looking up at him.

'Your father is the son of a king,' she whispered. Head on one side, he looked back, gurgling.

Now Gilbert needed to sit down on the stump where he had chided Eadric and Wulfstan for their idleness. Wulfstan the warrior, who had come and hunted and fallen, and who they had tended. Wulfstan who had loved Estraya, and been loved by her; who left for England, and did not return.

'Who knows this about Wulfstan, now Alfred is dead?' he asked Samra. 'Wulfstan himself? Or even Edward, since it was Alfred that told you?'

'Edward knows. But he knows too, that he can never tell him. For whoever tells Wulfstan ends his life.'

Gilbert and Estraya both looked at Samra in shock. Estraya held her son to her, wrapping him protectively in her arms. Gilbert was shaking his head.

'You cannot know—'

'I know.' Samra looked close to tears. 'And it is the hardest knowledge I will ever bear.'

In Estraya's arms, Ralf began to stir. Soon fully awake, he began to cry, moving his arms and legs as he had done in the water.

'I need to take him inside,' Estraya said, 'it is too hot out here.'

As her daughter walked away, Samra called to her.

'You do understand, my love, that even if Wulfstan should come back, you cannot tell him.'

Estraya stopped and turned back.

'You do not need to fear. I have always known that I will never see him again.' She hurried away, into the dark and quiet of the house.

When she had gone, Gilbert turned to Samra.

'Will you walk to the rocks with me? It should be a fine sunset this evening.'

Samra nodded and took his hand. And so they followed the same path uphill through the pine and beech trees to the rocky outcrop, and sat on a rock facing into the sun. Behind them, the light of the lowering sun through the edge of the forest was picking out the bole of every tree in a column of golden red. Gilbert put an arm round Samra and she rested her head on his shoulder; he felt her body against his, as lean as it had been twenty years before, in his cart on the way back to the Forest of Lyons.

'We used to come here with Estraya,' Gilbert said at length, 'when she was small. We'd play hide and seek in the rocks and trees.'

'And never find her.'

'I feel for her. She has a burden to carry, with the child, and now knowing about Wulfstan, yet knowing it must be hidden from him. As do you, with the book lost to you, and never able to tell Wulfstan he could be the next King of England. And this is what you couldn't tell me about Wulfstan.'

'I could not keep it from both of you any longer. "You are

of blood royal, and into your line blood royal shall come." But when Sophia spoke those words, she did not say it must be forever kept a secret.'

'Not so. Wulfstan may never be King of England. But Ralf might.'

Samra lifted her head and looked at him.

'You are right. We must look to Ralf now. Though how this will come about in the Forest of Valognes, I do not know.'

'Nor do I,' said Gilbert. 'William may have returned without Wulfstan, but he has come back with a prize: Edward's promise of the throne of England. Where does that leave your bloodline, and the foretelling?'

'In danger; for William will not entertain a rival to his claim.'

'He is not a man to be thwarted in anything. That day in the square, you said you didn't feel safe with William. He sent Jaco to kill you, didn't he?'

Samra looked at him. 'After what I told the duke about the book. I have not wanted to think about it; I know the love you have for him, and your loyalty.'

'If he can do that for a book, if he thought a rival to a kingdom was in his own forest warden's family, he would strike us all down.'

Samra shook her head. 'Then Ralf too must be kept secret,' she said sadly. 'And none of this will come about.'

Gilbert took Samra by the shoulders and looked into her eyes.

'Listen. Felip said to me once that nothing happens but for a purpose. "Everything begins and ends at its given time," he said. "Everyone comes into and leaves your life to set you on or change you from a path." Believe in that; and wait.'

Smiling, Samra said, 'You are wiser than you know, Gilbert.'

Gilbert thought for a minute. 'Does Felip know about Wulfstan?'

'My excuse was that I did not trust him enough to tell him.'

'You are right not to trust him, if he went to England to take the book for himself.'

'In truth, I wanted to keep what I knew about Wulfstan to myself.' Gilbert looked at her, surprised, and she shook her head. 'Whoever has the book covets it, and the knowledge it contains. I am not above this.'

Gilbert looked into Samra's eyes, and saw again the pain of her separation from the book. He took her hands in his.

'For his craving for the book, Hugh de Bayeux is lost. Now Felip may be, for his. They were blinded by their craving and their folly. You never will be; you have sight, Samra, sight of what is good and true.'

Return from Exile

Bosham, Sussex, August 1052

'Felip! Wake up!'

In the dawn, confused, Felip opened his eyes. For a moment he thought he was back in Berewic, with Cuthred sitting on the end of his bed – though that had been months ago, when he was barely healed of his wound, and the reeve was telling him he needed to go. He remembered seeing Cuthred's fleshy lips moving as he told him that the dull young woman who hung round Botulf was pregnant and she would be moving in, so the pair would need the bed. The pregnancy had been no great surprise; whenever no one else but Felip had been in the house they had been coupling noisily, like pigs; he grunting and she squealing. Fittingly, Cuthred had also told Felip that he had got his nephew a job as one of the village swineherds. In his oily voice, the man had made it clear that getting Botulf this position – involving taking the villagers' pigs to the autumn fattening grounds – was entirely due to his importance as reeve. So, after nearly three months of doing no more than walk around the house, Felip had found himself one night tottering down to the quay in Berewic, Cuthred before and Botulf behind him, making sure he was got onto a ship to be spirited unseen out of the village. If Felip had not been feeling half-dead, he might have noticed that the last coin leaving his purse to pay for his keep coincided with his own departing.

He had come into Bosham not in a small rowing boat this time, but in a large ship with slaves on its oars, heading up the approaches on a full tide; not looking around him in the sunshine but in a clinging mist, huddled on the deck against the cold; not finding the town teeming with Godwin energy, but sullen and subdued. Getting to the church with Osbern and his priests had felt like finding a sanctuary.

The time that had passed since then, Felip had spent regaining his strength, walking along the creeks and the mudflats, reading; and praying. Prostrate in the church before the altar, he had seen himself as he imagined God did, guilty of hubris so arrogant it was breathtaking. That he, a mere servant of the Lord, having heard everything Sophia had said under the dome in the observatory about the book, the knife and the family of Samra, had presumed to know better. *And the ruler I speak of will come from your bloodline.* He had ignored everything he was told and sought the book out for himself, craved it as a mere volume of instruction that would make him look greater in the eyes of princes and men. Well, he had paid for his hubris, and if he had not paid with his death, it must be for a purpose; to see that the part of the story he had ignored would come about. *You are of blood royal, and into your line blood royal shall come.* And Felip knew exactly who that incoming blood royal was.

Now Osbern was sitting on the end of his bed, shaking him awake.

'Get up! They are coming!'

Carefully, Felip sat up; his side was still tender. 'Who is coming?' he said dozily.

'The Godwins, of course. They have returned. The earl from Flanders, Harold from Ireland; the whole family. Raiding and taking hostages where people will not give them quarter; gathering men, arms and more ships where they will. Now their fleet is off the coast, with two ships ready to move up the approaches to Bosham.'

'Where will they be heading?'

'Along the coast; they know Sussex and Kent will give them more support still. Then to London, and to confront King Edward. God help us.'

'What do you mean?'

'The absence of the Godwins this last year has left the Normans Edward has given positions and favours to cruelly exposed. To many they seem like foreign leeches, feeding on England's rich and fatted body. Edward has done nothing to counter that view.'

'That is unjust,' Felip said. 'In your years here, you have done much – look around you. And you are not the only one. Men of ability who work hard are not leeches.'

'I will keep my head down, as always, and hope my Englishness saves me. But many of my countrymen will be in danger, when the rallying cry goes up: "Save England, and banish the outsiders!" And you should take care too, when we Normans are being sought out.'

Felip drew breath to point out that he was not Norman but from the Languedoc, but thought better of it. He began to get out of the bed and look for his clothes. Osbern looked at him.

'Where are you going?'

'To Berewic. If what you say is true, it will not be long before the Godwins are knocking on Hugh de Bayeux's door. If he is banished, the book could be lost, whether Hugh takes it with him or not.'

As Felip began to put on his habit, Osbern looked at the ugly scar on the monk's side.

'The man barred your way once to keep you from this book you have told me about, and left you for dead. Surely you cannot hope to succeed another time?'

'I must succeed, this time.'

'I do not pretend to understand your passion for this book.' Osbern nodded. 'But if it is as valuable as you say, I will provide you what you need for the journey. And you may bring the book here, now that Edward wants nothing to do with it.'

'No. I must return it to its rightful owner – the woman he stole it from in Normandy. And when I am there, I must find Wulfstan.'

'Wulfstan? Have you not heard? Wulfstan did not return with William. He is here, in England.'

'In England?'

'William left him behind, to be a guarantee that the hostages Edward holds against the Godwins' return would be delivered to Normandy.'

'Then he will be needed, and soon.'

'It is not as simple as that. In that time, he has taken up the Godwins' cause. He has pleaded with Edward for their return, and for the Lady Ædgytha not to be treated as they were.'

'That cannot have pleased Edward.'

'Edward has told me himself that he was reluctant

to let Wulfstan stay and not return with William. He said Wulfstan's father had promised the duke's father that Wulfstan would serve William for life, and only William's insistence that Wulfstan should remain here swayed him. Now it seems Wulfstan serves another lord.'

'And that will not please William. But where is Wulfstan?'

'They say, far from standing ready with the hostages, he has left London, hoping to meet with the earl and his sons, and urging the people to welcome them and give them every assistance.'

'Then when I have the book, I will seek Wulfstan. For I have something to tell him. And it will change the world.'

Osbern shrugged. 'I have heard that before.'

The Trap is Sprung

Berewic, Sussex, September 1052

It was hard to say who looked more surprised when Eadric opened the door of his house in answer to Felip's knocking: Eadric, to see again the man who had gone so quickly from Berewic, the quest for his book apparently abandoned; or the monk, when he looked past Eadric into the room, and saw Guðrun standing beyond him, fully pregnant. He knew little of childbirth, but he imagined she must be very close to being delivered.

Felip did not wait to be invited in, but pushed past Eadric and turned to speak to him. It was the end of a late summer heatwave, and the very warmth seemed to follow him into the room.

'Give me shelter for another two days, I beg you. And do not tell anyone I am here.'

Eadric motioned to Felip to sit at the table, where he joined him. Guðrun went to lie down on the bed, pulling the curtain around her as she did so.

'Two days?' Eadric asked.

'Within that time the Godwins will be here, and everything in Berewic will change.'

'Then the rumours are true; the earl and his family are restored to Edward's favour. It has, if anything, been quicker than I expected.'

'I must find the book before Hugh de Bayeux is banished.'

Eadric's eyes widened. 'Banished?'

'Normans everywhere are being rounded up and sent back. I doubt they will make an exception of the man who spurned the manor he was given, and its people. From what you told me before,' Felip added.

Eadric nodded. 'Before, you said you were leaving us without your book. If it was so important, why did you not take it then?'

'I lied to you. I stayed hidden and I found the book. But Hugh found me, and I was nearly killed.' Felip lifted his tunic, to show the scar on his side.

'Then why should you succeed this time?'

'Again, I lied. The book is not mine. I need to return it to its owner. And I must not fail in this.'

'The book belongs to the woman in Normandy; the one you told me about?'

Felip lowered his head. 'Yes,' he whispered. 'And I am ashamed that I ever pretended otherwise.'

Eadric got to his feet and quietly went over to the bed in the corner, parting the curtain just enough to see Guðrun dozing. Closing the curtain again, he came back to the table and stood, looking down at Felip.

'In the clearing in the Forest of Valognes, where Samra lives, do you remember a large tree stump?'

The monk looked up at Eadric, open-mouthed.

'How do you know the Forest of Valognes?' he managed at last. 'And how do you know—'

Eadric help up a hand to silence him.

'The stump – do you remember it?'

'Yes. There was a story… that Gilbert had given it to Wulfstan and Eadric – their manor, he called it – when the boys were so full of themselves about a manor in England they said they had claim to.' Felip got to his feet, staring at the face in front of him, trying to remember the boy he had last seen in the forest. 'Wait… the manor is Berewic, and you are Eadric; you are Wulfstan's brother!'

Eadric smiled. 'I exchanged that tree-stump manor for the few acres you see around me.' The smile vanished and his face hardened. 'But I have never given away my claim to Berewic. I am rightful thegn here. And if Hugh is banished, it will only bring me nearer to sitting in my hall house.'

Felip looked into Eadric's cold, grey eyes; it might have been a different man who, less than a year ago, had received him into his house. There was a noise from the bed, and at once the eyes softened.

'Eadric,' Guðrun was calling faintly.

Eadric stepped over to the bed and parted the curtain.

'Yes, my love?'

'Is the monk staying again?'

'No.'

Behind him, Felip jumped.

'But—'

'You will have your book today,' Eadric said, turning round. 'Hugh has been gone from the village for two days. He took his usual men with him to the woods, with horses and carts so laden they could hardly move. If you go now to the hall house, he will not be there to stop you.'

His final words were spoken to a swinging door. Felip had already gone.

Eadric turned back to the bed.

'How do you feel, my love?'

'In this heat, dreadful,' Guðrun groaned. 'Please God, let this baby come soon.'

'When it is ready,' Eadric said soothingly. 'All things in their own time.'

'Come here.' Guðrun patted the bed beside her.

Carefully, Eadric sat down next to her. Guðrun took his hand and placed it on the great mound of her belly beside him.

'There – a kick. Did you feel?'

And there it was, the child who would follow him, making a little lump in Guðrun's stomach under his hand, as if reaching out to him. He could not speak.

'You are a good man, Eadric,' Guðrun said, 'and you have been harshly treated. You will come to your birthright, one day. Berewic will be yours.' Her ice-blue eyes were shining with love, and hope.

Eadric smiled tenderly. But when he thought of Berewic, there was no tenderness in his heart. Yet he put that aside to move his hand over Guðrun's stomach.

'Will it be a boy or a girl?' he asked her.

'With a kick like that, it has to be a boy, of course!'

Guðrun gave a little laugh. Eadric knew this was despite the heat, and the heaviness making her body feel like lead, and her nervousness at what was to come; and he loved her all the more.

*

Moving quickly through the village, Felip looked around him, then opened the door to the hall house. The shutters were closed, but in the heat, the inside of the hall was still oppressively warm. When his eyes adjusted to the dark, Felip saw Æadgytha, seated behind the long table, sewing by the light of a candle. As she looked up, a servant made to confront the monk, but she waved the man away.

'Leave us.'

She motioned Felip to the table, where he stood resting his hands on it, wheezing. Flicking back the hair from over his eye, his hand came back wet with sweat.

Æadgytha stared at him. 'Why have you come back?'

'The Godwins are coming. And I must have the book.'

'The first, I have expected. But the second… Hugh said you had taken the book already.'

Felip lifted his tunic. 'I failed.'

If Æadgytha was moved at the sight of the scar, the flickering light of the candle on her face did not show it; but she gave a sharp gasp of breath.

'Since you came here, Hugh has redoubled his efforts to make gold. He has done nothing but buy lead, as much as he can, and charcoal. And I have seen other things – sulphur, mercury. We are penniless. He has even looted the church.'

'But have you seen him with the book?'

Æadgytha shook her head. Felip looked over at the door of the chamber.

'He must have hidden it.'

'If he has, you will not find it.'

'I have to find it. It does not belong to me, and I must return it.'

Æadgytha put down her sewing and passed him the

candle. Felip turned and went to the door of the chamber. He stepped inside, leaving her in near darkness.

*

In the Andredswald, Hugh de Bayeux was with two men from the village at the place in the woods where the Romans had an ironworks. On an open, level area above the stream in the valley he had set up his crucible, a large iron cauldron with an open top, bigger than any he had used before. It rested on a structure of stones, and a huge hearth of charcoal was blazing beneath it. A flash of lightning overhead revealed Hugh, bent over the crucible. He was adding a red powder through the open top, while two other men were stirring as hard as they could.

*

When Wulfstan of Wessex burst into the hall house, Æadgytha was still seated behind the long table. In the light that flooded in through the door, she looked up to see a man barely recognisable from the one who had come with Duke William the Christmas before. Wulfstan's fair hair was longer, and with his two-handed axe at his belt he was English, not Norman. His breathing was heavy, and he looked around him wildly.

'Where is Hugh de Bayeux?'

'I do not know. I have not seen him for two days.'

Æadgytha saw Wulfstan look over to the door of the chamber.

'I am here with Harold,' Wulfstan said, 'looking for Hugh. You do not need to harbour him.'

He moved towards the chamber door; inside, Felip blew out the candle.

'Hugh is not in there,' Æadgytha said firmly.

Wulfstan turned back and began to open the shutters on the windows.

'There is a storm coming. Soon you will need all the light you can get.' He turned to Æadgytha. 'It is over, Æadgytha; the Godwins are returned. And the Norman stooges King Edward foisted on our churches and manors are fleeing; they are declared outlaws, and we are come to drive out those who do not go willingly.'

'And Wulfstan of Wessex now serves the Godwins.'

'I would not have believed what Edward has done, if I had not seen it with my own eyes. Everywhere the people cry out against the incomers, and lament his gifting England to William. I joined Earl Godwin as soon as he alighted in Kent. In every landing he gathered more and more strength, and his people rose from the countryside too. When we came to London we opposed Edward with our fleet on the river, while our army marched towards him on the land. And Edward backed down and gave the Godwins back all he had taken.'

*

In the chamber, head against the wall, Felip listened to the muffled voices. *Wulfstan – did she say Wulfstan? I can tell him now who he really is.* He placed his hand on the chamber door. *No. First the book, then Wulfstan.* Felip opened the shutter to the window, and sunlight lit up the room, revealing the same objects the moonlight had the year before: shelf, table, bed and chest. There was nothing for it; he would have to search inch by inch.

*

The hall door opened again and Harold Godwinson came in, with Eadric following him.

'There is no sign of Hugh,' Harold said.

Ædgytha stood to greet her cousin. She got up awkwardly, weightily. And Wulfstan saw that she was heavily pregnant. At once he made to go over to her, but Harold stepped in front of him and embraced Ædgytha.

'How do you fare, cousin?' He turned back to Wulfstan. 'See, Wulfstan, Berewic will have an heir after all.'

Wulfstan stared at her, speechless, his mouth trying to form words, but Ædgytha looked away.

Harold turned to Eadric.

'And the cripple's woman is about to give birth too. All is well, in Berewic and in England. A pity that Archbishop Jumièges and some of the other Normans have made their escape, taking my brother and Hakon. But William will not keep them long, when he sees England has slipped from his grasp.'

Eadric showed no emotion, but his mind was racing. *The hostages gone, but Wulfstan not gone with them. William will never forgive this disloyalty… or that the Godwins have come between him and the throne of England.*

*

Now Hugh was riding back from the Andredswald, behind him a distant growl of thunder. Riding as hard as he could, still sweating from the heat of the crucible and with a burn mark on his temple, as he neared the village he could think of only one thing: *The book. I must get the book.*

*

Æadgytha looked at the three men in front of her, and her mind went back to the day nearly nine years ago when she had stood in her hall house with King Edward and the two Wessex.

'What do you want of me?' she asked Harold.

'Wulfstan wants me to drag Hugh out from wherever he is hiding and put him to the sword,' Harold answered. 'Berewic owes Hugh de Bayeux little, and you owe him even less. But he is the father of your child, and I am not a vindictive man. Your manor is in the gift of the king; Edward allowed you to choose when Hugh came here, and while he is king, I can do no less. Banish Hugh, or let him stay here as thegn; decide amongst you. And so there is no doubt, this time you must all be of one voice; if but one of you stays your hand against him, then thegn he will still be.'

He looked at Æadgytha and she knew he was testing her resolve, just as she had tested his that day they had gone hawking together two and a half years earlier. Harold turned and went outside.

*

Seeing Harold's men waiting in front of the hall, Hugh had gone around the side, to the chamber he and Æadgytha shared. Finding the window shutter open, he heaved his body into the opening. As the light was blotted out, Felip flung himself between the bed and a wall, trying to squeeze his rotund body into the narrow space. Hugh climbed through the window and into the chamber. Hearing a scraping sound on the floor, Felip lifted his head until he could see Hugh, pushing at the chest. He looked on astonished as Hugh de Bayeux moved the heavy chest across the floor, then lifted the boards underneath it. Straining to see what Hugh was doing, Felip had half lifted his body from out of the gap; through the wall he could distantly hear the voices of Æadgytha, Wulfstan and Eadric. Hugh was kneeling, crouched over the pit revealed by removing the boards. Then Hugh stood up, and he was holding something. He placed the object on top of the chest, and Felip saw the box that held the book.

Felip gasped, and fell out from between bed and wall to the floor, where he lay on his back, looking up at the box. In an instant, Hugh was beside him on the floor, with a hand over his mouth. He brought his face close to the monk's, and spoke in a low, urgent voice. As the sweat dripped from Hugh's forehead, Felip could feel the heat from the angry burn on his temple.

'Will you never give up? Has the book enslaved you, Felip, as it has me? It is time to end both our obsessions.'

Hugh got to his feet and opened the box. He took out the book, and turned it over in his hands, looking at the velvet cloth decorated with a moon and stars. Felip felt his scalp prickle. Hugh turned to Felip, as the monk was struggling to get up from the floor.

'You think you or Samra, or anyone, can own this?' Hugh said. 'You think you can use it, or even understand it? You look at it, and you think, "What it tells me, I can know; what it does, I can do too." You cannot. "For the wise, it is the way to treasure beyond price. For the foolish, it is the way to hell." Now I must free us both from hell.'

He put the book back in its box, and turned away. Felip moved to follow him.

'Where are you going? What will you do with the book?'

'What I should have done long ago. Burn it.'

'No!'

Felip was trying to keep his voice down, but he had half shouted the word, and now he was beside Hugh, with his hands on the box too.

'I cannot let you do this. The book has a purpose; one you cannot begin to understand, but it will change the world.'

Hugh pointed to the burn mark on his temple. 'I thought it my purpose to make gold from lead, but I was a fool. I held riches in my hands here, and I have thrown them away…'

Hugh's voice trailed off and he looked over at the bed. Leaving Felip with the box, he went to sit on the bed and put his head in his hands. Hugging the box to his chest like a baby, Felip stared at him.

Hugh looked up. 'The book… what purpose?'

'It concerns Wulfstan.' Felip glanced at the wall between them and the hall. 'Wulfstan has a destiny, that the book has revealed. The knife that Samra's daughter carries will bring it about. And I believe Estraya's fate is linked with Wulfstan's in this.'

'Wulfstan!' Hugh snorted. 'Wulfstan has betrayed William, and Edward. He serves our enemies, the Godwins, and he would see them on the throne of England.'

Felip shook his head. 'I know that your brother Ranulph met his end at Wulfstan's hands, at Val-ès-Dunes. But you must put that debt behind you, now. This thing is greater than all of us.'

'I am lucky that I was here, and not at Val-ès-Dunes, having to choose between my family and my duke. My brother was a traitor to William; that is a debt I must bear for the rest of my life.' Hugh pointed at the wall. 'But Wulfstan is here at my hall house, with Harold Godwinson. Whatever they are plotting through there, you can be sure we Normans will not profit from it.'

'Whatever is happening here is part of that destiny. Can you not realise this? I too thought I knew better, until the night here that you put a knife in my side. Now I know what I must do: take the book back to Normandy, and tell Wulfstan who he really is.'

'I know who Wulfstan is. The arrogant boy we knew in Normandy has become an arrogant man. And I know what I must do with the book.'

Hugh was quickly on his feet, and grabbed the box. As they held it between them, Felip struggled against the other man's strength, feeling the box slipping from his grasp as Hugh pulled on it.

'I will not let you take it; you will have to kill me this time.'

Hugh stopped pulling, and looked into the monk's face. Looking back, Felip saw the thegn's hard, blue-grey eyes betraying a torment that he would never have thought possible.

'Enough men have died here today,' Hugh said, and he wrenched the box with the book from Felip's grasp.

As Hugh moved to the window, Felip called out to him in desperation.

'I beg you, do not destroy the book!'

Hugh turned and Felip felt himself once again at the mountain pass in Spain, with Samra poised on the brink above the river, time standing still. The same moment of balance, from which everything would change, whichever way the scales tipped.

'If it is redemption you seek, let the book live. It is Samra's; let me return it to her.'

Hugh turned his face to the wall and pushed his forehead against it; for a moment he seemed about to collapse. Then he turned back to Felip and shook his head.

'Samra is dead.'

Felip stared at him. 'No... how?'

'By my order. When you came here last year searching for the book, I knew I could never be secure in it. To truly possess it, I had to take care of the woman who called herself its owner.'

The monk's head was spinning. 'The messenger... I saw you with him, in the paddock. You gave him the order, and money.'

'He had told me that before William would come to England, he had sent for his forest warden and his woman to come to Rouen. To strike at Samra in the Forest of Valognes would have been impossible. But Rouen... and I knew a man there who would do the deed. I thought God had given me the chance I needed. But it was the devil, taking me further in his grasp.'

Overwhelmed, Felip buried his face in his hands. *If I had not come here... I brought about Samra's death.* He looked up.

'She did not live to see the book again.'

'And you will not see it again.'

Felip wrenched himself from his misery to see Hugh beginning to climb through the window, and made a dash towards him. But he had forgotten about the pit; he fell headlong into it, striking his head on the far edge. Dimly, he saw Hugh's figure with the box in the window frame, before everything faded.

*

After Harold had left, there was silence in the hall house. Eadric, Wulfstan and Æadgytha looked at each other.

'Should we retire to your chamber, my lady,' Eadric said, 'as we did last time?'

'There is no need,' Æadgytha replied quickly. 'We are alone here.'

Eadric nodded. 'Then let us do this quickly. When Harold called me away, Guðrun was suffering. Her time is very close.'

Wulfstan spoke.

'It is clear. Hugh must go. And you will be Thegn of Berewic, Æadgytha.'

Æadgytha looked at Eadric. 'Do you agree?'

Just as he had the last time, Eadric chewed his lip. He turned away, and paced up and down. Then he turned back to the others.

'If you had lived here, Wulfstan, you would know what everyone knows; Æadgytha is as good as thegn here, and the child that follows her will be.' *Until William comes*, Eadric thought. 'I fear the disruption Hugh's removal will bring Berewic, when it needs stability.'

Wulfstan exploded. 'Are you mad, brother? The day we – you above all – have so long waited for... you will let this chance pass, to unseat Hugh?'

'What we have waited for is the chance to press the claim of the house of Wessex on Berewic,' Eadric retorted icily. 'I wonder that you throw yourself so mightily behind Æadgytha now, and not behind your own brother in his right? Or has her being with child changed your mind?'

Wulfstan shook his head. 'Like the *witan*, I believe we must make the best choice among those who would govern. And that is Æadgytha,' he said, looking at her, 'alone.'

Eadric paused, savouring the moment he had; to react to Wulfstan's disloyalty, to uphold Hugh de Bayeux, or to support Æadgytha.

'I admit, what our family has wanted is not the matter here,' he said, calmly, 'but the good of the manor of Berewic. And I can see the damage that Hugh's obsession and his greed have done. I know it cannot go on.' Turning to Æadgytha, he said hesitantly, 'Much as I know it must pain you, my lady, for the sake of Berewic, he must go.'

Wulfstan nodded his head. 'At last! My brother has shown some sense.' He looked to Æadgytha.

Æadgytha's senses were swimming. She felt the years roll back to when she was a girl, and her father had sat her on the branch of the moot tree. *Look around you*, he had said. *Berewic, its fields and its farms, its dwellings and its people, are all that matters. When you are thegn here, whatever you do, do it for the manor you hold dear.* And she knew what she must do. Fighting back the tears, she held herself upright and spoke firmly.

'Find Hugh, Wulfstan, and take him away.'

*

In the church, Father Brenier was lighting candles in the nave. He turned to see Hugh de Bayeux, dirty and sweltering, holding out a wooden box.

'Take it!' Hugh spat the words out, thrusting the box with the book in it on the priest. Brenier looked at it in his hands, then up at Hugh.

'What is it?'

'A book. Whoever possesses it has great power; too much power for a mortal man to own, and keep his soul.'

Brenier looked down at the box again. 'This is the book,' he said. 'The one Æadgytha has told me about. The one the monk was looking for, when I hid him here. Why are you giving it to me?'

'I want you to destroy it. But do not look into it; it will enthral you, as it has me.'

'Why do you not destroy it yourself?'

Before Hugh could answer, Brenier quickly put the wooden box on the church floor behind him. He turned back to see Hugh staring at it.

'When I go from here now, I will not get a hundred yards before I want to change my mind,' Hugh replied, his voice shaking. 'The moment I leave, the first thing you must do, is to hide the book. If I come back, you must not tell me where it is; if I beg, or bribe, or threaten, do not tell me! As soon as you can after that, burn it.'

The priest nodded calmly. As Hugh turned to go, he called after him.

'One more thing, Hugh de Bayeux.' Hugh turned back. 'Now put this back on your wife's hand.'

Brenier was holding out Æadgytha's wedding ring. Hugh nodded, and took the ring, anguish written on his face. Then he turned again, and left the church.

*

Hugh reached the hall house at the moment Wulfstan came out to join Harold. For a moment Wulfstan was shocked to see Hugh at all, and to see him so distraught and dishevelled he barely recognised him. Regaining himself, he called to Harold's men.

'Seize him!'

But Hugh dodged past him and into the hall. Seated again, Æadgytha was talking to Eadric. She turned to see Hugh falling to his knees in front of her and Wulfstan rushing into the hall after him. The breath went out of her; all her determination and strength ebbed away as she looked on the broken figure of her husband, clasping his hands together, weeping.

'Forgive me!' Hugh stuttered, head bowed, unable to look at Æadgytha. He was trying to take a ring from his little finger.

But Wulfstan already had him by an arm, and other men were rushing into the hall and began pulling him away.

'No! No, I beg you!' His boots scraped at the floor as he was dragged towards the door. At the threshold Hugh was just able to turn his head and look back. 'Æadgytha!'

Æadgytha shuddered. She put a hand over her mouth to stifle a cry. She held herself in her chair to stop herself from rushing to the door. She looked away. And when she looked back, he was gone.

*

Outside, Harold and Wulfstan watched from their horses as Harold's men bound Hugh and put him on a horse.

'The last thing I did before leaving London was put Edith back in Edward's bed,' Harold said. 'If he spends time on his knees now, he needs to do it between my sister's legs. Then all our problems will be over.' He turned to Wulfstan. 'They tell me you were eight years in Normandy with Duke William.'

Wulfstan nodded. 'My father pledged his father I would serve him for life. But that is ended.'

'You have done well today,' Harold said. 'I like a man who does not flinch. There is a place for you as one of my *huscarls*, if you want it.'

He turned at a noise behind him. From around the side of the hall house, a monk had appeared, staggering, dishevelled, and with a gash over one eye from which blood was streaming. As he made his slow progress along the wall of the house, with one hand he was holding on to it to keep himself upright. With the other, he pointed at Wulfstan.

'Wulfstan!' Felip's voice was a croak.

Harold stared at him. 'Do you know this monk?' he asked Wulfstan.

Wulfstan shook his head. At the corner of the hall house, Felip paused, then set off unsteadily towards Wulfstan as he sat on his horse.

'Wulfstan!' he called again.

Harold tensed and put his hand to the hilt of his word. Wulfstan dismounted, and stood watching Felip as he made his way across the space towards him. Felip stopped a few feet in front of him. Somewhere in the distance, thunder sounded. With a sleeve of his habit, Felip made a sweep across his face that took away most of the blood; but hair, matted with blood, had fallen over one eye. With one hand, Felip flicked it back.

'Felip!' Wulfstan stared at the messy, bloody figure in front of him. 'Why have you left Cerisy to come here?'

Before Felip could answer, Harold leant down to speak to Wulfstan.

'Cerisy?'

'In Normandy,' Wulfstan replied, without looking up.

'Another Norman!' Harold drew his sword. 'How many more of these rats must we chase from our barns?'

Wulfstan put up his hand to stay him.

'If you are here again, it must be about the book,' he said to the monk, stepping closer to him. 'Yet you left with it; Hugh said you had stolen it.'

Felip shook his head, and there were tears in his eyes.

'I left with only this,' he said, pulling up his tunic to show Wulfstan the scar. 'But I can leave you with the truth of who you are, Wulfstan of Wessex.'

Behind them, Harold had not seen the scar, or heard what Felip had said. He had seen only a Norman, reaching under his tunic, and his mind had gone back to the day on the beach at Hurst Head, and the man who had pulled the *seax* and run at Wulfstan. As Felip made to say more to Wulfstan, Harold heeled his horse and made a charge at him, sword above his head.

Hearing the noise, Wulfstan spun round.

'No! He means me no harm!'

And he put his body between Felip and the descending sword, while trying to reach for his axe. Harold watched in horror as his sword came down, and Wulfstan's arm came up, with his axe emerging from his belt. Just this movement of the arm that pushed Wulfstan's body slightly to one side, and the swerve of Harold's own arm away from Wulfstan, was enough. Harold's sword cut through the air an inch from Wulfstan's head, who with his axe went spinning to the ground one way, and Felip the other. As Wulfstan righted himself and Felip struggled in the dirt, Harold called to the men behind him.

'Take him! Two of you take the monk away. And keep him from Hugh de Bayeux. We do not want these Normans conspiring with each other.'

He sheathed his sword as, with two of Harold's men advancing on him, Felip tried to stand up.

'Wulfstan! Listen to me!' the monk called out. 'Your father—'

A blow from one of the men to the side of his head knocked Felip into the dirt again, where this time he stayed. Harold sighed.

'Let us be gone from here, before anything else happens.'

Harold heeled his horse on and rode away, with Wulfstan watching.

A huscarl; one of Harold's personal bodyguards. There can be no higher honour.

Wulfstan put his hands on his saddle, ready to pull himself up, then stopped, turned and looked yearningly back at the hall house, hesitating. Like with the lodestone Samra had once showed him in the Forest of Valognes, he felt his very soul being dragged towards it, and the magnetism of the woman who had had to make such an agonising choice. *A few steps, and I could be at her side.* Thinking of Samra brought another image into Wulfstan's mind, of a young woman, elfin-featured, dark-eyed, looking at him with mischievous longing: a second lodestone, pulling him back to Normandy. Panic and regret flooded through him, but he knew what he must do.

Oh, Estraya; forgive me. I will never see you again.

He mounted his horse and rode after Harold.

*

As the sounds of their departure receded, silence fell on the hall house once more, save for the far-off rumble of thunder. Eadric was standing next to Æadgytha. She looked up at him, face streaked with tears.

'I am thegn here now; the moment I yearned for all my young life. But I would not have come by it this way, if I had any other choice.' She looked over to the door through which her husband had been dragged.

Eadric nodded. 'You had no choice. We had no choice.'

'You have shown your loyalty today, Eadric, and I mean to reward it. I am alone, and soon I will have a child to look after. I need someone to manage the affairs of my household, to ensure it is furnished and provisioned as it should be. And that what is due to me is accounted for. I would like you to be my steward.'

Eadric paused long before answering. 'But Cuthred is responsible for gathering in your taxes and tithes, my lady.'

'And I trust him, of course. But I have not been able to oversee him as I would like. And in many things a reeve acts for the villagers in what he does. As my steward, you will act for me and in my interest.'

Again, Eadric seemed to take this in, before replying at length.

'Cuthred has his own lands to manage, as well as his duties. Guðrun will be busy with a new child, and I will struggle on my yardland...' he paused, savouring what he was about to say, 'with my damaged knee.'

He saw the flicker of distress on her face. *For which you are responsible.*

'You will have help,' Æadgytha said quickly. 'For as long as you need it.'

Eadric bowed. 'Then it will be my honour.'

'Only promise me this. The name Hugh de Bayeux will never be spoken in Berewic again. Not his name, not who he was, not where he came from.'

Eadric hesitated. 'A child should have a father, even if he—'

'My child will not know its father.'

Eadric nodded slowly, taken aback by the determination in her voice.

'Now,' Æadgytha went on more brightly, 'your first act as my steward.' She looked over at the door to the chamber. 'I heard a noise. I'm sure it's nothing, but this has been a day of turmoil and I want to be safe. Soon I will need to take to my bed.'

Æadgytha watched as Eadric went quietly into the chamber, closing the door behind him.

If Felip has found the book, he will be long gone. If not, let Eadric chase him away. Let the book stay hidden, where it can do no more harm. Let it not be spoken of, like the man I must now put out of my mind forever.

*

The first thing Eadric noticed was the open shutter, through which a little light was coming. There was a growl of thunder from outside, and then he saw the chest, the boards and the open pit. He had no doubt that this secret had been Hugh's, and no doubt either that Æadgytha knew nothing of it. Carefully he replaced the boards and dragged the heavy chest over them. He had no idea yet how it might serve him, but he knew that one day the hiding place would be part of his purpose. He pulled the shutter to, and went back into the hall.

'Just the shutter banging in the wind. I have closed it.'

Æadgytha smiled at him. 'Thank you. There is one other thing,' she went on. 'If I should die in childbirth, as my mother did—'

'God forbid, my lady,' Eadric cut in, looking shocked.

'If I should die, my daughter shall be called Ælfwyn.'

'You are sure of a girl?'

'I am.'

Eadric smiled. 'Guðrun is just as sure of a boy.'

But the look on Æadgytha's face told him she was not talking of a mere woman's instinct. Æadgytha was speaking again.

'And as a girl, to keep Berewic, she will need to be better than any man – stronger, cleverer, wiser.'

She had almost gasped the final words. Eadric looked at her again, and he could see she was in pain. Æadgytha winced, and put her hands on her belly.

'Now, please will you bring the midwife to me.'

*

As he hurried away from the hall house, Eadric was thinking. *The trap is sprung. Wulfstan and William are separated. Hugh is banished, and I appeared only to be loyal to Berewic in this. And now I am made steward. I will be at Æadgytha's right hand, and Cuthred will answer to me for what he does. Who knows; Æadgytha's child and Guðrun's might be born on the same day. Girl and boy, growing up together in the manor they both hold to be their birthright.*

He passed the church and stopped, imagining himself there with Æadgytha, both standing behind the son and daughter they had brought together in marriage, with the priest blessing the young couple.

Yes, I might come by Berewic another way. A way I never imagined in my years of struggle.

From the charcoal-black clouds massing behind him, the last shaft of sunlight lit his path in a golden glow. Eadric thought of Guðrun, his land and his life, and what he had. He felt blessed.

What do I gain from vengeance? Or from dreaming on what might never be? If I was put here to serve, I will serve Æadgytha and be content. The rest is in God's hands; if it is his will…

Eadric pushed himself on through the village, limping as fast as he could.

Arriving at the house the midwife shared with her son Botulf and her brother Cuthred, he found it empty. A vague chill came over him when a neighbour said that all three had gone to Eadric's house; Guðrun was being delivered of her child. But he put it down to the sun going – and with it almost at once, the heat of the day – not the look on the man's face.

Now he had to hurry to his house. As he came up the path through the vegetable garden, thunder echoing behind him, he saw Cuthred standing by the door. He reached him, and stopped. There was no sound from inside. Eadric looked at Cuthred, and the reeve put his hand on Eadric's arm.

'I'm sorry. There was nothing we could do.' His usually oily voice was toned down, almost friendly.

Eadric felt dizzy with shock. He steadied himself on the doorpost, staring at the ground. 'The child?'

Cuthred shook his head. 'It was... Botulf took it away. It was not something you should see.'

'What was it – boy, girl?'

But Cuthred only looked away. 'I'll leave you with her now,' he said.

Slowly, the reeve made his way down the path from the house, now and again looking up at the threatening sky.

Gently, Eadric opened his door. On the bed in the corner, he could see Guðrun, lying on her back with the curtain from the bed across her middle, arms folded across her chest as if asleep. The midwife was wiping her face. Eadric came across and looked down at her. Eyes closed, Guðrun looked pale but at peace; yet the blood-soaked bundle of sheets by the bed told another story. Summoning all the calm he could, Eadric turned to the midwife.

'You need to go to Æadgytha. Her time has come.'

Left alone, Eadric sat on the edge of the bed, on the very spot he had sat next to her such a little time – yet a lifetime – ago. He leant over and kissed Guðrun on the forehead. Seeing her twisted foot, he reached down and ran his hands around the deformity, gently caressing every curve. He remembered the day in the wretched village of Meresham when he had been duped into buying Guðrun. He remembered how he had hated those who had mocked Guðrun, and him; and how he had come to think that he had triumphed over them all. Finally, he gave himself to grief, his face buried in his hands, sobs wracking his body again and again, until he lifted his head, and let out a howl of anguish that was instantly drowned out by a massive peal of thunder.

He did not know how long he sat on the bed, with the darkness growing and the storm setting in until it was nearly overhead; the thunderclaps shaking the furniture in the little room, the lightning flashing again and again on Guðrun's face.

At last, Eadric got up. He went to the shelves and picked up the thimble, turning it in his hands, looking at the writing around the rim.

Love is stronger than iron, and a bond less easily broken.

For a moment he was minded to put it to be buried with her, then thought better of it and put it back. He stepped outside and stood looking across his yardland; the barley stubble looked grey and ragged under the dark clouds piled overhead. A few heavy raindrops began to fall. There was another clap of thunder and in the distance, a flash of lightning zigzagged into one his trees. The top of the tree burst into yellow, and the lightning flared down the trunk, severing a great limb, which crashed to the ground. Across the other side of a field, he could see his sheep huddled under some trees, motionless as stones as the rain began to fall on their backs. In a daze, Eadric went to see to his cow, fetching her inside and giving the animal some fodder, stroking her neck and rubbing her ears to calm her.

From outside, Eadric heard someone coming up the path and came out in time to see Father Brenier pushing open the door to his house. He followed the priest inside and saw him standing over Guðrun where she lay on the bed. Brenier looked round at him.

'Three this year. Three, and always some impediment to birth; mother too small, child too big or turned this way or that.' The priest's face was marked with anguish and horror; Eadric wondered if he himself had looked like that just now. 'I'm too late. I'm sorry – I came as soon as I was told.'

'What does it matter?' Eadric said, his voice flat. 'She is dead.'

'She was not shriven, before she died. I should have heard her confession, so she could make her peace with God.'

Brenier began to make the sign of the cross over Guðrun's body, its arms folded in submission to death. Grabbing him, Eadric wrenched his arm back until the priest's face was close to his own, now red with fury.

'God?' he shouted at him. 'God? Oh yes, we crowd into your church every day, Father, and hear you beyond the rood screen, intoning God's peace on us all. But where was your God when Guðrun was born so warped that it made every step of her life a struggle? Where was your God when she was taken for a slave? When the woman who owned her, sold her to be raped again and again?'

Every question he screamed at the priest forced Eadric's hot breath into his face, making his hair lift and forcing him to close his eyes.

'Where was He when she first came here, and people spat at her in the street? Just now, when the thing inside her took its own life, and hers – WHERE WAS YOUR GOD THEN?'

With this final scream, Eadric flung Brenier back against the wall. He stood looking at the other man's terrified face, while his breathing steadily subsided.

'No,' he said, more calmly now. 'We will do without your God.'

Eadric pushed his way out through the door and into the storm.

As the rain turned into a relentless downpour, Eadric walked back to the village. The last few to get home were bolting into their houses; some looked curiously at him as he limped slowly along, seemingly heedless of the storm and unaware of Father Brenier hurrying back to his church. By the time he reached the hall house, the streets were empty. He stood under the eaves, water running down his face and off his body. Lifting an arm to the door, from inside he heard a baby cry.

Eadric stepped back into the rain.

Berewic is mine. Mine by birth, mine by right, and mine by promise. I will be thegn here, if I have to step over the bodies of Æadgytha and her child.

He realised he was shouting into the thunder.

'Berewic is mine! Mine!'

*

As Father Brenier went into his church, he found Cuthred where he had left him, when the reeve came to tell him he was needed at Eadric's house. Or not quite; for Cuthred was standing by a wooden box on the church floor, next to which lay a cloth with a moon and stars. He was holding a book, a large leather-covered book, open at a page rich with symbols and diagrams. Cuthred barely seemed to notice the priest as he approached and stood with the rain dripping from his habit onto the hard earth floor. At last, the reeve looked up.

'What is this?'

'It is Hugh's. He left it with me, with the order to destroy it.'

'That would be a shame. It's a thing of beauty, though I can't understand any of it.'

Brenier frowned. 'An order from my thegn is an order.'

Cuthred smiled the smile of a man who had seen more success that day than he ever thought possible.

'Hugh de Bayeux has been taken away. He can't give you orders now.'

The priest looked at the book in the podgy hands of the ignorant reeve smirking in front of him. He looked at the symbols and diagrams, and held out his hands. The steel in his voice surprised him.

'Give it to me.'

Historical Note

The decades covered by *The Book and The Knife* novels are arguably the most momentous in the history of England. At their centre is the regime change of 1066, though this was not a simple 'English out, Normans in' process in either timespan or people concerned. And 1066 had its origins in another upheaval fifty years earlier, when the Danish King Cnut took the throne and the survivors of the previously ruling house of Wessex were exiled to Normandy. The power and ambition of the house of Godwin, which grew under Cnut, led to the fraught relationship between Edward of Wessex when he returned to become England's king and Earl Godwin and his son Harold – the man who, in succeeding Edward, triggered the invasion of England by William of Normandy.

In *The Book and The Knife*, this relationship is played out at a local level by the fictional characters in Berewic. When Sighere – a distant relative of Godwin – ousts Rædmund – a Wessex distantly related to Edward – as Thegn of Berewic in 1016, it triggers a feud between the families that will reverberate through the novels, with tragic consequences. And a returning Edward chooses not to give Berewic back to the Wessex – save for Eadric's peasant holding – but to his

Norman companion Hugh de Bayeux, and so the Book comes to Berewic too, while Wulfstan goes back to Normandy to serve William. This is a turbulent age in Normandy too, with William constantly beset – as he says in the book – by jealous nobles within and ambitious ones without, and having to own the King of France as his master.

My characters interact repeatedly with the historical characters such as Edward, Harold and William, sometimes influenced or directed by them, but also influencing them. The real historical events depicted in *The Book and The Knife* are a framework for these interactions, for the characters' dealings with each other and for the decisions they make.

Contemporary sources for this period are few and sometimes contradictory, depending on whether they took a supportive view of the Norman conquest or condemned its devastation of the defeated English. Only one such source mentions a visit to England by William of Normandy in late 1051, but it is widely accepted to have happened and it creates a pivotal scene in my novels when William visits Hugh in Berewic.

There were many books of knowledge in the Islamic world in the mid-eleventh century and the great scientist Alhacen wrote some of them. Alhacen also said there was no better way to be close to God than by searching for truth and knowledge. As to the Book in my story, if it reached England at that time it would have been in advance of the works later scholars were to discover in Islam, and which were to add hugely to our knowledge of subjects such as astronomy. And from his knowledge of optics, Alhacen could indeed have built a lens tube or telescope, long before Galileo.

Acknowledgements

My thanks to those who have read and commented on *The Book and The Knife*, and to the late great historian Ian Coulson, who pointed me to many of the sources for the period that I have drawn on in writing it. Thanks too to my publishers at Troubador for their help and support. Last but not least my love and gratitude to my wife Linda and my son Izaak for their encouragement.

This book is printed on paper from sustainable sources managed under the Forest Stewardship Council (FSC) scheme.

It has been printed in the UK to reduce transportation miles and their impact upon the environment.

For every new title that Troubador publishes, we plant a tree to offset CO_2, partnering with the More Trees scheme.

MORE TREES
LET'S PLANT A BILLION TREES

For more about how Troubador offsets its environmental impact, see www.troubador.co.uk/sustainability-and-community